CUCKOO SONG

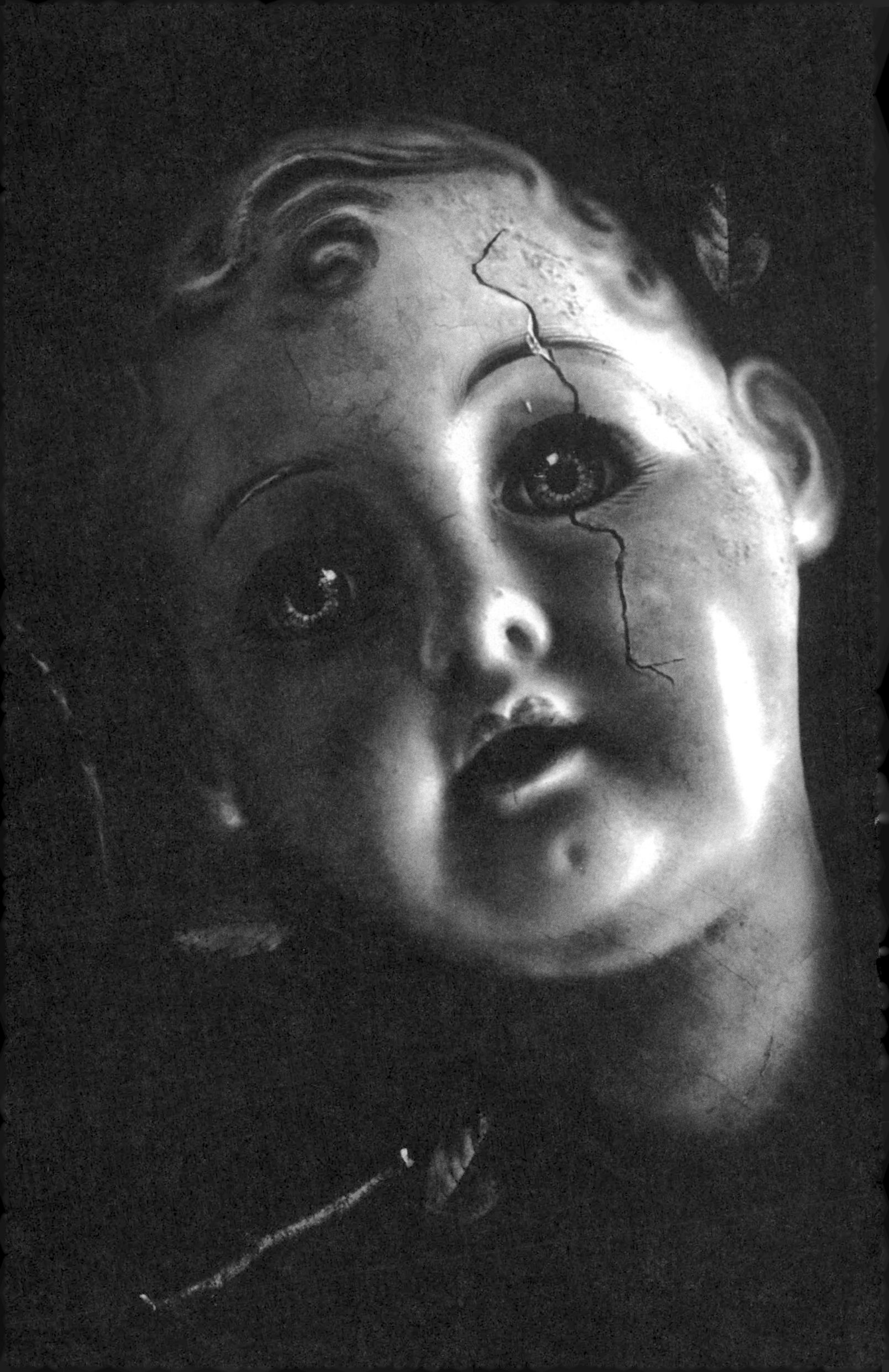

CUCKOO SONG

FRANCES HARDINGE

AMULET BOOKS
NEW YORK

Library of Congress Cataloging-in-Publication Data
Hardinge, Frances.
Cuckoo song / Frances Hardinge.
pages cm
First published in Great Britain in 2014 by Macmillan UK.
Summary: In post–World War I England, thirteen-year-old Triss nearly drowns in a millpond known as "The Grimmer" and emerges with memory gaps, aware that something is terribly wrong. To try to set things right, she must meet a twisted architect who has designs on her family.
ISBN 978-1-4197-1480-1 (hardback) — ISBN 978-1-61312-756-8 (ebook)
[1. Supernatural—Fiction. 2. Identity—Fiction. 3. Memory—Fiction. 4. Family life—England—Fiction. 5. Magicians—Fiction. 6. Great Britain—History—George V, 1910–1936—Fiction.]I. Title.
PZ7.H21834Cuc 2015
[Fic]—dc23
2014045264

Book design by Maria T. Middleton

First published in Great Britain in 2014 by Macmillan UK.

Printed and bound in U.S.A.
10 9 8 7 6 5 4 3 2 1

115 West 18th Street
New York, NY 10011
www.abramsbooks.com

To Dylan, my nephew and godson.
May you always regard the world's follies
with the same mellow calm.

Chapter 1

IN ONE PIECE

HER HEAD HURT. THERE WAS A SOUND GRATING against her mind, a music-less rasp like the rustling of paper. Somebody had taken a laugh, crumpled it into a great, crackly ball, and stuffed her skull with it. *Seven days*, it laughed. *Seven days*.

"Stop it," she croaked. And it did. The sound faded away, until even the words she thought she had heard vanished from her mind like breath from glass.

"Triss?" There was another voice that sounded much louder and closer than her own, a woman's voice. "Oh, Triss, love, love, it's all right, I'm here." Something was happening. Two warm hands had closed around hers, as if they were a nest.

"Don't let them laugh at me," she whispered. She swallowed, and found her throat dry and crackly as bracken.

"Nobody's laughing at you, darling," the woman said, her voice so hushed and gentle it was almost a sigh.

There were concerned mutterings a little farther away. Two male voices.

"Is she still delirious? Doctor, I thought you said—"

"Just an interrupted dream, I think. We'll see how young Theresa is when she has woken up properly."

Theresa. I'm Theresa. It was true, she knew it, but it just felt like a word. She didn't seem to know what it meant. *I'm Triss.* That seemed a bit more natural, like a book falling open on a much-viewed page. She managed to open her eyes a little, wincing at the brightness. She was in bed, propped up on a mound of pillows. It felt as if there was a vast expanse of her, weighted down with rocks, and it was a surprise to see herself stretched out as a normal-sized lump under the counterpane and blankets.

There was a woman seated beside her holding her hand gently. The woman's dark hair was short and arranged close to her head, molded into stiff, gleaming, crinkly waves. A faint flouring of face powder dusted over her cheeks, muffling the tired lines at the corners of her eyes. The blue glass beads of the woman's necklace caught the light from the window, casting frosty glints onto the pale skin of her neck and the underside of her chin.

Every inch of the woman was achingly familiar and yet strange, like a map of a half-forgotten home. A word drifted down from nowhere, and Triss's numb mind managed to catch at it.

"Muh . . ." she began.

"That's right, Mommy's got you, Triss."

Mommy. Mother.

"Muhm . . . muh . . ." She could manage only a croak. "I . . . I don't . . ." Triss trailed off helplessly. She didn't know what she didn't, but she was frightened by how much she didn't.

"It's all right, froglet." Her mother gave her hand a little squeeze and smiled softly. "You've just been ill again, that's all. You had a fever, so of course you feel rotten and a bit muddled. Do you remember what happened yesterday?"

"No." Yesterday was a great, dark hole, and Triss felt a throb of panic. What could she actually remember?

"You came home sopping wet. Do you remember that?" The bed creaked as a man came and sat on the other edge of it. He had a long, strong sort of face, with creases between his brows as if he was concentrating on everything very hard, and his hair was a tired blond. His voice was gentle, though, and Triss knew that she was getting his special kind look, the one only she ever received. Father. "We think you must have fallen into the Grimmer."

The word "Grimmer" made Theresa feel cold and shuddery, as if somebody had pressed frogskin against her neck. "I . . . I don't remember." She wanted to squirm away from the thought.

"Don't press her." There was another man standing at the foot of the bed. He was older, with a combed haze of colorless hair curving half an inch over his pink scalp, and gray tufty eyebrows that went everywhere. The veins on his hands had the bulgy, puddingy look that spoke of advanced years. "Children will play by water, it's what they do. Goodness knows I tumbled into enough streams when I was young. Now, young lady, you put your parents into a fine fright, wandering in last night with a towering fever, not knowing who they were. I suppose you know them well enough now?"

Triss hesitated and nodded her heavy head. She knew their smells now. Pipe ash and face powder.

The doctor nodded sagely and tapped his fingers on the foot of the bed. "What's the name of the king?" he rapped out sharply.

Triss jumped and was flustered for a moment. Then a recollection of childish schoolroom chanting swam obediently into her head. One Lord is King, One King is George, One George is Fifth . . .

"George the Fifth," she answered.

"Good. Where are we right now?"

"The old stone house, at Lower Bentling," Triss answered with growing confidence. "With the kingfisher pond." She recognized the smell of the place—damp walls, plus the fading scent of three generations of old, sick cats. "We're here on holiday. We . . . we come here every year."

"How old are you?"

"Thirteen."

"And where do you live?"

"The Beeches, Luther Square, Ellchester."

"Good girl. That's a lot better." He gave a wide, warm smile as if he was genuinely proud of her. "Now, you've been very ill, so I expect your brain feels as if it's full of cotton wool at the moment, doesn't it? Well, don't you panic—over the next couple of days all your wits will come home, I dare say, dragging their tails behind them. You're feeling better already, aren't you?"

Triss slowly nodded. Nobody was laughing in her head now. There was still a faint, irregular rustle, but looking across the room at the window opposite, she could easily see the culprit. A low-hanging branch was pressed against the pane, weighed down by clusters of green apples, leaves scuffling against the glass every time the wind stirred it.

The light that entered was shattered, shifting, broken into a mosaic by the foliage. The room itself was as green as the leaves. Green counterpane on the bed, green walls with little cream-colored diamonds on them, fussy green square-cornered cloths on the black wood tables. The gas was unlit, the white globes of the wall lamps dull and lightless.

And it was only now, when she looked around properly, that she realized that there was a fifth person in the room, lurking over by the door. It was another girl, younger than Triss, her hair dark and crimped so that she almost looked like a miniature version of Mother. But there was something quite different in her eyes, which were cold and hard like those of a thrush. She gripped the door handle as if she wanted to twist it off, and her narrow jaw was moving all the while, grinding her teeth.

Mother glanced over her shoulder to follow Triss's gaze.

"Oh, look, there's Penny come to see you. Poor Pen—I don't think she's eaten a thing since you got ill, for fretting about you. Come on in, Pen, come and sit next to your sister—"

"No!" screamed Penny, so suddenly that everybody jumped. "She's pretending! Can't you see? It's *fake*! Can't any of you tell the difference?" Her gaze was fixed on Triss's face with a look that could have splintered stone.

"Pen." There was a warning in their father's voice. "You come in right now and—"

"NO!" Pen looked mad and desperate, eyes wide as if she might bite someone, then tore out through the door. Rapid feet receded, echoing as they did so.

"Don't follow her," Father suggested gently, as Mother started to stand. "That's 'rewarding' her with attention—remember what they said?"

Mother sighed wearily but obediently seated herself again. She noticed that Triss was sitting with her shoulders hunched to her ears, staring toward the open door. "Don't you mind her," she said gently, squeezing Triss's hand. "You know what she's like."

Do I? Do I know what she's like?

She's my sister, Penny. Pen. She's eleven. She used to get tonsillitis. Her first milk tooth came out when she was biting somebody. She had a parakeet once and forgot to give it water and it died.

She lies. She steals. She screams and throws things. And . . .

. . . and she hates me. Really hates me. I can see it in her eyes. And I don't know why.

For a while, Mother stayed by her bedside and got Triss to help her cut out dress patterns with the big tortoiseshell-handled scissors from the sewing box that Mother insisted on bringing on holiday. The scissors snipped with a slow, throaty crunch, as if relishing every inch.

Triss knew that she had always loved pinning pattern to cloth, cutting out and then watching the fabric pieces slowly become a shape, bristling with pins and ribbed by frayed-edge seams. The patterns came with pictures of pastel-colored ladies, some in long coats and bell-shaped hats, some in turbans and long dresses that fell straight like tasseled pipes. They all leaned languorously, as if they were about to yawn in the most elegant way possible. She knew it was a treat to be allowed to help her mother with the sewing. It was the usual drill, she realized, for when she was ill.

Today, however, her hands were stupid and clumsy. The big scissors seemed impossibly heavy, and her grip on them kept slipping so that they almost seemed to twist rebelliously in her hand. After the second time that she had nearly caught her own knuckles between the blades, her mother took them back.

"Still not quite yourself, are you, love? Why don't you just read your comics?" There were well-thumbed copies of *Sunbeam* and *Golden Penny* on the bedside table.

But Triss could not concentrate on the pages before her. She had been ill before, she knew that. Many, many times. But she was sure she had never woken up with this terrible vagueness before.

What's wrong with my hands? What's wrong with my mind? She wanted to blurt it all out. *Mommy, help me, please help me, everything's strange and nothing's right, and my mind feels as if it's made up of pieces and some of them are missing . . .*

But when she thought of trying to describe the strangeness, her mind flinched away from the idea. *If I tell my parents,* she thought irrationally, *then they'll get worried, and if they're worried, that means it's serious. But if I don't, they'll keep telling me that everything's all right, and then maybe it will be.*

"Mommy . . ." Triss's voice came out very small. She stared at the pile of fabric pieces now lying on the bed. They looked wounded, limp and helpless. "I . . . I am all right, aren't I? It isn't . . . bad that . . . that I can't remember bits of our holiday, is it?"

Her mother examined her face carefully, and Triss was startled by how blue her eyes were, like the glass beads around her neck. Clear and fragile too, just like the beads. It was a kind, bright look that needed only the slightest change to become a frightened look.

"Oh, sweetheart, I'm sure it'll all come back to you. The doctor said so, didn't he?" Her mother finished pinning a seam, smiled, and stood. "Listen, I have an idea. Why don't you have a look through your diary? Maybe that will help you remember." From under the bed, Triss's mother pulled a small, faded red leather traveling case with the letters "TC" marked on one corner, and placed it on Triss's lap.

Birthday present. I know I love this case and take it everywhere. But I can't remember how the catch works. A little fiddling, however, and it clicked open.

Inside were more things that stung her memories to life, more of the pieces of being Triss. Clothes. Gloves. Other gloves in case of even colder days. A copy of the poem collection *Peacock*

Pie. A compact, like her mother's but smaller, with a mirror in the lid but no face powder. And there, beneath them, a book bound in blue leather.

Triss pulled out her diary, opened it, and gave a small croak of shock. Half the pages in the diary had been filled with her cramped, careful scrawl. She knew that. But those pages had been torn out, leaving a fringe of frayed paper, still marked by the occasional whorl or squiggle from the lost words. After them, blank pages confronted her. Her mother came over, summoned by her cry, and simply stared for a few seconds.

"I don't *believe* it," Triss's mother whispered at last. "Of all the stupid, spiteful pranks . . . Oh, that really is the *limit*." She marched from the room. "Pen? PEN!" Triss heard her feet rattle up the stairs and then the sound of a handle being shaken and a door shuddering in its frame.

"What is it?" inquired her father's voice at the top of the stairs.

"It's Pen *again*. This time she has ripped out half of Triss's diary. And her door won't open—I think she has moved some furniture against it."

"If she wants to imprison herself, let her," came her father's answer. "She'll have to come out and face the music sooner or later. And she knows it." All of this was said clearly and loudly, presumably so that the besieged party could overhear.

Triss's mother entered the sickroom once more. "Oh, froglet, I'm so sorry. Well . . . perhaps she has just hidden the pages, and we can stick them back in when we find them." She sat down on the bed next to Triss, sighed, and peered into the case. "Oh dear—we had better make sure that nothing else is missing."

Other things were missing, as it turned out. Triss's hairbrush was gone, as was a photograph of her riding a donkey on the beach, and a handkerchief into which she had proudly stitched her name.

"I know you had some of them yesterday afternoon, before the accident," muttered Triss's mother. "You were filling in your diary. I helped brush your hair. Oh, *Pen*! I don't know why she plagues you, love."

The sight of the ripped diary had filled Triss with the same cold, squirming feeling in the pit of her stomach that the mention of the Grimmer had given her. It had frightened her, and she did not know why, or want to think about it. *But it's OK*, she told herself. *It's just Pen being stupid and cruel.*

Triss guessed that perhaps she should feel angry about it, but in truth there was something comforting and familiar about her parents being angry on her behalf. It felt like being coddled inside a horse-chestnut shell, protected by its inward downy softness, while all the spikes pointed outward. It was, her recollections whispered to her, the natural way of things.

Now, if she let her mouth droop as if she was going to cry, the whole household would spin around her to try to make things up to her . . . and without even quite intending it, she felt her face start to pout sorrowfully.

"Oh, Triss!" Her mother hugged her. "How about something to eat? There's some mushroom soup, the sort you like, or steak-and-kidney pie if you can manage a little. Or what about jelly? And tinned pears?" The sick puckering feeling in her stomach intensified at the thought, and Triss realized that she was ravenously hungry.

She nodded.

Triss's mother went upstairs and knocked on Pen's door in an attempt to lure her down for lunch. Even from her sickroom, Triss could hear Pen's shrill, incoherent cries of refusal.

". . . not coming out . . . not *real* . . . you're all *stupid* . . ."

Triss's mother came down with a slight crinkle of exasperation on her brow.

"Now, that is willful, even for Pen. I have never known her to turn down food before." She looked at Triss and gave a weary little smile. "Well, at least *you* don't have her stubborn streak."

It turned out that Triss could more than "manage a little." As soon as she saw the first bowl of soup arrive, great crusty rolls on the side of the tray, her hands started to shake. The room around her ceased to matter. Once the tray was on her lap, she could not control herself and tore open the rolls, scattering crumbs, and pushed them into her mouth, where the wads of bread rolled drily against her tongue and champing teeth. The soup was gone as quickly as she could scoop it up, and she barely noticed it scalding her mouth. Pie, potatoes, and carrots were demolished in a frenzy, closely followed by jelly, pears, and a thick slice of almond cake. Only when she was reaching for the rest of the cake did her mother catch her wrist.

"Triss, Triss! Love, I'm so glad you have your appetite back so soon, but you'll make yourself sick!"

Triss stared back at her with bright, bewildered eyes, and gradually the room around her came back into focus. She did not feel sick. She felt as if she could have eaten a hippopotamus-sized slice of cake. Her crumb-covered hands were still shaking, but she made herself wipe them on her napkin and clasped them in her lap to stop them from snatching at anything more. As she was doing so, her father put his head around the door and caught her mother's eye.

"Celeste." His voice was deliberately calm and soft. "Can I

speak to you a moment?" He flicked a glance toward Triss and gave her a small, tender smile.

Mother tucked Triss into bed, took up the tray, and left the room to follow Father, taking her warmth, reassurance, and smell of face powder with her. Within seconds of the door closing, Triss felt twinges of creeping panic return. Something in her father's tone had stirred her instincts.

Can I speak to you a moment? Outside the room, where Triss can't hear you?

Triss swallowed and pulled the covers aside, then slid herself out of bed. Her legs felt stiff but not as weak as she had expected, and she crept as quietly as she could to her bedroom door and eased it open. From there she could just about make out voices in the parlor.

". . . and the inspector promised to ask some questions in the village, in case anybody saw how she came to fall into the water." Her father had a deep and pleasant voice, with a touch of hoarseness that made Triss think of rough animal fur. "He dropped by just now to speak to me. Apparently a couple of the local hands were passing near the village green at sunset last night. They didn't see any sign of Triss near the Grimmer, but they did catch sight of two men down at the water's edge. A short man in a bowler, and a taller man in a gray coat. And on the road near the green there was a car parked, Celeste."

"What kind of a car?" Her mother spoke with the hushed tone of one who already knows the answer.

"A big black Daimler."

There was a long pause.

"It can't be him." Her mother's voice was high and rapid now, as if her cloth scissors had clipped her words until they were short and frightened. “Perhaps it’s just a coincidence—there’s more than one Daimler in the world—”

“Out here? There are barely two cars in the village. Who could afford a Daimler?”

“You said it was all over!” There were warning sounds in the rising pitch of Mother’s voice, like the whistle of a kettle coming to a boil. “You said you were severing all ties with him—”

“I said that *I* was finished with *him*, and he’ll know that by now if he’s read this week’s paper. But perhaps he is not finished with me.”

Chapter 2

ROTTEN APPLES

HEARING MOTION IN THE PARLOR, TRISS CAREfully closed the door and scampered back to her bed, her mind whirling like a propeller.

They think somebody attacked me. Is that what happened? Again she tried to force her memory back to the Grimmer, and again there was nothing, just an inner shuddering and flinching.

Who was this "he" her parents had mentioned, the one that Father was "finished with"? If "he" was so terrible, why would Father have had "ties" with him anyway?

It all sounded like something from one of the crime films Pen loved so much, the sort where good, honest men became entangled with hoodlums and gangsters. But surely Father could not be involved in anything like that! Triss felt her chest grow tight at the very thought. More than anything else, she was proud of her father. She loved the impressed way everybody's eyebrows rose when they were introduced to him.

Mr. Piers Crescent? The civil engineer who designed the Three Maidens and Station Mount? It's an honor to meet you, sir—you've done wonderful things for our city.

Having a great civil engineer as a father meant seeing maps

of planned roads at the breakfast table. It meant watching her father open letters from the mayor's office about bridge construction and locations for new public buildings. Her father's designs were changing the face of Ellchester.

Triss jumped slightly when the door opened, and her mother entered the room. There was a touch more powder on her cheeks, a sure sign that she had stepped aside to calm herself and set her appearance straight.

"I've just been talking to your father," her mother declared with calm nonchalance, "and we think we should cut the holiday short and go home first thing tomorrow. Familiar surroundings—that's what you need to sort you out."

"Mommy . . ." Triss hesitated, unwilling to admit to eavesdropping, then went for a compromise. "You left the door open, and it was drafty so I went to shut it, and when I was there, I . . . overheard Daddy telling you that there was somebody else down at the Grimmer yesterday evening." Triss caught at her mother's sleeve. "Who was it?"

Her mother's hands halted for a second, then continued calming the creases out of the pillow.

"Oh, nobody, darling! Just some gypsies. Nothing for you to worry about."

Gypsies? In a bowler hat and a Daimler?

Perhaps some of her distress showed in Triss's face, for her mother sat down on the edge of her bed, took her by both hands, and met her eye at last.

"Nobody could want to harm you, froglet," she said very seriously, "and even if somebody did, your father and I would never, *never* let anything bad happen to you."

And this would have been reassuring if the crystal-blue eyes were not a little too bright. Every time she saw that fragile intensity in her mother's face, Triss knew that she was thinking of Sebastian.

He had been called up in February of 1918, not long after Triss's eighth birthday. Triss remembered all the celebrations with the flags and big hats when the war had ended later that year, and she had not really known how it would change everything, except that it had meant Sebastian would be coming back home. Then the news had come that Sebastian would not be coming back, and she had thought for a while, in a foggy, confused way, that the first news had been wrong, that the war was not over.

In a way she had been right. The war had ended, but it was not gone. Somehow it was still everywhere. Sebastian was the same. He had ended but he was not gone. His death had left invisible wreckage. His absence was a great hole tugging at everything. Even Pen, who barely remembered him, walked carefully round the edge of that hole.

Triss had started getting ill not long after the war ended, and in a hazy way she understood that this had something to do with Sebastian. It was her job to be ill. It was her job to be protected. And right now it was her job to nod.

She nodded.

"There's my girl," said her mother, stroking Triss's cheek.

Triss tried to smile. The conversation she had overheard still had its hooks in her mind.

"Mommy? I . . . I've read all my comics and books, hundreds of times. Can I . . . can I read Daddy's paper?"

Mother went to ask Father's permission, and then returned with a copy of the *Ellchester Watchman*. She lit the lamps, each glass globe giving a small, comforting *whump* as it started to glow, then left Triss to herself.

Triss carefully unfolded the paper, feeling treacherous for her small deception. What was it she had overheard her father say?

I said that I *was finished with* him*, and he'll know that by now if he's read this week's paper.*

In the paper, therefore, there was something from which the mysterious "he" might learn that her father no longer wanted dealings with him. If so, perhaps she could find it too.

The paper had already been read and handled enough to smudge the ink here and there, and her fever-wearied mind felt a bit smudged as well. Her mind slid over headline after headline, taking in so little that sometimes she had to read things several times to make sense of them. Most of them were just dull. Articles on the new omnibuses to be introduced in Ellchester after the London model. A photograph of a long line of unemployed men, flat caps pulled down over their grainy, sullen faces. A dance to collect money for the local hospital. And on the fifth page, a mention of Piers Crescent, Triss's father.

It was not very interesting. It described Meadowsweet, the new suburb her father was working on, just outside Ellchester but reachable by the new tramline. There were even diagrams showing how it would look, with all the houses in rows down the hill, facing out across the Ell estuary. Triss's father was helping to design the roads, the new boating lake, and the terracing of the hillside. The article said that this was "a departure" for an engineer "best known for his large and innovative constructions." However, it certainly didn't mention Piers Crescent throwing off gangster contacts, and Triss could not help but think that if it had, the story would probably have been nearer the front page.

Perhaps I misheard him. Perhaps I imagined the whole thing. Perhaps . . . perhaps I'm not well yet.

. . . . .

That night Triss lay awake, watching the dim flickering of the lowered lights and the chocolate-brown spiders edging across the ceiling. Every time she closed her eyes, she could sense dreams waiting at the mouse hole of her mind's edge, ready to catch her up in their soft cat-mouth and carry her off somewhere she did not want to go.

Suddenly the world was full of secrets, and she could feel them in her stomach like knots. She was frightened. She was confused. And she was *hungry*, too hungry to sleep. Too hungry, after a while, to think or worry about anything else. Several times she reached tentatively for the bell, but then recalled her mother's worried face watching as Triss wolfed down her supper, as wild with hunger as she had been at lunch. *No more now, froglet. Nothing more until breakfast, understand?*

But she was starving! How could she sleep like this? She thought of sneaking to the kitchen to raid the larder. The food would be missed, but for an unworthy, desperate moment she wondered if she could blame the theft on Pen. No, Triss had begged so hard for more food that her parents would surely suspect her.

Then what could she do? She sat up, gnawing at her nails, then jumped a little as the wind-swung foliage outside clattered against the window. In her mind's eye she saw the bough of the tree beyond, lush with leaves and heavy with apples . . .

The window had not been opened in years, but Triss gave the sash a frantic yank and it juddered upward, spitting a fine spray of dust and paint flakes. Cold air rushed in, rippling the newspaper by her bedside, but she had no thought for anything but the young apples bobbing among the leaves, glossy with the dim gaslight behind her. She snatched at them, tearing them from their stems and cramming them into her mouth one by one, feeling her teeth cleave into them with a shuddering relief. They were unripe and so sharp that her tongue went numb, but she did not care. Soon she was staring at nothing but stripped stems, and her hunger was still thundering its demands, a raw gaping chasm at her core.

The bedroom was on the ground floor, and there was nothing more natural, more necessary, than clambering her way out to sit on the sill and dropping the short distance to the ground. The grass was downy-pale with dew. The cold of it stung the skin of her feet, but it did not seem important.

Only a few boughs were low enough for her to snatch the fruit from them, and when these were bare, she dropped to all fours and scrabbled at the early windfalls. Some were recent, merely speckled with rot, others caramel-colored and slack, riddled with insect holes. Their pulp squeezed between her fingers as she caught them up and crammed them into her mouth. They were sweet and bitter and mushy in the wrong ways and she did not care.

Only when at long last there were no more rotten apples to be found nestling in the grass did the frenzy start to fade, and then Triss became aware of her own shivering, her scraped knees, the taste in her mouth. She sat back on her haunches, gasping in deep ragged breaths, not knowing whether to retch or sob as her shaky hands wiped the sour stickiness from her cheeks, chin, and tongue. She dared not look at the half-guzzled windfalls in case she saw white shapes writhing in the pulp.

What's wrong with me? Even now, after this wild glut, she knew that another surge of hunger was hanging somewhere like a wave, just waiting for its chance to break over her.

Her unsteady steps took her to the garden wall. It was crumbling and old, and all too easy for her to climb and sit upon, knees knocking under her thin nightdress. Before her was the grainy, gravelly road that passed the cottage, and following it with her eye she could see it curve and dwindle down the rough, tussocky hillside until it reached the distant village, now not much more than a cluster of lights. Before them, though, she could see the triangle of the village green, a dull pencil gray in the moonlight. Beyond it quivered a faint floss of pale willows, and behind them . . . a narrow streak of deeper blackness, like an open seam.

The Grimmer.

She felt as if she was falling apart. All the little patches and pieces of how-to-be-Triss that she had been carefully fitting together all day were coming unpinned again, all at once.

Something happened to me at the Grimmer. I have to see it. I have to remember.

She took the shortcut down the hill over the hummocky grass, rather than following the wide swing of the road. By the time she reached the green, the Grimmer was no longer a mere slit in the land but a lean lake, long enough to swallow four buses whole. Over its waters the willows drooped their long hair, bucking in the gusts as if with sobs. Against the dark surface she could make out the white water lily buds, like small hands reaching up from beneath the surface.

Shaky steps took her across the green to the water's edge, where she halted and felt the cold properly for the first time. This was where they had dunked witches hundreds of years ago. This was where suicides came to drown themselves.

At one place on the bank the mud was ravaged, tussocks of the grass pulled away, the earth finger-gouged. *That's where I dragged myself out. It must be. But why did I fall in?*

She had hoped that if she found memories here, they would provide solid ground at last under her feet. But when memory came, it brought no comfort. Here was only fear and falling.

Triss recalled an icy darkness, cold water choking her nose, mouth, and throat. It seemed that she remembered looking up through a shifting brown murk, while her limbs slowly flailed, and seeing two dark shapes above her, their outlines wavering and wobbling with the motion of the water. Two figures standing on the bank above, one taller than the other. But there was another memory trying to surface, something that had happened just before that . . .

Something bad happened here, something that should never have taken place.

I've changed my mind. I don't want to remember.

But it was too late, she was there and the Grimmer was watching her with its vast, lightless slit of an eye, as if it might open the eye wide and stare into her gaze at any moment. Then, as the panic rose, her mind flapped shut like a book and instinct took over. She turned and ran, fleeing from the water, sprinting across the green and tearing back up the hill to the cottage with all the speed and panic of a coursed hare.

Chapter 3

THE WRONG KIND OF ILL

SIX DAYS, CAME THE LAUGHTER. *SIX DAYS*, IT snickered like old paper in a draft. As Triss woke, however, the words melted and became nothing but the whisper of leaves against the window.

Triss's eyes opened. Something scratchy was touching her cheek. She reached up, pulled the dead leaf out of her hair, and stared at it. One by one, she recalled her actions the previous evening. Had she really climbed out her window, gobbled windfalls, and then stood on the banks of the Grimmer, feeling that it might speak to her? She picked her way through the memories with disbelief, like a householder surveying rubbish scattered by foxes overnight.

There were more dead leaves in her hair, so she hastily pulled them out and pushed them through the window. Her muddy feet she wiped clean with a handkerchief. Her nightdress was grimy and grass-stained, but perhaps she could smuggle it into the laundry without anybody knowing.

Nobody saw me. Nobody knows what I did. And so if I don't tell anyone, it's like it didn't happen. And I won't do it again—

I'm better this morning. I'll get dressed and go down to breakfast, and everybody will say how much better I'm looking today . . . and that'll make it true.

Sure enough, as she creaked her way down the stairs, she was met with relief and joy in her mother's voice.

"Triss! You're up! Oh, it's so good to see that you're looking better . . ."

Hunger had finally broken Pen's siege. She scraped her chair as far from the rest of the family as she could and sat with her head bowed resentfully over the plate. She ate with all the good humor of a condemned prisoner.

Fresh eggs from the farm had been brought in and boiled, and now sat freckled in their cups beside the racks of toast. The pack of wolves that seemed to have taken over Triss's stomach was still baying for food, but she managed to eat slowly and steadily, and stop when she had finished her share.

There. See? I'm better today.

They were going home after breakfast. Everything would be normal once they were home.

Back in her room Triss quickly piled her possessions into her little red traveling case and last of all stooped to pick up Angelina, her doll. Angelina was a fine, large, German-made doll, about the size of a human baby. Her bisque skin was not glossy like porcelain but had a dull shine like real skin, and she had carefully painted lashes and gracefully curved brows. Her painted lips were parted to show tiny white teeth. Her curling hair was light brown, like Triss's own, and she wore a green-and-white dress with an ivy-pattern print.

Triss's mind performed an odd little twist, so that she seemed to see her possessions as a stranger might. An unfamiliar thought crept unbidden into her mind. *It's as if I'm still eight years old. It's as if I'm still the age I was when Sebastian died.*

She stared down at Angelina with a slight squirming in her stomach, a tiny worm of shame and wonder.

"What are you doing here?" she asked under her breath. "I'm thirteen. Why do I still carry a doll around?"

And it was while these words were still hanging in the air that the doll moved in her hands.

The first things to shift were the eyes, the beautiful gray-green glass eyes. Slowly they swiveled, until their gaze was resting on Triss's face. Then the tiny mouth moved, opened to speak.

"What are you doing here?" It was an echo of Triss's words, uttered in tones of outrage and surprise, and in a voice as cold and musical as thc clinking of cups. "Who do you think you arc? This is *my* family."

All the breath had left Triss's lungs. Her whole body had frozen; otherwise, the doll would doubtless have dropped from her hands. *It's a trick*, she told herself frantically. *Pen must have done this somehow. It's a trick.*

She felt the doll move in her grasp as it gripped at her sleeves with its delicate hands and hauled itself a little more upright, jutting its head forward to peer at her more closely. Its glass eyes seemed to come into proper focus, and then the doll flinched and started to shake. Its mouth fell open, emitting a low, eerie mewl of horror and fear.

"No," it moaned, and then started to thrash, its voice rising to a wail. "You're not right! Don't touch me! Help! Help! Get her away from me!" It flailed at her with tiny china fists, its scream rising to a single eerie note that went on and on like a siren. Through the window, Triss saw the house martins burst in terror from their nest in the eaves, and the wall plaster crack slightly, spitting powder into the air. The doll's jaw dropped wider, and its scream became ear-rending, until Triss was sure that everybody in the house and beyond must be stopping in wonder.

"Stop it! Stop it!" She shook the doll, but to no avail. "Please!" In panic she tried to smother the small screaming face with a fistful of woolen shawl, but it only muffled the sound a little. At last, in sheer desperation, she threw the doll across the room as hard as she could. It hit the wall headfirst with a crack like a gunshot, and the scream cut out, leaving a chilling silence.

Triss walked over to Angelina. *Thump, thump, thump* went her heart, like a policeman beating at a criminal's door. She turned the doll over with her foot. Angelina's face was cracked from one side to the other. Her mouth was still open, as were her eyes.

Triss dropped to her knees. "I'm sorry," she whispered uselessly. "I . . . I didn't mean to . . ."

She would be found kneeling over Angelina like a murderer over a corpse, she thought. Panicking, she pulled a couple of logs out of the basket by the hearth, pushed the broken doll into the basket's base, and piled the wood back on top.

The door opened unexpectedly, just as Triss was straightening again. She spun around guiltily, mouth dry. Somebody had come to investigate the terrible screaming, of course they had. What explanation could she possibly give them?

"Are you nearly ready?" Her father wore his coat and driving gloves.

Triss nodded mutely.

He glanced toward the window. "Birds have been making quite a racket this morning, haven't they?"

Out in the sunshine a few moments later, Triss kept her hands stuffed deep in her pockets so nobody would see them shaking.

Angelina moved and spoke and screamed. And I killed her.

That didn't happen that didn't happen that didn't happen . . .

But if it didn't . . . then it was all in my head. Which means there's something wrong with me. It means I'm really, badly ill.

Ordinary ill was fine, comforting even. But this was the wrong kind of ill. She didn't want to be ill in her mind. *I don't want to be taken away and hypnotized or have holes drilled in my head . . .*

So Triss stood in silence by the car, hunched in the golden light of the morning, and felt like a monster. Every time her parents went into the house to retrieve one last thing, she tensed. *Please don't look in the log basket. Please let's go, let's just go . . .*

She jumped out of her skin when a loud screaming became audible inside the house.

"I've found her!" It was her father's voice, sounding strained and at his temper's edge. Triss's heart lurched. But it was not Angelina that her father carried out into the daylight. It was Pen, sobbing, roaring, and doing her best to stamp her heels into his kneecaps. "She tried to hide in the attic."

"I'm not coming!" It was hard to make out Pen's words. She screamed herself hoarse, a few half-comprehensible words lost in the tornado of her rage. ". . . see she's lying . . . can't make me sit with her . . . hate you all!"

Triss slipped into the backseat through one door, and Pen was bundled in next to her through the opposite door. Once there, Pen curled herself into a tight, hostile ball and flinched up against the door to be as far from Triss as possible.

She thinks I'm pretending to be ill, thought Triss limply. *Pretending so I can get everybody's attention. The attention that* she *wants. I wish she was right.* Triss's father climbed into the driver's seat and pressed the starter motor button. There was a whine, then the main engine chuckled and purred. At last, at long last, they were on their way in their mint-green Sunbeam.

With a relief almost painful, Triss saw the cottage recede behind them, and then they were buzzing down lane after lane at a giddy thirty miles an hour. Triss's hair whipped around her face, and as the scene of her crime receded behind her, the knots in her stomach started to loosen. Perhaps illnesses could be left behind, just like small, badly concealed china corpses.

Hills reared under them like bad-tempered beach donkeys, and the road twisted as if trying to throw them. Dry stone walls wriggled, rose, and fell on either side. Then a white-painted sign tore past. Oxford that way, 85 miles, Ellchester this way, 20 miles.

Triss leaned her cheek against the cool wooden paneling inside the car door, clinging to the sense of familiarity.

I'm safe. I'm going home to Ellchester.

The first thing anybody noticed on the approach to Ellchester was the Three Maidens.

The most impressive of the trio of bridges spanned the width of the Ell estuary in one long, elegant stride, its smooth arc and sandy-gold paint visible for miles against the glittering blue of the water. The second bridge cut a lofty line across and over the city itself, supported by three of Ellchester's eight hills, one of which was now capped with a pyramid-shaped building in dull pink stone, the city's soon-to-be-completed railway station. The last stretched out to join the rising slope of the valley on the other side. Between them, they held aloft the recently constructed railway line.

Everyone agreed that before the Three Maidens were built, Ellchester had been "in a decline," which seemed to mean a slow, sorry sort of collapse like a sandcastle in the rain.

Then Piers Crescent, her father, had come forward with his plans for the Three Maidens and shown that, in spite of the intervening estuary and awkward hills, the railway could be brought to Ellchester. Everybody called the bridges "a miracle of engineering." They had changed everything and brought money to the city, and now his was one of the best-known and most popular names in Ellchester.

Triss never saw the Three Maidens hove into view without feeling a surge of pride. Today, however, the surge of warmth was followed by a bitter aftertaste, as she remembered the overheard conversation and the newspaper article. If somebody *was* trying to frighten her father, did it have anything to do with his work?

Triss's father did not steer into the busy, hillocky heart of Ellchester, with its maze of bridges and zigzag steps. Instead he drove into the quieter districts, where grand three-story houses were arranged in squares, each with a little park in the center. The Sunbeam pulled up in one such square in front of one such house, and in the backseat Triss let out her breath slowly. Home.

As she followed the rest of her family through the front door, Triss felt her heart sink. She had expected everything to click back into place once she was home. The crowded hatstand, the waxed parquet floor, and the twilight-yellow Chinese-style wallpaper were familiar, or felt as if they should be, but the click did not come.

"Oh, now, who did that?" Triss's mother pointed at some little flakes of earth on the smooth, clean floor. "Which one of you forgot to brush her feet? Pen?"

"Why are you looking at me?" exploded Pen. Her glance of incandescent rage, however, was darted at Triss, not her mother. "Why does everybody always think it's me?" She thundered away up the stairs, and a door could be heard slamming with shattering force.

Their mother sighed. "Because it always is, Pen," she muttered wearily, pinching the bridge of her nose.

"Margaret will take care of the floors when she comes in tomorrow," said her husband, placing a reassuring hand on his wife's shoulder. Margaret was the "woman who did" for the Crescents, coming in to clean for a few hours each morning.

"Oh—I must warn Margaret that we have returned early," their mother said with an exhausted air. "And find Cook and tell her that we are home after all and will need her. I had told her that she could take a few days off while we were away—if she has gone to see her sister in Chesterfield, I do not know *what* we will do. I must make sure that Donovan girl has moved out, and send letters to the recruitment agency, asking them for another governess. And if I do not send word to the butcher and baker, there will be no deliveries tomorrow."

Triss's recollections stirred. The "Donovan girl" was Miss Donovan, the Crescent daughters' last governess, who had just been turned away for being "flighty." Triss's mother had given previous governesses notice for "dumb insolence," for being "too confident," or for taking the girls out to museums or parks, where Triss might catch a chill. Triss no longer bothered much with the governesses. If she let herself like them, or care about their lessons, it was a wrench when they left.

"Celeste," Triss's father murmured in a quiet and deliberately even voice, "perhaps first of all you could look to see whether any new letters arrived for us while we were away."

Triss's mother cast a puzzled look toward the empty basket where the family's post was always kept, and then realization seemed to dawn in her spring-blue eyes. She wet her lips, then turned to Triss with a warm, soft smile.

"Darling, why don't you run upstairs, unpack your things, and then lie down for a while?"

Triss nodded and headed up the stairs. As she stepped onto the landing and passed out of her parents' view, however, she halted. It was happening again. A conversation was waiting to be had behind her back.

Chewing her lip, she opened the nearest door and then closed it again, so it would sound as if she had withdrawn into her room. Leaning against the wall she waited, and sure enough was soon rewarded with the sound of voices.

"Piers, do you mean *those* letters? I thought we agreed not to read anything else sent by that man—"

"I know, but right now we need to understand whether he was the one who attacked Triss. If he *is* trying to bully me, then perhaps there will be a letter from the man himself, instead of the usual. If he has written to us with demands or threats, at least then we will know."

Hearing steps on the stairs, Triss turned to flee, and felt panic creeping into her soul like cold water into her socks.

Which room is mine?

There was no time to lose. The steps were reaching the head of the stairs. Triss jerked open the nearest door and slipped within, closing it quickly but quietly behind her.

The room beyond was dim, illuminated only by the little sunlight soaking through the thick amber curtains. The air smelled tired, like old clothes packed away for a special occasion that had never come.

Triss held her breath and pressed her ear to the door. Outside she could hear footsteps striding along the landing, heavy steps that she easily identified as belonging to her father. Soon she could hear the muffled sounds of him talking in the study, using his loud, careful telephone voice. The telephone was a relatively recent addition to the house and still jarred with its newness and brashly insistent bell. Sometimes it seemed that Triss's father felt he had to overbear it with force of personality, in case it had a mind to take over the house.

Triss felt a slow wash of relief. *He didn't hear me. But where am I? This isn't my room. This is too big to be my room.*

Her eyes slowly adjusted to the gloom, and with a wash of alarm she realized how badly she had mistaken her way.

Oh no—not here! I'm not supposed to be here!

She knew the room now, of course. Nothing had changed since she had last seen it. Nothing had been moved.

The bed was made, with clean sheets. The dented surface of the desk had been dusted and polished. A telescope moped in a corner, its tripod folded in like the legs of a dead crane fly. The top shelf held books on Arctic exploration, astronomy, and fighter planes, with a cluster of peeling green-and-yellow detective novels at the end. On the bottom shelf a series of photographs had been carefully arranged edge to edge. As her eye glided across, boy became youth became man, the last photo showing him in a military uniform.

Sebastian.

Occasionally Triss had been brought in to see this room, as if it was a sick relative. Entering without permission, on the other hand, would be the worst kind of trespass, almost a blasphemy.

Triss knew she should leave at once but found herself overwhelmed by a guilty fascination. She moved farther into the room.

The bedroom had a churchy feel. You could tell that this was a sacred place full of rules you might break. Sebastian was a lot like church, with everyone solemnly knowing what they were meant to feel and when.

We will now consider mercy. We will now pity the poor. We will now forgive our enemies.

We all loved Sebastian very much. We are all very sad he has gone. We all remember him daily.

But do I? Triss ran a curious fingertip over the glass of the uniformed photo. It left no smudge of dust on her finger. *Do I love him? Am I sad? Do I remember him?*

Triss did have a strong but unfocused sense that everything had once been better, and that everyone had once been happier. Sebastian was tied in her mind to that betterness and happiness.

She remembered laughing. Sebastian had said the sort of things nobody else dared say, and it had made her laugh.

Now, however, Sebastian was their other, special sibling, the one who needed help with his possessions even more than she did. The one who said nothing during family discussions but whose absence left eddies and whorls in what other people said.

If Triss were found here, even *she* would be in trouble. She might have special privileges for loitering near death's door, but Sebastian had passed through it and so outranked her.

The atmosphere was so overpowering that it took Triss a second to realize that she could now hear her mother's distinctive, rapid step climbing the stairs. The landing outside creaked, and then to her horror Triss saw the doorknob turn.

Mother's coming in here!

There was only one place to hide. Triss dropped to the floor and scrambled under the bed even as the door opened.

I don't do things like this, Triss thought helplessly as she watched her mother's silk-stockinged ankles and buckled shoes come into view. *I don't sneak into places and hide and spy.* And yet she stayed still as a mouse and watched as her mother lit the gas, seated herself at the desk, and unlocked the drawer.

Peering from under the tasseled counterpane, Triss could see her mother carefully pull the desk drawer open a mere half an inch. Immediately the crack bristled with paper corners, as if a host of envelopes had been crammed in by force and were in a hurry to burst out. Her mother's mouth tightened, and her hand made a nervous motion as if the envelopes were hot and she was afraid to touch them. Then she clenched her jaw, tweaked out one envelope, and ripped it open.

Nothing happened in her mother's face. Nothing happened, except that Triss had a feeling that staying expressionless was taking a lot of effort.

Triss was too far away to make out the words on the letter, but she was struck by the whiteness of the paper. It looked clean, crisp, and new, in a room where nothing was supposed to be clean, crisp, or new.

Her mother's hands were shaking. At last she made a sound of utter misery, somewhere between a moan and a gulp, and crammed both letter and envelope back with its fellows before forcing the drawer shut and shakily locking it.

Letters. Sebastian's desk was full of recently arrived letters. Her mother had gone to see if any new ones had arrived. But why would they appear in Sebastian's desk? Who would put them there? And how could they get into the house and sneak themselves into a locked desk?

The scene was like a dream, nonsensical but drenched with ominous and unfathomed meaning, full of the familiar turned alien. All of a sudden the entire world seemed to be the Wrong Kind of Ill.

Chapter 4

WAR

THERE WAS SOMETHING TERRIBLE AND UNCOMfortable about hearing her mother sob.

It was a relief when at last Triss's mother sniffed and rallied, carefully wiping away tears with the very tips of two fingers, so as not to smudge her makeup. She locked the drawer again and pocketed the key, then stood and left the room, closing the door carefully, as if an invalid slept in the empty bed.

Triss remained where she was, listening as her mother's tread moved away across the landing.

A distant door closed, and from behind it came the dull murmur of voices. At last Triss dared to crawl out from under the bed. The locked drawer taunted her, and she gave its handle a small, futile tug, but the drawer would not yield.

Taking a deep breath, she softly opened the door and slipped out, closing it behind her. The landing was empty, and Triss uttered a quiet prayer as she slipped across to the door opposite.

Please let it be the right one this time . . . To her relief, it opened onto a little room that she recognized instantly. Patchwork quilt on the bed, new *Flower Fairies* book on the bedside table, primrose wallpaper . . . yes, it was her room. It smelled faintly of cod-liver oil and the potpourri in the drawers. An old tongue-shaped cocoa stain that had never been entirely cleaned out of the carpet was a familiar roughness under her foot.

A wave of relief broke over her, then lost its bubbling momentum and drained away, leaving her cold and uncertain. Even this, her own little lair, gave her no sense of comfort or security.

Mother said the letters were from that man, the one they're worried about. They think he attacked me, so they whisked me home, where I'd be safe. But if he left letters in Sebastian's desk, then he must have been in the room somehow.

Home isn't safe. Whoever he is, he can get in.

Her wardrobe loomed at her from the corner of the room. Triss's imagination instantly crowded it with creeping assassins. When she threw open the door, however, nothing but innocuous dresses stared back at her.

On impulse, she ran her fingers over lace collars and cotton frocks, trying to tease out her own memories. Her hand paused on a small, cream-colored blazer, with a straw boater hung over the same hanger. These did stir a memory, but also a painful briar-tangle of feelings.

Two years ago, Triss had worn this uniform during her brief time at St. Bridget's Preparatory School. She had loved going to the school, but it had made her ill.

Triss had not noticed it making her ill. In fact, she had thought she was getting better, brighter, and happier. After spending so much of her life in one house, leaving it each morning filled her with an almost painful excitement. Her parents had changed, however, seeming discontented and short of temper. Everything had turned wrong and sour, and she sensed deep in her gut that it was her doing. Often they had felt her brow at breakfast, then decided she was *too* excited and kept her home. Every day they interrogated her about the school, and declared that the teachers had been negligent in some way that she had missed.

One day Triss was caught gossiping in class and was kept back after school. It was only for ten minutes, but her parents were in an uproar. After bitter recriminations the Crescents had taken both their daughters out of the school. Triss had begged her father to let her stay, which made him more agitated than she had ever seen him before or since. He was doing all of this for *her*. He was defending *her*. Why was she trying to turn her back on her home? She had wept and wept for hours afterward, until her stomach turned sick and her head ached. Then, of course, she had realized that she *must* be ill, and that her parents must have been right all along.

Knowing that the uniform no longer fit filled Triss with a saddened yearning, and a twist of guilt at the feeling. She closed the wardrobe door to block it from sight. Even as she did so, she thought she glimpsed a tiny hint of movement in her peripheral vision. She tensed and stared around the room, senses tingling.

Everything around her was still, but her gaze was returned. From the dresser and side table stared the rag dolls her mother had sewn her, the cherry-mouthed French *bébé* doll, and a china ballerina her father had given her after her first serious fever, almost like a reward. On any other day their presence should have been comforting, but now as Triss looked at them, all she could think of was Angelina's shattered face.

They were motionless, nothing but dumb, soft bundles of cloth and china. Or perhaps they were rigid, watching her, waiting for her to look away so that they could move again . . .

Stop looking at me.

She could not bear the thought that all of them might slowly turn their heads to stare at her, chime out china words, or start to scream. Scrambling off the bed, Triss snatched up a pillowcase. She hastily swept all the dolls into it and knotted the top. Looking for somewhere to hide the bundle, she dragged open a drawer, then froze, staring down into it.

Within it she could see the diaries she had kept for years, each with its different leather or fabric cover. Every one lay open, a ravaged paper frill showing where all their pages had been torn out. They had been ripped in just the same way as the diary she had taken on holiday.

This changed everything. One destroyed diary smacked of an act of impulsive spite, the sort of thing that Pen might well do if she had the chance. The destruction of seven diaries in two different places suggested method and planning. Was Pen really that organized?

Perhaps Pen had not done it at all. Perhaps her father's mysterious enemy had been in Triss's room and gone through her things.

"Mommy!" It was meant to be a call, but it turned into a croak instead, as the force left her voice. The next moment Triss felt frightened and embarrassed by the tortured books and shut the drawer quickly, glad that nobody had heard her.

She hurled the pillowcase of dolls into her wardrobe instead, and dived back into her bed. For a long while she stayed perfectly still, listening for any sound from within. There was nothing but silence.

Even in Triss's quilt-fortress the scents of cooking found her out. Evidently Mrs. Basset, the cook, had been tracked down after all. However hard Triss tried to focus on understanding everything that had happened, her mind was soon a slave of her stomach, and her attention fixed on the yawning emptiness inside her.

When lunch was called, it took all her willpower to walk down the stairs instead of running. Her parents were fortunately distracted and did not appear to notice her meal vanishing almost as soon as it was set in front of her, nor did they catch her stealthily ladling more onto her plate.

Triss could not understand how they could sit so mildly and calmly at the table and talk about boring, ordinary things as if they mattered. Her mother was complaining that Cook had asked for the whole of Tuesday off, in lieu of the break she had been promised.

Once again, Pen did not come down to lunch, and Triss was tortured by the sight of her sister's food gradually cooling and congealing on the table. Only by clasping her hands tightly together in her lap did she prevent herself from snatching at it.

"She'll get weak at this rate," sighed their mother. "Triss—could you be a love and take it up to her room? If she won't answer, leave it by her door."

"Yes!" Triss struggled to suppress her eagerness while her mother fetched a tray.

Carrying Pen's lunch up the stairs, Triss managed to wait until she was unobserved before furtively picking at it. *Just a potato—she won't miss one. And . . . that piece of bacon. And a carrot.* It took a lot of self-control to leave it at that, and Triss proceeded to Pen's room with haste so that she could put the rest of the meal out of temptation's way.

"Pen?" she called quietly, knocking on what she believed and hoped was Pen's door. "Your lunch is out here!" There was no response. Triss wondered if Pen was sitting sullenly within, ignoring her, or whether the younger girl had climbed out her window and run off in yet another fit of truancy. She laid the tray on the ground. "Pen, I'm leaving it by your door."

Please come to the door and take the food, Pen. Please—I don't think I can resist it if you don't.

No Pen appeared. The scented steam from the plate was in Triss's nose, and even when she closed her eyes, she could still see the golden-crusted pie with its glossy gravy, and the pepper freckles on the potatoes' creamy flesh . . .

It was too much for her. With a small, helpless sob, Triss dropped to her knees and snatched up the fork. Pen's food tasted better than hers had, better than anything. She tried to make every mouthful last, but could not. She tried to stop, but could not.

And as she was shakily licking the plate, she heard the faint sound of a voice in her father's study, the study that should have been empty.

Triss set down the empty plate on the tray, then gingerly drew closer to the study. When she put her ear to the door, she heard what sounded a good deal like Pen, talking in a low, steady, furtive tone. Peering in through the keyhole, Triss could indeed see Pen. The younger girl was facing away, but Triss could still see exactly what she was doing. She was making free with that most august and sacrosanct of objects, the family phone. Triss felt her eyebrows rise. She could not have been much more surprised if she had caught Pen borrowing the family car.

It was a tall black candlestick telephone and was fixed to the wall for ease of use, so that you needed only one hand to use it instead of two. It was placed at a height convenient for Triss's father, but Pen was standing on tiptoe on a chair to bring her face level with the mouthpiece. Her right hand held the little conical earpiece to her ear.

Triss could not make out her sister's murmured words. Pen looked absurd perched there, like a tiny child playing at being the parent in a game of make-believe. Only Pen's hushed tones made the matter seem more serious.

As Triss watched, Pen hung the little earpiece back on its hook and stepped down. Triss straightened up, and a few seconds later Pen opened the study door. Finding herself face-to-face with Triss, Pen froze, her face a mask of guilty terror.

"Who were you talking to, Pen?" asked Triss.

Pen took a deep breath but found no words. Her face reddened and twitched, and Triss could almost see her sister hastily auditioning a range of lies and denials to figure out whether any of them would do. Then Pen's eye fell on the empty plate by her door, and when her gaze returned to Triss's face, the terror had been replaced by outrage and disbelief.

"You ate my lunch!" Her voice was so shrill it was almost a squeak. "You did, didn't you? You ate it! You stole my lunch!"

"You didn't come down for it!" Triss protested, feeling her hackles rise defensively. "I knocked—I tried to give it to you—"

"I . . . I'm going to tell Mother and Father . . ." Pen was gasping in angry breaths as if she might explode at any moment.

"They won't believe you." Triss had not meant to say it. She had been thinking it, but she had never intended the words to leave her head. It was true, though, and Triss could see the same knowledge reflected in the frustration and rage on Pen's face.

"You think you can do anything you like, don't you?" snapped Pen, in a tight, bitter little voice. "You think you've won already. But you haven't."

"Pen"—Triss struggled to undo the damage—"I'm sorry I ate your lunch. I'll . . ." She steeled herself to promise Pen part of her own dinner, but knew this was a promise she could not keep. "I'll make it up to you. Please, can't we just stop this? Why do you hate me so much?" All at once Triss felt that she could not bear Pen's relentless animosity on top of everything else.

"Who do you think you're kidding?" Pen's face was a map of disbelief. She leaned forward to peer into Triss's eyes, her own gaze pit-bull fierce. "*I know about you*. I know what you are. I saw you when you climbed out of the Grimmer. *I was there*."

"You were there?" Triss took a step forward, only to see her sister flinch back. "Pen, you have to tell me everything you saw! Did you see me fall in? What happened?"

"Oh, stop it!" snapped Pen. "You think you're really clever, don't you?" She swallowed hard and clenched her jaw as if there was nothing she wanted more than to bite somebody. "You know what? You're not as clever as you think. You're getting everything just a bit wrong. Everything. All the time. And sooner or later they'll notice. They'll see."

In Pen's face Triss could see nothing but a declaration of war. The younger girl's incomprehensible words boiled and seethed in Triss's mind like a shoal of piranhas, and Triss's desperation was swiftly replaced by a flood of frustration and resentment. She had wanted to be sorry about eating Pen's lunch, had wanted to talk it out with her, but all of these feelings were now swallowed up by bitterness and a stinging sense of unfairness. It was always this way, she remembered that now. She would try to reach out, only to be knocked back by Pen's ingenious and relentless hatred.

"You're lying, aren't you?" Triss hissed. "You didn't see anything at all. You're just trying to scare me. Liar!"

She was filled with a seething desire to strike back, and with a honey-sweet throb of power realized that, if she wanted, she could get Pen into trouble without even trying. *I can tell them she screamed at me and made my head hurt.* As the thought passed through her mind, it started to seem to her that her head *did* hurt, that Pen *had* made her feel ill. *And I can tell them she saw something the day I fell in the Grimmer; they'll make her tell.*

"Girls?" Their mother appeared at the head of the stairs. "Girls—are you having a row up here?"

Both girls froze and involuntarily glanced across at each other, more like conspirators than opponents. If there was no row, neither of them would be in trouble. On the other hand, if either of them wanted to plead a grievance, the other would have to do the same, louder and harder. Who had more to lose from a cascade of blame?

Triss had been on the verge of calling down the stairs to her parents, to tell them what Pen had said and report the illicit phone use. Now, however, her nerve failed her. Despite her rage, there was a creeping fear that perhaps Pen really did know something terrible about her, something that Triss would not want her parents to know.

"No," answered Pen sullenly. "We're not rowing. I was just . . . telling Triss something I thought she ought to do. Loudly."

"Really?" Triss's mother raised both eyebrows.

"Yes. You see"—Pen's gaze crept sideways to Triss's face—"Triss brought me up my lunch, and I told her I wasn't hungry. And . . . she was. So I told her to eat it. And so she did."

Triss's mother looked to Triss, a question in her eyes. Triss's mouth was dry. She had been braced for Pen to accuse her of lunch theft. Now, for no obvious reason, Pen seemed to be letting her off the hook. Feeling a little as if somebody had poked her in the eye with an olive branch, Triss slowly nodded, confirming Pen's story.

"Oh, Triss!" her mother said, sounding half scandalized, half concerned.

"You see, she's really hungry all the time," continued Pen,

frowning deeply at her scuffed shoes. "*Really* hungry. And just now I was saying that she ought to tell you, in case it meant she was still ill, only she didn't want to because it might worry you."

"Triss! Darling!" Her mother dropped down onto her knees and gave Triss a tight, brief hug. "Oh, you should have said! You should always tell me things that are worrying you, poor froglet!"

"Mommy," Pen asked in the smallest of voices, "is Triss going to be all right?" Her brow puckered and her mouth drooped a little, as if she was a much younger child, frightened by the dark. "Is she still sick? Only . . . I got really scared last night. When I saw her in the garden. She was acting all funny."

Triss's blood turned cold. *That little snake. She saw me under the apple tree last night. She must have seen me from her window.*

Their mother looked at Triss again, no suspicion or accusation in her gaze, only the beginnings of a bewildered smile. "In the *garden*?"

"I have no idea what she's talking about." Triss was amazed that she managed to keep her voice so level, so convincingly bemused.

"Yes—that's the scariest bit," mumbled Pen. She reached out and wound one finger round a fold of their mother's skirt, as if for comfort. "I really don't think Triss remembers. But I saw her, and she was crawling around in the mud and stinky apples for ages. She looked all starey, and her nightdress was mucky . . ."

"Triss, darling." Her mother's voice was very soft, and with a sinking of the heart Triss knew what she was going to ask. "Can you fetch your nightdress? There's a love."

Inside her room, Triss tried to scratch off some of the mud and grass stains with her fingernails, but to little avail. There was no spare nightdress she could substitute. Her neck and face felt hot as she carried the grimy, crumpled mess out to her mother, who unfolded it and surveyed it in silence.

For the briefest moment, Triss caught Pen flashing her a hard, appraising glance. The whole conversation had been a trap. Triss could see only now that the pit was gaping in front of her.

"Pen was using Father's telephone." The words fell from Triss's mouth like stones, hard, cold, and bitter tasting.

"I didn't!" Pen's face took on a look of simple blank incomprehension, so realistic that for a moment Triss half believed in it. "Mommy—why is Triss saying that?"

"She's lying!" protested Triss. "She's always lying!" For the first time, however, she saw her mother's seesaw teeter and threaten to settle in a new direction.

"I didn't!" Pen sounded as if she was close to tears. "Triss did say something about hearing voices coming from the study when she came up, and said it sounded like somebody on the telephone, but there wasn't anyone there! There weren't any voices! Mommy—she's scaring me!"

"Girls, I want you to wait here." Their mother half walked, half ran to the stairs and returned a few moments later with their father, who gave them both a brief, distracted smile that did not reach his eyes. He walked into the study, and then Triss could hear him talking loudly to the operator, asking what other calls there had been in the last day.

When he returned, he knelt down before Triss, sighed, and looked her straight in the eye.

"Think carefully, Triss. When was it you thought you saw Pen using the telephone?"

"Just now," whispered Triss. His words had already told her all she needed to know, however. Not, "When was it you saw Pen using the telephone," but "When was it you *thought* you saw Pen using the telephone."

The operator must have told him that there had been no call made from their house. What could that mean? Had Pen been playacting with the phone after all? Could she even have put on a performance, to trick Triss into looking crazy? Or . . . was it possible that Pen never had been in the study, and that Triss really had imagined it?

Triss's mother put her arms around her.

"You're not in trouble," she said very, very gently. Triss's blood ran cold.

Chapter 5

SWALLOWED MARBLES

TRISS'S PARENTS WERE KIND. TOO KIND. THEY talked everything over with her in the front room, after her father had phoned the doctor to make an appointment for the next day. There was nothing to worry about, they told her. She hadn't done anything wrong. It was just a silly leftover bit of illness, but they would take her to the doctor and he would take care of it.

The doctor would see through her, she was sure of it. He would be able to tell at a glance how ill she really was. *Seeing-things* ill. Doll-killing ill. Windfall-guzzling ill. But none of Triss's tried and tested strategies worked. *I don't want to go to the doctor, I don't feel like it, it would make my head hurt, his office smells funny, it scares me . . .*

In the end, what made her stop trying to squirm off the hook was the expression on her father's face. It was pained and drawn in a way she had not seen before, and it made him look older. She could not bear making her father look older.

"Triss, there's no need to be scared." He pulled her over to sit in his lap and hugged her. "You trust me, don't you?"

Triss nodded mutely, her cheek against his lapel. Even as she did so, though, the memory of the strange conversations she had overheard stung her, like a forgotten splinter in her skin nudged by a careless gesture. Her nod was a lie. She did not, could not, completely trust him.

"And if you're very good and very brave, then after we see the doctor, I'll take you down Marley Street and we can buy you a new nightdress. And a nice new party dress at the same time. Would you like that?"

Triss hesitated and then nodded again, slowly. A new party dress meant that he still loved her and that she was still Triss in his eyes. Party dresses meant parties, which meant not being locked up in a mental hospital.

Triss felt her mother's hand stroking her head, and with a rush of relief she felt a sense of her own power return to her. They were worried about her, but they were still on her side. They would still do anything they could to stop her lip from trembling. The feeling of safety was fleeting, however. Pen would be planning something new, and Triss felt her own rage and resources rallying in preparation for battle.

Triss suffered a largely sleepless night, kept awake by her thoughts and the pattering of the rain. Even when she dipped into sleep, it was puddle-thin and streaked with dreams. She dreamed that she was in a dressmaker's shop to be measured, but that when she took off her own frock to try on the new one, she found she had another dress on underneath. She took off that one as well, only to find yet another dress beneath that one. Dress after dress she removed, becoming thinner and thinner all the while, until it came to her that in the end there would be nothing left of her, except a pile of discarded clothes and a disembodied wail.

But the dressmaker kept making her take off dress after dress, and snickered all the while, with a laugh like the rustling of leaves.

"Five," it rasped as it shivered with mirth. "Only five left to go."

Triss woke with a lurch. Her heart banged a terrified tattoo until she worked out where she was and satisfied herself that her limbs were not made of dress fabric.

"Triss! Pen! Breakfast!" Hearing her mother calling from downstairs, Triss roused her wits, scrambled out of bed, and dressed quickly. As she was dragging a brush through her hair, however, little brown fragments of something tumbled from one of the tangles. With sudden foreboding, Triss peered into the mirror of her little dressing table. Her shaking fingers teased a crinkled brown shape from her hair. It was a dead leaf.

"But . . . but I didn't go out last night!" she exclaimed helplessly. "Not this time! I didn't! I didn't! That's . . . that's . . . not *fair*!" Her gaze misted and her eyes stung, but tears would not come. Blinking was difficult and painful.

I couldn't have gone out last night without remembering . . . Could I?

There were no grass stains on her discarded nightshirt, but when Triss examined the floor, she found wisps of straw and little crumbs of what looked like dried mud. Perhaps it meant nothing. Perhaps she had brought them in on her shoes the day before. When she dragged open her sash window it was reassuringly stiff and yielded only with a grating of paint, suggesting that it had not been opened in a long time.

In the square below, she watched the leaves of the park trees bouncing under the onslaught of the rain. Down on the slick, dark pavement she could see tiny, pale flickers as each unseen raindrop struck home.

It was raining all night. I could hear the pattering whenever I couldn't sleep. So if I had gone out, my hair and nightshirt would be wet. And that would be wet mud on the floor, not dry. I couldn't *have gone out.*

Her mind had been fighting off the image of herself leaping out the window like a mad thing and rampaging through garden after garden, guzzling squash and going through dustbins like a starved cat. Now another image sprang to mind, that of Pen sneaking into her room with fistfuls of grit and dead leaves, in order to sprinkle them on the floor and in Triss's hair.

Would she really do that?

Pen hates *me. She'd love it if I ran down the stairs right now in tears, sobbing about dead leaves in my hair. She wants me to look mad so I'll get sent away and locked up. Then she'd have all the attention she ever wanted.*

But I'm not going to let her get rid of me.

Triss brushed her hair with great care, cleaned the grit off the floor, and walked down the stairs with all the calm she could feign. She had a battle to fight.

In the late afternoon Triss's father drove her into town, the rain thudding against the canvas roof of the car. Every time they stopped at a junction, awaiting the wave of the white-gloved policeman ordering the traffic, a small gaggle of boys and girls in hand-me-down clothes would gather by the road to gawk at the Sunbeam.

For all they knew, she might be a princess or a movie star.

But today she could not feel glamorous and did not want to be special or mysterious. She felt small and miserable, and this morning the world outside seemed large, alarming, and dreamlike. The road was chaos. Carts lurched, and horse flanks gleamed like varnish. Trams clanged and shuddered along their shining tracks, the faces clustered inside them as unsmiling as soapsuds.

Ellchester was a city of bridges, and had been even before the Three Maidens were built. Her crooked hills demanded it so that the biggest roads did not need to dip, climb, or buck but could sail serenely from summit to summit. The nethermost streets weaved through old arched bridges in ancient walls that bulged like dough, while above them stretched bold Victorian bridges with the city's crest carved in the sides.

Dr. Mellows's office was on a steep street to the north of town, full of tall houses of murky brown brick with long, gawping windows. Triss's father parked carefully, turning the large wheels so that they lodged against the curb and hauling hard on the brake so that the car would not roll downhill.

The hall and reception were pill-pink and pill-green, and smelled of clean. The receptionist with the bobbing curls over one eye remembered Triss and gave her a big scarlet-painted smile.

"Yes, Dr. Mellows is expecting you. Do you want to go through now?"

"I'd like to talk to Dr. Mellows first, if you don't mind," Triss's father said quickly.

Triss was left in the waiting room, where she sat feeling sick.

Five minutes later her father came out, gave her his special smile, and stroked back her hair.

"Dr. Mellows is ready for you now. I'll be right here."

Triss was shown into the doctor's office and found Dr. Mellows sitting at his desk. He was a tall, grizzled man in his early fifties, with a comforting rumble of a voice that seemed to come from somewhere deep under his rib cage. She had seen him so often over the years that he was almost like an extra uncle who was brought out for special occasions.

"So. How's my little hero? How's my smallest soldier?" It was his typical greeting. His eyes were alive with the usual mixture of twinkle and appraisal. The only thing that was different was that there were three large books on his desk, one of which was open. "Oh, now, don't look so frightened! No pills or needles today—nothing to scare you. We're just going to have a little talk. Sit down."

Triss sat in a comfortable chair on the other side of the desk, her gaze dropping briefly to the books in front of the doctor. The title along the spine of one of the closed books read *Studies in Hysteria*. The open book had the words "The Ego and the Id" across the top of each page.

"Now, I hear that you've had a nasty fever. How are you feeling now?"

"Oh, much better." Triss made her voice bubble-bright.

"But . . . not all better? Some things still don't feel quite right, do they?" Dr. Mellows watched her with that same steady, unblinking twinkle, the pad of his thumb teasing at a corner of a page. "Why don't you tell me about it?"

So Triss told him. She told him that she was feeling fine, but a bit hungrier than usual. She told him that she thought she might have walked in her sleep back at the holiday cottage, and it scared her a bit. When he asked her if there was anything else that worried her, she spent a few moments with her head on one side, as if racking her brains, then blithely shook her head.

When Dr. Mellows asked her about her claim to have heard Pen talking on the telephone the day before, Triss crumpled her brow, looking rueful and reluctant to speak.

"You . . . you won't make everybody angry with Pen, will you? Only . . . I think it might have been a sort of a . . . a joke. I think maybe she pretended she was talking on the phone, so I'd tell people and then look stupid. She . . . does things like that sometimes. But you won't say anything, will you? You won't get her into trouble?"

She bit her lip and looked across at the doctor, and could see from his face how he saw her. Brave but beleaguered, the long-suffering victim of a more spiteful sibling.

"And you're afraid that if she gets in trouble, she'll take it out on you, I'll warrant." He sighed. "Yes, I see. Don't worry, you leave that with me."

Triss let out her breath slowly, trying not to show how her pulse was racing. *Two can play at your game, Pen.*

"Well, good, good." Dr. Mellows smiled at Triss, and despite his words she wondered if there was the tiniest hint of disappointment in his gaze.

"Can you stop me from sleepwalking?" she asked carefully. "Everybody seems really worried about it, and I don't want to make anybody upset."

"Of course you don't." He smiled at her kindly. "Well, let's see what we can do. Young Theresa, your father tells me that before you were ill, you fell into some kind of a millpond, and that you don't remember doing so—that you don't remember any of that day, in fact. Is that true?"

Triss nodded.

"Now, how shall I explain this?" The doctor smiled warmly and gently. "Suppose one day you swallowed a big marble. Not that I'm saying a big girl like you would do anything so silly. Well, after you'd done so, that marble would cause you all sorts of trouble until it was out in the open again. You wouldn't be able to see it, you might not even work out what was causing the problem, but you'd have a deuce of a tummy ache.

"The funny thing is, sometimes memories can be like that. If something happens that scares us, or that we don't want to remember, we swallow it down, just like that marble." He was talking slowly and carefully now. "We can't see the memory anymore, but there it is deep inside us, creating problems. I think that's what causes your sleepwalking. The trick is to *remember*. Bring the marble back into the light of day. Then it won't bother you anymore."

"But having this marble doesn't mean I'm mad, does it?"

The doctor looked up at her in surprise, then gave a short gust of laughter. "No, no, no! Lots of people sleepwalk, particularly youngsters like you. Don't you worry about that. It's not like you're seeing pixies in your porridge, is it?"

Seeing things! Seeing things! He knows! He knew all the time!

There was no challenge or scrutiny in the doctor's eyes, however, as he smiled and shut his book.

No. No, he doesn't know at all. That was supposed to make me feel better.

"Now, just hop up on the scales over there, and after that I'll set you free."

Triss obeyed, and barely noticed the way the doctor's eyebrows rose as the needle wobbled across the painted numerals.

As she followed her father out of the doctor's office, Triss felt a warm wash of relief, followed by a cold current of deep anxiety and self-loathing.

Well done, Triss, murmured a small voice in the depths of her gut. *You tricked him. You tricked the person who was trying to help you. So now he can't.*

Chapter 6

SCISSORS

MARLEY STREET WAS ONE OF THE HIGHEST thoroughfares in Ellchester and was now lit by electricity instead of gas. It transformed the street and made everything larger, louder, more vivid and exciting, as if all the shopping throngs were onstage and knew it

"Lambent's as usual?" her father asked. It was her favorite dress shop, Triss recalled after a moment's confusion. All her best-loved dresses had been bought there, after fits of illness. Her whooping-cough blue chiffon. Her three-day-fever cotton with the primrose print.

They halted before Lambent's, the golden letters reading LAMBENT & DAUGHTERS gleaming above the window in the light from the streetlamps. Beyond the glass posed five sleek plaster mannequins with pale silver skin. They were languorous and inhumanly slender, in the very latest style, and had utterly featureless faces.

Triss was just admiring their pastel-colored tasseled dresses when all five of the figures stirred. Very slowly they turned their eyeless heads to stare at her, and then hunched their shoulders slightly and leaned forward with an attitude of intense interest.

"No!" Triss leaped backward into the rain. Her father turned to her in surprise. She swallowed hard and forced her gaze away from the shop window. If her father saw her staring, he might look over his shoulder to investigate. What if he saw them move? Or what if he saw nothing strange at all? "Can't we go somewhere else this time? I heard there was a better shop, down . . . *that* way." She pointed blindly along the street, hoping that she could find some dressmaker in that direction to lend her story credence.

"Really? Yes, if you like." Her father opened his umbrella again. "What was this other dressmaker called?"

"I . . . I can't quite remember," said Triss, just relieved to find herself walking away from the ominous, watching mannequins. She strode on without looking back, her heart bouncing in her chest. "The name was something like . . . like . . . It was this one!" To her delight and relief she realized that they were passing a shop with a big metal pair of scissors suspended above the door by a slender chain, a sure sign of a tailor or dressmaker. Most of the clothes on the wire-frame dummies in the window seemed to be for men, but there were some women's clothes too. Triss's eyes flitted quickly to the twirly sky-blue letters over the door. "Grace and Scarp—yes, that was it!"

"All right." Her father smoothed back her damp hair. "Let's see what they have, shall we?"

Only as she was mounting the steps to the shop door did Triss felt a tickle of disquiet. It was not exactly fear, just a tug of unease, as if she had forgotten something important. A thought flashed into her mind, but it was not a terrible one, just odd. It was the memory of wrestling with her mother's scissors the morning after her fever, the tool sullenly uncooperative in her hands.

As Triss pushed the shop door open, there was a loud and sudden bang. Something clattered to the ground at her feet. She found herself staring down at the enormous pair of iron scissors that had been hanging over the door.

Her father had been holding his umbrella over her, and only this had prevented the blades from falling onto her head. The world around Triss seemed to bleach, and for a few moments she lost the ability to understand it. The great scissors at her feet were the only real thing. There was a lot of fuss all around her, and it sounded as if her father was making most of it. Everybody else seemed to be doing a lot of apologizing.

"No idea how the chain snapped . . . It was brand-new just a year ago . . ."

Triss and her father were hurried into the gleaming shop, and somebody made a great business of dabbing the raindrops off Triss's shoulders with a handkerchief, as if that would undo the scissor attack.

"My daughter," her father was declaring in tones of incandescent rage, "is in a state of delicate health. Her nerves cannot stand this sort of shock!"

One portly man managed to raise his voice above the chorus of apology. "Sir, we are most heartily and profoundly sorry. No excuse can be made for such an accident, but perhaps you will let us make some small amends. Perhaps a dress for your daughter with our compliments . . . and maybe a suit for yourself at a discount?"

Triss's father hesitated, the lid tottering on the boiling pot of his temper. Then he knelt down beside her.

"Triss—how are you? What do you want to do? Do you want to stay here and see what their dresses are like, or shall we go somewhere else?"

"It's all right," piped up Triss. "I don't mind if we stay here." It was true, she realized. She was shaken but did not feel bodily affected by the shock the way her father seemed to expect. Triss even felt slightly guilty about it, as if after his speech she had a duty to be more stricken.

"If you are sure." Her father briefly glanced across at the stout man who had offered the dress and discounted suit. "Triss, I need to talk to the manager about a few things. If I leave you to be measured, will you be all right?"

"But we know my measurements," Triss exclaimed, surprised.

"I think you should be measured again, love," her father said quietly but firmly, and again Triss saw the ghost of anxiety stalk past behind his smile. "Dr. Mellow says . . . that you may have lost a little weight."

Lost weight? *Lost* weight? With incredulity Triss recalled all the food she had devoured over the last three days. How could she have *lost* weight? Now that she thought about it, though, the doctor had looked rather taken aback when she climbed on the scales.

Still turning this revelation over in her head, Triss was led through a door marked RESERVED FOR SPECIAL GUESTS OF GRACE & SCARP. The room on the other side was small but much grander than the main shop floor and startlingly empty of people. The walls were patterned in serious-looking dark blue and silver-gray, and the furniture was mostly chrome and glossy leather. From racks along one wall hung folded bolts of black, brown, and navy-blue cloth. It was all very sensible and gentlemanly, and made Triss feel silly and out of place, like a dollop of jam on a newspaper.

"Please, do take a seat." The man who had shown her into this grand room pulled forward a large leather chair for her.

"This is our VIP room—reserved for royalty, the extravagant, and those we attack with scissors."

At first glance Triss had thought that the man was quite young. His hair was oiled to a fashionable treacly gleam. His smile was youthful as well, quick and humorous. Now that she took the time to look at him, however, she noticed horizontal lines creasing his forehead and a touch of grayness in his cheeks. His motions had a slight stiffness as well, and she realized that he must be older than her father. His manner was playful, but it was the careful playfulness of an old dog who no longer chases every ball. When he crossed the room, he walked with a shadow of a limp, though it was almost hidden by the neatness of his step.

"My name is Joseph Grace," he continued, "and since my partner is arranging your father's fitting, I shall be looking after you."

Triss seated herself on the throne-like chair. Now that the door had been closed behind her, cutting out the babble of voices in the main shop, she found she could hear music. It was a lilting violin piece, so clear that Triss cast a glance around, just in case there were live musicians like in the Lyons tea shops, but instead her eye fell on a gramophone in the corner, its turntable spinning, the mouth of its curved horn pointing into the room.

"Now," continued Mr. Grace, "what will you have? Tea and cake? Lemonade? Cocktails and oysters?"

Triss gave a little surprised squeak of laughter. "Tea—just tea, please. And . . . cake."

"Of course." Mr. Grace called through a door, and a little later a short young woman in a trim blue dress suit tripped in with a plate heaped with angel cakes, and tea in a bone-china cup.

Triss grinned, forgetting her duty to look woebegone. Perhaps the room seemed surprised to find a frilly thirteen-year-old in it, but Mr. Grace was not treating her with pained, nervous courtesy, as if she was some brittle brat who might fall into convulsions or tantrums at any moment. He was smiling at her gently and easily, as though they were old friends who had unexpectedly run into each other. He put a stylebook in Triss's hands, filled with fashion plates and pinned fabric swatches. He flicked past countless pages of elegant men-about-town and oblongs of dull suit fabric until he reached the brightly colored ladies' pages at the back. Triss turned the pages, feeling a fizz of power as she made her choices.

A smart young woman with stiffly curled golden hair led Triss to a changing room and took her measurements. After this, Triss was escorted back to the VIP room, where rolls of fabric were brought for her to feel. All of this made her feel quite queenly.

She did not notice how quickly the cakes beside her were vanishing until her groping hand found an empty plate.

"Oh! I . . . I'm sorry." Triss realized how rude she must seem.

"Please do not trouble yourself." The tailor waved away her apology. "VIPs are allowed infinite cake. Would you . . . care for more?"

Triss nodded, and watched hypnotized as two further platters arrived, stacked with fruitcake lined with royal icing. When she managed to unglue her eyes from the sight, she found that the tailor was studying her, a look of wry speculation in his large, serious brown eyes.

"Recovering your strength after an illness, isn't that right?" he asked quietly.

"Yes . . ." Triss became aware that her massacre of the cake plate was not really in keeping with the picture of delicacy her father had painted. "I've lost weight," she declared, defensively.

"Cake is the very best medicine." He gave Triss a small, confidential smile. "I'm sure a doctor told me that once. Personally I *always* take cake for my leg." He glanced ruefully at his slightly lame left leg. "And if one of our VIP guests decided to eat six plates' worth or more, nobody will hear of it from me."

Triss stripped the newly arrived plates of their cargo in minutes, and another three plates were brought in almost immediately, loaded with muffins. Triss attacked them without hesitation. It was such a relief not to have to hold back that she could have cried. *If I can eat enough here, without my family knowing, then perhaps I won't need more than an ordinary dinner tonight. I can seem normal.*

"Your leg—was that from the war?" Triss did not exactly mean to ask the question, but it slipped out.

"Yes," said Mr. Grace calmly. "A little souvenir from France."

Triss thought of Sebastian. She wondered how life would have been if he had come home from the war, saddened and limping but still kind and clever. The thought gave her a surprising hollow pain in her middle. She liked Mr. Grace, she decided.

As she was thinking this, she noticed for the first time that the tailor was wearing a black silk armband, almost camouflaged against his dark sleeve. It looked like a mourning band. Mr. Grace noticed the direction of her gaze.

"Ah." He touched the silk with a fingertip. "Another old wound. Older than the war, in fact."

"That's a long time." Triss had never heard of anybody wearing a mourning band for years.

"Somebody I loved passed on because I put my faith in a doctor who told me not to worry," Mr. Grace said quietly. "I wear it to remind myself that blind trust has consequences."

He stared through Triss for a second or two, then gave her a rueful smile. "Forgive me—and let me find an antidote to such a melancholy subject."

The tailor walked over to the gramophone and delicately lifted the needle so that the violins stopped mid-warble. He lifted out the record and tucked it back into its waiting sleeve, then pulled out another disc and placed it on the turntable. When the needle was lowered onto the record, it gave a short cough of static, as if clearing its throat, and then music began to play.

But this was not proper music! All the instruments plunged in at once, as if they had been holding a party and somebody had opened a door on them. There were trumpets and horns, but they didn't sound solemn in the way they did when they boomed out against a background of silence to remind everyone of the dead. Instead they were as noisy and irrepressible as a farmyard—they whinnied and squawked and mooed and didn't care what anyone thought.

And nothing stopped and nobody breathed and there was no to-and-fro pat-a-cake pattern and instead it was a tangle of noise with threads winding through and over each other and it was exhausting to listen to and it made her feel she could never be exhausted again.

And Triss knew what it was. She had heard the wireless spit out the starting chords of such wild, blaring music, only to have her father tut and turn it off.

This was jazz.

"Do you like it?" asked Mr. Grace.

Triss could barely answer and became aware that her heels were drumming against the chair legs, in an excitable, seated dance. She wondered if this was what drunk felt like. Perhaps she *was* drunk. Cake-drunk.

She was having *fun*. When had she last had fun? Treats, pampering, protection, oh yes, she had all these things in abundance. But fun?

Jazz was not respectable. She was not supposed to hear it, and nobody was meant to play it to her. She was sure that Mr. Grace knew that, and she gave him a look of glee. His feet were not tapping, she noticed. He simply stood by the gramophone, watching her and smiling.

One of the shop women put her head round the door, and Mr. Grace quickly lifted the needle from the record.

"The young lady's father is ready to take her home," she said.

Triss felt a throb of disappointment. Mr. Grace grabbed a clothes brush and helped her dust off the cake crumbs, even taking a moment to pluck a loose hair from her sleeve.

When Triss was taken back to her father, she knew that her eyes must still be shining and her face pink from icing and jazz. Her father looked her over, frowned very slightly, and touched his fingers briefly to her forehead to check for fever. Despite herself, Triss felt a tiny pang of resentment. Couldn't she be happy without it being a sign of a temperature?

"If you would like to bring Theresa back in a week for a first fitting . . ." Hearing these words, Triss's mouth twitched. She was coming back here. Instantly she was filled with a rush of guilty glee.

Only as she was leaving did her spirits cool a little. Over on the reception desk she could see the scissors that had nearly fallen on her. A bright cloth had been thrown over them, but the tips of the blades still pointed out. The weather-worn iron was blackened and unforgiving, and the points looked sharp.

Chapter 7

A LATE CALLER

TRISS RODE HOME WITH JAZZ IN HER BLOOD. More than once she caught herself trying to hum one of the strange leaping melodies under her breath, but it came out as a tuneless murmur. She was filled with a wild sense that everything was possible.

As she neared home, however, this strange new confidence peeled away. Her Trissness closed in around her again, like cold, damp swaddling clothes. As she saw her house hove into view, the last fizz of enthusiasm left her.

Her mind was so crowded with thoughts that for a moment she could not quite work out why the house looked different. Then she realized that there was a dark angular blot in front of the garage door. A motorcycle had been parked there with an insolent obstructiveness, blocking the Sunbeam's easy cruise into the garage itself.

"Of all the nerve!" exclaimed her father, bringing the car to a sharp stop at the curb.

The motorbike was a lean black creature with a tan body and sidecar. It was mud-spattered and looked as out of place in the prim, trimmed square as a footprint on an embroidered tablecloth. There was something bold and ugly about the way it let you see right into its metal works. It had the rough cockiness of a stray dog one hairsbreadth away from snarling.

At the sight of it, Triss felt her spirits sink further, though it took her a moment or two to remember why. She had seen the motorbike before, and its presence meant trouble. It meant scenes; it meant both her parents being angry and upset.

As Triss's father made a great show of laboriously parking on the pavement, Triss caught sight of the motorcycle's owner, standing with hands on hips and an air of impatience. The tall, slender figure was dressed in a long, earth-brown overcoat with a high collar, thick leather gloves, and a tight black leather driving cap trimmed with fleece. Beneath the coat, however, divided skirts revealed themselves, and jaw-length dark hair peeped out from under the cap. Legs were visible almost up to the knee, and were shiny with nylon. It was unmistakably a woman, a woman with a long pale face and forward-jutting chin. As the intruder shielded her eyes to peer past the Sunbeam's headlights, Triss recognized her.

It was Violet Parish. Violet Parish, who had been Sebastian's fiancée when he went off to war. Once, she had been "Violet." After Sebastian's departure, she had been "poor Violet." And then somehow, in the years since his death, her name had blackened and speckled in Triss's family home, like a fruit left to rot, until it was thrown out and no longer allowed in the house.

"Stay in the car," Triss's father murmured, then opened his car door and climbed out. Triss peered out through the windscreen, her stomach tensing as if for impact.

"Mr. Crescent!" called Violet as he approached. Her voice had a studied, London-ish drawl to it, but with an underlying bite of anger. "Do you know that your wife has left me on your doorstep for over an hour?"

"Miss Parish, what are you doing here?" Triss's father was clearly trying to moderate his tone so that Triss would not hear, but he was not doing it very well. "I told you to visit my office next week to discuss your so-called grievance. How dare you come here and bother my family!"

"Yes, you did tell me you couldn't meet me until next week—something about the whole family being on holiday, wasn't it?" Violet's London drawl was rubbing off like old paint, showing the rough metal of an Ellchester accent underneath. "And then today I saw your car in town. I know when I'm being sold a line, Mr. Crescent."

"If you must know, Theresa was taken ill, so we came home early."

Violet's dark gaze flicked to the car and Triss sitting muffled in the backseat. Out of instinctive loyalty to her father, Triss wrinkled her brow and thought sickly, woebegone thoughts. A look of impatient contempt flashed across Violet's face; Triss could not tell if it was contempt for her or for her father's words.

"Really? And what would the excuse be next week? For years you refused even to talk to me about my request, or admit that all of Sebastian's belongings were brought home to you. And now that you can't deny it anymore, you're finding every way to avoid talking to me about it. I turned up here because then you *can't* ignore me."

"Oh, I rather think I can," snapped Triss's father. "What made you believe that you could turn up at this time in the evening, on *that*, and be allowed inside my house? Perhaps this passes for a reasonable visiting hour among your crowd, but nobody with an ounce of consideration would dream of calling this late, without warning or invitation, and expect to be let in."

"Just give me what's mine," Violet continued, through her teeth, "and you never have to see me again. Only the things

Sebastian's letter said he wanted me to have if he died—the service watch, the cigarette case, and his ring."

"So that you can sell them, the way you have sold your engagement ring, my son's books, and everything else of his you could lay your hands on?" Triss's father was now bitterly, quiveringly angry. It terrified Triss and sent her thoughts scattering like rabbits. "To us, all these things are precious beyond all measure, because they were *his*. To you, they are worth nothing more than their shop value. I gave you money at the end of the war, to help you find your feet, and since then all you have done is make demands. We owe you nothing."

"Who are you to tell me whether I can sell what is mine? Sebastian *wanted* me to have those things!"

"Because he mistakenly thought you would value them. He had no idea what a cold-blooded vulture you could be."

"Do you think I care what you call me?" shouted Violet. "Do you think I care what you think of me?" She did not look as if she did not care. For the moment she was like the motorcycle, all her angry, grimy inner workings visible to the eye.

"No, I think you are quite dead to the feelings of others. *I* must consider my son's wishes, however, and I know he would have wanted his possessions to remain with those who would treasure them." Triss's father stepped back with an air of finality.

"Oh, that tune again!" Violet snarled and drew herself up as if preparing to trade punches. "Yes, I can see why you love him so much. He's the perfect son now, isn't he? He can't argue with you anymore. You can make him agree with whatever you say, forever and ever—"

But this was too much for Triss's father. He abruptly turned away from Violet Parish and strode back to the car, opening the rear door.

"Come on, Triss," he said, his voice vivid with an anger that Triss knew was not meant for her but that still made something in her stomach shrivel like a petal in a frost. She got out quickly. The atmosphere outside the car turned out to be frosty in more ways than one. There was an unseasonable chill and a sharp, minty bite to the air. Triss could see her breath.

"Don't walk away from me—" Violet began, but broke off abruptly just as Triss's father was slamming the car door. Glancing past her father, Triss realized that Violet was no longer looking at them. Instead her eyes were following something small, white, and feathery that had floated down from above to land between the toes of her patent leather shoes. Violet hastily stepped back from it, as if it was a cinder that might burn her.

"This conversation is at an end," Triss's father announced to Violet as he guided Triss briskly to the front door. "If I ever find you here again, I will call the police."

But Violet no longer appeared to be listening. Even before the last threat was uttered, she was pulling her goggles back down to cover her eyes and hastily buttoning her coat. As she followed her father indoors, Triss could see Violet hurriedly straddling her motorcycle. The door shut, and then there came the sound of an engine starting, somewhere between a roar and a loud, lazy rattle of gunfire.

Triss's mother was waiting just inside, her hands clasped in a fretful knot.

"That *dreadful* girl," she began immediately, her voice high with tension. "I told her you were out, but she would not go—I do not think she believed me. Piers, I . . . I did not know what to do! But I did not think you would wish me to let her into the house. After all, it would set a precedent—"

"You were quite right." Her husband patted her hand. "Unconscionable behavior. We cannot let such things go."

That dreadful girl. It was the only name Violet Parish was allowed nowadays in the Crescent household. The nature of her dreadfulness had never been openly discussed in front of Triss, but she had pieced together a little from her parents' veiled remarks. The word they used a lot was "fast," and Triss did not think they were talking just about the motorcycle. Violet *did* look fast, Triss reflected, lean like her motorcycle, pared to the sleek basics, with no softness to slow her down. Even her bobbed hair had sharp corners.

"I can't believe how *cold* she is," Triss's mother said, peering fearfully out through the window. "Could you ever think that was the same girl?"

After Sebastian's death the Crescent family had been braced to catch "poor Violet" in its welcoming and supportive arms, but Violet had failed to reel or fall back into them. Instead of going into a proper, decent mourning, she had hacked off her hair, then started smoking and wearing dresses that let men see her calves. She had also started bothering Triss's father for money, and Triss's mother always shook her head and murmured about funds squandered on cocktails and "the high life."

Triss let her hand rest against the inside of the front door, almost expecting it to be chilly to the touch. Violet had indeed seemed cold—cold, selfish, and ugly. Her visit had ripped a hole in the fragile calm of the house, like the scratch of a careless nail over tissue paper. It had torn away the last remaining shreds of Triss's brief sense of joy. She had seen herself through Violet's eyes, a pallid, simpering accomplice to her father's claims.

Perhaps if you're cold enough, you make the world around you cold . . .

Triss's father had shown no sign of noticing the tiny white something that had floated down to land at Violet's feet. However, Triss was almost certain that the frail scrap of white that had fallen out of the cloudless September sky had been a solitary snowflake.

Chapter 8

THE MIDNIGHT POST

WHEN PEN APPEARED AT THE HEAD OF THE stairs, Triss could not prevent a small smile from creeping across her face. The younger girl looked thunderous and disappointed at seeing Triss standing there in the hall. Perhaps she had really thought that the doctor would instantly order Triss to be taken away in a straitjacket, leaving their father to return home alone.

Pen's first words reflected nothing of this, however.

"Where's Violet?" she demanded. "That was Violet outside, wasn't it?"

"Hush, Pen," her mother answered firmly. "It was, and she's gone, I'm glad to say."

"Why didn't she come in?"

Pen's question was not dignified with a response, so the younger girl stamped off down the landing again. This was one of Pen's many small acts of rebellion, an occasional perverse insistence that she liked Violet. Triss was fairly sure Pen only said it to shock, just as when she had claimed to have drunk gin or seen a dead body.

"Really," muttered their mother, "that child." She trailed her fingertips lightly over her temples. "Sometimes I just cannot . . ."

She did not say what she "could not," but there was a tone of utter weariness in her voice.

Triss had hoped that her cake frenzy would dull the edge of her appetite, but as the smell of dinner reached her nose, she was again swept up by dizzying waves of hunger. A pleasant surprise awaited her, however.

"Dr. Mellow says that you've lost some weight, so we should let you eat as much as you like for now," her mother told her, heaping Triss's plate with steak-and-kidney pie. Pen glared poison over her more meager serving, but Triss had no thought to spare for her. She wanted to weep with relief, and mentally sent a hundred thanks to Dr. Mellow. For a while she was incapable of thought, so utterly submerged was she in the joyous, helpless, compulsive task of eating. Pie, potatoes, mashed parsnips, buttered peas, bread and butter, fruit, jam sponge, tinned pears, bananas, preserved cherries . . .

Only gradually did the bliss of it start to develop a bitter edge. There was something dreamlike about it, a continual ritual of disappointment. It seemed to her that every time she reached for a serving bowl, she found it empty. She was vaguely aware that full plates were being brought in to replace these, but they were not brought fast enough, and eventually she awoke to the dull, horrified realization that the arrival of loaded dishes had trickled to a halt.

She stared at all the empty plates before her, breathing heavily. What was wrong? Why had they stopped bringing more food? She looked around, aware for the first time that all sounds of dining had ceased around the table, that the rest of her family was mutely observing her as she scraped at each bowl for crumbs or traces of sauce.

"That's enough, Triss," her mother said gently, with the tiniest touch of panic in her voice. "That *must* be enough."

Enough? Triss could barely understand the word. She might as well have been asked whether she had had enough air and was ready to stop breathing.

"But I'm *still hungry*!" she exclaimed. There was nothing in her head except need, and it made her angry, terrified, and childish. "You said I could eat as much as I liked! I'm still hungry!" Her voice was louder than she intended, but why not? She was desperate. And they had promised her all the dinner she wanted! If they loved her, why was there not more food?

"Darling," her mother said, gently and shakily, "you've eaten half the pantry. Now, unless you want to eat dry oats or flour . . ."

"Oats—I could have porridge! Porridge!"

"No!" snapped her mother, then closed her eyes and smoothed her own hair. "No," she added more gently. "That . . . that really is enough, Triss."

"You promised!" The yell tore its way out of Triss as she jumped to her feet. "You promised I could have as much as I wanted!" She felt impossibly angry, as if she had been tricked into giving full rein to her appetite. Her plate was gripped tightly in her hands, and it seemed possible that she might smash it on the table, watch its little blue-white Chinese scene shatter into bits. Why were her parents starving her? What was wrong with them?

"Triss!" It was her father's voice, and it was sharp enough to penetrate the fury and desperation that had enveloped her. It was not a tone he had ever used toward her before, and it stung her to the quick.

She became abruptly aware of herself, standing by an overturned chair, gripping a plate, white-knuckled. Her mother had one hand raised protectively to her throat, a sign that she was particularly nervous or shocked. Pen was struggling to keep a look of mock shock on her face, her eyes alive with glee, fascination, and triumph.

The plate rattled as Triss hastily set it back on the table. Her mouth was too dry to form words. She mutely fled the dining room.

Back in her room, Triss lay on her bed, curled into a ball.

When a knock sounded, she raised her head but could not face opening the door.

"Triss?" It was her father's voice. It was gentler than before, but Triss did not want to see his face, in case it wore some of the hardness and disappointment she often saw when he looked at Pen.

"I'm . . . I'm sorry," she croaked.

The door opened. Her father entered, and his face was not hard. It was tired and sad, which made Triss feel even worse.

"That sort of behavior was not something I expected from my Triss," he said softly. "My Triss is a sweet, quiet, well-behaved girl. She doesn't stamp and scream at the dinner table."

"I'm so sorry," whispered Triss. "I couldn't . . ." *I couldn't help it, I think I went a bit mad, I felt like you were starving me and I was going to die, I felt like you hated me and I hated you.* "I think I might be . . . running a bit of a temperature." It was the easy lie, the much-stamped passport to forgiveness, and Triss felt sick as she heard herself say the words.

"Yes." Some of the sober tension went out of her father's posture, and he came over to sit next to her on the bed. "Yes, that's probably it. I did think you looked a bit flushed when we left the dressmakers'." He touched the back of his hand to her forehead and seemed satisfied. "It has been a long day, hasn't it? Lots of shocks too."

He put an arm around her and she threw both of hers around him, clinging on as if otherwise she might drown, her face buried in his waistcoat.

Help me help me help me . . .

"What you need," her father said at last, "is an early night. You'll feel a lot better after a good, long rest."

He gave her a brief squeeze and stood up, pausing to gaze fondly down at her. Triss managed to force a smile and nod.

The door closed behind him, and Triss was alone and at the mercy of her thoughts.

Pen had told Triss that she was doing everything a little bit wrong. *It's true,* she reflected, *I am doing everything wrong. I lied to the doctor when he tried to help me, and it didn't even do any good—if I keep screaming at everybody, they're going to decide I'm crazy anyway.*

So what can I do? I have to get better without the doctor's help. I have to get better really quickly before they realize just how sick I am. I can't go on like this.

She *had* to get well. Perhaps it was all a matter of willpower. Perhaps she could force herself not to eat everything in the house. Maybe she could make herself stop seeing strange things that could not exist.

Perhaps when Angelina had started screaming, she should just have ignored it and carried on packing. Perhaps if she had stared down the shifting shop mannequins instead of running away, they would have returned to being decently inanimate again. Perhaps the dolls in her room had not really been moving in her peripheral vision . . .

Her eye strayed toward the wardrobe, where she had hastily bundled all her dolls, and she sat irresolute, chewing her lip.

They won't move, she told herself as she edged gingerly toward the door. *And even if they do, I'll know it's not real. I'll just stare at them and stare at them until they go back to being normal.*

When she opened the wardrobe door, the lumpy pillowcase bundle within showed a reassuring disinclination to writhe or struggle. With her foot, Triss nudged it onto its side, stepping back quickly. As it slouched and came open, a single doll fell out of the opening. It was a china half-doll with a glazed pompadour hairstyle, a narrow-waisted blue dress, and a pincushion where its lower body should be.

Very slowly and deliberately, Triss crouched beside the bundle and picked up the doll. The pincushion was just small enough to fit into her splayed hand, the china head, neck, and torso four inches tall altogether. The doll had its eyes lowered so that they looked shut, and its delicate little hands rested on its lace neckline and the rose on its bodice, as if it was adjusting its dress.

You're just a doll. You're just a doll. You're just a . . .

The first movement was very slight. A tiny hand, delicate as a minnow's fin, shifted its position on the porcelain lace. Slowly, stealthily, it reached out toward Triss's encircling hand, and Triss felt tiny, cold fingertips grate lightly down the fine grain of her thumb pad. It did not turn its head. Its eyes were closed, and it moved its hands like a blind thing, searchingly.

It took all of Triss's willpower not to hurl it away. There was a horror in the idea of it smashing, however, the elegant neck snapping like a celery stick. Her hand shook, but she tried to focus all her attention on the idea that what she was seeing was not real.

At last the small, questing fingers nudged against one of the pins in the pincushion and closed around the white glass bobble of its head. Before Triss could react, it grasped the pin with both hands, tweaked it out of the cushion, and drove it into the flesh of Triss's thumb.

"Ow!" Triss jerked her hand but managed not to drop the doll. *It's not real,* she tried to tell herself, even as a bead of blood began to swell from the tiny puncture. *This pain can't be real, it can't.* A moment later she was suffering more unreal pain, as the half-doll raised the pin high and drove it into Triss's thumb again. "Ow—stop it!"

In spite of all her resolutions, Triss found herself using her free hand to tweak the pin from her tiny attacker's grasp. *I shouldn't have done that, it isn't real, it isn't real.* But mind over matter had seemed much easier when the matter was not actually stabbing her.

Triss became aware that the half-doll was making a faint musical rattling noise, like the sound of cups tottering on saucers. Its jaw was moving rapidly up and down, but she could not tell whether it was cackling, gnashing its teeth, or trying to talk. Its hands were now stroking the surface of the pincushion in search of another weapon.

"Stop it!" hissed Triss. She shook the doll, and her blood ran cold at the way its big-wigged head wobbled forward and backward. "Stop it, or . . ." A flood of panic filled her, and with it the tide of hunger that had been driven back but not defeated. "Stop it, or I'll . . . *eat* you!"

The little doll's voice increased to a crockery snarl. A black well of terror swallowed Triss. She closed her eyes and opened her mouth wide, then wider.

The china slid over her tongue like ice cream. The pincushion was harder, and for an alarming moment it lodged in her mouth, filling it, the saggy velvet stale-tasting and dusty. Then Triss did something that sent a shiver through her throat: the next moment she swallowed the cushion down. For a second or two she could feel the cold knobbly sensation of the pinheads grazing her insides as they traveled downward.

Afterward Triss sat for a long minute, staring down at her empty hands.

I can't have done that.

Coming to her senses, she slammed the wardrobe door with trembling hands. Then she rose unsteadily, walked over to her dresser, and dropped into her chair. Staring into the mirror, she opened her mouth as wide as she could, closed it again, opened it, closed it.

Seeing dolls move was crazy. Swallowing dolls whole was impossible. There was no way that she could have opened her mouth wide enough to fit the entire doll inside it, let alone force it down her gullet. She watched her face in the reflection crumple with confusion, fear, and misery, but tears did not come.

It was only slowly that she realized that the howling quicksand in her stomach was now silent. For now, she was no longer hungry.

Hours passed, and at last Triss admitted to herself that there was no hope of sleeping. She lay in bed, staring at the ceiling, while her thoughts traced out dark kaleidoscope patterns across it. *I'm ill, I'm mad, I'm horrible, I have to get better.*

What had the doctor said? Remembering his words, Triss felt a tiny sting of hope. What if he was right, and her illness was just caused by a memory that she had swallowed like a marble? What if she could get better just by remembering whatever it was that she had forgotten?

If so, then the "swallowed" memory must be of the day that she had lost, the day she had fallen into the Grimmer. Before that day, everything had been normal, she was almost sure of it—no strange hallucinations, no terrible hunger. Triss focused all her energy on trying to remember the missing day, but in vain. She sat up and pressed the heels of her hands against her eyelids until red flowers starting exploding against the blackness. She tried to recapture the sense of certainty and imminent recollection that she had felt on the nocturnal banks of the Grimmer, the memory of icy cloudy water, but to no avail.

As quietly as possible, Triss rose from her bed. After taking a pair of tweezers from her dresser, she eased open her bedroom door and listened hard.

Houses breathe in their sleep as people do, and the only noises in the silence were such soft ticks and settling creaks. The rest of the family had long since gone to bed, and Triss could hear no sounds of movement from their rooms. There was nobody else in the house except Cook, whose room was down in the basement. Usually the Crescents' governess would have a room near the family, but at the moment there was no governess.

Triss knew next to nothing about the mysterious "he" whom her parents had discussed, but she did know one thing. He had sent dozens of letters to the family, all of which had somehow found their way into the desk drawer in Sebastian's room.

Triss padded carefully across the landing, alert for any sound from the other rooms, any mattress creaks or waking murmurs. Sebastian's door opened smoothly, and once again Triss crept into the forbidden room.

She did not dare light the gas, but her eyes had adjusted somewhat to the dark and she made her way to the desk without bumping into anything. Dropping to her knees, she ran her fingers over the front faces of the drawers, their ornate metal handles cold to the touch. Yes, it was *this* one, and she knew it was full to bursting with letters, so many that some had been visible through the crack at the top of the drawer.

She found that her tweezers fit through the gap only if she turned them sideways. Trying to grab the corner of an envelope by touch alone proved difficult and frustrating. Time and again she felt her tweezers tentatively grip a papery edge, only to slide off it again.

It was then that Triss heard a sound out in the corridor. She acted reflexively, scooting on all fours back to her previous hiding place under the bed and rolling under it. Only when she was hunched behind the fringe of coverlet did she realize that the sound beyond the door was not a footstep at all.

It was a dry, wispy flutter-tap, like the noise a dying fly makes against a window, but louder. It drew closer and closer, until Triss was certain that whatever made it must be right outside the door and braced herself for the handle to rattle or turn. It remained motionless, however. Instead the stealthy sound abruptly became much clearer. The door had not opened, but the unseen intruder was no longer out on the landing. It was in the room with Triss.

Peering from beneath the hanging counterpane, Triss caught glimpses of the intruder, enough to be sure that it was definitely an "it" and not a "he" or a "she." It flitted in heavy, clumsy arcs around the room, grazing the walls with what she thought might be wings, bumping gently against furniture, halting now and then to perch.

The creature was hard to see, and not just because of the dark. Whenever it paused for a moment and she was able to stare at it directly, it seemed to melt away before her vision. When it flitted to and fro, however, it left dark, fleeting streaks across her sight.

At last it came to rest on the handle of the drawer full of letters, and Triss heard a papery rustling. From nowhere the creature produced a slim, pale oblong. As Triss squinted, the duskily unseeable something leaned back and smoothly slid the envelope in through the crack at the top of the drawer to join the other letters.

It glanced around itself once, and Triss thought she glimpsed a tiny pallid face, no bigger than an egg, with sparks for eyes. Then there was a roar of air and rapid flapping, like a flag in the wind, and it was gone.

Long after the sound of its wings had faded, Triss lay still, carpet rough against her chin. She was seeing the impossible again. But somehow, alone at midnight in her dead brother's darkened room, the impossible was easier to handle.

Mouth dry, she crept back to the desk. One corner of the latest delivery was just visible, jutting out of the crack. She pulled it out using the tweezers, then scurried back to her own room, where she ripped it open and pulled out the letter. It bore the date of that very day, and the handwriting was achingly familiar.

Dear Father, Mother, Triss, Pen,

I am writing again, even though I know it is hopeless. I no longer believe that any of these notes are reaching you, let alone that I will ever receive a reply. I cannot stop myself, however. Writing these letters is all that I have, even though now it is just a make-believe game I play to make the cold less bitter.

Even if I thought that you would actually see this letter, I no longer have the strength to put on a brave face for you. This is a place where all bravery is broken on the rack.

This winter never ends. I can no longer remember when it started. It seems to me that I have been suffering the same bleak skies and bitter snows for years. Perhaps it is the same day, stretching on and on forever like barbed wire. I have lost track of everything. My friends are all dead. The men who fight alongside me are strangers, always dying before I can learn their names. Their faces are nothing but a smudge in my mind.

My hands and feet are in agony from the cold, but at least pain is better than thought. I am a shattered thing now, I know it. I can feel my soul sticking out at twisted angles like a broken limb. All I can hope for is numbness and an end.

Forgive me,

Sebastian

Chapter 9

A STITCH IN TIME

"SEBASTIAN . . ." TRISS WAS BARELY AWARE THAT she had whispered the name aloud.

What had she expected? A list of demands from the mysteri ous "him," perhaps. She had not been ready for *this.*

Triss held Sebastian's letter in unsteady hands, shaken by how much and how little she remembered him. Triss had already known that there had been special days that she had enjoyed with him, such as the birthday when he had helped her dress as an Egyptian queen, and a picnic outing where he had carried her on his shoulders for hours. These were family folklore, recited by her parents in a solemn ritual fashion on the few occasions when they felt it appropriate to mention their lost son. Over the years her parents had herded Triss's woolly memories into the neat pens of their stories, until she no longer knew what she actually remembered.

This was different. This was shocking, like the warmth of a teardrop falling on her skin. Suddenly Sebastian was a person, a lost, frightened, desperate person in pain. It caused her a deep pang of sympathetic horror, and she realized that she *did* feel love for the lost Sebastian, despite the fog of the years.

But he's dead.

Sebastian had died five years before, during a bitter winter. There had been a letter from his commanding officer, talking about a detonation in his side of the trench, his deepest regrets, no possibility that anybody could have survived. There could be no mistake.

Triss could make no sense of her parents' behavior. The drawer was crammed full of envelopes. For months, then, or perhaps even years, Sebastian's messages had been arriving, and her parents had known about it. They had traded solemn words about their long-lost son, and all the while they had been locking his heartfelt letters in a drawer and pretending they did not exist. Their dignified grief was a lie. Everything was a lie.

Her parents had talked about the letters being sent by "that man," the mysterious "he" who they thought might have attacked Triss. Now that she thought about it, though, they had never said that "he" had actually written them. "If he is trying to bully me," her father had said, "then perhaps there will be a letter from the man himself, instead of the usual." That suggested that the "usual" letters were *not* written by the mysterious enemy.

How could Sebastian still be fighting in a war that had been over for five years, and how could he write letters from beyond the grave? If they were not cruel and clever fakes, and if Sebastian really had written that desperate note, he needed help. Either way, Triss needed to understand the riddle of the letters.

The beginnings of an idea started to form in Triss's mind. The drawer was crammed to bursting. How often had this strange flitting thing been invading their house to deliver letters? Every month? Every week? Or every night?

Whatever it is, it's weird and scary, but it's also smaller than me. So if it comes again tomorrow night, maybe I can catch it.

. . . . .

It was raining steadily, and the raindrops fell with a rustle, not a splash. They fell right into the house, settling on the carpet and furniture, and Triss could see that they were actually dead leaves. They landed on the heads and shoulders of the family as they sat at the breakfast table, all trying to pretend that nothing was happening.

"Triss did it!" Pen was shouting, strident with glee. "Look!" The younger girl pointed toward the ceiling, and when Triss glanced upward, she realized to her horror that great holes had been gnawed in the ceilings and the roof, so that the sky glowered grayly through. Triss could even make out her own teeth marks on some of the rafters.

I didn't, she tried to protest. But it was a lie, and she knew it. She had no voice, only a dry rustling like a forest path underfoot.

"Triss ate the ceilings!" shouted Pen. "Triss ate the walls! There are only four left now! Only four!"

Triss woke with a jerk and spent a long minute panting and waiting for her heart to slow. A dream, just a dream. She rolled over onto her side, and her cheek pressed against something rough that crackled with the pressure. She sat up with a gasp.

There were dead leaves on her pillow, several of them. Slowly she raked her fingers through her hair, and her hand came away with another fistful of brown, broken leaves. Her eye crept to the chair she had propped against her door, and her heart sank. Only then did she realize how much she had been hoping that the ever-malicious Pen had been responsible for the mysteriously appearing leaves.

Triss sat up, carefully, and pulled back the covers. There were more leaves on the sheet around her, some inside her nightdress, and a few tiny twigs and wisps of hay.

Mouth dry, she cleaned away the debris once again, then moved to the dresser for her hairbrush. To her surprise, she found tiny flakes of dead leaf clinging to the bristles, despite the fact that she was certain she had removed from it everything but a few strands of her own hair. As she stared at it, however, a horrible suspicion crept spider-like into her mind.

No. It can't be.

She had to know. After shaking off all the leaf fragments, Triss plucked a few hairs from her own head and trailed them over the brush. Then she forced herself to look away for a time, counting to three hundred under her breath. When she looked back, her spirits plummeted like a stone. There were no hairs draped across the brush's bristles. Instead there was a piece of a skeleton leaf, moth-wing dry and more frail than any lace.

The leaves in my hair, the dirt on my floor—I didn't bring them in from outside. And Pen didn't scatter them over my room.

They're me.

"Triss looks pale. Doesn't Triss look pale?" Pen's voice rang out again and again at the breakfast table. "Is Triss all right? What did the doctor say? Does she need to see him again?"

Triss sat carefully dissecting her egg and found herself almost hating Pen. It was all too close to the dream from which she had struggled. At least she was not ravenously hungry, but it was hard to feel relieved about that when she remembered eating the half-doll. She wanted to cry, but her tears seemed to be trapped in a gluey mass behind her eyes. Her mind was haunted by the leaves on her hairbrush, and the thought of Sebastian's letter, now hidden beneath her mattress.

Hazily she managed to follow some of her parents' conversation. Her father had to work that day after all, and was going into

Ellchester. The new station he had designed was nearly finished. It was shaped like a pyramid, following the craze for all things Egyptian that had followed the discovery of the Tutankhamun tomb the year before. Somehow ten years ago was dead history, but anything ancient Egyptian was now the most modern thing imaginable.

"Holiday over, I'm afraid." Triss's father sighed. "They want me at the building site to approve everything, which means that if anything goes wrong afterward, they can blame their handiwork on me. And of course once the main structure is complete, they want me to be present for the Capping Ceremony so that the press can take pictures." The "Capping Ceremony" involved using a crane to lower the pointed tip into place at the top of the pyramid, symbolizing the building's completion.

"More hullabaloo," murmured Triss's mother, in a tone that combined martyrdom and pride.

"I know, I know." Triss's father gave her a quick smile. "But it is only four days more. Then it will all be over."

Triss flinched violently and started shaking. The words recalled too vividly those from her nightmare, and for some reason they filled her with an uncontrollable terror.

"Triss! What's wrong?" Her mother started to reach out a hand toward her, but Triss recoiled.

"Headache!" she managed to squeak out, and fled from the room.

The medical cabinet was raided for all its emergency troops. Now there were rows of bottles lined up on Triss's bedside. Lying muffled to the chin in her bedclothes, Triss surveyed their ranks without feeling much reassurance. Would any of those bottles prevent her from crumbling into leaves? Would syrup of figs rescue Sebastian? She didn't think so. Nor did she hold out much hope for the effectiveness of the camphor in the bowl of hot water by her bed, or the moistened flannel across her forehead.

She was to spend the day in bed. In the past, she would have accepted this. Now watching the hours roll by was torture. What was she doing—waiting to fall apart or go mad? *Four days, four days, four days* . . . Why did those words keep going through her head? She could not understand how she had ever been able to bear just *lying there* in bed, getting paler and frailer while the world went on without her.

Triss heard the clocks strike two and kicked off the covers, feeling too hot to stand them. When she pressed her face against the window, the coolness gave her some relief. Her room smelled stale, and the gray, impatient energy of the wind outside drew her, making her want to fling open her window.

Triss heard a car door slam. There was a small, blue Morris parked on the other side of the square, she realized, and somebody had just gotten out, his figure somewhat obscured by the trees on the central green.

As he drew closer, Triss recognized him. It was Mr. Grace, the tailor who had played her jazz and told her to eat cake the day before. She watched him walk up to the Crescents' front door, and a moment later she heard the bell sound.

Triss's initial fizz of joyful recognition turned a moment later to confusion. Why was he here? What if her parents met him and found out that he was a jazz sort of a person? Perhaps she would not be allowed to go back to his shop.

What *was* he doing here?

With a stealth that was becoming second nature, Triss slipped out of her room and to the head of the stairs. Since Margaret had departed for the day, it was her mother who had answered the door. Cook was notoriously deaf and claimed that she could never hear the bell. Triss did not dare peer around the corner for fear of being seen, but remained where she was, listening.

". . . so sorry to disturb you." The tailor's voice was just audible. "Mrs. Piers Crescent? My name is Jacob Grace of Grace and Scarp—your husband and daughter visited our establishment yesterday."

"Oh—you're from the dressmakers'?" Triss's mother sounded perplexed and a bit flustered. "But . . . I understood the first fitting appointment was set for next week . . ."

"Yes, indeed. But it seems your daughter left her gloves in our VIP room, and since I was passing by, I thought I would drop them off."

"Oh, I see! How very kind." Pause. "Er . . . I am sorry, Mr. Grace, but these do not actually belong to Triss."

"Really?" The tailor sounded taken aback. "Oh. Well, how very stupid of me! They were so small I thought they must be hers. In that case, my sincere apologies for bothering you."

"I'm sorry you've had a wasted journey." Her mother's tone had thawed a little.

"Oh, not at all, I was glad of a chance to ask how the young lady was faring today in any case."

"Theresa is . . . well, I think that she has recovered from the shock she received in your shop, if that is what you are asking."

"Actually, that was not what I was asking." For the first time Mr. Grace sounded serious and somewhat hesitant. "Mrs. Crescent, I had the good fortune to spend some time with your daughter while she was visiting our shop, and I noticed certain . . . symptoms. Symptoms that concerned me because they . . . reminded me of another case. But if your daughter is doing well today and is quite herself again, then that is a weight off my mind."

"Mr. Grace," asked Triss's mother with a nervous sharpness, "what do you mean?"

There was a long pause.

"Please accept my apologies," came the response, so softly that Triss had difficulty making out the words. "I am so very sorry, Mrs. Crescent. I had no place offering comments on your daughter's health. You are obviously both loving parents and no doubt are arranging the best of medical help for her. I am not a doctor, nor even a friend of the family. Please excuse me, and pass on my good wishes to young Theresa."

"Stop! Wait!" Her mother's voice became slightly more distant and less echoing, as if she had followed the departing tailor a step or two out through the front door. "My daughter . . . is not completely well yet. If you recognize her symptoms and have any idea what might be causing them . . ."

"You would not thank me, Mrs. Crescent." A sigh, and then another pause, during which Triss thought she heard the faint scritch of pen on paper. "Here. The shop has a telephone—if you or your husband need me, call this number and ask for me by name. But, Mrs. Crescent? Contact me only when you are desperate. Not before."

Clipped steps receded, and a few moments later Triss heard the front door close. She crept back to her room, her mind in a helpless tumult.

What did any of this mean? What was Mr. Grace *doing* here? He must have seen her put on her own gloves when she left. Had he pretended to think the stray gloves were hers so he had an excuse to drop by?

He wanted to talk to Mother about me. Her first feeling was a sense of betrayal. She had been so sure that she and Mr. Grace had a bond of secrecy, and that he would not say anything about the six plates of cakes. What other symptom could he be talking about? But sometimes adults were like that. They decided that promises to a child didn't matter, as long as they thought they were doing something for the child's own good.

Triss's second feeling was a small, tremulous snowdrop of hope. What if Mr. Grace really *did* know what was wrong with her? What if he could do something to make it better?

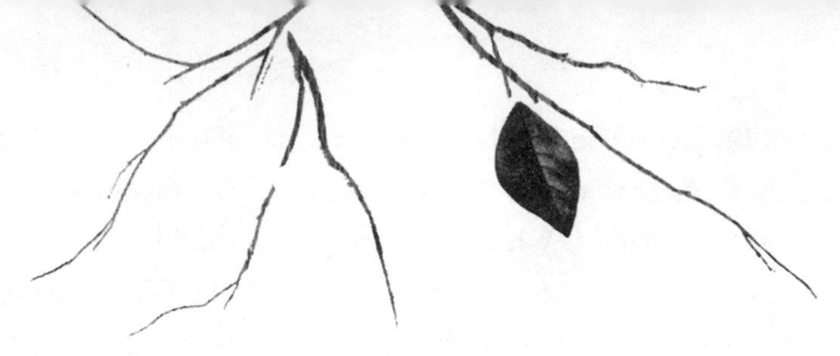

Chapter 10

ABSENT WITHOUT LEAVE

HEARING FOOTSTEPS CREAK UP THE STAIRS AND along the landing, Triss leaped back under the covers, hastily arranging her damp cloth across her forehead and a drowsy look over her face.

When the door opened and her mother peered around it, Triss made sleepy, mumbling noises as if she had just woken.

"Sorry, darling. I won't bother you for long. I . . . just wanted to ask you something. You talked to one of the gentlemen at the dressmakers'. A Mr. Grace?"

Triss blinked a few times and nodded.

"What did you talk about?" Her mother hesitated, wetting her upper lip with the tip of her tongue. "That is, did he seem . . . ?" She hesitated, as if uncertain what she wanted to ask.

"He was nice," Triss answered, hoping she did not sound too keen. "We talked about dresses and things. I said I'd been ill and was getting better. He seemed concerned. He seemed . . ."

What do I have to say to make you call him?

"All very peculiar," muttered Triss's mother, and Triss's heart sank.

Triss immediately realized that she had played her cards

wrong. She should have said that Mr. Grace was clever and sensible. She should not have admitted that she *liked* him. It was, a clammy, uncomfortable voice in her head told her, the same as it had been with the governesses. She was not supposed to *like* them. Showing that she liked a governess or any other servant guaranteed their dismissal.

Her mother sighed and gently rubbed at her own temple. "Froglet, Mommy is coming down with a bit of a headache too, so I will be taking my restorative, then having a little sleep. But if you need me, I shall be in my room."

Triss knew what this meant. The family medicine cabinet was almost entirely dedicated to the war against Triss's own ailments, but there were always a few bottles of her mother's "restorative" in there as well. They had WINCARNIS written on the label, and a picture of a hearty-looking woman in a red hat raising a glass. It had been explained to Triss that "wine tonic" was completely different from ordinary wine, even if it smelled the same. A doctor had once prescribed it for her mother's nerves after Pen was born. Ever since, her mother had resorted to it when feeling particularly agitated.

"I'll be quite all right," Triss said, and managed to keep her tone soft, sleepy, and unconcerned. An idea had pushed its way into her head, setting her heart thundering.

After her mother had withdrawn and closed the door, Triss lay listening intently. Even after she heard her mother return to her own room, she waited for a while, to give her mother time to drink her tonic and settle down in bed. Only when all was reassuringly silent did she scramble out of bed.

Triss yanked open the chest of drawers, piling their contents on her bed. She arranged the blankets over the top so that the whole looked a bit like a sleeping shape.

She would probably have a few hours before her mother woke. If she was lucky, this might give her enough time to head into the center of Ellchester. She would find the dressmakers' and invent some excuse to talk to Mr. Grace.

I have to know what's wrong with me. He must *tell me—he* liked *me.*

Triss dressed quickly, donning her outdoor coat, hat, and gloves. She dared not risk going through the front door, for fear that the neighbors might notice the Crescents' sickly daughter slipping out on her own and ask questions about it. There was a back door, however, which opened out onto the small strip of garden and the alley beyond. The only challenge would be dodging past Cook without being seen.

As she crept downstairs, Triss was almost stopped in her tracks by the thought of her father's quiet, reproachful words. *My Triss is a sweet, quiet, well-behaved girl.* What would he think if he saw her slipping out of the house without permission?

"Sorry, Daddy," she whispered under her breath.

She tiptoed through the dining room and peered into the kitchen. She could see nothing of Cook, but there were reassuring sounds of splashing and scrubbing from the little scullery. Evidently Cook was busy washing up after lunch in the big cement sink.

A rattle and bang made Triss jump. Startled, she looked across at the house's back door, which was usually kept locked, the key hanging from a nail on the inside wall. The key was now in the lock and the door slightly open, so that it rattled against the jamb in the impatient wind. Triss stared, then tiptoed across the kitchen and peered out into the garden.

A familiar figure was hurrying between the cucumber frames and nasturtium beds, padded out like a very short Eskimo in her pale cream fleece-trimmed coat. It was Pen. As the younger girl unfastened the gate at the back of the garden, she flashed a fierce and furtive grin toward the upper stories of the house. Then the gate closed, concealing her from sight.

Clearly Triss was not the only person who had decided to take advantage of their mother's nap. Triss slipped out through the back door, taking care to close it more carefully than Pen had done.

What is she doing? Where is she going?

Pen's eyes had been watchful but alive with anger and a hint of triumph. It reminded Triss of her sister's face when she had forced Triss to show her grass-stained nightdress.

Whatever she's planning, it's something to do with me.

Triss scampered across the garden to the gate, opened it a crack, and peered through into the alley beyond, just in time to see Pen's familiar form disappearing around a corner. Triss made haste to the same turning, thankful her steps were drowned by the bluster of the wind. And there was Pen, strutting down Lime Street with her hands in her pockets, as if she had every right to do so.

At a distance, keeping Pen just within sight all the way, Triss followed.

How strange it was, to be outside alone, without permission! Triss was sure that at any moment she would bump into some friend of the family. Thankfully the wind gave her an excuse to keep her collar turned up, her hat pulled down, and her scarf wrapped around her face. Again her father's words haunted her.

My Triss is a sweet, quiet, well-behaved girl.

But, she promised herself, she would be *his* Triss again soon, once she found out what was wrong with her and made it better.

Wherever Pen was going, the route was clearly not new to

her. She knew which railings were loose and could be pulled out so that you could sneak into the park and take a shortcut. She slipped down tiny behind-house alleys, where you could fight your way through the hanging washing and come out on main streets. She was familiar with the little zigzag lanes that crept up the sides of the hills and spat you out onto footbridges with a view across the city, then swallowed you up in alleys again.

Eventually Pen came to a junction that Triss recognized. To the right lay the broad street that ran up the hill toward the better shopping districts, including Marley Street, where Mr. Grace's dressmaking shop was. The left-hand road ran downhill toward the Puttens, the area of Ellchester that the younger people of the city had claimed for their own. There the lines of shops were interspersed with dance halls, bars, and cinemas.

Pen turned left.

Triss felt a knot of conflict in her stomach. Mr. Grace's shop was so close now, a mere handful of turnings away, but if she lost sight of Pen she would never know what the younger girl was up to. Again, Triss remembered the look of guilty terror on her sister's face when she had been overheard using the phone. Had Pen just been pretending, to trap her? Or . . . did Pen have a part in the strangeness that had consumed everything?

I hate you, Pen, Triss murmured silently, as she turned left, down the hill, keeping the smaller girl's figure in sight. *I hate you.*

At last Pen halted before a curious building that had been built on a hairpin bend and was therefore wedge-shaped. High above, under a row of lightbulbs, was a sign painted with the words THE SLICE OF LIFE. The walls were cream colored, increasing the resemblance to a piece of cake. They were covered with posters, on which Theda Bara offered a sultry glare, John Barrymore showed off his famous nose, and Rudolph Valentino fiercely clutched a young woman who did not seem to mind too much.

It was a cinema, a strange little cinema that Triss could not remember ever having seen or heard mentioned. As she was wondering at this, Pen walked up the front steps and in through the glass swing-door.

Triss halted in the street, irresolute. Could this be the answer? Had Pen really fled the house on an illicit filmgoing trip? Now that she thought about it, Saturday afternoon was the time that most cinemas held their "tuppenny rush" showing, with cheap tickets for children.

Her eye slid to a board near the door. Sure enough, it advertised a children's matinee. The main picture was *Murder at the Midnight Casino*, and the serial was something called *The Unseen Blade*. Both sounded exactly to Pen's taste. Pen was addicted to gangster films, and any other picture that involved people shooting each other or falling off cliffs.

With severe misgivings, Triss walked up the steps and into the cinema.

The Crescent family's cinema trips had always been to the Rhapsody, on the edge of town. It was large and grand like an Egyptian palace, full of reds and golds, with a piano that rose up on a special platform just before the film began. Mother had always insisted that the other cinemas were "bug huts," where one "was jostled by all sorts and came home with fleas."

The entrance was close to the "point" of the cinema's wedge, so Triss was unsurprised to find that the foyer was very small.

It was a strange mixture of old and new, grand and dingy. The carpet was bright red and had the raspy, exciting feeling of nylon, but the dark paint of the walls was peeling. Behind a battered desk sat a pretty young woman with a mouth painted like a cherry and white-gold hair that looked like whipped cream.

There was no sign of Pen. Behind the woman was a doorway with a velvet rope across it, from beyond which Triss could hear a cacophony of voices.

Triss's mouth dried as the woman gave her a special warm "for children" smile.

"Don't look so worried!" she said in a confidential tone. "It's just beginning. If you sneak in now, you'll catch the start of the serial." She said the word "sneak" with a small, charming wrinkle of her nose. "That's three ha'pennies for the stalls, thruppence for the gallery." She paused and seemed to take stock of Triss's clothes. "You'll be for the gallery, won't you?"

Triss floundered for an instant, before remembering that she had a purse with a little money in her coat pocket. She hesitated, then fished out three pennies, received a metal token in return, and headed through the door behind the desk. From the gallery she would have a much better view of the auditorium, and a good chance of spotting Pen.

She passed through a door labeled TO THE GALLERY, pausing to hand her token to a silent, sallow-faced attendant, then climbed a set of stairs, the sound of ruckus ahead growing ever louder.

She emerged onto the gallery, which appeared to be empty. The auditorium below, however, was seething. The hard wooden benches were crammed with children of every age, from heartily screaming infants to teenage girls who sat gossiping and peeling potatoes at the back. Children threw nutshells or stood on benches to yell across to each other. Others stamped their feet and whistled, calling for the film to start. Peering down, Triss tried to make out Pen's diminutive shape among them, but in vain.

As Triss watched, a woman with her hair in a stern bun walked down the aisles, spraying something into the air above the children's heads. All of them seemed to accept this as a matter of course. A chemical scent of lavender drifted up to Triss, and she wondered if the woman was spraying for fleas.

When a solitary man sat down at the piano and began to thump out a tune, the audience erupted with excitement. The room darkened, and the silvery screen began to move in its magical way, showing the latest news events. Mr. Baldwin, the prime minister, was talking silently in a big coat, the silver sunlight making him blink.

Then the serial episode began, showing a young woman trapped in a cellar rapidly filling with water. Most of the audience had clearly been following this story avidly and were soon shouting warnings to her by name, or calling out the titles on the screen for friends hard of reading. As the heroine made her unlikely and ingenious escape, there were cheers, gasps, laughter, and catcalls.

On another day, Triss would have been drawn in as well, the shimmer of the great screen filling her with an almost unbearable excitement. Today, however, she was too busy scanning the figures below bathed in the screen's flickering light, searching in vain for Pen.

Could Pen have paid thruppence for a seat upstairs? There was a large central pillar blocking Triss's view of the other half of the gallery. She sidled along the row of seats, and gingerly peered round the pillar.

In a seat at the far end of the gallery sat Pen.

The smaller girl was fidgeting and seemed to be paying no

attention to the screen at all. Over and over again she glanced to her left, toward the wall directly opposite Triss. There was nothing there, though, only a darkened wall painted a rich, deep red.

And then, quite suddenly, there was.

A small, open door appeared in the wall, offering a rectangle of faint illumination. As Triss watched, Pen saw it and stiffened, then rose stealthily, made her way down the row of seats, and vanished through it.

There was something about that dimly lit doorway that sent Triss's instincts twitching. She could smell something. No, taste something. No, neither of those, but there was something in the air that furred her tongue and made her teeth tingle. It was strange. It was familiar. It made her think of the Grimmer. She did not want to follow Pen into that mysterious half-light.

But she knew she would.

The serial had yielded to a cartoon. Boggle-eyed, Felix the Cat crept past a sleeping dog, his shoulders hunched, each step an exaggerated lurch. As his adventures bathed the auditorium in a storm-flicker light, Triss crept on silent feet toward the waiting door.

Chapter 11

THE ARCHITECT

AS TRISS APPROACHED THE MYSTERIOUS DOORway, the sounds of joyful uproar in the auditorium seemed to dull. The roar of voices became foggy, the piano music muted to a tinny chiming like distant cowbells. Beyond the doorway lay a narrow corridor running from left to right, carpeted in a drab earthy gray and with patterned wallpaper of the same color on the walls.

Triss gingerly leaned in to peer. To the left, the corridor led to a set of stairs stretching downward. To the right, it ended at a distant white-painted door, before which stood Pen. As Triss watched, Pen knocked. A moment or two later, the door was opened, and the younger girl vanished within.

The carpet crunched strangely under Triss's feet as she advanced down the corridor, soft but prickly, delicate but fibrous. The wallpaper looked a lot like velvet with some of its pile shaved to create patterns. When she put out her hand to touch it, however, she found her fingertips stroking feathers. As she brushed the wall, a tiny tremor seemed to flutter through the pattern, as though the wall was a living thing and had stirred its plumage.

Pen had left the white door slightly open, so Triss settled herself by the jamb so that she could peer in through the crack. She found herself looking into a small, dim room partially obscured by the figure of Pen, who was still hovering just beyond the threshold. The lighting in the room was bleached and palpitating, like that in the auditorium she had just left.

"Miss Penelope Crescent." Somebody was striding forward to shake Pen by the hand, somebody male and very tall. His voice was educated, confident, and designed to carry. At the same time, there was an edginess in his tone, as if he was being distracted by thoughts of something very exciting. He stepped backward again, fully into Triss's line of sight, and she saw him clearly.

Her first reaction was shock. The stranger was not just handsome, he was *movie star* handsome. His short, carefully combed hair gleamed like honey, and he had a small, fair, Douglas Fairbanks mustache that curled up at the ends. He did not wear a proper daytime suit with jacket and vest of the sort her father always donned on weekdays. Instead he was dressed in the latest fanatically casual fashion among those her parents called "the sporty set." He wore a V-necked sweater over his crisp white shirt, the comfortable, loose trousers known as "Oxford bags," and two-toned, tan-and-white "spectator" shoes. Over these hung a sleekly tailored gray-brown overcoat, and Triss could only assume that he had just arrived from some much more glamorous engagement.

"Always a pleasure. Please." He took another step back and spread his arm in a broad, welcoming gesture. As he did so, Triss thought she caught a gleam under his shirt cuff, a hint of metal on his wrist. Pen accepted the tacit invitation, passing him to move farther into the room.

Triss swallowed, then pushed both her luck and the door an inch or two more so that the crack widened and she gained a better view.

It was easy to make out the source of the fitful lighting. To the right, the whole of one wide wall was a seething, quivering mass of silver-and-gray action. It was a movie, there was no doubt about that, but there was no projector in sight, no blanched beam of light from across the room slanting down to strike the wall. Triss watched the great moving picture in bewilderment as some mute heroine, bristling with ringlety virtue, shook her head rapidly and shunned the gifts of a Lothario with seal-sleek hair. Only when a title card flashed up on the screen with the words back-to-front did Triss realize that she must be looking at the back of the auditorium's screen.

Triss had heard that some cheap fleapits whose screens were nothing but hung sheets sometimes put a few audience seats behind the sheet, charging half price to those who saw the film back-to-front. But the surface on which this film flickered looked like a wall, not a sheet. And if it were thin enough for the light to pierce, why could she no longer hear the piano music or the murmur of the audience?

The rest of the room was extraordinary for its ordinariness. Aside from its walls, which were lined with the same feathery paper as the corridor, it seemed to be a perfectly normal parlor, complete with floral-patterned chairs, a grandmother clock, and a cloth-covered table sporting a tea set and a wireless radio. Triss could not imagine why such a room would be lurking behind a cinema screen, however, and the light made everything look restless. Shadows jumped and beat like wings.

Pen settled herself a little awkwardly on one large gilt-edged armchair facing toward the reverse screen. Her feet did not touch the ground, and she had pulled her sleeves down over her knuckles, a sure sign that she was on edge.

"A good choice. The best seat in the house." The stranger with the movie-star mustache moved over to stand beside her chair, gazing at the back-to-front film. "But then, the clearest way to see things always *is* from the hidden side. Creep up on the world from behind, catch it unawares, and then you see it for what it really is—"

"Mr. Architect," Pen interrupted in a small, determined voice, "I wanted to talk to you."

Mr. Architect? Triss stared at the stranger with renewed interest. Her father had spoken as if somebody he knew through his work might have been responsible for her fall into the Grimmer. As a civil engineer, her father worked with a lot of architects. Could this man be one of them? Somehow 'architect' seemed more like a title than a name.

As Triss stared at the Architect, she experienced a growing sense of discomfort. He was handsome, she could see that, but when she thought about it, it was difficult to say *how* he was handsome. His charm was like a sunbeam right in the eyes, smudging out all detail. When she did squint hard with her mind, she found herself glimpsing bits and pieces through the glare that were not really like Douglas Fairbanks after all. His eyes were very pale, she realized, a light shade of a color that she could not remember from one moment to the next. There was a kink at the corner of his smile that made her think of a treacherous raised nail on a stair carpet.

"So I understood from our telephone call." The Architect surveyed Pen for a long moment. "You asked for an appointment . . . and here we are."

Triss's mind flashed back to Pen's furtive departure from their father's study. *She* did *use the telephone! She used it to call this man! But . . . why didn't the operator have any record of it? And why was she calling him, anyway?*

"They say that a picture is worth a thousand words," continued the Architect, "and your face, Miss Crescent, is a picture. By now I would expect it to have a thousand happy words to say, but it seems not."

"Of course I'm not happy!" snapped Pen, finding her confidence in her ever-to-hand satchel of rage.

"No." He regarded her with his pale eyes. "I suppose you are the sort who will never be happy, but who will make the world far more interesting in your attempts to become so. Ah well. Never mind."

Pen blinked, and Triss could almost feel the Architect's clever words simply flowing past her, like elegant brook eddies around a small and determined rock.

"I'm not happy," Pen went on doggedly, "and you *know* why. You tricked me!"

"Tricked." It was not a question, nor an expression of outrage. The Architect let the word fall flatly, rather as he might have dropped an unidentified oddment on the table to examine it. He paused for a few seconds, raising his eyebrows in contemplation, then shook his head. "I am not sure what you mean by that."

"Yes, you are!" Pen scowled, and her heels kicked hard at the leg of the regal chair. "We made a deal! And I did everything you asked! I got you the diary pages and the brush and all the other things! I even got Triss to come to the Grimmer! You said if I did all of that, you'd take her away!"

Hiding behind the door, Triss had to cover her mouth with both hands to stop a cry of outrage from escaping.

The anger was so overwhelming that it seemed to be something outside her, like a vast animal watching over her shoulder, breathing on her neck and making her skin hot.

"Well?" The Architect looked about as concerned as a cat on a summer wall.

"I thought you'd take her, and that would be the end of it! I just wanted her gone. I never asked for . . . for *that*!" Pen made a wild, rather unfocused gesture, as though waving toward a thought present only to her mind's eye.

"I always keep my bargains." The tall man smiled. "She *will* be gone. In mere days."

Triss swallowed, anger yielding once again to fear. She was still in danger, then.

"Days?" exploded Pen. "Days of *that*? This isn't what I wanted, and you know it! It's horrible! I hate it!"

"I'm not responsible for giving you what you *wanted*, just what you *asked for*." The man shrugged noncommittally. Perhaps it was a trick of the light, but it seemed to Triss that the fibers of his coat shrugged too, a ripple running down through it from his collar to the bottom hem. It struck her that the coat was the same color as the peculiar carpet and wallpaper.

"You can't treat me like this!" Pen clenched her nails into her palms, face like a crumpled dishcloth. "You have to get rid of that thing and put things right, or I'll . . . I'll tell!"

The Architect, who had been turning away with a smile on his face, stopped moving altogether. So did the dust motes waltzing in the flickering light. So did the pendulum of the clock. Even the figures on the silver screen behind Pen stopped mid-soiree, gripping their champagne glasses as they turned to stare at her, huddling together as if expecting a storm or an explosion.

"Tell?" His voice was very, very soft. He turned to face Pen, and in doing so appeared to grow a few inches. His coat bristled and brindled, like the fur of an angry cat, and it seemed to Triss that a light shone in his pale eyes, as if they were reflecting a wild sky that nobody else could see. *"TELL?"* He did not simply shout the word, he screamed it at the top of his lungs, with the terrible force of a thwarted infant. "But that would be *breaking our bargain*!"

Somehow it was not funny. The very childishness made it strange and terrifying. Seeing an adult give in to temper without shame was like seeing a chain falling from the collar of a large and dangerous dog.

Pen hunched into a ball in her chair, knees to her chest, both hands raised in defensive fists before her face.

"I don't care!" she shrieked. "I'll tell them what happened to Triss! I'll tell them where you are! I'll tell them about all your friends, and the bird-things, and the telephones!"

There was a long, long second during which a hundred winter winds drew in a silent breath and the Architect was not handsome at all. Then the dust motes eased back into their luminous meanderings, the pendulum resumed its broken swing, and the film characters went back to gliding around and ignoring the parlor.

"Ah, never a dull moment in your company, Miss Crescent." He lowered his shoulders and straightened his back, then smiled down under his blond lashes at his toffee-and-milk-colored shoes. "Well, never let it be said that I left somebody unsatisfied with their bargain. I take such things seriously. Very seriously. Since you are so insistent, it seems I will have to talk to some people, change some arrangements. Will you excuse me?"

Pen nodded, slowly lowering her fists, watching the Architect all the time over her jutted chin. He moved toward a door near the far corner of the room, then hesitated, apparently in two minds about whether to say something.

"My dear," he began at last, "I . . . must ask you not to touch anything while I am gone. The items in this room, simple as they are, are important to me."

As the Architect disappeared through the other door, Triss saw the younger girl look at the room around her with a new and fierce curiosity.

Does he know who he just said that to?

Pen listened for a few seconds, then wriggled out of her chair and started walking around the room, scrutinizing the wireless and ducking to all fours to look at the underside of the table. Thus it was only Triss who noticed when the figures on the flickering screen first abandoned their duties and edged forward to peer out at Pen.

There were six of them, three men and three women. The scene was a countryside picnic, so all the characters were dressed in outdoor clothes and overcoats. The background was silvery hills and rippling, blossom-filled trees.

One of the women raised a fist and knocked, as if she was banging against her side of an invisible barrier. She called something short, and a title card flashed up. It was of course back-to-front, but it stayed up long enough for Triss to squint and read it backward.

HEY!

Several more of the figures began to beat on their side of the screen, calling out with increased urgency, all eyes on Pen. The title cards followed, with ever-larger lettering.

HEY! HEY, YOU! OVER HERE!

The title cards lingered for longer and longer, plunging the room into relative darkness each time, so that at last Pen looked up at the screen in annoyance, and did a double take.

YES, YOU! YOU'RE IN DANGER!

Pen leaned forward, mouth moving as she worked out what the words said, and then she straightened, eyebrows rising and mouth pursing into a small pout of doubt.

HE LIED TO YOU.

HE HAS GONE TO GET THE GRIPPERS.

"Grippers? What are the Grippers?" Pen asked aloud. The film figures gave furtive glances toward the door through which the Architect had left and flapped their hands in "quiet, quiet" motions. Pen took a step toward the door behind which Triss was hiding, but the silver coterie all jerked with alarm and flailed their arms in warning.

NO, NOT THAT WAY!

THEY'RE WAITING FOR YOU!

Pen halted, irresolute. Triss, who had tensed at the prospect of Pen rushing out of the door and straight into her, now glanced apprehensively down the corridor. No mysterious "Grippers" could be seen advancing on her position, however.

Back in the film scene, one of the men ran back to his car, which was parked almost out of the shot. He pulled open the door, then looked back at Pen expectantly. The other film folk remained close to the screen, all beckoning furiously.

THIS WAY! QUICK! INTO THE CAR!

YOU CAN ESCAPE WITH US!

Pen hesitated, her face a battleground of different emotions. Then she tightened her jaw and scampered forward until she was a pace from the flickering image. She stretched out one uncertain hand and patted at the wall.

Instantly the figures made a lunge for her, their colorless hands tightening on her arm, her shoulders, her clothes. Their faces slid into identical smiles of triumph. No title card flashed up this time, but it was not hard to make out the words they were mouthing.

GOT YOU!

Pen screamed. Where the colorless flickering hands touched her, Triss could see Pen's own skin and clothes start to mottle and spot, as if a gleaming, silver lichen was spreading across her. Pen was yanked off her feet and pulled through the frame into the country scene to lie on the gray grass. She made a desperate lunge back toward the parlor but only managed to catch at the edge of the image "frame" with one hand. The grinning picnickers hauled on her clothes and limbs, and Triss could see Pen's grip on the edge of her world starting to weaken.

Pen was now almost entirely consumed by gray, except for that one tenacious hand, and even there the flesh was dulling and losing its color. Her screams were silent, and her cheeks were shiny with tears.

It serves her right. It serves her right, the little horror. She brought it all on herself.

Oh . . . Pen, you little pig. I hate you. I hate *you.*

Triss broke cover and sprinted into the room. She lunged forward toward the screen just as Pen lost her grip, and managed to seize the younger girl's wrist in both hands. Triss could feel a pins-and-needles sensation creeping over her fingers and, looking down, found that speckles were spreading across them like drops of mercury. The gloating look of the picnickers changed to confusion and rage as Triss yanked at Pen's arm with all the strength in her body and dragged her sister, still silvery and silent, halfway out of the flickering picture.

There were a few seconds of desperate tug-of-war. Glowing fingers prized at Triss's grip on Pen's arm, pulling one of her hands free. Desperate, Triss lashed out and felt her fingers tear something. One of the men reeled away, clutching his face. The others stared at Triss with new fear, and she grabbed her moment.

The heave took all her strength, and she felt her shoulders creak under the strain. A moment later Pen was lying on the parlor floor beside her, still colorless and voiceless, but alive.

Chapter 12

MONSTER

THERE WAS NO TIME TO LIE PRONE AND BREATHless. The figures behind the screen were edging forward again.

"Run!" Triss scrambled to her feet, and beside her the small, flickering figure of her sister did likewise. As Triss dragged Pen toward the door, she cast a glance over her shoulder and caught sight of the picnickers, all reaching groping hands toward the fleeing girls. The gaggle now all shared one form, one face. They were all the Architect, eyes ice-bright with fury, screaming in silent rage.

The audience of children in the auditorium was making too much noise to notice two girls charging across the gallery. Even as the pair pelted down the stairs, Pen's feet made no sound at all, and it occurred to Triss's distracted mind that her own were not ringing out as loudly as she would have expected. Then they crashed through the door into the lobby, rushed past the woman at the counter before she could react, and burst out into the street.

The panic halted Triss for a second, then spurred her into a sprint, back the way they had come. As she ran up the hill, Pen kept pace with her like a stumpy silver shadow.

Only when they were cutting across a park did they dare slow. Ducking into the shadow of a small huddle of trees, they waited for a moment or two to recover their breath, peering all the while to see if any gray figures were lurching after them. There was nothing.

Pen doubled up, resting her hands on her knees, and silently coughed up clouds of silver dust. Her skin was still colorless and luminous. As Triss watched, a moth circled giddily around Pen's head before settling on her cheek, evidently drawn by the light. Pen brushed it off and continued gasping, until at last patches of sallow pink started to reappear in her face.

Triss could feel the cold breeze on the back of her neck. She was no longer panting from the run; now her breath was heaving with the storm of feelings that filled her when she looked at Pen. In the end she could not contain them. She grabbed her sister by the shoulders and shook her hard.

"You little *monster*! You asked that man to kidnap me!"

Pen stared at Triss for a second, then, without warning, launched herself forward and threw her arms around Triss's middle.

"Triss! Is it really you?" It was the tiniest croak. Pen's voice was choked by tears but also sounded oddly distant, as if beyond a wall. "Triss, Triss, Triss! You don't know how glad I am to see you!"

Triss, furious and thwarted, stared down at the top of Pen's disheveled silver head. She had wanted to hit Pen, but it now felt strangely difficult.

"Oh, stop it!" she hissed instead, with all the venom she could muster. "You tricked me out to the Grimmer! Did you hope he'd drown me?"

"No!" Pen let go and pulled back a few steps, looking wild-eyed. "He just said he'd take you away! It was supposed to make things better! It was supposed to make Mother and Father better—instead of angry and miserable all the time!" It was rather hard to follow Pen's words. Her voice cut in and out like a faulty engine. During the patches of silence, Triss thought she could see white lettering trying to appear behind her, curling around the bark of the nearest tree and glistening on a few of the leaves.

"You *stupid* . . ." Triss trailed off, as if she too had been tainted with silence.

Pen scowled hard and muttered something. It looked a bit like "sorry," but it was soundless, and the lighted word that appeared behind was scattered by the leaves, a small galaxy of unreadable glimmers.

"But you're here!" Pen continued, more audibly. "Triss. Triss—what happened? Where have you been? How did you get back?"

"Back?" Triss stared at her. "Where have I been? I've been following *you*. I saw you sneaking out of the house, so I came out after you and tailed you to the cinema. What did you think I'd been doing?"

Across Pen's face a collage of silver moved and danced, as if some invisible moon was casting its light on her through shifting foliage. As Triss watched, the younger girl's expression changed to one of realization, her eyes becoming hard and wretched. The silvering seemed to get worse again as she grew more distressed.

Pen screamed a single silent word. This time the letters that curled across the bark behind her were large enough to be read, despite the rough bark and daylight.

YOU!

Pen backed away a few steps, her expression tormented.

IT'S YOU! YOU TRICKED ME!

"Me?" Triss screamed, no longer caring that they were in a public park. "*I* tricked *you*? Look what *you* did to *me*!"

Triss grabbed at a few strands of her own hair, yanked them out, hardly feeling the pain, and held them up. Within seconds she could feel them changing in her grip, becoming dry and crumbling. Then the wind was teasing fragments of filigree leaf from between her fingers, bearing them away like brown confetti.

"I'm falling apart!" Triss could hear all her anguish escaping into her voice, making it so harsh she barely recognized it. "Why is this happening to me?"

Still wearing the same bright, half-mad look, Pen watched the last brown specks fall from Triss's fingers. Triss sensed the change in the younger girl's posture even before Pen turned to flee, and pounced quickly enough to catch her by the arm. Pen screamed silently and tried to claw away Triss's restraining hand, even tried to bite her sister's knuckles. There was no mistaking the desperation in her eyes. But Triss was desperate too. With a force she had not quite intended, she stepped forward and pushed Pen hard so that she fell down into a tangle of tree roots. Pen gave a smothered yelp and lay there clutching her arm.

"What did he do?" screamed Triss. "What happened at the Grimmer? Tell me!"

"Leave me alone!" shouted Pen, her voice returning with a shrillness that sounded almost angry. "You know what happened! You were there!"

"But I don't remember! I don't remember anything about that day! I don't remember lots of things . . . I hardly knew who *you* were at first, or Mother, or Father. And home looks strange, and I keep seeing things that can't be real, and I'm hungry all the time—and it's all your fault! *What did that man do to me?"*

Realization washed across Pen's face, leaving behind it a look of hypnotized horror.

"You *don't know*?" she whispered. "But . . . but you *must*! You must remember coming out of the Grimmer!"

Triss hesitated as the odd impressions bobbed to the surface of her mind again, like dead fish. *Surrounded by cold, murky water, light overhead, the silhouettes of two men above . . .*

"No!" she erupted. "It's just . . . pieces! And I don't remember how I fell in at all!"

"That's because," Pen said, in a tight and tiny voice, "*you didn't*."

And Triss was standing on the brink again, just as she had been during her midnight excursion to the Grimmer. Standing on the edge of a terrible truth, something that she did not want to know after all. But she had drawn too close this time, and turning to run and run and run would not help.

"What?" she heard herself ask faintly.

Pen was breathing heavily. Her eyes still wore that hard, bright look that made her look mad and desperate.

"They put a big bag over her," she said rapidly. "She tried to kick them, but they bundled her up and put her in a car. And then they came back with all the things I gave them—the brush and the diaries and everything—and they threw them in the Grimmer.

"And then they brought out this big doll, made of leaves and twisted sticks and briars, and they threw that in too. Then the short man made some noises that sounded like the wind in the trees. And the wind answered. And then there were ripples, and something started coming out of the water. Walking out. And it was made of sticks and paper and bits and bobs and thorns and painted eyes, but after the water ran off it, it started to look like Triss.

"And then it climbed out onto the bank and stood up. And it smiled. And I ran away, back to the cottage. But it came after me. It turned up at the cottage, dripping. And everybody thought it was Triss."

The ground no longer seemed steady under Triss's feet. Some stealthy sea seemed to be stirring under the turf, its waves rising and falling with each of her breaths.

"But I *am* Triss," she said. Now it was her own voice that sounded distant and unreal.

Pen said nothing, but just stared up at her, her eyes as hard as bullets.

"I *am* Triss!" Triss tried to give the words more force.

And still Pen's dark eyes just stared and stared.

"I *am* Triss!" screamed Triss, using all the power in her lungs, as if she could force the words to be true. "You're lying!" The wind was building, and as the clamor of the leaves increased, it sounded as if the very air was seething.

Pen made a lunge to the side, scrambling over the exposed roots, away from Triss. As the younger girl stumbled to her feet, Triss leaped forward and lashed out, slapping Pen across the face as hard as she could. Pen gave a high, thin shriek of shock and pain and reeled back against a tree, clutching her cheek. She gave Triss one last hard-eyed, maddened glance, and far too late Triss realized what the look meant, what it had always meant. Not anger, not hatred at all, but terror.

Then Pen turned and fled unsteadily toward the park gate, the film light still coruscating over her small form.

The girl who had been left behind did not chase her. Slowly she turned her hand and stared down at it, noticing the hint of red dampness on the tips of her middle three fingers.

I hurt Pen. I really hurt her somehow. I made her bleed.

She stared at those faint brown-red smudges for a long time, while the wind roared like a great page tearing in two.

"I'm Triss," she whispered.

But she knew it was not true.

Chapter 13

THE BRINK

NOT-TRISS STOOD IN THE PARK WITH REDDENED fingertips and wanted to run. Run, run, run from the monster. How could she, though? She was the monster.

But she ran anyway, pounding street after gray street into numb thunder with her soles. The wind blasted into her face, and she bared her teeth against it until they ached with the cold.

Where could she run? Home?

Mommy Daddy make it better make it not be true . . .

But they could not make it better. They could not change the truth. And she was not their little girl. Why would they even try to help her? If she told them what she was, they would surely recoil in horror.

Not-Triss tore her way into an alley across which washing lines zigzagged. As she raced through this rippling labyrinth, she wailed and lashed out, feeling cloth rend under her fingers. The sound that came from her mouth was not one a human girl could have produced. In it she heard the splintering lament of wind-felled trees, the steel cacophony of gulls, the whining note at the heart of a storm wind.

On all sides she heard doors slam and voices raised in consternation. She hurled herself onward, making herself scarce before anybody could come to investigate.

She burst out of the alley and into the next, and her feet carried her through one walled byway after another. There was a reek in her nose, a slick dark green smell of water that was old enough to be clever and dangerous. The paving stones gave way to worn cobbles, and then her feet were drumming on a wooden jetty and the wind felt as clammy as a dead man's kiss. The sky opened out before her like a wide white page scrawled with tiny bird shapes. And there surged the Ell, its gray skin rippled and scuffed, so broad that the far shore was fringed with toy trees and matchbox houses.

At the jetty's edge Not-Triss's legs gave way and she dropped to her knees. Her sobs sounded more human, at least. Tears misted her vision now, but they stung bitterly and clogged her lashes. When she dabbed at her eyes, the tears came away in long, clinging strands, not blots of saltwater. She stared at the gleaming, gluey threads in confusion before realizing what they were.

Spider silk. She was weeping spider silk.

Numb with despair, she stared down at the glossy coffee-colored river, hearing it click and lick against the quay supports.

She felt as if it had been lying in wait for her. She had climbed out of the Grimmer. Perhaps these waters before her were destined to close over her head, completing the circle.

Triss's parents could not make everything go away. The river could. Perhaps it would be better for everybody else if Not-Triss did let herself tumble forward into the water and took the monster out of the world . . .

"But *I* don't want that!" she exclaimed aloud, frantically rubbing the cobwebs from her cheeks. "Even if I'm not Triss, I'm still real! I'm still somebody, even if I don't have a name! And I don't *want* to drown myself or fall apart! I don't want to die!"

And, whispered a sly voice in her head, *the real Triss is gone. Why can't* I *be Triss now instead? If I fix myself and don't tell anyone where I came from, I could be a really* good *Triss—help round the house, maybe even be kind to Pen. I could be a better Triss than the real one.*

Almost as soon as this thought formed in her mind, however, Not-Triss recalled Pen's description of the kidnap, of her other self being bundled into a car despite her struggles. Where was the real Triss now? What was happening to her? Was she in danger?

"I don't care!" Not-Triss clamped her hands over her ears, as if she could shut out her own thoughts. "It's not my fault! And . . . and *I'm* Triss too! They're *my* family too! It's *my* home too! I've got nowhere else to go!"

But she did care. She could not help it. Somewhere her namesake was the captive of the Architect, and might be weeping just as bitterly. Perhaps she was tearfully waiting to be rescued by her loved ones, unaware that nobody knew she was even missing.

Nobody. Nobody except me and Pen. If I don't do anything, she'll be murdered, or eaten by cinema screens.

"But . . . if she comes home, what happens to me?" Not-Triss whispered, her face in her hands, tear strands tickling at her fingers. "What am I supposed to do?"

It was fairly plain that she needed to do something. If she did not, soon there might be no Trisses left whatsoever.

The world looked different as Not-Triss walked back. It was as if she was letting herself see with her true eyes for the first time, no longer trying to convince herself that things looked normal. There was a new glisten to everything. Walls and trees conspired as she passed, their silent murmurs spreading through the air like blood into water. She was noticing things, like the way her own feet made little sound however fast she walked.

Before, she had felt desperate and terrified, but all the while she had at least sensed the safety net of her parents' love stretched invisibly below her. Now she knew how small a tug would be needed to drag it from beneath her. Her thoughts performed the same manic carousel all the way home.

I have to find out what's going on. Then maybe I can discover what's wrong with me. Maybe I can find a way to rescue the real Triss, and help Sebastian. And maybe . . . maybe . . . maybe . . . if I do that, then they won't mind there being two Trisses.

But she could not believe it, and when at last the Crescents' home came into view, her emotions leaped and flapped like a washline in a tornado.

I can't let them know what I am, I can't, I can't! But Pen knows! How can I stop her from telling everybody? No, Pen won't tell. She can't, not without admitting what she did.

I hurt her. I hurt Pen. Maybe I hurt her badly.

Not-Triss stared at her fingertips again, still uncertain how she had managed to draw blood. Perhaps she had claws that hid, like those of a cat. She did not want to think about hurting Pen or consider the possibility that she had scarred her small face. Even as her stomach squirmed at the thought, a more fearful, selfish concern slipped into her mind. What if Pen had run home and been interrogated about her injuries? What if she had broken down in pain and terror and told the truth? What if her parents were waiting, even now, for the imposter?

Not-Triss had the presence of mind to enter by the back door.

Thankfully it was still unlocked. Cook had finished washing up but had evidently retreated to her own room in the basement. Not-Triss crept in, slid off her boots, and tiptoed through the kitchen. The house was silent, so she eased her way back up the stairs and hurried to Triss's room.

She was just reaching for the handle of the door, when it opened and her mother stepped out.

"Triss." Her mother's voice had a tone she had never heard before, faint and winded-sounding. "Where in the *world* have you been?"

Not-Triss boggled at her. Somehow, amid the torrent of fears and feelings, she had not thought to put together a story that would serve if she was caught.

"I . . ." Not-Triss thought about claiming that she had seen Pen sneaking out and had gone after her to bring her back. But what if they asked Pen to corroborate? "I . . . was sleepwalking." She could feel her face becoming hot.

"Sleepwalking?" whispered her mother, in the same tense, breathless voice. "Did you say 'sleepwalking'?" She swallowed, then held the door fully open. "Then what is that?" Not-Triss was treated to a view of her own bed, and her heart sank as her eye fell on the covers, still clumped to look like a sleeping figure.

Not-Triss had no answer. Her own precaution had incriminated her.

"I . . . don't know" were the words she mouthed, but she seemed to have no voice for them. It was a baby's excuse, transparent as gauze.

"You went *outside.* Without telling anybody. Why would you do that, Triss? Why would you betray my trust in you? Look at me!" Not-Triss risked only the briefest glance at her mother and was stricken to see that she was actually trembling, a great tear gleaming under one of her eyes. Not-Triss dropped her gaze again, fearful that her mother might look into her eyes and see a monster lurking there.

"I said, look at me!" Firm hands took a tight grip on her shoulders. "Did Pen talk you into this? Where has she run off to now?"

So Pen had not returned after all, and Not-Triss had a chance to blame the whole escapade on the younger girl. She could even feel the right words curling into shape on her tongue, and her mother's ear waiting for them. But instead, quite unexpectedly, amid the pity, guilt, and alarm, a tiny spark of outrage managed to flare in Not-Triss's mind.

"No," she said. "It wasn't Pen."

There was a pause, and a gasp, then Not-Triss felt herself shaken slightly by the shoulders.

"You know it was! You would *never* treat me this way unless Pen had made you do it!" There was almost a tone of pleading in her mother's voice.

"It wasn't her!" Not-Triss felt choked by claustrophobia. "I just . . . felt better. And . . . I really wanted to go for a walk. And . . . I knew you wouldn't let me go. You *never* let me go anywhere." The words were out before she could do anything about them.

"Triss!" Her mother's voice had a choked, tear-mangled tone. "Enough! You are *ill*! Now . . . go back to bed. You've made me very unhappy, Triss, and you *knew* I already felt under par."

There was nothing Not-Triss wanted to do more than to leap into the woman's arms, but there was no safety there, no hope.

Help me, she begged her silently as the door closed between them. *Help me help me help me . . .*

Chapter 14

SILENT TREATMENT

THERE WAS NO HELP. THERE WAS NO HELP FROM anybody. Not-Triss had nobody to trust but herself.

She wiped the cobwebs from her eyes with the heel of her hand and listened. Her mother's steps were moving into the study at the end of the landing. The door closed, and then she could make out the very faint sound of her voice.

The telephone. Her mother was using the family telephone. After a moment's confusion, Not-Triss realized that this was to be expected. Pen was missing. Her mother would doubtlessly wish to tell their father. But would she report their other daughter's disgrace at the same time?

Not-Triss crept out and along the landing. She was aware now of the ease with which she softened her steps. The floorboards were her accomplices, swallowing their creaks as her soles pressed them. Her breath made no more sound than a flower petal falling.

With her ear to the door she could make out her mother's half of the conversation in the room beyond. Her tearful tone tugged at Not-Triss's heart. But was it really her heart that was tugged? Did she even have one? She could not be sure.

". . . oh, I know that I should not be calling you like this, while you are at work. Believe me, I would not have done so if I were not quite, quite desperate. I *must* talk to you."

Pause.

"Yes . . . yes, it is! And I am completely at my wits' end. I thought . . . I thought she seemed better. I really did. But . . . there is something terribly wrong. Ever since the fever. And as time goes by, I am ever more certain of it."

Not-Triss stiffened against the door. Whatever she had in the place of blood ran cold. Her mother had not phoned her father to report Pen's disappearance. She had called to talk about Triss.

"What makes me certain? A hundred things!" her mother went on, now sounding almost hysterical. "I would be anxious enough if it were just the weight loss, or the way she eats, eats, eats like a mad thing—like a plague of locusts! But . . . there's something more than that. She is *different*. There's something slow and strange about the way she talks to me. It's as if she is pausing to listen to somebody else before she answers. It's more than just a worrying symptom, it's . . . *eerie*.

"She never used to have a temper, and now she does. Sometimes in her eyes I see this . . . this wild thing I don't recognize! I don't know what it is! I don't know what it is doing in the face of my little girl!

"And she *creeps* everywhere." Her mother's voice dropped to a hushed, oppressed almost-whisper. "Over and over she startles me half to death by turning up unexpectedly without a sound. Even now . . . even now I almost want to go to the door to make sure she is not behind it, listening."

Behind it, listening, Not-Triss held her breath, remembering Pen's words.

You're getting everything just a bit wrong. And sooner or later they'll notice.

"And this afternoon," her mother continued, "she crept out of the house. She claimed that she had a headache and was taking a nap. Then she made this . . . this lump out of her bedclothes, so if anybody peered in through the door, it would look as if she was still sleeping, and she sneaked out into the cold and wind. I don't know why. I don't know where. I caught her coming back, but she wouldn't tell me where she had been. She just stared at her feet with this cold, stony expression . . ." There was a pause while Triss's mother gulped down tears. "And when she finally looked at me, there was such anger in her eyes . . . This . . . this just isn't like her. This isn't Triss at all."

Every sobbed word was caught by the girl who wasn't Triss at all. The girl would have given every dress in Triss's wardrobe to hear the other end of the conversation. Was her father agreeing? Was he soothing her mother's fears, or laughing at them?

"Oh yes . . . That would be . . . I really can't go on like this." Pause. "Yes. Yes, please do. When?" Pause. "Could you not leave work a little early? Just today?" Pause. "I . . . I see. Yes. No, I do appreciate that. Thank . . . thank you. Yes. Yes, I . . . I might have a little tonic to settle myself. We will talk this evening, then."

Not-Triss was back in her room before her mother had set the earpiece back on its hook. She listened as steps creaked unsteadily back down the landing again and the door of her mother's bedroom closed.

She knows! She knows I'm not the real Triss!

No. She suspects something, that's all. She doesn't know what she suspects. And she's a bit hysterical and she's been drinking her wine tonic. So maybe Father won't have taken her seriously.

It was small comfort. Over and over, Not-Triss kept remembering the fear and distress in her mother's voice. She was torn between utter misery at being the cause of her mother's unhappiness and selfish panic at the prospect of discovery.

I have to be normal. I have to be as normal as normal can be, just until I know what's going on.

But I'm so scared. I'm so confused. I'm so . . . hungry.

Oh no, oh no! I can't afford to be hungry again! I can't afford to start eating like a plague of locusts, not now!

But there was no hiding from it. The clawing hole in Not-Triss's stomach was back. What could she eat? The panic seemed to make it more intense. Her eyes turned involuntarily toward the wardrobe, where she had hurriedly thrown the rest of her dolls. She took a few hesitant steps toward it, even reached for the wardrobe door, then flinched back as within it she heard a rattle like the gnashing of wooden teeth.

"I can't!" she whispered in despair. "I can't! Oh, isn't there something else here I can eat? Something that doesn't scream?" She tugged open drawers, dragging out the contents and throwing them on the floor. At last, amid the heaps of clothes, she saw a small box shaped like a wooden treasure chest. As she flipped the catch open, the hunger inside her stirred, like a deep-lurking pike sensing a ripple on the surface.

The box was filled with small glittering treasures, a tangle of brooches, ribbons, and glass beads. Her borrowed memories told her that they had been gifts from school friends, cousins, and Sunday-school acquaintances.

She could almost smell the real Triss's love for them, like steam from a cooking pot.

Not-Triss drew a long necklace from the box, fascinated by the bluish pallor of the mock pearls. She closed her eyes and tipped back her head, slowly lowering the string into her mouth, then swallowed once, twice. The beads were hard as gobstoppers against her tongue, and mint-cold. Then the whole string of them vanished down her throat with a swoop, as if they had found a life of their own.

A brooch followed shortly afterward, its glass jewels fizzing on her tongue like champagne. Then she was snatching up a bracelet with one tiny boat-shaped charm. A part of her cried out that she *couldn't* eat that, anything but that, even as she was gulping it down, the tarnished silver like sugar frosting.

Her frenzy ebbed. A wave of terrible sadness took its place. She had devoured things that could never be replaced, she realized. With a shaking finger she stirred the remaining items in the box. So many gifts, so many friends. But how many of these friends were still in Triss's life? None, she realized. Her mother had considered some "too exuberant" for Triss's health, and her father had argued with the parents of others. Somehow, every time Triss had formed a connection, it had been severed. These gifts were the stumps of friendships hacked short.

The little silver boat, however, had been a present from Sebastian.

It had been a promise as well. Sebastian had told Triss that when he got back from France, he would take her out boating again. To her surprise, Not-Triss found she had cloudy recollections of bright days out on the estuary in a little wooden boat, Sebastian rowing while Pen and Triss giggled and splashed each other with river water. How had that laughing girl become Triss of the sniffles, who needed to be protected from every breeze?

The box held the relics of a dozen dead friendships and one dead brother. Not-Triss closed it with a sting of self-loathing and guilt, knowing how much the little treasures meant to Triss. But, she realized, that was precisely why they were so irresistible. They were soaked with an essence of Trissness that made them delicious, and Not-Triss almost wept with relief when she realized that her hunger was now sated. Perhaps she did not need screaming dolls to satisfy her appetite after all.

"I'm ready," she told her ashen reflection in the dresser mirror. "I'm ready to be normal now."

Father came home at the usual time, and when she heard the Sunbeam draw up, Not-Triss felt her stomach twist with anxiety. She peered down from her window as he walked from his car through the increasing rain, but she could not tell from his face how he had reacted to the afternoon's telephone call.

After he had entered the house, Not-Triss could just make out the sound of a conversation below. She pressed her ear to the floor of her bedroom, hoping to make out what was being said, but the voices remained a bee hum, just recognizable as the tones of her parents. They went on for more than an hour, her father's voice sometimes rising in volume, but not enough for her to make out what he was saying.

By the time she was called down to supper, Not-Triss was almost trembling with apprehension. To her surprise she found her father seated quite calmly at the table and her mother absent. She had expected to find both her parents waiting side by side, ready for an inquisition.

"Where's Mother?"

"She has gone to talk to the neighbors, to see if they have seen anything of Pen." For Pen, "running away" often meant fleeing to somewhere safe and dry where she could stay until she felt that her absence had been long enough to worry people. The usual procedure when Pen disappeared, therefore, was to check with nearby friends and relations to find out whether she had unexpectedly turned up at their house.

"Triss, sit down," her father went on, his voice quiet and firm, and Not-Triss realized that the inquisition had come for her after all. He took some time folding his paper, then looked across at her. Only two places had been set at the table, she realized now. There was a plate before her father, steam rising from the buttered potatoes and grilled mackerel. However, no food had been set down at the other place.

Not-Triss understood the meaning of this immediately. She remembered seeing Pen sit down to an empty place on many occasions. It meant that she was in disgrace, and that unless she could explain herself properly, or offer appropriate remorse, there would be no supper.

She sat, keeping her head lowered so that her hair fell forward over her face.

"Triss, I hear you frightened your mother badly today—"

"I'm sorry." The moment the words were past her lips, Not-Triss knew that she had spoken them too soon. An immediate apology would look like a greedy bid for supper. There was a disapproving pause, and then her father went on as if she had not interrupted.

"Your mother tells me that you left the house, without telling anybody, and tried to hide the fact—and when you returned, you lied to her about it and then raised your voice. What could make you do that, Triss?"

"I'm . . . sorry. I . . ." Not-Triss thought about telling him the headache had made her do it, but her instincts told her that she was close to rubbing the gilt off that excuse. "I . . . don't really know. My room just started to smell of . . . being ill. I was hot. And I really, really, really wanted to go out all of a sudden. So I did."

There was another long pause, and Not-Triss heard her father sigh.

"So. Where did you go?"

"I . . . just walked around."

"Walked around?" Her father's prompt was so very gentle that Not-Triss felt her heart break. All she could give him was a nod, and the silence stretched and stretched as he waited for her to fill it with something more. She tried to think of a suitable lie, but the day had left her mind too battered to fashion one on the fly.

"Just . . . around," she heard herself mumble.

"Was Pen with you? Do you know where she has gone?"

Not-Triss shook her head to both questions, and there was another pause.

"Triss, you're hiding something from me." Her father's voice was level but wounded-sounding. "Look at me."

And she could not. She could not let him see that she had cobwebs softly oozing down her cheeks. She kept her chin ducked low to her chest, her hair a stubborn curtain before her face. The tears at the back of her throat tasted like sour cherries. Her fingers gripped the table edge until they ached.

"Am I a monster?" he asked, and Not-Triss nearly looked up at him out of sheer surprise.

She shook her head. *No, I am.*

"Have I ever given you a reason to lie to me, or hide things from me?"

Not-Triss shook her head again.

"Then don't you think I deserve an answer?" He waited a long time, knowing that his Triss would have to raise her eyes sooner or later. When she did not, he gave a long, somewhat pained sigh, then picked up his cutlery and began to eat.

Not-Triss wanted to sob at the thought of hurting her father. Her mind was a tempest, however, and she could not be sure that a human sound would come out if she parted her lips. She turned her head away so that her father would not see her face when she wiped her eyes, and it was then that she glanced at the window and saw Pen.

The younger girl was outside, beating on the window. She was a creature of coruscating silver once again, and her fists made no sound against the glass. Behind her, against the wall of the garage, Not-Triss could see occasional flickering words appear.

BANG

BANG BANG BANG

WHY WON'T ANYBODY LET ME IN?

The sight ruptured Not Triss's thoughts like a spade driving into a mosaic. Her first feeling was disbelief and horror. What was Pen thinking, trying to get everybody's attention while she looked like *that*? Even Pen with her talent for mendacity would have trouble explaining her transformation.

Then Not-Triss noticed that Pen's clothes were sodden, her hair bedraggled, and her face crumpled with exhaustion and despair. Slowly the truth dawned. She must have been out in the rain for hours to get that wet. What if their mother had locked the back door again after Not-Triss's stealthy entry so that Pen would be forced to knock at the front door on her return and face the music? If so, who could say how long Pen had been beating in vain on doors and windows, producing nothing but silver words hanging in the air?

With a frisson of guilt, Not-Triss saw that there were three long, dark parallel marks scoring Pen's left cheek.

WHY CAN'T ANYBODY HEAR ME?

I DON'T CARE ANYMORE, I JUST WANT TO COME IN.

I'M COLD.

She's eleven years old. Not-Triss had almost forgotten this fact, so busy had she been thinking of Pen as a threat. *It doesn't matter how clever she is, she's a little girl, and right now she's cold and scared and wants her mother.*

Without meaning to, Not-Triss made eye contact with Pen, and instantly regretted it. The younger girl's face changed and took on a look of pure frustration, resentment, and despair. Pen could not possibly guess at the icy tension around the supper table. She would see only a usurping monster seated in *her* house, with *her* father, presumably eating *her* dinner, and enjoying light, warmth, and love while Pen herself was shut out in the cold.

Not-Triss sat paralyzed with indecision and guilt. She felt a wrench of pity for the small, soaked figure outside, but what was she supposed to do? If she pointed Pen out to her father, what good would that do? He would demand an explanation, and if Pen was miserable enough, she might just break down and provide one. How would that make things any better for Pen or for herself?

Hoping she was unobserved by her father, Not-Triss risked a small shake of her head, willing Pen to read her mind. However, there was no sign that Pen had noticed the subtle signal.

"May I be excused?" Not-Triss asked impulsively, the tension becoming too much for her.

There was no answer but the scrape of fork on china. The words Not-Triss had spoken were not the explanation for which her father was waiting. His silence was a cold, gray sea of disappointment and chilled her to the bone. Eventually he did give a small nod, and she fled the dinner table.

As soon as she was out of sight of her father, Not-Triss slipped down the hall, unlocked the front door, and stepped out into the rain.

"Pen!" she called out as loudly as she dared. "This way! I've unlocked the front door!" There was no response, however, and after a few minutes she ducked back indoors, leaving the door ajar so that it would be obvious from outside.

Just as she was passing back along the hallway, a short silvery figure barreled past her from the direction of the front door, colliding soddenly with her and knocking her aside. Crumple-faced with misery, Pen thundered up the stairs, or would have if her steps had not been completely silent. The floating words behind her retreating figure were a poor substitute as an expression of rage.

STAMP

STAMP

STAMP

STAMP

STAMP

And then, a few seconds after she had disappeared from view—

SLAM

Just as Not-Triss was recovering her balance, her father appeared in the hallway. He was confronted by the sight of Not-Triss hovering at the end of the hall and the trail of small muddy footprints that ran past her and up the stairs.

"Pen's back," said Not-Triss, suspecting that she might be stating the obvious.

"So I see." Her father let out a long breath. "Well, that's one less worry at least." He walked past to close the front door, and Not-Triss retreated upstairs, not wanting to give him time to wonder why she was still downstairs or to notice the raindrops nestling in her hair.

Upstairs in her room, as she rubbed her hair dry with a

blanket, she heard a faint rap of the front-door knocker, then the sound of the door opening and closing. Hushed murmurs moved down the hall and into the sitting room, where they were muffled by the closing of the door. One voice was that of her father, the other that of another man, and she could not shake off the feeling that it was familiar. Half an hour later she heard the sound of the front door opening again, and shortly after, her mother's voice joined the muted conversation below.

For a long time Not-Triss lay on her bedroom floor, listening to the buzz of three voices, which rose, fell, and interweaved without ever becoming comprehensible to her. They went on for two hours, and when at last the stranger left the house, it was too dark for Not-Triss to make out more than a solitary, male figure walking away with a purposeful step.

Chapter 15

AMBUSH

OUTSIDE TRISS'S ROOM, THE EVENING CAME TO an end. There was movement on the landing, muffled voices, door percussion. The faint rustles and ticks of the sleep-time rituals. And then, over the next two hours, quiet settled upon the house by infinitesimal degrees, like dust.

And this fine dust of silence lay undisturbed, even as Not-Triss opened her bedroom door and glided out onto the landing. She might have been a figure floating across a cinema screen.

Over one arm hung a woolen shawl, which she hoped might serve as a net to throw over her winged quarry. In her hands she carried her sewing box, a gift from her mother. It was made of wood and painted with forest scenes. The inside was lined with silk, the sewing tools housed in sheaths in the underside of the lid. Not-Triss had emptied out the box's store of cotton reels and wool balls, and could only hope that it would be large and sturdy enough to act as an improvised cage. The night was thistle-sharp, spiderweb-tense. Not-Triss was part of its secrecy and danger now, but she sensed that she was not the most secretive or dangerous thing abroad. The night had no favorites. She could almost sense it curled around the world, dispassionate as a dragon, the stars mere glints in its black scales.

Not-Triss slipped into the forbidden room and found it much as she had last seen it. Once again, she slid under Sebastian's bed to hide and wait.

Whatever that bird-thing is, it comes at midnight. If I can catch it, and if it's able to talk, perhaps I can force it to tell me what's going on. Maybe it knows what happened to the real Triss, and to Sebastian.

The little mantel clock downstairs could just be heard chiming twelve.

After the last chimes had hung in the air for a few seconds, the sound Not-Triss was waiting to hear reached her ears. It was the same dry, wispy flutter-tap as before. It was out in the corridor. It was growing nearer. And then, with a whirr like the wind through dry wheat husks, it was in the bedroom.

The room was too dark to see it clearly, but now and then she could just make out the small airborne shape careering hither and thither. A dark shuttlecock in an invisible game, each wing-brush like a rasped breath, the motions unnerving in their unpredictability. Not-Triss *could* predict it, though. That was her one advantage. She knew that it had come to deliver a letter, and that sooner or later it would have to perch on the drawer handle in order to do so.

Flutter-tap, flutter-rasp-bangitty-flap, flappety-flap. Flap. And perch.

There it was, a tiny shape perched on the drawer handle, so small that she would not have seen it if she had not been looking for it. Even now it melted into shadow before her direct gaze and kept its outline only when she looked slightly away. It was distracted for the moment, sliding an envelope in through the narrow gap above the drawer.

Her instincts prickled in her veins like a thousand tiny thorns, causing her muscles to tense and coil.

Now.

Not-Triss sprang from cover, the motion as easy as falling. The only sound she made was the faint flap from the counterpane, stirred by her passing. Nonetheless the perching thing heard it and looked around in time to see her landing neatly on her bare feet. Its shocked cry sounded the way a scar looks. The thing spread its wings, but Not-Triss was already hurling the shawl.

The fabric swamped the creature, but even the heavy wool was not enough to keep it down. A moment later there was a shawl-smothered shape crashing blindly around the room, bouncing off walls. All the while it hissed and screamed, in a voice like hot embers dropped down a well. Not-Triss could just make out gabbled curses and muffled abuse.

Not-Triss made a few jumps in an attempt to catch it, only to have the trailing fronds tease through her fingertips. She bounded onto the desk, landing so lightly that it did not even shudder, and leaped out into the center of the room, seizing the loose ends of the shawl with both hands. She landed with a triumphant huff of breath, but the next moment her feet were dragged from the floor again as the thing fought its way back into the air and Not-Triss clung to the shawl like grim death as she was lifted from the ground, swung against shelves, and then dropped floorward by sudden cruel swoops so that she landed awkwardly.

"Twig-minx!" it screamed. "Scrap-brat!"

It tired in time, though its torrent of shrieked abuse continued. When Not-Triss found her feet on the ground, she threw herself on top of the struggling mass of increasingly ragged shawl and then forced the bundle into her sewing box. Before it could burst out of her grip again, she slammed the lid and sat on it.

There was a wail of utter horror, like a wind change before a storm.

"Let me out! Let me out or I'll bonfire you! I'll make nests of your bones!"

The box jumped under Not-Triss, and she could hear rending within. She could picture the wicked little beak tearing the shawl apart.

"Not till you tell me what I want to know!" she hissed back. "What are you?"

"Just a messenger! Deliver letters!"

"Where's the man who wrote the letters? Where's Sebastian?"

"Don't know! Don't know any Sebastian! Don't know what is in letters! Not my fault! Not my fault!"

"Whose fault, then? Who sent you?"

The response the creature gave might have been a name. It slithered over the eardrum the way moonlight slides over the surface of a rippling pool. It was unfamiliar, but Not-Triss already had an idea who might have sent the bird-thing.

"Is that the same man they call the Architect?"

"Yes! Brick-magic. Insidey-outsidey-hiding-magic. Let me out!"

"Did he steal away the other me—the real Theresa?"

"Yes! Needles and pins, they burn! Let me out!"

"Where is she?"

"I don't know—only a messenger. Architect would know. The Shrike might know."

"The Shrike?" The box was rattling so badly that Not-Triss had to brace her feet against the floor to stop herself from tumbling off.

"The one who made you. Skraaark!"

The one who made me. It's true, then. It's really true. An unacknowledged shoot of hope that Pen had been wrong withered and died.

"What *am* I?"

"Rag doll, thorn-doll, seven-day doll! Cruel doll! Killing doll!"

"Stop it!" snapped Not-Triss, bouncing hard on the box lid, her mind a simmering turbulence of rage and fear once more.

"Killing me!" insisted the voice again, now rising in what sounded like pain and panic. "Killing me! Let me out! Stop killing me!"

"Well, stop flapping if you don't want to hurt yourself!" Not-Triss whispered back, but the sounds from the box were becoming troubling. The wingbeats were more frenzied and intermittent, and there was a rattle now and then as if something hard and heavy was lurching about inside.

"Please!" For all the voice's strangeness, the panic sounded real. "Get it away from me! It's killing me!" There followed an incoherent susurration that sounded like *sizzizzizzizzizz* . . .

Scissors.

With a stone-cold jolt, Not-Triss remembered her mother's scissors twisting antagonistically in her hand, the vast cast-iron shears falling down toward her head outside the dressmakers' shop . . . and the sewing scissors sheathed in the silk-lined lid of the sewing box. Scissors had turned on Not-Triss, wanting to hurt her. If this creature was like her in some ways, perhaps she had just shut it in a box with a tool that wanted to kill it . . .

Her conscience smote her. Whatever this creature was, even if it was sent by her enemies, she had not seen it do anything that deserved death at her hands.

"Promise you won't attack me!" she whispered.

"I swear!" came the shriek.

"Promise you won't lie to me!"

"I swear!"

"Promise me you'll stay and answer my questions!"

"Three questions, three answers—I swear!"

Not-Triss would have liked to insist on more promises, but there was a terrible breathy wailing and whimpering coming from within the box, and she was afraid if she waited a moment more the creature within might actually perish. She had no idea whether her captive would really consider promises binding, but she slid off the sewing box and flung open the lid.

No flutter of wings erupted into the room, and for a moment she feared that she might have been too slow. Peering into the box, however, she discovered a pitiable sight. Somehow the scissors had managed to fall from their sheath in such a way that the two points were embedded in the base, one on either side of the bird-thing's throat. It appeared to be unhurt but was clearly too terrified to move for fear of shredding itself on the hostile blades.

"Help . . ." it whispered. When she looked at it directly Not-Triss could see only a pattern of staining on the silk lining. When she peered intently at the scissors, however, the figure became visible, and she could see that it had the face of a lean old woman ashen with terror, brows threadbare and pimpled.

Not-Triss reached toward the handles, then hesitated. It occurred to her that pulling the scissors free might not be the best idea, in case they were waiting for a chance to close on the captive creature's neck with a self-satisfied snip. Snatching a small award cup from one of the shelves, she popped it over the bird-thing's head, to its evident confusion and outrage. When she tugged the blades free they did indeed close, but clinked harmlessly off the metal. They then settled for twisting in her grip, scraping the skin from her knuckles until she flung them away across the room.

There was a lather of wings, and the bird-thing was not in the box anymore. Not-Triss stared around the room in vain, fearing that it had fled in spite of its promises. Then she became aware that there was something bobbing in her peripheral vision. The creature was perched on the silver frame of Sebastian's soldier photograph, gripping the metal with tiny pale hands.

They looked at each other for a long second, bird-thing and thorn-doll, and then the former flew sullenly down to perch on the desk with an air of concession.

"Friends now," it whispered, its voice as soothing as a rattlesnake lullaby. "You won't tell anybody about this? Not them?" It jerked a head toward the door, the bedrooms beyond. "Not . . . him?" A fearful glance toward the night-filled window, and Not-Triss thought of the Architect.

Not-Triss said nothing. Instinct told her there was danger in making promises, and she was suspicious of the creature's sudden good humor.

"I know what you're thinking of asking," the bird-thing continued, edging closer to her along the desk in small, companionable sideways hops. "You want to know where you can find *him*. Do not ask that, for I cannot answer it. Our beaks are bound on that matter, and we could not say anything of it if we wished. And anyway, if you have wits, you will not *want* to find him. Of all the Besiders in these parts, he is the most powerful and dangerous. He would tear you to pieces."

Besiders? Not-Triss nearly asked the question aloud but bit back the word at the last moment. She had almost used up one of her three precious questions.

"*He's* not the one you want to talk to," the bird-thing continued. "I will tell you that for free. You want to talk to the Shrike. The Shrike created you—he will know how he made you and why. He will know something of the Architect's plans. And he doesn't *belong* to the Architect, the way we do. He just works for him when the price is right. So he might not kill you. If you're clever. And if you know where he can be found."

Not-Triss closed her eyes and sighed. The hint was obvious. But was there anything more useful she should ask? The bird-thing had already told her that it had never heard of Sebastian, did not know where the real Triss could be found, could not reveal the location of the Architect, and was ignorant concerning the letters it delivered.

"All right," she muttered, "where can the Shrike be found?"

"He lives in the Underbelly, beneath the Victory Bridge," the thing answered, in crisp, triumphant tones. "Of course," it continued, with a hint of mockery, "knowing where he is will not be enough to get you there."

Not-Triss could have kicked herself. Now she had little choice but to ask the trailing second question. Without it, the first piece of information was useless.

"How can I get into the Underbelly to find the Shrike?" she asked through clenched teeth.

"Go down Meddlar's Lane under the bridge's end, turn your face to the bricks, and start walking. Then keep walking until the sound of the traffic grows faint and you can understand the gulls. Of course"—and now there was clearly a suppressed snigger in the voice—"knowing how to reach the Underbelly is not the same as knowing how to enter it and leave again *safely*."

Not-Triss hesitated a long moment. Her brief advantage over the invisible sniggerer was slipping through her fingers.

However, she had already committed herself with her first two questions, and there was no going back.

"Tell me," she said at last, giving in, "how do I enter and leave the Underbelly safely?"

The creature leaned forward, and its grin of pleasure was diluted by a gleam of earnestness.

"Find yourself a cockerel, and a dagger or knife. Before you enter the Underbelly, drive the blade into the ground by any means you can. That is the only way to keep the path open behind you for when you need to leave. Pay no heed to any music that you hear playing. And whatever happens, remember why you are there. If you have questions to ask, keep asking, and make it plain that you will not be gone until they are answered. Keep the cockerel wrapped and dumb until you think you are in danger."

It watched her face for a few seconds more, and the sparks in its eyes became gleams of malicious delight.

"But hurry, scrap-brat! You have only three days left! Three days! Three days!"

And then it was gone, with only the briefest rasp of sound, like somebody running a thumbnail down a notepad.

Too late, Not-Triss realized that the dead of night was no longer as dead as it had been. From down on the street she could hear the sound of hushed and puzzled voices and the barking of excitable dogs. Even so, she was slow to make sense of it, her mind still shaken by the bird-thing's words.

Thus it was that she was quite unprepared when the door suddenly opened, and she found herself bathed in candlelight.

Chapter 16

CAUGHT

THERE WAS NO TIME TO DIVE UNDER THE BED. Her eyes had adjusted to the dark, and the candle dazzled her, so that she could scarcely make out the two figures standing behind it.

"Triss!" Her mother's tone was beyond anger or incredulity. There was awe and fear in her voice.

Not-Triss could only gape into the light. How stupid she was! For some reason she had assumed that her ferocious battle with the bird-thing would have been inaudible to ordinary ears, like Angelina's screaming back in the cottage. Now she realized that it had been very, very audible indeed, loud enough to wake the whole street.

The light advanced slowly into the room, and Not-Triss could see that it was held by her father. Not-Triss wondered how she looked to them—a glaring, disheveled specimen perhaps, hunched like a church gargoyle on the scuffed rug.

"Triss—what are you doing here?" Her father's voice was very, very level.

"Nothing," she whispered. A stupid lie, but she scarcely cared anymore. What was one more stupid lie in this house full of stupid lies?

Her mother still hovered in the darkened doorway, and Not-Triss could just make out shocked stars of candlelight reflected in her eyes. Glancing around, Not-Triss could understand her aghast silence. The sacred room was in chaos. Most of Sebastian's award cups had been jogged off their stands during her battle with the bird-thing, and several photographs had fallen face-first. The rug was chaotically rucked, and the wood of the shelves and desk was gouged here and there with fine, deep scratches.

"Triss," her father began again, "I'm trying to give you a chance. Why did you come in this room? What . . . happened just now? Was there something else in here with you?"

Yes. I fought a bird-thing and forced promises out of it at scissor-point.

Not-Triss looked down at her own hands, clenching at her cloth-covered knees. She shook her head.

"Then where on *earth* did that terrible noise come from?" demanded her mother.

Not-Triss did not need to look up to know what expression her mother would be wearing. A hesitant, brittle look, eyes brilliant with uncertainty and nerves.

"Oh, why don't we blame it on Pen?" Not-Triss heard herself snap, in a voice that sounded harsher and more brutal than her own. Something had burst, and the words welled up in spite of all her attempts to dam them. "That's what we always do, isn't it? That's what she's for, isn't it? We blame everything on Pen and then we change the subject. And nothing matters as long as we don't *talk* about it."

The following silence was terrible. There had been a whole conversation she might have had, she knew that now. It was no longer there to be had. She had ripped out the remaining pages of the script and had fallen off the ragged edge of the paper.

For a moment there was nothing she wanted more than to break loose, scream at them for lying to her for so many years, and demand an explanation. Here they were, acting as if *she* had behaved in a strange and treacherous fashion, and all the while they had been hiding the letters sent by their dead son. The unfairness of it filled her with Pen-like rage.

The next moment she remembered that it was Triss they had lied to for years, and that she herself had many dangerous secrets that needed to be kept. If she gave vent to her temper, would she give herself away for the monster she was? Had she given away too much already?

"Go to your room, Triss." Her father's voice was so distant that it took Not-Triss a moment to understand that his words were directed at her.

Very slowly, Not-Triss got to her feet. As her unsteady steps carried her back to her room, her mind crowded with all the excuses and stories she should have used when asked for an explanation.

I was sleepwalking. I had a nightmare. I think maybe I cried out in my sleep. A lot.

There was a bird in the room. It was squawking and banging around. I came in here to help it out through the window.

I dreamed that Sebastian came back, so I came in here to see if he was sleeping in his bed. But he wasn't there, and I was really upset. And cried a lot.

Why hadn't she said something like that? Anything, just so that her parents could force themselves to believe her and could go to bed with their minds somewhat at rest. That was the whole problem, though, she realized. Right at that moment, she had not wanted their minds to be at rest. She had not wanted to make things easy for them, or to add yet another lie to the stack of comfortable lies that seemed to be the only thing holding up the roof.

"Stupid," she whispered, feeling her eyes sting and her lashes clog with cobweb. "Stupid! What's wrong with me? Why couldn't I just lie? Now they'll think . . ." She could hardly begin to imagine what her parents might think.

The excitement of her little victory over the bird-thing had dissolved, leaving only dread. She had learned something from its answers, perhaps enough for her to continue her investigation, but at what price? It was too late for her to offer her parents an innocent-sounding explanation for her presence in Sebastian's room, the strange shrieking and upheaval that had taken place and the long scratches on the furniture. Any plausible excuse she gave from now on would smack of a tale invented in retrospect, and for very good reasons.

But I have to think of a story, she realized. *By tomorrow. Something that will explain everything, even why I shouted at them, and why I wouldn't explain myself at the time. Or I'll be knee-deep in doctors for the next three days, and I've only* got *three days. That's what the bird-thing said.*

Only three days.

Chapter 17
QUIET

NOT-TRISS MANAGED ONLY SNATCHES OF SLEEP during the night. Her mind sparked and spun relentlessly like a Catherine wheel, trying to come up with stories that would save her.

In the early hours she was woken by sounds of furtive, shuffled movement that appeared to come from Pen's room. To Not-Triss's surprise, they did not appear to wake anybody else. But, she considered after a moment, perhaps they were not as loud as she imagined. Perhaps she could hear them so clearly because her own senses were peculiarly sharp, or because she was in tune with the sounds of the night.

Another thought crossed her mind. If Pen was making any noise at all, then right now she was not suffering from her eerie state of silence. If Not-Triss wished to speak to Pen, this might be her best chance.

It was risky, but Not-Triss slipped out of her room anyway and very gently tapped on Pen's door.

"Pen!" Not-Triss tried to make her whisper eiderdown-soft. "I know you're awake!"

There was a short, sharp movement within, as if somebody had started.

"Don't be scared—I'm not going to hurt you." Once more Not-Triss was haunted by the image of the scratched lines in the younger girl's cheek. "I'm sorry about your face. I didn't mean to. I was just . . . scared. I . . . only meant to slap you." Somehow that had sounded better in her head.

There were no more noises of motion within, though Not-Triss thought she heard the sound of slow, careful breathing.

"Pen, I know you can hear me! We have to talk. Can I come in?"

No answer. Not-Triss reached for the handle and gently turned it. The door refused to open, however. Evidently Pen had wedged a chair or something against it. Not-Triss wondered if the smaller girl was hunched in a corner of the room, staring hypnotized at the silent, menacing turning of the handle. She sighed and rested her forehead against the wood.

"*Please* let me in, Pen! I know you hate me, but you need my help, and I need *your* help. You have to tell me everything you know about the Architect—what he's doing, how you got in touch with him, where he lives. Think about Triss—you want to get her back, don't you? What do you think will happen if we don't work together?"

There was an abrupt snuffle, like somebody resolutely sniffing back a sob.

"Go away!" came the snapped whisper. "I . . . I've got a gun! Don't you break this door in, or . . . or I'll shoot you!"

"You haven't got a gun." Not-Triss fought against all the years of Triss's frustration and hurt and focused on the memory of Pen standing alone and drenched in the rain. "And I'm not going to break into your room. But I can't keep talking through the door like this—sooner or later I'll wake everybody up!" There followed a few seconds of silence while her words were digested.

"Go away," hissed the unseen Pen again, this time with venom and more confidence. "Get away from me, or I'll *scream*."

And that threat, more than the menace of imaginary firearms, was enough to drive Not-Triss from the door. She could not afford to be discovered roaming the nocturnal house a second time, not after her first ignominious capture. Once again, holding out a hand to Pen had been about as rewarding as plunging it into a nettle patch.

Day crept in like a disgraced cat, with a thin, mewling wind and fine, slanting rain. Her face pressed against her window, Not-Triss watched it come. The birdsong sounded hard and metallic.

Not-Triss was not ready for this day. She hated it. She wanted to send it back. Something inside her was squirming so hard she felt she might burst. Everything was wrong. Everything was going to go wrong.

Breakfast was left on a tray outside Not-Triss's room, and she did not know whether to feel relieved or hurt. The eggs were soft-boiled the way she liked them, but with a sense of disorientation she noticed that the fruit juice was not in her favorite, pink-tinted glass.

She stared at it, as though making sense of the change would help her understand her parents, and allow her to save herself. The pink glass was Triss's glass. Had they really decided to deprive her of her favorite glass as part of her punishment, or had they instinctively felt that Triss's glass was no longer rightly hers? Did disobedient Triss no longer count as Triss? Was crazy Triss no longer Triss? Or . . . could they possibly suspect the truth?

Not-Triss braced herself and used the fruit juice to wash down a hairpin and two screwed-up pages from Triss's favorite comics, but her stomach continued to growl.

It was Sunday, so Not-Triss changed carefully into her smart church clothes.

By the time she went downstairs, she had an explanation rehearsed in her head. It was a good lie, with a fair dollop of the truth in it to stop it from curdling. As she meekly sat down beside her father on the sedan, however, she saw his face, and her story cooled in her mind. He had clearly slept less than she had. Not-Triss plunged in anyway, but her explanation sounded stilted, her words as cold and mechanical as beads on an abacus bar. She was not sure he was even listening.

Her father said nothing when she had finished, but gently laid a hand on her head. He was looking at her face, she knew it, and still she dared not meet his eye. If she did so, the spine of her story would break and the beads would clatter to the floor.

"All right, Triss." She could not tell from his tone whether he had accepted her story or merely accepted that it would be the only story forthcoming.

Not-Triss became aware of her mother having a hushed conversation in the hall with Miss Soames, a young woman who sometimes came to babysit when the Crescent parents went out to parties.

"Thank you for coming at such short notice. We should be back tomorrow, so we only need you to stay over the one night. It's just a matter of looking after Penelope this time. She will need to be taken to church, and you will need to consult Mrs. Basset about meals."

We should be back tomorrow.

It's just a matter of looking after Penelope.

"Are we going away somewhere?" Not-Triss asked. She kept her eyes fixed on her father's shoes, so that they would not stray to his face. His feet moved slightly, perhaps uncomfortably.

"It's going to be rather a long day, I'm afraid." His hand settled over one of hers. It was warm but did not squeeze hers. Perhaps he was afraid of breaking her. "We're going to drive out on a trip to Wenwick—you, me, and your mother. We're going to talk to one or two people, to see if they know . . . ways to help you get over these . . . night troubles. Most of them are friends of friends. Kind people. You'll like them."

Not-Triss gnawed at her lip, her small, scattered fears becoming large, specific fears, like raindrops merging on a windowpane.

No pink glass for crazy Triss.

"I don't want to!" she blurted out, still fixing the innocent shoes with a stare that might have kindled wood. "I don't want to talk to them! I don't want to go away! Not . . . not now!"

I can't go away now, I can't! I need to find the Shrike! I need to talk to Pen!

"And you're busy right now!" she went on, scrabbling for arguments. "You have lots of work—getting ready for the Capping Ceremony in three days' time—you said so! So we can't! Why don't we talk to them next week?"

"Triss." He put his arms around her, as carefully as if he was hugging a child of smoke. "I love you very much, you know that?"

Not-Triss nodded, sick with panic. "Don't make me go! Please, please let me stay here!" She clenched her eyes shut, willing him to feel her desperation even if he could not understand it.

"I love you," he continued, tenderly relentless, "and that's *why* we have to go."

As Not-Triss stepped out through the front door and heard it click shut behind her, she felt a sudden superstitious pang. Into her head came an unreasonable fear that she would never see it open again. She felt as if it had closed like scissor blades, snipping away her past and everything she knew.

The little travel case in her hand she had crammed to bursting, for she knew she would be away for at least one night. It was filled with treasured trinkets, comics, and hair ribbons. Not-Triss could only hope these provisions would be enough to stop her from becoming feral.

Before her, the world wore a gray veil of rain. The air was clammy and unseasonably cold. There were grains of something in Not-Triss's socks, and she guessed that they must be earth crumbs that had broken away from her soles. The gutters tutted, and the Sunbeam was slick as new paint.

Her mother had a yellow scarf around her head and hesitated on the step under her umbrella while Triss's father readied the car.

Not-Triss could hear the cool, solemn chiming of church bells over the growl and gossip of the traffic and could see other people stepping stiffly out into the drizzle in their best clothes. The raindrops glistened on straw hats and buttoned gloves. But Not-Triss was not going to church, and it made her feel all the more out of step with the world.

Not-Triss stared up at the windows of the house, but the one face she expected to see did not stare down at her. Somehow she had been certain that she would be confronted with Pen's coal-hard gaze. With triumph in her eyes, perhaps? Or fear, or resentment? But perhaps Pen was still given to flashes of silver and would not be coming out of hiding for a while.

To her surprise, Not-Triss found that she was disappointed. In spite of the way the younger girl hated her, she realized that she had counted on that exchanged look to strengthen her nerve.

They shared secrets, if nothing else, and a mutual interest in keeping them. That made Pen the nearest thing she had to a coconspirator.

Not-Triss approached the car feeling betrayed. The rear seat was covered in luggage, and she was offered a place in the front, between her parents. Usually this would have been a treat, and even the crush would have made her feel warm and protected. Today she wondered whether they wanted to keep an eye on her.

The Sunbeam's engine stuttered its objections to the rain, then found its voice. Not-Triss smudged herself a spyhole in the clouded windscreen and watched mutely as Ellchester slid damply by and then was left behind.

Wenwick was fifty miles' drive away, an old-fashioned resort with long, arcing streets of wide-windowed, staring houses. Even though the Wenwick baths were no longer considered to cure everything from gout to toothache, the place still bristled with doctors, like a crust of barnacles marking a high-water point after the tide had gone out.

Each doctor the Crescents visited spent half an hour talking to Triss's parents and then ten minutes or so talking to Not-Triss herself in private, "so they could get to know each other."

The first one was a very kindly elderly man who talked to her about the "rest cure," in a conservatory that looked out onto a garden. Sometimes people had too many worries and needed *rest*. Even wonderful things like families and friends could be too tiring sometimes. So you needed a *rest* from them, so that your mind had a chance to calm down. A few weeks of lovely bed rest, perhaps. And sometimes it was best to avoid other excitements, just for a while. Reading, writing, talking . . .

The second doctor was much younger, and believed in the "talking cure." He told Not-Triss that he was there to help her defeat her secret "monsters." Sometimes you had monsters that frightened you, and so you pretended they weren't there and didn't look at them. But the strange and magical thing was, if you *did* look at the monsters, they just vanished away, and you were perfectly safe. The young doctor had the clear, earnest eyes of a man who had never seen a monster in his life.

The third doctor was really a nurse, a big, boisterous woman with a voice that could have drowned out a foghorn.

"Fresh air!" she explained in tones that might have been heard as far as Denmark. "We move the beds outside, so they have fresh air all the time. And they can see the sea. You'd like that, wouldn't you?"

Each time, something about Not-Triss's spiny stillness and strangeness infected the room, draining the certainty from both doctors' voices. As she left each doctor, Not-Triss clung to her father's arm and buried her face in his coat.

"I don't want to go to this place—I *hate* it. I don't *need* to come here. I want to go home!"

She could hear that she was whining like a six-year-old. However, she could not help it. Every moment wasted here was a precious grain of sand slipping through the hourglass of her life.

After they left the "fresh air" woman, they drove out of Wenwick along the narrow coast road. Not-Triss's spirits rose a little when she saw a signpost promising Ellchester in nineteen miles, then dropped away as they drove past it in the wrong direction.

"Why aren't we going home?" she exclaimed, alarmed.

"We're staying at a little seaside cottage, just for tonight," her mother answered promptly. Her eyes were shiny, and Not-Triss wondered if she had brought some of her tonic with her. "Think of it as a tiny holiday, to make up for the one that was cut short. We thought a change and some sea air might do you good."

"I don't believe you!" The panic that Not-Triss had been fighting down exploded from her. "It's a trick! You're going to take me to a rest-cure place and leave me there!"

"Triss!" The tone of exhaustion in her father's voice silenced her. "It's just a cottage that was recommended to us. It sounded . . . quiet. Peaceful. No doctors, I promise."

He sounded as though he had been carrying a great weight for miles and had just realized that the road ahead of him wound its way up a mountain. Not-Triss felt a pained pity, but also confusion.

"And . . . and we're going home tomorrow?" she could not help asking in a whisper.

There was a pause as her father maneuvered the car around a corner onto a narrow, sloping driveway.

"Yes. First thing tomorrow."

The drive twisted down through a little wood of dripping silver birches, the black crusts on their white barks like healing cuts. The woods had a rich, energetic smell of rot and the thirsty scent of moss. At the bottom a gray-stone cottage lurked at the base of a small cliff, as if trying to shelter from the rain. Beyond it the ground sloped downward to a beach, where the sea pawed at loose pebbles, hushing and hushing the scene to an ever-deeper quiet.

Chapter 18

EGGSHELLS

GETTING OUT OF THE CAR, NOT-TRISS WAS struck by the chill of the down-beach wind, and the wet, salt smells of weed and rock pools. She felt as if the tide of the year had gone out unexpectedly and left them in autumn. The light was ebbing, the cloud-smothered sun spreading dull white wings above the horizon.

Then, quite unexpectedly, the door of the little cottage opened, and a homey orange light bloomed in the doorway. A young woman with tousled hair stood there, holding up an oil lamp.

"Mr. and Mrs. Crescent?" It was so strange to hear such a warm, human sound in this gray scene. "Thought I heard the car coming down. I just put the kettle on—come on in!"

While Not-Triss's father hauled at the family's cases, Not-Triss and her mother dashed for the bright doorway, then stood dripping in a narrow hall. Now that she was closer, Not-Triss could see that the "woman" at the door was younger than she had thought, perhaps no more than sixteen.

"I'm Dot," declared the oil-lamp girl, as if this explained everything. Her face was skinny but vital, with large dark eyes and a pointed, mischievous chin. "Come through—I've stoked up the fire." She led them into a small sitting room with faded curtains and walls paneled in dark wood. There was a low, scratched table and five large, saggy brocade chairs that smelled of dogs. "If you give me your over-things, I'll hang 'em up to dry."

Dot was dressed in a plain, practical blue frock with an apron over the top rather than a proper servant's uniform. Her manner was surprisingly friendly too, and this confused Not-Triss. She seemed too bold for a maid, but her Ellshire countryside accent was thick as custard and her knees grubby from scrubbing floors. Not-Triss expected her mother to stiffen and give clipped, disapproving responses to put the girl in her place. To her surprise, however, she simply gave a faint murmur of consent, surrendered her coat, and allowed herself to be shown to a chair.

The room was lit by the blaze from the hearth and a series of small candles and lanterns arranged along the mantel and the table. Glancing around her, Not-Triss realized that she could see no gas fittings.

"Where are the gaslights?"

"Oh, there's no gas in the cottage," Dot declared cheerfully. "Wasn't worth their while, building the pipes down the hill just for this place. But there's good hearths in most of the rooms and a decent stock of candles."

By the time Not-Triss's father had heaved the cases into the house, both Not-Triss and her mother were sipping hot cocoa and watching their coats dry.

"Look at that! The rain's letting up. Always the way. Stops as soon as you're indoors . . ." Dot continued her warm, effortless prattle, and Not-Triss found herself feeling profoundly grateful to her, as bridge after bridge of Dot's words were strung out over the gaping chasms of the waiting silences.

"I expect you'd like to see your rooms?"

The staircase was dark, cramped, and narrow, the stairs dipping smoothly in the center where they had been worn by centuries of feet. The bedroom doorframes were short and irregular, and her father had to stoop to pass through them. "Sir, ma'am, this is your room. There's a family of house martins in the eaves by the window, and they chirrup something frightful of a morning, but if you close the shutter it cuts out the sound. This little room is yours, miss. You can look out and see the lighthouse of Wellweather Island." The chamber was small, low-ceilinged, and wood-paneled, half-comforting, half-claustrophobic. The only light came from another oil lamp on the table. "I'll leave you to get settled. If you need anything, I'll be in the kitchen preparing dinner."

At the word "dinner" Not-Triss felt her terrible hunger stir once more, like a great mastiff rousing itself from slumber.

Left alone in her room to "refresh," Not-Triss waited for a few seconds, listening to the creaks of her parents edging their way back down the stairs. Only when these sounds faded did she unlatch her case and fling its contents onto her bed. She snatched up and swallowed an embroidered handkerchief, a bundle of postcards, and a pair of gloves, then leaned against the wall, trying to rally her mental forces.

The fire in the hearth was only just gathering life, and the air was cold enough that each breath summoned a brief flicker of vapor.

Why had her parents brought her here?

Perhaps this was still a trick. Perhaps this was a "rest cure" after all. Perhaps doctors didn't think that gas was "restful" enough.

The house was still as snow. Not-Triss strained to hear her parents' voices, and could not. How long had it been since they had left their room? Gripped by panic, she tore down the stairs, nearly stumbling on the sloping steps, and crashed into the sitting room. It was empty. There was nobody in the neighboring parlor, nor in the poky eating room.

Dot looked up from chopping vegetables as Not-Triss hurtled into the long stone-flagged kitchen. She seemed surprised, her narrow face sidelit by the blaze from the great hearth.

"What's wrong?"

"They're gone!" Not-Triss was shaking with a mixture of terror and anger. "They've left me behind, haven't they?"

"Who have?" Dot frowned, wiping onion juice from her hands. "Do you mean your parents? They stepped out for a walk, lambkin. They'll be back soon enough."

"I don't believe you!" shouted Not-Triss, fighting back the silken tears that threatened to creep into her eyes.

Dot didn't seem at all upset by this outburst. Instead she pushed her tongue into her cheek thoughtfully.

"Well, if they headed back to Ellchester, they've got a long walk ahead of them. I didn't hear the car leave, did you?" She laughed as Not-Triss's face flushed with new hope. "You go and have a look, put your mind at rest."

Not-Triss scampered back to the front door and eased it open. With colossal relief she saw that the Sunbeam was still parked outside, its flanks darkening to cedar green in the deepening twilight.

Farther down the beach, distinct against the leaden gray of the sea, she could make out the figures of her parents. Her mother's head had drooped to rest against her father's chest, and he was holding her tightly against him. Not-Triss remembered seeing her father wrap his arms around her mother many times, but usually gently and firmly, as if he was holding together a broken thing long enough for the glue to set. This time there was something fierce and desperate about it, as if he needed the contact as much as she did.

Not-Triss's mother raised her head and said something too soft to be overheard, and Not-Triss's father nodded slowly and kissed his wife's forehead with absolute tenderness.

Not-Triss carefully closed the door and returned to the kitchen, where she hovered shame-faced in the doorway.

"I'm sorry," she muttered. "Sorry I shouted at you."

"I'm used to it," Dot answered, flashing her a grin. "I come from a big family. Nothing but shouting, all day long. Only way to make yourself heard." She blew a stray tress out of her eyes and took stock of Not-Triss's trembling uncertainty. "Do you want to come in and watch me make dinner? It's warmer by the fire than it is over there. If you're really worried about your parents driving away, you can leave the door open so you'll hear the engine."

Not-Triss ventured into the kitchen, fascinated by the great black kettle next to the hearth, the butter molds, the blackened patches on the white plaster ceiling. She had never been invited to watch Mrs. Basset cooking. It had been something that she knew she was not really supposed to look at, like ladies dipping into their powder compacts. On the table was a pile of crisp, dark spinach leaves and some turnips shaggy with black earth. Beside these lay a dead rabbit. The head and feet had been removed, but with a creeping of the skin Not-Triss knew what it was.

"Did you ever see anybody skin a rabbit?" asked Dot, picking up a small, sharp knife.

Not-Triss shook her head, mouth dry. *But I don't want to see it.* Those were the words waiting on her tongue, but somehow she did not get them out in time.

It was all so quick, deft, and no-nonsense. Dot slit it down the middle, then made a workmanlike cut across, and the next moment she was peeling the fur off the body, just as if she was taking off a jacket. Not-Triss stared at what was left. It was strangely bloodless, a glossy misshapen thing that looked absolutely nothing like a rabbit at all. She wanted to unsee what she had just seen, but she could not stop looking at it.

"Are you all right?" asked Dot, looking her up and down. "Not going to faint, are you?"

Not-Triss shook her head. The sight had been shocking, but Dot's directness was curiously comforting. Seeing somebody dealing so calmly with horrible things made her feel that perhaps she herself was not so terrible, and might not strike fear into every heart.

"No," Dot went on, "I don't reckon *you're* the fainter in the family, are you?" She gave Not-Triss a conspiratorial smirk. "Your mother came over nervous, so your father took her out to find some air. And they said *you* were highly strung. All I can say is, *you're* not the one I'd be dragging to doctors."

Not-Triss could only gape. She was so used to everybody treating Piers Crescent and his family as sacred. And yet here was this odd girl fearlessly dissecting the Crescents' private affairs, as swiftly and matter-of-factly as she had skinned the rabbit. Not-Triss was shocked and horrified but also excited and fascinated, in an uncomfortable, pins-and-needles way. Dot was doing something else with the rabbit and the knife now, and Not-Triss looked away for a bit.

When she looked back, the rabbit was becoming chunks

of pink meat, some pale, some darkly marbled. After that, the turnips were diced, the cubes glowing amber in the firelight. The greens were shredded. From time to time Dot muttered and added more wood to the fire.

"What's the point of having a great hearth like this if you don't use it?" she asked, and laughed when it spat sparks on her feet.

As Dot finished preparing the ingredients, Not-Triss looked around and realized for the first time that there was something missing among the bound herbs and long spoons hanging from the beams.

"Where are your pots and pans?"

"I haven't got them out yet. Wait a moment   I'll show them to you." Dot receded into a dark corner of the room and returned with a square box, about six inches across. She set it down carefully before the hearth and lifted the lid. Inside, Not-Triss could just make out white, rounded shapes nestling in a bed of fine, wispy straw.

Slowly and respectfully, Dot pulled out pale shape after pale shape and set them next to each other on the floor. They were eggshells, their crowns broken away and their insides scooped out. The ragged hole of each shell was spanned by a loop of cotton like a miniature handle. Although they were perfectly clean, Dot pulled out a handkerchief and began delicately wiping them, inside and out.

Then, as if she was performing the most ordinary act in the world, she took one of the shells to the table and very carefully pushed some shreds of spinach into it, followed by a cube of turnip, a piece of rabbit, and a tiny dribble of stock.

Not-Triss stared at her, looking for the flicker of a smile to show that this was a joke, but Dot's manner remained perfectly serious and offhand as she carried the shell back to the hearth and used the cotton handle to hang it from a hook over the fire, just as if it was a tiny cooking pot.

Not-Triss gave a snort of laughter as Dot began doing the same with a second eggshell.

"You're not cooking dinner in those!"

"Why not?" Dot raised her eyebrows, looking surprised. "They're my pots and pans. Don't you like them?" And she continued her task. Some shreds of spinach, a cube of turnip, a piece of rabbit meat, a dribble of stock . . .

Something about Dot's poker face set Not-Triss giggling helplessly. She looked away, but the sight of the tiny cooking pots over the fire made things worse. They just looked so absurd dangling there, dripping stock into the flames. Suddenly everything seemed incredibly funny, far funnier than it had any right to be. She rocked silently, web-tears rising to her eyes.

She smothered her mouth with her hands, but she was full of a great swelling laugh and there was nothing her small frame could do to keep it in. It swelled, and swelled, and swelled, and it was only in the moment before it broke forth that she was afraid, and knew it was not *her* laugh, not *her* hilarity that was bursting out of her.

Then the Laugh escaped. Not-Triss rolled on the bench, laughing with the creak and thrash of a forest in a gale. She laughed until the windows rattled and the flames of the hearth dipped and quivered. Words came from her mouth, but they were not hers, nor could the voice that spoke them be mistaken for human.

Oh, we are leaves of the Perspell Wood
That grew before old London stood

Yet never have we seen a sight so strange
As eggshell stewpots on the range.

Dot stood motionless, her face set and unreadable, watching Not-Triss until her helpless mirth subsided. Then she looked past her toward the door, her expression suddenly youthful and uncertain.

"Will that do?" she asked, in a surprisingly respectful tone.

"Thank you, Dot, that will do very well," said Mr. Grace the tailor. He stood just within the doorway, and a pace behind him Not-Triss could see her parents, gazing aghast into the kitchen.

Dot gathered up her kitchen knives, gave Not-Triss one glance of thinly veiled fear and revulsion, and hurried for the door. She pushed hastily past the Crescents and vanished from view.

"Eggshells used as cooking pots," Mr. Grace said, as he advanced slowly and carefully into the room. "It never fails, for some reason. The sight always makes them laugh so hard that they give themselves away. They just can't help it." He sighed. "I promised you proof, my friends. Now you have seen the truth. *This is not your child.*"

Not-Triss was breathing hard, but there did not seem to be any air in her lungs. There were stone flags under her feet, and yet she felt as if she was falling.

"I'm . . . ill." Her voice was a breathless, helpless creak. Everything she had fought so hard to find out—she wanted none of it now. She wanted to be wrong after all, anything to stop her parents from looking at her that way. She *was* wrong. She had to be. "I've been ill, that's all. You said so. You all did. I'm just ill. I'll . . . I'll get better. I . . . I promise I will." Her eyes began to mist.

"Stop!" The tailor threw out an arm to stop her mother from stepping forward. "Don't play into its hands. I'm sorry, but you have to be strong. It's cornered—it knows that its only hope is to tug at your emotions."

"But . . ." Her mother cast an uncertain glance at Not-Triss's face, her gaze bluer and more fragile than ever before. "But look at her!"

"I *am* looking at her," murmured the tailor, and gave a short, dark laugh, a bit like a cough. Before Triss could react, he had sprinted forward and grabbed her by the chin, and she gave a squawk of shock and fear. Both her parents cried out and stepped forward to intervene, but the tailor's expression stopped them in their tracks. His face was that of a man bracing himself for battle, or staring into a hurricane. "You think those are tears shining in her eyes?" he demanded. "Let me show you these 'tears.'" With his free hand he tweaked out a handkerchief, and as Not-Triss tried to jerk her chin free, he gently dabbed at the corner of her eye, catching a long silvery strand and drawing it out for her parents to see.

"What . . . ?" Her father had turned ashen.

"Spiderweb," the tailor replied curtly. "That's all. Just another part of the disguise. This creature *has* no tears."

Not-Triss dug her fingernails into the tailor's hand. When his grip on her chin slipped, she bit him and sprinted away to the far corner of the room. There was a small scream of horror from her mother.

"Her teeth!"

"You saw that?" The tailor was wrapping his handkerchief around his hand. The back of it was marked by small bleeding puncture wounds, not like the dents left by normal teeth at all. Not-Triss raised hesitant fingers to her mouth, and their questing tips touched tooth-points that were slender and unbelievably sharp. "Thorns for teeth. Yes, that's its real appearance. Sometimes they revert when they're frightened or angry. I am so sorry you had to see that, Mrs. Crescent, but now at least you know. *This is not your daughter.*"

"I . . ." Not-Triss looked from face to face in desperation, feeling the cradle of love disintegrating around her. "I *am* Triss! I . . . I *can* be! I *want* to be! Let me try again—I'll get it right this time! Please . . ." They were backing away; her parents were backing away.

"Triss." There was a soft, broken look on the face of her mother.

But she's not your mother, her wits told her, in a voice as soft and terrible as thunder. Too late, Not-Triss realized how blind she had been. Even after she had found out that she was an imposter, she had still been thinking of this man and woman as *her* father, *her* mother. It had been second nature. She had not even noticed herself doing it.

It was Triss's mother who stood before her now, Triss's mother who was flinching away from her in horror, Triss's mother whose expression was ebbing into pale shaking rage.

"Triss—where is she?" Celeste Crescent's throat bobbed as she swallowed. "You little monster, what have you done with her? Where's my little girl?"

"Mother . . ." With a sick feeling in her stomach, Not-Triss could feel her mouth drooping into the little sob-shape that always worked, that always made everybody soften and look after her. But it was a stolen mannerism, and today it only made things worse.

"Tell us what we have to do," asked Piers Crescent through his teeth.

"It will be unpleasant," answered the tailor, "so we should spare Mrs. Crescent. She's been brave enough already."

"Celeste"—Piers gave his wife a look of tender appeal—"love, please, can you leave us? Triss will need you strong and well, when we get her back."

"Don't go!" Not-Triss knew at once that something terrible was going to happen, something that the tailor was not willing to do in front of Mrs. Crescent. "Don't leave me!"

But her mouth was full of thorns, and her voice came out wrong. With one last white-faced, appalled look at Not-Triss, Celeste Crescent tottered weakly from the room and closed the door behind her.

"Now, Mr. Crescent," continued the tailor in a deliberately calm and steady voice, "I will need you to stoke up the fire. Make it as fierce as you can."

Not-Triss leaped toward the door by which Mrs. Crescent had left, but the tailor seized her, wrapping both arms around her so that her own were pinned to her sides.

"It's the only way," he added through clenched teeth as Not-Triss scratched, struggled, and tried to bite him with her thorn-teeth. "The only way to show the Besiders that we mean business. This creature is either one of their own children, or it is even less than that—a doll made of dead leaves, perhaps, or carved from a block of wood. If it is a child of theirs, the Besiders will not wish to see it hurt. The best ways of dealing with a changeling—the oldest, tried, and tested ways—are to force them to save it. Beat it with a switch till it screams. Throw it into fast-flowing water. Or push it into a blazing fire."

"God above," whispered Piers, as he shakily piled more wood on the fire and nursed it to a roar. "Isn't there any other way?"

Not-Triss gave a wordless wail of terror, but it sounded ghastly even to her ears. There was the whickering of bat wings in it, the whistle of November winds, the scream of gulls. The kindling in the hearth snapped with a sound like castanets, spitting sparks to dance lazily up the flue.

"It won't kill it," answered the tailor curtly. "Mark my words, if it's a Besider child, either it will jump up the chimney, or its parents will come for it. Either way, the Besiders will bring back your child to make sure you never trouble their family again."

"And if it's a wooden doll?" Piers was ashen-faced and shaking. He stared at his own hands tending the fire as if they horrified him. He did not look at the tailor, or at Not-Triss wrestling in his arms. He kept his gaze on the rising flames the way a drowning man clings to a timber.

"Then the outcome is less certain. The Besiders will not bother to rescue a doll, but if you destroy it, they may well lose interest in their game and return your child anyway. Or they may not—but you will still have rid your house of a monster."

"He's wrong!" Not-Triss called through her sobs, willing her not-father to look at her. "He's wrong! I'm real! I'm real, and if you put me on the fire I'll die!" She could feel cobweb tears oozing out of her eyes and down her cheeks, leaving long, shining, incriminating strands.

"Don't listen." The tailor was maneuvering her closer and closer to the hearth, an inch at a time. "Mr. Crescent, remember this: It doesn't feel pain the way we do; it doesn't feel fear. However much it screams, none of it is real. Are you ready?"

"Oh God." Piers stepped back from the fire, and at last turned his dismayed gaze toward Not-Triss. His face softened for an instant, with the kind look he saved for only one person. Not-Triss felt a small dewdrop of hope before she realized that he was looking through her, not at her. “For Triss,” he said under his breath. “For Triss I can do this. Yes. I’m ready.”

“Then on a count of three, help me force it into the fire,” murmured the tailor. “I’ll need your assistance. Even their children can be inhumanly strong and agile.”

His face was drawn and pained. With a deep despair Not-Triss realized that he was a good man, and that good men sometimes did terrible things.

“One . . .”

Not-Triss struggled and wailed until the roof tiles popped and cracked like hot chestnuts. She screamed until the grain pots shattered on the shelves.

“Two . . .”

She fought, clawed, and tried to bite, all pretense forgotten.

“Thr . . .”

But the rest of the “three” never arrived. Suddenly there came a drenching rush of icy water from behind, soaking her back and shoulder and cascading down onto the hearth. There was a deafening hiss, a blinding surge of smoke and steam, and the room was plunged into near darkness.

Not-Triss felt the tailor’s grip slacken in surprise. In one wild, convulsive motion she burst from his grasp, nearly losing her balance. Before she could fall, however, a small hand snatched at hers and yanked her in the direction of the door.

Instinct took over, and she ran. Out of the kitchen door, through room after room. Then out through the front door into the cold, sea-scented darkness, sprinting all but blind over the shifting pebbles, with the short dark figure of Pen by her side.

Chapter 19

RUNNING FROM THE SCISSOR MAN

PEBBLES CLACKED UNDER THEIR HASTY STEPS with a cold, disapproving sound. The wind was against them. Overhead the clouds rolled by, solemn, smoky, and vast, the pale face of the moon surfacing now and then. The black waves seethed unseen against the black beach, only occasional frills of white foam visible in the gloom.

Pen ran alongside Not-Triss, panting fiercely. Her silveriness of the day before seemed to have worn off, and she was now as dark and solid as she had ever been. Not-Triss could not even start to guess how Pen had contrived to suddenly appear here, let alone why the younger girl had decided to save her.

Panic had led them down the beach, because it was flat, and panic told them they needed to run fast. Panic had nothing to suggest when the beach ran out and they found themselves staring at the cliff-face of the headland that formed the end of the cove. They halted for a second, staring and gasping for breath, and Not-Triss recovered enough of her wits to realize how exposed they were.

"Head inland!" she hissed. "Into the woods!"

The pair of them scrambled up the beach, over some slippery

wave-worn boulders and into the birch wood beyond. Staring up the steep, tree-covered slope that seemed to climb forever, Not-Triss felt the clammy touch of despair.

The woods were thick with wet rust-colored bracken, which soaked them as they struggled up the slope, and hid their own feet from them. The damp moss and leaf-rot were softly treacherous underfoot. The silver-birch trunks gleamed in the darkness like lean and elegant ghosts.

There was no sound of pursuit behind them yet, but there would be. Not-Triss was sure of that. Mr. Grace and Piers Crescent must have gone to find light sources. *And scissors*, said a fearful part of her mind. She tried to silence it, but she could not rid herself of a mental picture of Mr. Grace bounding up the slope after her with a pair of enormous scissors, like the "long, red-legged scissorman" from the old story, who cut off children's thumbs.

They tried to throw me on the fire.

Her lungs started jerking with sobs. She couldn't think about *that*. Not now. Not when she needed every ounce of breath for climbing. If they could just reach the road . . .

But Pen kept falling down. Her legs were shorter. The bracken came up to her waist, not her hips. Not-Triss caught her and helped pull her back to her feet over and over and over. At last, when Not-Triss stooped to drag her upright for the twentieth time, Pen pushed her away hard, and Not-Triss nearly slid back down the slope.

"I hate you!" Pen's would-be shout was muffled by breathlessness, and Not-Triss realized that the younger girl was sobbing with exhaustion and rage. "I hate you! You stupid . . . Why did *you* have to happen? I never asked for a stupid . . . stupid . . . toothy . . . stupid . . . monster thing."

"I know," whispered Not-Triss. It was all she could do to

keep her voice quiet and calm. Her mind was a thundercloud, waiting for the first crack.

"You spoil everything! Always! Even when you're just *fake* you, you still spoil everything. And now you've made me run away again!"

There were lights farther down the slope, tame white-yellow lights that swiveled and scanned, foliage feathering their beams. Hand lamps, perhaps, or electric torches.

"Pen," breathed Not-Triss, "they're coming. They're coming after us, Pen." With despair she stared down at Pen's round, stubborn face.

Please, Pen, please! I'm so close to screaming. Don't make me carry you! I can't! I can't do that as well!

"We've got to get up to the road, Pen," she heard herself say. "It'll be easier then. And we're nearly there."

"Liar," growled Pen, as she scrambled to her feet with painful slowness. "Lying . . . monster-face." Nonetheless she continued her struggle up the slope, sobbing for breath.

When the rain descended, at first Not-Triss did not know what it was. All she knew was that the air suddenly rushed downward, waterfall-cold, and the forest gave a long exhalation like a sigh of relief. Then she felt the chill, heavy finger-taps of fat raindrops on her skull and understood.

She closed her eyes in an instant of gratitude. The weather was on her side for once. Their scuffles and rustles would be much harder for their pursuers to hear now.

We must be near the top. Please let us be near the top.

It became a chant in her head, and the words had almost lost meaning by the time she scrambled over one more tussock and found herself staring at the winding, puddle-silvered road. Her legs burned, and her head felt light.

"We're here." She could force no triumph into her voice. She realized that she had no idea what to do next.

"Triss," said Pen in a small voice, looking back down the slope.

Not-Triss followed her gaze and felt a tingle of panic pass through her whole frame. The following lights were closer now. She could even make out the dark shapes of figures behind them. So what if their pursuers could not hear them over the rain? They knew that the girls had nowhere to head but the road.

Not-Triss stared up and down the lane, searching blindly for inspiration, but it was Pen who spoke first, through the dripping fuzz of her hair.

"We need to catch a lift. We need a car."

As if Pen had spoken some summoning spell, Not-Triss realized that near the bend in the road the puddles were brightening. A moment later, two circular yellow headlights swung round the corner, their radiance dimpled by the rain.

Both girls desperately waved their arms at the oncoming car, and Pen whooped to get the driver's attention. The car showed no sign of slowing, however, and swerved to the other side of the road.

Before Not-Triss could stop her, Pen broke away from her and sprinted into the road, so that she was standing in the middle of it as the sedan sliced past—

Bang.

There was a high-pitched, childish scream. Not-Triss stood gasping amid the rain as the car screeched to a halt ten yards on. There was a small figure lying behind it on the road, faceup. Not-Triss's skin seemed to be covered in ants, and she could not feel her insides.

It was a few seconds before she recovered the use of her

limbs, and by then the driver was getting out and staring in horror at Pen's fallen form.

"She . . . she . . . ran out," he stammered helplessly.

"She's got a pulse!" Not-Triss had insides again, though they seemed to have been jumbled and turned over like the contents of a manhandled crate. "She needs a hospital! You need to take her to a hospital!"

The driver crouched to examine Pen. He was young, with a nice enough face, somewhat crumpled by uncertainty.

"Where are your parents?" he asked.

"They're not here! There's just you, and you have to do something! She's cold and she's got rain falling on her face and she's been hit by a car!" Not-Triss could feel herself losing control. If she was not careful, soon her screams would be tearing the forests apart like a cyclone. "We need to take her to a hospital!"

"Yes—yes, we will. Don't be scared." The driver smoothed back his wet hair as if ordering his thoughts, then carefully scooped up Pen in his arms. He put her in the backseat, and Not-Triss climbed in next to her.

This car did not have a starter button like the Sunbeam, and Not-Triss had to watch while the driver wrestled with a crank handle on the front of the car to get the engine started again. She was close to breaking by the time he climbed back into the driver's seat.

As the car drove away, Not-Triss saw two lights emerge from the woods and pan after them. Her mind was so full of Pen that it took her a moment to even realize what they had been, and by then they were disappearing around the darkened bend.

Don't you dare die, Pen. It was all Not-Triss could think, over and over. *I'll never forgive you if you die.*

"There's a hospital near Ellchester," the driver said, obviously fighting to keep his voice calm. "It's about twenty miles. Just twenty miles. It won't take long."

He kept up a countdown as he drove. Each time they passed a signpost, he let Not-Triss know how close they were.

"Three miles," he said at last. "We're just passing Bobbeck Ridge . . ."

It was at this point that something completely unexpected happened. Pen suddenly sat bolt upright, peered out through the wet glass at the signpost, then thumped the back of the driver's seat.

"Here! You can let us out here! I'm . . . feeling better now."

The driver jumped out of his skin and nearly hit the signpost. He pulled the car up by the side of the road and turned to stare over his shoulder.

"What?"

Pen looked meek.

"I'm all right now. I just fainted. And now I'm better. And we live down there." She pointed to a cluster of seedy-looking buildings on the banks of the estuary. "Thank you for the lift!"

"Hey!" The driver's face reddened. "Were you faking back there?"

Pen did not wait to continue the conversation but opened the door and leaped out into the rain with no obvious sign of injury. Not-Triss followed as quickly as she could. They splashed quickly away from the car as the driver gave them a suspicious scowl and began the slow and awkward task of wrestling his vehicle back onto the road.

"You *were* faking!" exclaimed Not-Triss in disbelief. "But . . . there was a bang!"

Pen shrugged. "I threw a rock at the side of the car, then I screamed. Cars always stop when they think they've hit you.

You don't know anything, do you?" Her determinedly complacent look faded a little after a second, and her teeth started to chatter. "I need to use the bathroom," she announced without preamble, then turned and started slithering her unsteady way down the wet wooden steps to the riverside.

Not-Triss stared after her, the rain beating drums on the boardwalk before her. She wanted to throw up. She wanted to laugh.

Pen, she thought in the quiet of her own head, *you are amazing*.

Chapter 20

FROSTY WELCOME

AS NOT-TRISS EDGED AND SLIPPED HER WAY down the wet boardwalk steps, she realized that the buildings on the riverside were surprisingly well lit and crowded for the time of night. All three buildings were made of wood and had the words J. WILKINSON & SONS BOATBUILDERS painted on the sides in tall, honest blue letters. The people Not-Triss could see through the windows, however, did not seem to be dressed for boatbuilding. She could make out sequins, bow ties, and bare shoulders, and everybody seemed to be laughing about something.

Behind the drumming of the rain, music was audible. It reminded Not-Triss of the record that Mr. Grace had played, and her heart gave a leap of fear. However, this was not the same crazy, breathless sound, as she quickly realized with a mixture of relief and disappointment. This was jazz that had wiped its feet and put on its best manners to meet somebody's mother.

Over a door somebody had nailed a wooden plaque with the word PINK'S painted across it in green and white, next to little black silhouettes of a man and woman dancing.

As Not-Triss was examining the sign, Pen emerged from a little outhouse nearby. She approached one of the windows and stood on tiptoe to peer in, her breath clouding the pane. As the light from the window fell on Pen's face, Not-Triss again noticed three fine scratches that ran slantwise across the younger girl's cheek. They were shallow but dark with dried blood, and Not-Triss felt a guilty pang.

"I can't see her," Pen muttered in an annoyed tone. "But she *has* to be here!" The younger girl pushed her way in through the door, and with some apprehension Not-Triss followed, feeling uncertain and exposed.

There were no boats inside. Instead it was filled with dozens of people, all large and loud and moving around. From a central beam above hung a series of gently swinging lanterns made of chrome and pink glass, which bathed the hall in a patchy rosy glow and made everybody look flushed and a bit otherworldly. Lots of the women wore dresses that fell from tiny shoulder straps, and some carried feathered fans. Everybody's hair seemed to be short and very shiny. The walls were partially concealed by hanging cloths, creamy white with fine vertical stripes of cerise.

The music lurched into loudness, and Not-Triss could see that there were actual musicians at the far side of the hall, one plinking at a piano, one nodding away with a cornet, and a third pouting plump-cheeked into his clarinet. They wore evening dress, bow ties neat against their shining shirtfronts.

Just for a moment it reminded Not-Triss of drawings she had seen in magazines and on book jackets, of pastel-colored parties where languid, fashionable women slunk and posed, slim and elegant as fish, and gentlemen passed them flutes of fat-bubbled champagne.

The impression did not last long, however. The scene around her was too jarringly and robustly real. The accents were all too

Ellchester, and some of the girls had knobbly ankles. Two of the musicians were tubby and shiny-faced, as if they regretted having to wear their jackets. People did not glide, and the floorboards creaked under them. Aside from the smell of the river and cigarette smoke, there was another scent that reminded Not-Triss of Celeste's wine tonic, but also of the way the family car smelled after the tank had been filled. It seemed to come from the large cluster of glasses on a trestle table by the wall.

Not-Triss was uncomfortably aware that Pen and herself were drawing quite a few odd looks. They were not exactly hostile, but rather the sort of crinkled-brow glances that somebody might direct toward a banging door or a dropped cigarette. The girls were clearly a minor problem that somebody needed to deal with, but nobody had yet worked out who. Not-Triss had a strong feeling that this was not the kind of party that welcomed sudden damp children.

One of the women nudged a young man with a large reddish nose and looked pointedly at the new arrivals. He glanced across at Pen and Not-Triss, then wandered over and stooped to peer at them as if they were so small that he needed to focus to see them properly.

"Hello there." His voice was a bit slurred and his eyes shiny, as if it was raining inside his head as well. "Are you looking for somebody?"

"Hello, Doggerel," Pen answered promptly. "We're looking for Violet. Is she here?"

Violet? Violet Parish? Why are we looking for her, of all people? Not-Triss tried to catch Pen's eye, but in vain.

Doggerel shut his mouth with a snap, and Not-Triss could see him sorting through scattered memories looking for Pen's face and name.

"Oh . . . It's Penny, isn't it? Yes . . . yes, I remember. Violet's, er, little friend. Yes, Violet was here. But you've just missed her. She's gone."

"What?" Pen's eyes widened with dismay. "But she'll be back, won't she?" She was glaring at him now, willing him to agree, willing the world to agree. "She *has* to come back." There was a slight edge of angry panic in her voice.

Doggerel winced sympathetically and drew his breath in through his teeth. "Probably not—you know what she's like." He swooped one of his hands to and fro and made whooshing noises. "Five minutes in a place, then off again!" He seemed to notice the look of increasing desperation on Pen's face. "Look, ah, is something wrong? Do you need somebody to drive you two home?"

Both girls shook their heads, perhaps a little too urgently. Not-Triss did not much like the idea of throwing herself on the mercy of Violet Parish, but what other options did they have? If the party came to an end and they were still out in this lonely spot, either some well-meaning adult would insist on taking them home, or they would be on the run again, with nowhere to hide.

"Where is she?" asked Pen. "Where did she go? We need to find her!" She was looking younger by the second.

As Doggerel opened his mouth to answer, the door banged open, making any response from him unnecessary.

"Here it is!" a voice called out above the hubbub. "Kid Oliver's 'Dippermouth Blues'! I drove back for it, so you had all better bloody well appreciate this." In the doorway stood a figure in a rain-darkened tan coat and a fleece-lined motoring cap. Above her head she held a gramophone record, still in its sleeve. "Pinky—wind up that croaky machine of yours!"

It was Violet Parish, removing her cap and shaking out her cropped hair, tufty as a fledgling from the rain. Everybody seemed to know her, and there were calls and whistles of approval at her return. A dense gaggle gathered around her, and Not-Triss noticed that a lot of them seemed to be men.

"Somebody get me a drink and a cigarette!" Violet said as she dragged off her coat, revealing a long dark-green dress with split skirts. It was not a sultry request, more like a mechanic asking to be passed a wrench. Nobody seemed offended, and soon she had a glass in one hand and was drawing on a cigarette as somebody lit it for her. Her face was still shiny from rain, but she did not seem to care.

The musicians looked a bit aggrieved at first as a wind-up gramophone was produced, but took the opportunity to seek out drinks and mop their brows.

"Thank God they've stopped," Violet said quite audibly. "Music as hot as a dead frog."

As the needle dipped to the record there was a white-noise hiss, and even after the first rude blare of brass there were still spit-spots of static. This was a record that had been places and come back scratched, and somehow the roughness made it seem all the more itself. *This* jazz had not wiped its feet; it crunched right into the room with gravel on its shoes.

Pen tried to call out to Violet but was hushed. Everyone in the boathouse had drawn closer, listening until the mischievous, lawless song ended with a half-mocking salute and a last long note.

"That," said Violet, stubbing out her cigarette, "is how you do it." The remark was partially directed at the musicians, who seemed to take it as a challenge. When they started up with their instruments again, the rhythm was fiercer and more defiant than before.

"Violet!" called Pen again, but Violet did not hear. She went out with the tide of dancers to the floor, and Not-Triss was unsure whether she drew the tide, or whether the tide drew her.

Half the windows looked out over the river, and it made Not-Triss feel as if she was on a boat. As the dancing began again and the floorboards started to thunder, it was easy to believe that there was no ground under them. Nobody was steering the boat, everybody was dancing, and nobody danced more wildly than Violet. There was something desperate about it, as if dancing would stop the boat from sinking. There was something fierce about it, as if she wanted to drive her foot through the hull and sink the boat faster.

So this was Violet's world. The *fast* world. "The high life," as Celeste Crescent would put it. In spite of everything, it made Not-Triss nervous, as if wickedness was something she could breathe in like smoke, and which might leave a scent on her clothes.

Even though she was out of the rain, Not-Triss realized that she was starting to shiver. The more people looked at her, the worse the trembling became. She did not want anybody to stare too hard, in case they saw something monstrous in her face and reeled away in search of flames to destroy her. All these people could turn in a moment, she knew it.

"Violet!" At last Pen's perseverance paid off, and as the musicians finished their piece she managed to force her way through the crowd. "Violet, it's me!" Violet's eye fell upon Pen, and she paused in the middle of drawing from her cigarette, then closed her eyes and let out the smoke in a long exasperated breath.

"Oh Lord," she muttered. "Pen, for . . . Pete's sake, what are you doing here?" Once again, her mock-London drawl grated on Not-Triss's nerves.

"I *had* to come!" exclaimed Pen. "It was life and death!"

"Of course it was. Isn't it always?" Violet sighed and drew Pen aside. Not-Triss followed at a small distance, still loath to draw attention to herself. "Pen—have you run away *again*? And how did you get here from Ellchester? You haven't been throwing rocks at cars again, have you?"

Pen opened her mouth wide, made a small not-quite-squeak, and shut it again.

"And what's happened to your face?" continued Violet. "Where did you get those bramble scratches on your cheek?"

Pen's eyes crept across to Not-Triss. Violet followed her gaze and stiffened, her long jaw dropping.

"Oh—you have to be joking." She stared, then shook her head in disbelief. "This evening is just . . . you brought your *sister* out *here*? Pen! What—"

"It was the only place I could think of to go! You said I should! You said I should always come to you—"

"I said that *if* you ran away, then you should come and stay with me until you were ready to go home, instead of sleeping in hedges or getting into strange cars. And I could get into trouble for saying *that*." Violet gave Not-Triss another glance, as if assessing the likelihood that she might run to the police straightaway. "This is different. If *both* of you are missing, your parents will be calling everybody short of the prime minister. I need to take the pair of you home right now."

"No!" shouted both girls, with enough volume that several people looked round in curiosity.

"Please don't!" blurted out Not-Triss. "I'm sorry we interrupted your party, but please, please don't take us home. Our parents . . ." She trailed off, desperately trying to think of a good story.

"They tried to burn Triss alive!" Pen leaped into the gap.

Violet raised her eyebrows and just looked at Pen. Not-Triss's spirits sank. Violet didn't like Mr. and Mrs. Crescent, but adults believed adults. Adults believed *in* adults. Violet evidently liked Pen, but Pen told lies, and Violet clearly knew that.

Pen took hold of Violet's arm.

"Please!" she said through her teeth, her eyes bright with the effort of willing Violet to listen to her. "Really. Truly. Cross my heart and hope to die."

"It's *true*," Not-Triss whispered, uncertain how much her word was worth. "I know how it sounds . . . but we can't go home. We're in danger."

There was nothing warm about Violet's long-jawed face as she scowled at them. She was an adult looking at two silly girls who had come to her with a silly lie. Then she gave an annoyed sigh and closed her eyes. When she opened them again she looked angry but tired.

"One night," she said simply, and it took Not-Triss a moment to understand what she meant. "I really shouldn't do this . . . but you can stay at my lodgings tonight. I'll take you there now and drop you off. But first thing tomorrow, you are going to tell me what is going on. Is that clear?"

Not-Triss nodded, hardly daring to believe in the reprieve.

"Where are your coats? Don't you even have coats? Wait here and I'll get you blankets, or you'll catch your death in the side-car." It was becoming chilly, Not-Triss couldn't help but notice. A number of the women in the hall were pouting a little, rubbing at their bare shoulders and looking for their shawls.

After Violet had departed in search of blankets and her coat, Not-Triss stole a glance at Pen.

"Violet's your friend, then? Are you . . . are you sure we can trust her? You're sure she won't pretend to help us, then drive us back home?"

Pen nodded confidently.

"You don't know her. If she was going to take us back, she'd tell us. Really loudly."

Nobody wanted to see Violet leave, but nobody seemed surprised. Her record was passed back to her, and she tucked it under her coat.

"Don't go, Violet!" A drunk young man kept trying to haul her back to the dance floor. His drawl made her name sound like "Varlet." "Stay for once! Why do you never stay anywhere?"

"Because I'm avoiding *you*, Ben," Violet declared calmly, pushing him aside. "It's all personal." There was a burst of laughter.

"Give up, Ben," somebody shouted. "Don't tangle with old Frosty over there."

Violet gave a short laugh, and for a moment her face held an odd mixture of pride and something less happy. She led Not-Triss and Pen out of the dance hall into the darkness, where the rain was slicingly cold against the skin.

Chapter 21

CANNED CHEESE AND BANANAS

VIOLET'S MOTORBIKE WAS STANDING AMID THE parked cars like a grimy fox in a field of cows.

"The sidecar's only meant for one person," she muttered, "but we'll have to squeeze you both in." It was shaped like a fat little canoe with a big wheel on the side, a tapering enclosed nose to contain one's legs, and a seat under the opening. It proved possible for both girls to fit inside, with Pen sitting on Not-Triss's lap.

Violet donned her goggles, tethered her cap, and straddled her motorbike. Then, with visible effort and using most of her weight, she drove her foot down on the kick-starter, wrenching a startlingly loud rattle-roar from the engine. The smell of oil made Not-Triss feel sick. When the bike lurched forward and swerved out onto the road, Not-Triss reflexively gripped at the sides of the sidecar, teeth clenched with apprehension.

The road felt very close. On one side roared the bike, so loud that it made her right ear ache. On the other she could see the mudguard over the sidecar's great wheel vibrating with the ruggedness of the road, and she was afraid to let her hands near it. The icy rain was now rushing horizontally, straight into her face, and the wind was merciless. Worst of all, Pen wouldn't stay still but wanted to wriggle, twist, lean, and stare around her, in ways that always seemed to involve elbowing or squashing Not-Triss.

A gentle and exhausted numbness settled upon Not-Triss's mind as she watched the occasional car rattle past, the headlights carving shafts of light out of the darkness, streaked with bright rain. The recent past was a fading ache. Only this was real, this long moment of being shaken around like a shoe in a box, and even this was not *very* real.

At last the motorbike stopped in front of an old terraced house on a narrow unlit street, and Violet cut the engine.

"Try to be quiet," she whispered as she clambered off the bike and set about extricating the two girls. "My landlady's an old crab, and I'm not supposed to have guests."

Not-Triss and Pen followed Violet up the steps and watched as she slowly turned her key in the lock, with the concentration of a safecracker, and led them into a shadowy hall. The two girls were a step behind as she tiptoed up the stairs, unlocked another door, and stepped through into a darkened room.

As Violet put coins in the gas meter and lit the lamps, Not-Triss looked around her at the primrose-patterned wallpaper dimpled with damp, the scuffed elderly furniture, and the curtains that stopped two inches short of the sill. Celeste Crescent had talked about Violet living "the high life," but the only valuable-looking objects in the room were a small wireless set, a wind-up gramophone, and a few records.

Every drawer in the room was open, as if somebody had been interrupted in the act of searching the place, but Violet did not seem surprised by this. A half-open door in the opposite wall looked onto a disheveled bed. A row of stockings dangled from the mantelpiece, their toes held in place by various ornaments. Not-Triss wondered if they were "artificial silk," the new stocking stuff that Celeste Crescent sniffed at as "shopgirl silk."

When Violet knelt by the small tiled hearth and started to load it with coal, Not-Triss watched her with a blank, hypnotized fascination. At the first lick of flame, however, she could not help flinching back a step and drawing in a panicky breath. Her skin seemed to tingle with terrible warmth once more, as it had when she had been forced close to the cottage fireplace. Violet cast a surprised glance over her shoulder at Not-Triss, taking stock of her mute, trembling paralysis, and frowned a little. She turned back to the hearth but shifted her position across so that she blocked Not-Triss's view of the flames. When Violet put the fireguard in place, Not-Triss felt her pulse slow a little.

Meanwhile, Pen busied herself collecting blankets and cushions from here and there, dropping them in front of the fire to make a sort of nest, with the confidence of practice.

"Violet!" Pen whispered loudly, when their reluctant hostess was sitting back, wiping soot from her hands. "We need food. We haven't eaten anything for hours!"

"So next time perhaps you should wait until after dinner before running away," Violet muttered, without obvious sympathy.

"But I'm *starving*!" exclaimed Pen. "I haven't eaten anything *all day*!"

"Well, you needn't sound as if that's my fault," Violet growled, heading over to a wooden box near the wall. "I'm not your mother."

"Good," Pen answered without hesitation. "I wouldn't *want* you to be my mother. I'd run away from you too."

Not-Triss listened agape to this exchange, tensing for the inevitable thunderclap. It did not come.

"Canned cheese and bananas," murmured Violet, returning to the hearth and dropping to her haunches. "It's all there is."

Pen shrugged. "I like canned cheese."

Not-Triss watched as Violet dug her opener into the cheese can and started cutting a jagged hole in the top. Her long face was still jeweled with rain, her nose blue from the cold, and the straps of her motoring cap hung down below her ears. For the first time Not-Triss started to understand why Pen might come here when she ran away. In the Crescent family home you had to be careful all the time, because if you did or said the wrong thing, it never went away. It just hung there forever, an invisible black mark that everybody knew was there. Pen had found a place where you could say things that were rude and grumpy, and where the other person would just be rude and grumpy back, and afterward you could sit eating bananas without an ounce of ill feeling.

The three of them ate the cheese off tea-set saucers. It had a slight metallic taste but nobody seemed to care. The bananas were brown-skinned, but the flesh inside was still mostly pale and firm.

At last Violet stood, fastening the chinstrap of her cap again.

"I'll be back in a few hours, and I'll try not to wake you. Don't burn down the house while I'm gone unless absolutely necessary. And when I'm back, don't wake me until at least ten."

"Where are you going?" In spite of everything, a hundred suspicions and fears crowded back into Not-Triss's head. "Why are you going out again? You're not going to our parents or the police, are you?"

"Oh, for pity's sake! No. No, I won't." At the door she paused, her eyes lingering on Not-Triss again, her narrow, painted mouth drooping into its habitual frown. "Triss, do you need any . . . any medicine or anything before you go to bed?"

"No." Not-Triss shook her head, feeling abashed at her outburst, but still only half reassured. "No, thank you. I . . . I don't think they really help."

The door closed behind Violet, and Not-Triss sank down to sit on the cushions near the now-caged fire.

"It's all right," Pen said, pulling blankets over her own knees. "I've stayed here before. She *always* does that. Last time she stayed out until *seven in the morning*. I know because she woke me up coming in. She sleeps till ten, then gets up and goes to work."

Work. Again not entirely the "high life" Celeste Crescent had described. Apparently Violet Parish did not spend her whole time sitting around and drinking cocktails at the Crescent family's expense. Not-Triss had a dozen new thoughts about Violet Parish, and yet these were not the most important things on her mind.

She glanced across at Pen, who was nestling herself in the blankets like a dormouse and refusing to meet her eye.

"Pen," she said gently, "I think we need to talk. About everything. About the Architect."

Pen chewed hard on her upper lip, and for a few seconds Not-Triss thought the younger girl might ignore her, or give vent to one of her fits of temper. Instead she wound the blanket tassels around one finger and shrugged.

"You have to promise not to get angry," she mumbled belligerently, "or scratch me with your claws or bite me with your thorn-teeth."

"I promise," said Not-Triss. "And I'm really sorry I hurt your face."

"Good," answered Pen sullenly.

"So," Not-Triss prompted, as patiently as she could, "the Architect. Where did you meet him?"

Pen gave her a sly sideways glance. Perhaps she was weighing up a lie, like a snowball in her hand, seeing if it would hold together. Or perhaps she was trying to judge whether Not-Triss might become a screaming thorn-monster at a moment's notice if she said the wrong thing.

"He just turned up one day. Three weeks ago. The day after my birthday. And Mother and Father promised we would all go to Bowgate's Picture House, because they were showing *Peril on Park Avenue*. But then when we were about to go, you said—I mean, *real* Triss said that she had a headache and a fever. She did it on *purpose*, so we couldn't go, I know it, I saw her looking at me, I *know* it. So I called her a liar and a rat, and then everybody shouted at me and I wasn't allowed to go to the cinema at all."

Not-Triss said nothing. She could vaguely remember the incident, could recall a sense of outrage at being yelled at while she was ill. Had there been a certain hint of spiteful satisfaction as well at seeing Pen robbed of her birthday treat? Perhaps there had.

"I ran away again," Pen whispered. "I hated you *all*. I went and sat on the seesaw on Gramhill Park, and it was raining, and I hated you all so much I wished I had a *weapon*. Or a gang, so I could go home and you'd all be scared. But then I thought I didn't want to make Mother and Father scared, just you, because it was all your fault, and you *made* them like that. And when I was thinking that, a big black car stopped by the park, and a man got out and came right up to me. He called me 'Miss Penelope Crescent' and held his umbrella over me, and said no gentleman should let a lady sit in the rain."

"And that was the Architect?" asked Not-Triss, trying to untangle her thoughts. She had wondered how Pen had managed to contact the Architect in the first place.

Pen nodded. "I was a bit scared of him at first, particularly when he said he'd been watching us for some time. But then he said he didn't like the way everybody else treated me, that it wasn't fair, and he wanted to help me. He said sometimes families are like fruit bowls, and if one of the pieces of fruit is rotten, it makes everything rotten. So you have to take that fruit out of the bowl, and that makes everything better. And I said that you—I mean, the *real* Triss—were rotten and made everybody unhappy. And he agreed."

Not-Triss could feel some of her previous anger and hurt stirring in her, but the misery was so vivid in Pen's face that she forced herself to rein it in.

"He wanted to know if our family would be going to the countryside anytime soon, and I told him about the holiday. Then he said he wanted to make a bargain with me. I had to give him lots of things belonging to Triss—he said the diary pages were the most important bit—and then, when we were on holiday, I had to get Triss to come with me to the Grimmer. He said that if I did that, then he . . ." Pen paused, biting her lip. It was hard to tell in the firelight, but Not-Triss thought she might be flushing somewhat. "He said he'd take Triss away so she'd never come back and everything would be better," she said, adding in a mumble, "and neither of us would ever talk about it to anybody."

"So you lured the real Triss down to the Grimmer—"

"Don't say it like that!" hissed Pen. "And don't look at me like it's all my fault! I just wanted everything to stop being horrible, and that's *your* fault. Well, real Triss's fault, but you're just like her!"

"Well, if you hate me so much, why did you bother saving me?" snapped Not-Triss. Her paper-thin self-control was stretched to the tearing point, and there was a sea of grief behind it.

Pen glared at Not-Triss. Her eyes were shiny with angry tears.

"I didn't *mean* to," she muttered fiercely. "This morning, when everybody was driving away without me, I thought you might do something horrible to Mother and Father if I wasn't there. So I hid in the back—down on the floor under the blanket. Then when the car was stopped outside the cottage for ages, I got bored and cold, so I sneaked out and hid in the kitchen. Then everybody found out you were a monster and caught you, and at first I was really glad, because it meant you wouldn't come home and scratch my face and try to break into my room." Her tone held a mixture of malice and fear. "But . . . then they wanted to burn you. And you started crying. And it wasn't real tears, but it was real crying. You were *really scared*, even though they kept saying you weren't."

"Then why couldn't Father see that?" Not-Triss felt despair and hurt welling up inside her again, and it was all she could do to stop her teeth from sharpening. "Why couldn't Mother see it?"

"Because they're stupid," growled Pen, rubbing at her nose with her sleeve. "They can't tell when real Triss is fake-crying, so of course they can't tell when fake Triss is real-crying."

"Don't call me that!" It was hard to say why the words stung so much.

"If you don't like it, that's too bad," retorted Pen with a sudden gleam in her eye, "because that's what you are. Fake Triss. In fact, that's your name now. You don't have a name, and I saved your life, so I get to choose what your name is. And it's Fake Triss."

"I'm not—"

"Shut up, Fake Triss. You're lucky I'm letting you have a name at all."

Not-Triss closed her eyes and took a deep breath. She thought of Pen dragging her by the hand from the cottage kitchen. She thought of Pen sprinting by her side through the moonlight.

"Tell me more about the Architect." Not-Triss thought it safest to change the subject. "He gave you a way of calling him on the phone, didn't he?"

Pen gave a short nod.

"I had to say, 'Waste, wither, want,' before I picked up the earpiece, and then when I pressed the button for the switchboard, the voice on the line wasn't a normal operator. There was this whispery woman instead, and I just had to ask her for the Architect, and she put me through."

At last Not-Triss understood why there had been no record of Pen's mysterious phone call from the Crescent household. It had not gone through the usual switchboard at all. No wonder the operators knew nothing of it.

"Did he ever tell you where he lived, or anything else about him?" continued Not-Triss.

"Not really, just that he was an architect." Pen scowled in concentration. "Wait—he said that's why he was watching us. Because he knew Father. Through their work. But he said he'd decided he liked me better than Father, because I seemed more 'honorable.'"

A blizzard of fragments was flurrying through Not-Triss's mind and trying to form a picture. She remembered the overheard conversation between Piers and Celeste Crescent, regarding the mysterious *he* that Piers wanted nothing more to do with. She remembered the article in the newspaper concerning Piers's new building project. Last of all, there was the mystery of the envelopes in the desk drawer, their existence so carefully concealed. Her mind was too tired to make further sense of the fragments, however.

“We have to find out more about the Architect, Pen.” Not-Triss saw her not-sister flinch and, after a moment’s hesitation, aimed a comforting pat at the smaller girl’s foot. “I know you don’t want to, and I don’t really want to either. But we have to. He doesn’t just have Triss. He has Sebastian.”

Chapter 22

THE UNDERBELLY

NOT-TRISS WAS WOKEN BY THE SOUND OF A solitary cock crowing. She lay on the floor staring at the dim, cracked ceiling and listened, remembering where she was. No, she was not in the countryside. The bird she could hear must be in somebody's backyard coop. It was a bold, brass sound nonetheless. It would not be cowed into silence by the invention of alarm clocks, the subdued buzz of the city or the fact that it was still hours before dawn.

Memories of the previous evening crept back into her head, but did so numbly. They made her feel scraped out and empty. She wondered if soldiers felt this kind of blankness when they looked out at battlefields that had been pounded into mud and stark wasteland. There was no grieving for the lush valley that had been. Its destruction was too complete.

From this dull desolation surfaced a single thought.

I have only two days left.

As the cock crowed again, it brought with it another set of recollections, from her conversation with the bird-thing. What had the creature said?

Find yourself a cockerel, and a dagger or knife . . . Go down

Meddlar's Lane under the bridge's end, turn your face to the bricks, and start walking . . .

You want to talk to the Shrike.

The Shrike had made Not-Triss. *Perhaps*, whispered a stubborn voice in Not-Triss's head, *perhaps he knows a way to stop me from falling apart. Perhaps I don't have to die in two days.*

Even if he had no such answer for her, she knew she had to talk to him. He had worked for the Architect and might know about his plans. He might know what had happened to the real Triss, and perhaps even something of Sebastian's fate. Whatever had befallen them, it sounded as if both were in desperate need of rescue.

I don't want to die. I'll fight to the last moment to stop myself from falling apart. But if all I have are two days, I'll make them count. Every last minute of them.

Not-Triss sat up, accidentally nudging Pen, who was curled up next to her.

Pen scowled bitterly and rolled into a tight ball like a sullen hedgehog.

"Go 'way" was her barely comprehensible response. "*Hate* you."

Not-Triss gazed down at her not-sister, and in spite of herself found a smile creeping onto her face. Pen was still managing belligerence even while asleep, but the frown made her look vulnerable, young, and a bit comical.

"All right." Not-Triss slipped out from the small portion of blanket she had retained and tucked it around Pen. "You stay here and sleep."

Violet's coat and motoring cap were slung over a chair, a sign that their owner had returned and gone to bed. Not-Triss tiptoed to the window, shivering at the cold, and pulled back the curtain. When she rubbed at the clouded pane with her sleeve, the latter came away with a crumbly smudge of white. The mistiness of the window was not steam, she realized to her surprise, but a thin layer of ice. Beyond the cleared pane the sky was low and gray with a yellowish tinge, the street deserted.

According to the clock it was ten past four. With every passing hour, there would be more people abroad on the streets. If she wanted to sneak through Ellchester without a risk of family friends spotting the eldest Crescent daughter, it had to be sooner rather than later. Not-Triss dug through the boxes of Violet's belongings by the wall until she found a carving knife and a cloth bag that she could borrow.

It's best to leave Pen behind, she thought, as she donned her jacket and started looking for her shoes. *She's only little, and she talks too much, and I might be going somewhere dangerous—*

There was a rustle of blankets behind her. She turned to find Pen sitting up, rubbing at her hair in a disgruntled way.

"Where are you going?"

Not-Triss hesitated. Her tongue seemed to have run out of lies.

"I'm going to steal a cockerel, then walk to the Victory Bridge," she admitted. "But I'll be back in a few hours. Go back to sleep—it's four in the morning."

"You have to let me come! You were sneaking out without me!" Pen rubbed her eyes, scowling, and Not-Triss could not tell how far her own words had penetrated. "And I'm hungry," Pen added as an afterthought.

"Then stay here," answered Not-Triss, almost keeping the snappishness out of her voice as she continued the search for her shoes. "Violet will feed you when she gets up."

"But I'm hungry *now,*" Pen declared obstinately. "Aren't you?"

Slightly to her surprise, Not-Triss realized that she *wasn't* hungry. But she had been, at one point in the night, ravenously so. She had sat up, wildly famished, and the first thing her eyes had settled upon had been . . .

Oh.

She stooped and picked up a solitary shoe buckle from the floor. It was somewhat bent, and there was a row of tiny dents that looked like the marks of pointed teeth. Pen moved over to peer at the buckle, then gawped at Not-Triss with awe and horror.

"You ate Triss's shoes!"

"It doesn't matter," Not-Triss answered firmly, putting the buckle in her pocket. "I'm faster barefoot."

Oddly, once Pen properly understood that Not-Triss proposed to steal a cockerel, this seemed to put all thoughts of sleep or breakfast completely out of her mind. It soon became clear that if Not-Triss tried to leave Pen behind, she would risk a row that would wake Violet and probably the rest of Ellchester.

"You *need* me," Pen explained. "I'm your lookout. If I see the coppers coming, I'll make a sound like an owl."

They slipped out of Violet's rooms, down the stairs, and out through the boardinghouse front door, which thankfully had a key on a wall hook. As the door closed behind them Not-Triss paused, peering at the front door's tinted windows, then rubbed at one of them experimentally.

"What is it?" whispered Pen.

"Nothing." Not-Triss bit her lip. "There's no ice on the outside of these windows. And in Violet's rooms there was—on the *inside*." Once again she recalled the single snowflake that had fallen out of a flawless sky and landed between Violet's feet.

. . . . .

The cockerel never knew what hit him. One moment he was king of a small but dusty yard, patrolling between a row of runner-bean poles and his ginger-feathered harem. The next moment something landed behind him as softly as a moth, and a perfumed bag was thrown over his head.

As she leaped back up onto the fence, Not-Triss gripped the top with her toes and was glad of her bare feet. The rooster was larger than she had expected, and its struggles hard to control. After a while, though, it stopped twisting and squawking so much and settled for a subdued, nervous fluttering and twitching.

As she dropped down to street level once more, Pen watched her with a mixture of excitement, fascination, and disapproval.

"Your toes are strange" was her only comment.

A few streets later, Not-Triss was no longer so sorry to have Pen with her. The younger girl did at least seem to know where they were, and the quickest route to get to Meddlar's Lane under the Victory Bridge. Once again, Pen's career of running away seemed to be standing them in good stead.

Meddlar's Lane was a steep cobbled zigzag of a road that climbed the hill, and at its crest passed under one end of the Victory Bridge before weaving unsteadily down the other side. It was flanked by dour buildings the color of tobacco, plain as aprons and dull-eyed as morning-after drunks. Some were homes, and celebrated the fact by stringing washing-line bunting between their upper stories. Many lay empty, however, having been bought up by the city at the same time as the land for the bridge, still "awaiting development." They were split husks, waiting for the seed of the new to germinate and make them into something better.

Arching over all stretched the Victory Bridge, which cast the highest portion of the street into shadow. Gazing up at it on the approach, Not-Triss realized for the first time how truly vast it was, many houses high, its sandstone hues still murky in the half-light.

The two girls walked into the shadow of the bridge. There was a sound of dripping, and Pen's footsteps began to echo. Not-Triss's soles made no sound at all.

Not-Triss produced the carving knife.

"Are you going to kill the cockerel?" Pen asked, her eyes round.

"No." Not-Triss sat down and managed to find a crack between two of the pavement slabs. With considerable difficulty she worked free some of the mortar and slid the blade into the crack so that it remained jutting out when she let go. It looked like a cut-price Sword in the Stone.

"Why are you doing that?" asked Pen.

"We're going somewhere, and this will help us get out again," answered Not-Triss, hoping it was true.

"What happens if it falls out of the hole?"

"Then we can't get out," Not-Triss answered, with as much patience as she could manage.

"What if somebody pulls it out?"

"Then we can't get out," Not-Triss repeated, with slightly less patience.

"This is a stupid plan," Pen told her, helpfully.

"Then go back to Violet's house and eat canned cheese!" snapped Not-Triss. "I didn't ask you to come! I didn't *want* you to come! It's going to be dangerous and . . . and if anybody's going to be hurt . . . then it's best if it's just me." She had not really planned the sentence, and when she ended it, her face burned with shame and annoyance.

Pen's face also looked like it might be flushed, but it was hard to tell in the shadow of the bridge.

"I *hate* canned cheese," she growled. "It tastes like I bit my tongue. Anyway, don't be stupid. Go on—tell me. How do we get in?"

"Are you sure you want to come?" Not-Triss felt like crying but was uncertain why.

Pen nodded.

"Then you'd better take my hand." She reached out and was a little surprised when Pen's small, cold hand was indeed placed in hers. "Walk forward, just the way I do."

Facing the wall that formed one of the great pillars of the bridge, she began to advance. As the two girls passed the embedded knife, Not-Triss thought she heard a faint musical whine, a sound as frail as a moonlit hair. *Go down Meddlar's Lane under the bridge's end,* the bird-thing had said, *turn your face to the bricks, and start walking. Then keep walking until the sound of the traffic grows faint and you can understand the gulls . . .*

Step after step. The brick wall approached, but as it did so, it seemed to lean back, so that it was not a sheer face but an impossibly steep upward slope. They took another step, and the slope was less steep, almost climbable. Another step brought them to the base of the brick wall, and now it was only a mild climb, like a hilly path.

Instinct told Not-Triss to avoid looking either left or right, and she was glad that she had Pen by the hand. She stepped out onto the brick "slope," and it tipped to become a level, horizontal surface under her feet. Ignoring the internal voices that screamed that she was walking up a sheer wall, Not-Triss strode on. She ignored them again when the brick gave way to sandstone and concrete and they screamed that she must be walking along the underside of the bridge.

The faint sounds of the early-morning city were fading. The

distant rumbles of the first trams, the rattle of handcarts—these sounds were dissolving like salt grains in water. A strong wind blew around them, and the peals of the gulls became louder.

And as they walked and walked, it seemed to Not-Triss that she heard something new in the voices of the gulls. It was not that the sound changed, rather that it was unsheathed like a blade so that its edges were bared. Or perhaps it was her ears that were unsheathed and her hearing that grew sharper.

"Child!" she could hear the gulls shouting. "One child, two child! Pink cheek childs with eyes in their heads! Soft eye childs with hearts like fruit!"

Not-Triss knew that Pen could hear them too. The smaller hand did not shake but gripped hers like a vise. Not-Triss squeezed it back as they matched each other, step for step.

Chapter 23

SHIFTS AND SHIMMERS

NOT-TRISS TOLD HERSELF THAT SHE WAS WALKing along the top of a bridge, not the underside. That was the only way to stay calm. The path before her was so broad that thirty men could have stood shoulder to shoulder across it. There were curve-topped walls to either side, and they threw the walkway into ever-deepening shadow. Beyond these side walls the sky had a dull luster like oiled lead, and against it shapes could be seen circling and skimming. They were swift as ice skates and called with their almost-gull voices.

And ahead . . .

"What's that?" whispered Pen.

About thirty yards away, the shadowy path disappeared into a large dark mound that blocked the way entirely, like a giant molehill. *Or a house martin's nest under the eaves*, thought Not-Triss as she remembered for an instant which way was up. It was so dark that she seemed to hear the hiss as it sucked light out of the air.

As they drew closer, though, the inkiness seemed to drain away. The opaque mound resolved itself into a cluster of small, dun-colored buildings, which clustered and jostled and sat on one another's shoulders, as if somebody had piled them into a cairn. The windows were squint-thin and without glass, the roofs sagged and dimpled like damp bread, and some had steps cut into them so that one could reach other huts farther up the mound. There were spires, not lofty like those on a church but wickedly slender and topped with weather vanes that moved independent of the wind.

"It's a village," Not-Triss answered, unable to keep the surprise out of her voice.

"But we're under the bridge, aren't we?" Pen scowled. "Why is there a village under Father's bridge? Does he know?"

It was a surprisingly good question.

"I don't know," Not-Triss answered. "But I wish I did."

There was motion in the house mound. It was not a single flash of activity to draw the eye but rather a universal stirring, like the subtle seething of an anthill, or the heat shimmer of a summer day. Now and then pennants flapped with idle deliberation, like horsetails slapping at a gnat's bite. The outlines of the roofs shifted, as if low, scarcely seen shapes were scurrying along them. There were faces at the windows too. Not-Triss never saw any of them directly—they were too quick for her—but their fleeting appearances left a smudge upon her eye.

"I think there are people looking at us," hissed Pen. "Who *are* they?"

Not-Triss recalled what the captive bird-thing had said about the Architect. *Of all the Besiders in these parts, he is the most powerful and dangerous.* Mr. Grace had used the same term back in the cottage, when he had talked of throwing her in the fire. *The only way to show the Besiders that we mean business.* He had believed that Not-Triss herself was a child of the Besiders, or a doll of their creation. If the Shrike *had* made her, then presumably *he* was a Besider too.

"Besiders," she said aloud, trying out the word.

"What does that mean?" demanded Pen.

Not-Triss shrugged, trying to seem calm despite the hammering of her heart. "I think we're about to find out."

The wind's tone changed and rippled, and now there was music riding on its back. Not-Triss had known at blood level that there would be, but the sound of it still surprised her. She realized now that she had been expecting old-fashioned instruments—pipes, fifes, fiddles, and tinny drums. Instead there came the cocksure, brassy warble of a saxophone, the blare of a cornet, and the squeak and trill of a clarinet being made to work for its living.

Not-Triss had heard jazz with neatly wiped shoes and jazz with gritty soles and a grin. And this too was jazz, but barefoot on the grass and blank-eyed with bliss, its musical strands irregular as wind gusts and unending as ivy vines. It was not human music; she could tell that in an instant. This was truer, purer, and more chaotic, but also . . . colder. Human jazz was a clumsy imitation of this music, but it had blood, breath, and warmth to it.

The melodies called to her, but she knew she should not answer. Her feet were full of pins, but if she let them twitch even an inch, she would start dancing and never be able to stop.

Pay no heed to any music that you hear playing, the bird-thing had told her.

"Don't listen to the music!" she whispered. "Don't dance!"

In spite of her determination, however, her pace was increasing, trying to find a match in the rhythm of the music. Pen was speeding up beside her as well, until they were pelting along at a syncopated sprint. And then, all of a sudden, they were no longer approaching the village, they were in the midst of it, and Not-Triss had the eerie feeling they had been there for some time.

A man bowed low to them, as if thanking them for a dance. Not-Triss caught only a glimpse of his face as he straightened. His long, pointed nose and chin met and merged, making a loop like a cup handle. Then he had moved away, losing himself in a crowd that was full of cheerful noise but baffled her eye when she tried to gaze upon any part of it. The throng flowed around the two girls, apparently unconcerned by their presence. Not-Triss felt her determination waver, dissolving into the shyness and uncertainty of a child lost in the adult whirl of an unknown town.

Her everyday mind tried to tell her that she was on an ordinary street, clean and gleaming with sunlight after rain. However, her sharp eyes noticed the strangeness in the puddles, the way individual drops would swell on the surface and then fly upward, obeying the call of thwarted gravity. Her everyday mind was dazzled by the brilliant displays in the shop windows and the sweet, crimson smiles of the immaculate shopgirls. However, her eyes noted the bizarreness of the wares, the gold clocks whose hands moved backward, the arrays of tiny arrowheads made of flint, silver, and glass, the cages of goats as small as mice.

None of this was wasted on Pen either.

"Look!" The younger girl surged toward the nearest shop window, nearly pulling Not-Triss off balance as she did so.

A moment before, Not-Triss could have sworn that the shop had been an ironmonger's. Now the window display held angel cakes, strawberry puffs, and glossy Bakewell puddings clustered obsequiously around vast iced creations in the shape of sleeping swans and full-skirted maidens glittering with candied fruits. Beyond them were great jars of gleaming, multicolored sweets—gobstoppers, lollipops, barley sugars, fruit bonbons, caramels, licorice allsorts, and the floury, jelly blobs of Peace Babies. There were other sweets that were unfamiliar, however—tiny silvery eggs, mint-freckled pebbles, and what looked like pale yellow strawberries with black leaves.

"*Look*," Pen said again, in tones of awe, her eyes as large and round as Ferris wheels. "Triss—do you have any money?"

"No—and we don't have time to go shopping!" Not-Triss could have kicked herself for letting the easily distracted Pen come with her. That the younger girl had absentmindedly fallen back into calling her "Triss" again did not reassure her much either.

"I'm *really* hungry," declared Pen stubbornly, resisting Not-Triss's attempts to draw her away. "I could go in and . . . you could make a distraction out here. Pretend to be ill, or—"

"No!" hissed Not-Triss, scandalized. "I'm not helping you steal sweets!" She cast a glance over her shoulder to make sure that nobody was listening. "Pen—things aren't the same here. If they catch you stealing, they won't just call your parents or the police. They'll . . ." She trailed off, sure of her instincts but not her facts. "They'll . . . *eat* you!"

"Don't be stupid," mumbled Pen, but the seeds of doubt had been sown. A moment later she flinched back from the window, eyes bright with shock. Not-Triss glanced back toward the display, and a motion caught her eye. The caramels in one of the great jars were in scuttling motion, their foil wrappers gleaming like beetle carapaces. Face reddening, Pen at last let herself be dragged away from the sweetshop.

"Where *are* we?" asked Pen. "What *is* this place? What's wrong with it?"

"I don't think any of it is real," Not-Triss whispered back. "Or maybe it's real, but isn't the way it looks. I think everything and everybody here is . . . strange and dangerous. Like the Architect. And the cinema screen that tried to eat you. And like me. We need to hurry—"

But Pen's attention had already moved on, closely followed by the rest of her. It was all that Not-Triss could do to keep up, and more than she could do to stop Pen from tugging on ropes, straining to pluck peaches from iron trees, or leaning into brine barrels and splashing the water so that she could watch the sky-blue fish within leap and shimmer.

With every new distraction that drew Pen on, Not-Triss felt a creeping and increasing sense of panic. The pins and needles of a hundred gazes prickled across her skin. She knew in her blood that she and Pen were perches in a pond full of pike, and that every thoughtless word or action from her small companion was drawing in grinning predators. Soon they would cast off all friendly disguise . . .

But we've been noticed from the start, she realized. *It's all a lie and a game. The people around us, they're only pretending to go about their business.*

The truth is, they're watching us. All of them.

What had the bird-thing said to her about staying safe in the Underbelly?

Pay no heed to any music that you hear playing. And whatever happens, remember why you are there.

"Pen, we mustn't get distracted!" she exclaimed. Pushing through the crowd, she found Pen standing before an imp-adorned fountain, staring at its crystal arcs of water with mute fascination. Not-Triss grabbed at the smaller girl's hand for the tenth time and tried to pull her away.

Pen did not move. She continued to gaze straight ahead, as if mesmerized.

"What's wrong with you?" whispered Not-Triss with rising alarm and concern. "Oh, please, please, *please*, Pen—we have to stay on the move! They're closing in—I can *feel* it!" She dragged on Pen's arm with increased urgency. Her efforts were of no avail. Pen stirred not a step, not a muscle.

Pen's hand was very cold. Not-Triss realized that the smaller girl was neither blinking nor breathing.

Not-Triss's thoughts somersaulted and fell into place. She took a deep breath and closed her eyes tightly for a few seconds. When she opened them again, her vision was clear. She was standing on the street unaccompanied, and firmly gripping the handle of an old pump. In height and bulk it was almost the same size as Pen, and was painted the same blue as her jacket.

She spun around, and was just in time to see the real Pen disappearing around the corner of the street, following a tall and stately woman in a long green coat. Not-Triss pursued at a sprint and caught up with them just as the woman was opening the front door of a honeysuckle-draped house. Warmth and the smell of a roast dinner drifted from within.

"Where are you taking her?" Not-Triss seized Pen's shoulder, bringing her to a halt at the very threshold. Pen wore a puzzled frown, as she often did when she was not completely awake.

"My little girl is tired and hungry," said the woman. She was taller than Triss's father, and yet her height did not look freakish. Her smile was sunlight on the skin. Her gray, summer-mist eyes understood everything, forgave everything. "I am just taking her home to supper, and then a nice, long sleep in a goose-feather bed."

Not-Triss could hear the gulls laughing and laughing.

Seven years' slavery, they mocked. *Seven years scrubbing her floors and grinding her flour. Seven years nursing her brats as they bite and scratch.*

"She's not your little girl," Not-Triss declared, dragging the sleepwalking Pen away from the door, "and we're not here to see *you*!"

The woman gave the kindest of smiles, and without moving or changing she became taller. Or perhaps Not-Triss was becoming smaller, frailer, fading away before the warmth of that smile like steam on a window.

"Triss?" Pen blinked, still sounding sleepy. "What's happening? Where are we?"

All around the false city sounds became muted, as if the crowd had ceased all pretense at milling and had halted in their tracks to gaze silently on the two girls. The buildings lost their cheerful, daylight appearance and once again became the strange toadstool tumble Not-Triss had first glimpsed, drab as old bones. She was gripped by a terrible fear.

A cold and stinging pain tore through her side. With a short shriek she spun around, and as she did so, a few dead leaves fluttered to her feet like brown confetti.

Looking down, she saw a tear in her dress, where it covered her flank. To her horror, she realized that through the rip she could see no skin, only dead leaves, fern fronds, and twists of paper. Something had torn right into *her*, and her stuffing was falling out.

As she clapped her free hand to her side, she felt a similar rending pain in her other flank. She turned in time to catch a couple of child-sized figures stooped to peer at her exposed insides, teasing out leaves with their long fingers. She could feel the scrape of their fingernails like glass shards in her stomach.

"Get away from me!" She backed away, helplessly shrill. But the crowd was closing in now, weary of watching and laying traps. Her gaze still would not settle on their faces, but she could see and feel their eyes—hard, childlike, and multicolored, like toy marbles. No matter which way she turned, there were always wicked fingers behind her, tugging at her wounds. One of her arms was taken up with gripping the rooster bundle, so it was impossible to defend herself properly.

A long, dry vine was tweaked from her flank and carried away by a cackling figure. The pain was shocking, but worse was the dizzy weakness that followed, the sense of having lost part of her very self.

They're all monsters. I'm going to be torn apart by monsters.

But I'm a monster too.

As cruel fingers plucked and poked at her once more, she rounded on her tormentors and hissed as loudly as she could, showing her thorn-teeth.

"Don't touch me!" Not-Triss raised her voice for the benefit of the surrounding crowd. "I bite!" She felt the tingle of her thorn-claws pushing out through her fingertips.

The throng around her receded sharply, like chaff before a breeze. The cold, hard eyes around her lost their glitter and became wary, appraising. For a moment she thought she had them at bay, but then an insistent whisper hissed its way through the crowd.

"They know how to enter!"

"They know where we are!"

"They will tell everybody! We cannot let them leave!"

The throng started to close in once more. Not-Triss knew that she had only seconds to act. She pulled the drowsy Pen behind her, turned to face the crowd . . . and yanked the cloth from the head of the rooster. Finding itself abruptly returned to the world, it bucked, flapped, and crowed.

The sound was deafening and set the very streets shuddering like a struck bell. On all sides rose an unearthly howl as Not-Triss's erstwhile foes doubled up, hands clamped to their ears, and shrieked as if in torment.

"We want to see the Shrike!" Not-Triss shouted, fighting to make herself heard over the din.

These were not human screams. This was like the sound she had heard leave her own mouth during her worst anguish, but multiplied a hundredfold.

"Get out!" bayed the mob. "Get out, or we'll tear you! We'll flay you!"

Not-Triss realized that the hostile crowd was parting, offering her a route of escape.

But Not-Triss had not come all this way just to flee. She gritted her teeth.

"We want to see the Shrike!" she shouted again.

The din became so terrible that her ears ached. The crowd surged to envelop the two girls, and Not-Triss was pinched, poked, scraped, scratched, clawed, and nipped on all sides. Around her whirled a crazy mosaic of half-seen faces. Pointed features with chestnut skin.

Puckered bat-faces with human eyes. Colorless girls with wet hair.

It took every ounce of Not-Triss's will to stop herself from breaking into a run. It took all her strength to hold on to the legs of the cockerel. But hold on she did, while the bird stretched its neck to crow, and crow, and crow.

The cockerel's feathers gleamed a brilliant bronze, and its comb was flame. It shook its plumage, scattering sunbeams. Those whom the beams touched screamed and backed away, as if singed by embers.

All around, the buildings shivered and shuddered like a coop full of frightened hens. Stray tiles and lumps of thatch shook themselves free and fell upward, leaving ragged holes in the roofs. Cracks appeared in the street, leaking gravel and loose cobbles, which also flew up and disappeared. Puddles flung themselves upward in a brown rain. Some of the smaller figures were hurled from the ground and had to clutch at house eaves to stop themselves from rising out of view.

Not-Triss could feel her own body becoming weightless, giddy. There was a perilous drop somewhere above, beckoning to her. She clenched her eyes shut.

"We want," she bellowed at the top of her lungs, "to speak to the Shrike!"

A voice cut through the uproar. It was not loud, but it made itself heard, like a cello note through the roar of a storm.

"Leave them be. I'll talk to the ladies . . . if they'll hood their bird."

The pinching and scratching stopped abruptly, and Not-Triss opened her eyes to see the crowd withdrawing from her with a reluctant hiss. With a shaking hand, she flung the cloth over the cockerel's head once more.

It took a second or two for the world to settle on its axis with a jerk and a rattle. When her head stopped spinning, Not-Triss found that she was staring down a deserted street, haunted only by flickers of movement at windows and street corners. Pen was clinging to her arm and taking tiny, rapid, terrified breaths.

Farther down the street, Not-Triss could see a workshop with an open door. Just outside it stood a short, stocky man in a bowler hat. He was in his shirtsleeves, looking for all the world as if he had just stepped out for a smoke. As she stared, he raised a hand in a casual-looking wave, then beckoned.

Warily, and with Pen gripping her arm, Not-Triss advanced toward the hatted figure.

Chapter 24

THE SHRIKE

AS NOT-TRISS DREW CLOSER, SHE SAW THAT THE workshop wore a dull gray mop of thatch, streaked with dank green. The man did not wait for them but ducked back under the low eaves and disappeared into the shop.

The idea of following this stranger into his lair was unappealing, but Not-Triss was even less keen on staying out on the street.

Pen was shivering slightly. Her face was still pale, but to Not-Triss's relief, her expression was recovering some of its usual uncertain, belligerent glare.

"That was him!" exclaimed Pen shakily. "He's the other man from the Grimmer—the Architect's friend—the one who called you out of the water!"

Not-Triss had guessed as much. Her hazy recollection of her view from beneath the Grimmer's surface had shown her the dim outlines of two men standing on the bank above her. The taller of the two had doubtless been the Architect, but beside him there had been a shorter and stouter man.

"Yes. He's the Shrike—and we're going to ask him about the Architect. He might not be our enemy. But he's probably not our friend." Not-Triss wet her lips as the doorway neared. "Pen—hold on to me tightly. Everything here is a trick and a trap. Don't eat anything. Don't dance to any music. Don't touch anything. And," she added quickly, as Pen's expression became mulish, "don't let *me* do any of those things either. We have to watch out for each other."

With one arm firmly tucked around the rooster bundle and the other gripped fiercely by Pen, Not-Triss advanced into the workshop.

Within, the light was dim, most of it pouring in through the door, with a few pallid shafts from the narrow windows. Above, Not-Triss could make out the thorny thatch past the heavy rafters. There were a dozen tables, all cluttered with tools, china hands, herbs, and feathers. On stands and sideboards were displayed dozens of dolls, nearly all of them incomplete. The majority were fashioned from a mixture of green twigs, leaves, porcelain, and wood. All of them were life-size, mostly babies, but there were occasional effigies of older children or even full-grown women, their bellies swollen to suggest pregnancy.

Not-Triss was uncomfortably aware that the nearest dolls were turning their incomplete faces toward her, regarding her with hostile eyes of glass.

The man who had greeted them sat in a small rocking chair and watched them with dark gray eyes, brighter than a soldier's buttons. Now that she saw him up close, Not-Triss realized that he was scarcely taller than she was. He had a heavy, bulldog cast to his face. The curls beneath his bowler hat were gray. His nose was particularly long, with a slight downward curve that made Not-Triss think of predatory birds.

"Mr. . . . Mr. Shrike?" asked Not-Triss. She was not sure how manners worked in this strange place.

"Just Shrike." The man grinned. For the tiniest flash of a second, Not-Triss thought she saw something that was not a man's face. A bird's beak snapping shut. A curved beak—clever, wise, but possibly cruel. Then the impression was gone, and the bowler-hatted man was smiling at her again.

He waved them to two worn-looking stools with blue velvet cushions. As they sat, he appraised them with raised eyebrows.

"Well. This *is* unexpected." The Shrike sounded interested and genuinely delighted. "Yes, I can promise you that I did *not* expect to see *you* here. And with little sister in tow! Now, that's a team I would never have predicted." He leaned toward Not-Triss with a confidential wrinkle in his brow. "You do know what young Penny did, don't you? To poor, trusting Theresa?"

"Yes," Not-Triss answered quickly, noticing the way Pen was flushing.

The Shrike nodded, seeming if anything even more pleased, and glanced across at Pen. "And you—you're happy skipping down lanes with this one, are you? She doesn't frighten you?"

"I'm not scared of anything," Pen declared icily.

"Marvelous." The Shrike looked pointedly at the claw-marks on Pen's cheek and gave a snicker of pure glee, touched with something like admiration. "Why not? What's a little maiming and treachery between friends? Oh, don't look so sour. I'm impressed. I don't remember the last time I was so impressed."

As he spoke, he flashed occasional glances at Pen, but most of the time his gaze was fixed on Not-Triss. There was curiosity in his bright eyes, and approval, but also a hint of pride.

"Wonderful," he said under his breath. "You're wonderful, if I say so myself."

"You're the one who made me, aren't you?" asked Not-Triss. It came out sounding like an accusation. The idea also made her feel vulnerable, as if she was a book and somebody had seen all her secret pages.

"Yes." The Shrike twinkled at her, pulling what looked like a silver snuffbox out of his top pocket. "And when I did, I surpassed myself, I must say. I just never realized how *far* I had surpassed myself until now." He opened the box, and to Not-Triss's surprise she saw that it did not contain snuff at all. Instead there was a small pat of butter on a wad of muslin. The Shrike licked at it with a slim black tongue and studied her with narrowed, speculative eyes. "I would love—dearly love—to know how you came to find us here. Not to mention how you knew to stick a dirk in the ground and bring that bird with you."

Not-Triss had no intention of revealing the way she had gained her information, however.

"Perhaps my leaves and twigs knew," she suggested in what she hoped was a confident tone. "You made me in this workshop, didn't you? Perhaps they remembered."

"Perhaps." The Shrike did not look particularly convinced, but he inclined his head, conceding the possibility. "But . . . the fact is, by coming here you have put us all in a bit of a pickle. A pretty little dilemma. I might go so far as to call it 'a spot.'

"Here's the hub of it. This place is secret, and for good reason. The safety of everybody here depends on it. So you really shouldn't be here. You definitely shouldn't know that *we're* here. And now that you do know, we can't let you leave. The problem being, of course, that thanks to your cockerel there, we can't actually *stop* you from leaving."

"If we did tell everybody, and the police came and arrested you, it would serve you all right!" said Pen, with venom.

The Shrike ignored her outburst and paused to lick at his

butter again. It seemed that he was waiting for something, and Not-Triss did not know what.

"So . . . what are you going to do?" she asked at last.

He gave a shrug. "That, my dear, depends on you. You must have come here for a reason. What is it you want with me?"

"I have questions," Not-Triss replied. "Questions about the Architect, about me, and about . . . other-me."

"Yes, I'm sure you do." The Shrike twinkled thoughtfully, and his black tongue scraped another smear of butter. "Dangerous questions, with dangerous answers."

"You want to make a bargain, don't you?" she said.

"It's that, or sit here staring at each other until the final trump," the Shrike responded placidly. "You want questions answered. I want to protect my people here. So we bargain. You hold your tongue, and I loosen mine. Everybody is happy."

"Triss, I don't trust him!" Pen declared. "He was working with the Architect! He'll lie to us and betray us. We should just set the cockerel on him and run away!"

The Shrike gave Pen a hard, flat flash of a smile. "You remind me of a little girl I knew years ago. One day, all of a sudden, her head fell off. It was very sad."

"But we *don't* know if we can trust you!" Not-Triss cut in quickly, before hostilities could escalate.

"That we can mend," answered the Shrike. "How shall I explain this? There is . . . a special promise that can be made. If somebody breaks such a promise, then a terrible curse descends upon them. I am willing to promise to answer all your questions truthfully, if the pair of you will promise never to reveal to another living soul anything you have learned here in the Underbelly."

"That's not fair!" Pen announced. "That's two promises for

one! If Triss and me are both promising, then you should promise *two* things!"

"She's right." Not-Triss nibbled at her lower lip. "You're asking us not to warn people in Ellchester that there's a camp of . . . of magical, dangerous things living right over their heads! You have to promise that none of the people living here will cause trouble in Ellchester. No stealing children, or hurting people, or laying traps—"

"I can't promise that." The Shrike's smile was gone, and he looked quite serious.

"Then you admit it—that's exactly what they're going to do!" Not-Triss's spirits plummeted as she imagined the hissing, half-seen Underbelly mob descending upon the streets of Ellchester.

"Some of them, yes." There was something disarming about the Shrike's bluntness. "And usually—not always, but usually—it's because a human has wronged them, intruded upon them . . . or invited them." He cocked an eyebrow and glanced pointedly at Pen. "Do you think *that* one is the first to make a deal with one of my people?"

Pen reddened furiously under his gaze, but the Shrike continued with more earnestness.

"And what promises could you make for the rest of your kind, human girl? Could you promise that nobody in Ellchester would lie, steal, kidnap, harm, or kill? No. Of course not. Because Ellchester is a town. Well, so is this. A hotchpotch of the helpful, the harmless, the mischievous, and the malicious.

"Believe me, we did not choose to be mingled so, or even to live so close to your kind. This town is a refugee camp. We are all here not because we wish to be, but because we have *nowhere else to go*. The places that were ours . . . we can no longer survive there."

"Why not?" asked Pen.

"That's a long story." The Shrike gave a wry smile, and Not-Triss thought she understood his meaning. *One I will tell you if we make our bargain.*

"And . . . if we do tell people you're here?" Not-Triss had the feeling that everything had just become much more complicated.

The Shrike stayed silent for a second or two, then closed his butter box. "We would have to leave. I . . . would survive. So would a few of the others, the clever and adaptable ones. The rest . . ." There was nothing plaintive about his small shrug. Indeed he seemed rather cold and analytical. "Most of them would not find a way to live. Some are too old, or too lost in the past, some too strange, or too stupid. One or two are . . . unpleasant things, and perhaps they would be better off dead. But they are my people, and this is their last chance to change, and find a place in this new world. I would like to see them have this chance. And if they fail to take advantage of it . . . then let them join the lizard bones in your museums."

Not-Triss glanced at Pen and saw the same splinters of indecision in the other girl's frown as she felt.

"I can see you both still bear a grudge for the welcome you received when you arrived here," remarked the Shrike. "I don't much blame you." He glanced at the rips in Not-Triss's side and tutted. Again Not-Triss had a fleeting image of a strong beak cracking something small. "The children weren't kind to you, were they?"

"Children?"

"What else could be so cruel? Wait here." He went to the door and whistled, then Not-Triss could hear him talking. "The lady's innards—bring them in. No, *all* of them. I'll know if anything is missing. Enter in your own skins—no guises, no shapes."

And into the workshop trooped a parade of figures with scowls and bowed heads, misshapen things with skinny flanks and ragged clothing. Many were dressed in coats made entirely of dull-colored feathers. One had hare's ears and a cleft between nose and mouth like that on an animal's muzzle. Some had paws, and one a long, trailing rat's tail. However, the slouch was that of children in disgrace. Each in turn trudged up to Not-Triss and placed something in her hand—leaves, twigs, twists of paper, and finally the long piece of vine she had seen tugged from her side.

They were children. Monstrous children perhaps, but Not-Triss felt that she was in no position to criticize.

"Little horrors," the Shrike said with affection, and gave the familiar phrase new meaning. "But what do you expect? Drop a wounded bird into a box full of kittens, and what you see will not be pretty. They are just doing what they do."

"Did you see them?" whispered Pen. "They looked scared, Triss. Scared of *us*."

It was true, Not-Triss realized, and she finally understood the enormity of the decision before her. Some of the people in the Underbelly were terrifying, but did she really want to destroy them all? What if the Shrike was right, and some of them were harmless, or helpless, or stupid, or just too young to realize what they were doing?

I'm a monster too. And they probably can't help it either.

She leaned over and whispered into Pen's ear.

"Pen . . . I don't want to force them all out so they die. Do you?"

There was a pause.

"No," Pen whispered back, in a grudging tone. "They're just stupid. And . . . we can always come back with more cockerels. I think *he's* the scariest one. I don't like him."

Not-Triss realized that she did like the Shrike, but then again she had liked Mr. Grace. Both had the same air of candor, the same sense that she was being allowed into their confidence.

"Shrike," she said slowly, "maybe we'll make the promise you want . . . but Pen's right. We need two promises from you. One is answering all our questions truly. The second one . . . is that you never act against either of us. In any way. Ever."

The Shrike was silent for a long time and appeared to be thinking hard. The harsh, beaked look of his face intensified.

"Clever little vixens," he said at last, rather sharply.

Not-Triss suspected that that counted as a yes.

Chapter 25

THE PACT

"THEN WE ARE AGREED?" ASKED THE SHRIKE, and received a nod from both girls. He took a deep breath and started to speak. It was a slippery, musical language that sounded like the bird-thing's attempt to speak the Architect's true name. The words were unknown to Not-Triss, but then she sensed that they were not directed at her. The Shrike was speaking to gain something else's attention, and as he spoke, the whole room developed a thickening storm-tingle, as if something enormous was turning its ancient, passionless stare upon them.

It waited for their promises. It heard them. Something indefinable in the world changed with a silent click, like a key turning in an imaginary lock. Even the Shrike paled, his face puckering for a few seconds as if he was struggling to hide his discomfort.

"So," said the Shrike, once he had recovered his color, his smile, and his sangfroid. "Ask away." There was still something a little forced in his tone.

Not-Triss had to swallow before she could speak. There were too many questions in her head, trying to crowd out all at once.

"What am I, really?" she asked. "And . . . and why was I

made? Why did the Architect take away the *real* me? And where did he take her? What's he doing?"

"And where's Sebastian?" demanded Pen. "And what are you all doing here under Father's bridge? And why is everything upside down?"

"Slow, slow!" The Shrike held up a hand to halt their flow, then dropped his voice to a confidential murmur. "I had better start at the beginning, or we will be running in circles." The Shrike looked Not-Triss up and down, and again she was struck by the mixture of pride and cold appraisal. "And while we talk, I'll stitch up those rips in your sides, if you'll let me," he added. "It goes against the grain to leave those holes gaping."

Not-Triss remembered his promise not to act against her and warily drew her stool closer to him. As she did so, the nearest dolls shifted as well. Some flinched away from her. Some reached out slender jointed hands of wood.

"Stop that!" squeaked Pen, glaring at the Shrike. "Stop making them do that!"

"I'm not." The Shrike's eyes gleamed like stars in mist, as he threaded his needle. "*She's* doing it." He nodded toward Not-Triss, to her alarm and confusion. "But we'll come to that.

"I told you before, that my people have found it harder and harder to live in the places that were once our homes—"

"Why?" Pen's question broke through his words like a bullet through a windowpane. The Shrike's gaze flickered, and Not-Triss suspected that she had just seen a veiled wince. Certainly, when he started speaking again, there was a good deal of reluctance in his voice. The point of his needle stung slightly as he set about darning her flanks.

"Maps." He cleared his throat. "Mostly maps. We . . . used to live in the wilds, the deep forests, the bleak mountains, the unused places. Because they were unknown. Mysterious. Lost. Uncharted. And . . . we need that. We can't survive anywhere that is governed by certainty, where everything is known and mapped and written about and divided into columns. Certainty poisons us, slowly."

The Shrike gave Pen a small cool glance in which there was a good deal of dislike, and Not-Triss felt certain that her question was one he had hoped not to answer.

"Or sometimes quickly," he added, and darted Not-Triss a questioning look. "I dare say you've noticed by now that there's a certain human tool that has a quarrel with us?" With his second and third fingers he mimed scissorish snipping motions. Not-Triss flinched, and the Shrike nodded. She noticed that he was trimming his sewing thread with a tiny serrated bone knife rather than scissors.

"A knife is made with a hundred tasks in mind," he continued, threading his bone needle. "Stab. Slice. Flay. Carve. But scissors are really intended for one job alone—snipping things in two. Dividing by force. Everything on one side or the other, and nothing in between. Certainty. We're in-between folk, so scissors hate us. They want to snip us through and make sense of us, and there's no sense to be made without killing us. Watch out for old pairs of scissors in particular, or scissors made in old ways."

"Yes," Not-Triss admitted reluctantly. "They do seem to hate me . . . and I think it's been getting worse."

"The more you act and think like one of us, the more they'll see you as one of us." The Shrike was feeding the stolen vine back in through her torn side, and she could feel it moving amid her vitals like a dry snake.

"Anyway," he went on, "we ran into the same sort of fix when your people started making better maps. Planes flew over and could see everything, and the railways went everywhere, and ramblers started wanting charts so they could follow the paths into the remote places. We withdrew and withdrew, until there was nowhere left *to* withdraw.

"Some tried to defend their territory from the certainty, some tore each other apart fighting over the last scraps of land . . ." The Shrike gave a dismissive wave of his hand, idly brushing away decades of bloody history. "We were losing. We were dying. And then one of us—the man you call the Architect—came to the rest of us with a plan.

"He had noticed something that the rest of us had missed, because we had been skulking farther and farther away from the villages and towns. He dared to walk right past them and into the fringes of the nearest *city*. And one Sunday he discovered something. *The church bells there no longer hurt him.*"

"Church bells?" asked Not-Triss.

The Shrike nodded. "We have always avoided them. They sicken us, make our heads ring—"

"It's because you're *evil*," Pen suggested promptly.

"It's the *certainty*," the Shrike contradicted her. "Every Sunday, people have always trooped to that cold crypt of a building to share their faith, their *certainty*—God's in His heaven, the vicar is His postman, and all's right with the world." There was a glint of mirth in his eye that was not pleasant.

"But everybody *does* still believe that!" Not-Triss exclaimed.

"Do they? Oh, they still troop in, good as gold, and listen to the vicar's sermon. But they remember that same vicar telling them that the war was *God's* war, that all pious young men should be dropping their hoes and grabbing a gun. And they wonder, *Was it? That hell-beast that ate our sons whole, was that really God's war?*"

The Shrike grinned, and Not-Triss found that she did not like him after all.

"I do not pretend to know if there *is* a God," he went on, "or whether the cold stars go on forever. The war belonged to humanity, and nobody else. But for us it was a *godsend*, that much I can tell you. The war crushed *faith*. All kinds of faith. Before the war, everybody had their rung on the ladder, and they didn't look much below or above it. But now? Low and high died side by side in Flanders Fields, and looked much the same facedown in the mud. And the heroes who came back from hell didn't fancy tugging their forelocks as they starved on the streets.

"And the women! Once, they kept to their pretty little path and didn't step on the grass. But those who worked in the farms and factories during the war have a taste for running their own lives now, haven't they? So all their menfolk are panicking. Frightened. *Uncertain*. And all of this doubt, this shaking up of the foundations, there was more of it in the cities."

"Why?" asked Not-Triss, scarcely wanting to interrupt the Shrike's flow.

"Because cities are beautiful . . . *chaos*. They're not like villages, where everybody knows each other and the ruts run deep. They mix hundreds of people and ideas like chemicals in a flask, till things go *bang*! You can get *lost* in cities. The walls rise high and swallow all the landmarks, and you're nearly always surrounded by strangers. And there are *automobiles*. Everybody knows where they are with a horse, but motorcars? Nobody knows what they're doing with them! And nobody driving them bothers with the rules! And they churn up great dust clouds so that *everything* is uncharted and impossible to predict. It's beautiful."

"So that's why you're here?" Not-Triss tried to steer the Shrike back to the main topic. "It was the Architect's idea?"

"Yes." The Shrike grinned. "He *is* an architect of sorts, you see. A brilliant one. He can whisper bricks and mortar into shapes that twist your eye and your mind if you stare at them. He can build a palace with a hundred rooms and make its outer shell no bigger than an outhouse. He realized that the best way to find uncharted places for us in a city would be to *build* the places in ways that would show up on no maps.

"But he knew that he could not do it alone. He needed an ally, a human architect—or better still a civil engineer—to pose as the creator of his designs, or they would never be accepted."

"What does he mean?" Pen was glaring at the Shrike accusingly. "He's talking about Father, isn't he?"

Not-Triss, however, could guess all too clearly what he meant, though she did not want to. She still felt the real Triss's pride in her famous father, the Three Maidens bridges, all the landmarks that had put Ellchester on the map . . .

"All those buildings, the ones that made Fath—Mr. Crescent famous." She took a deep breath. "He didn't design any of them, did he?"

"What?" Pen stared, appalled as the Shrike shook his head.

"No," confirmed the Shrike. "But he did rather well out of the deal."

"What was his side of the bargain?" Not-Triss thought of poor, misled Triss, who worshipped her father, and felt an unexpected spark of anger on her behalf. "What did Mr. Crescent have to do in return?"

"Oh, you don't understand," answered the Shrike. "That *was* his side of the bargain, building to the Architect's plans. He was very reluctant, actually. Thought the whole business very queer. It took quite an offer to bring him round."

"What was . . . ?" Not-Triss did not end the sentence, because already her mind was spiraling away from her toward the truth.

"It was just after the end of the war," the Shrike explained. "Thousands of young men still stranded out in Europe, waiting to be brought home. Their families over here combing through the bulletins, looking for news. But sometimes it was the *wrong* kind of news.

"Your parents received a letter from your brother's commanding officer. The usual kind of letter, along with your brother's personal effects. But they did not want to believe it. And then the Architect told your father that if he made a deal with him and gave him one of your brother's effects, *he would hear from his son again.*"

At last the terrible letters from Sebastian started to make sense.

"But . . . where is he?" exploded Pen. "Where's Sebastian? Why didn't he come home?"

"Because he died," answered the Shrike, calmly and mercilessly. "He is not *gone*, but he is not alive either. Sorry. He is just . . . stopped."

"Stopped?" Not-Triss's mouth was dry.

"How do we unstop him?" asked Pen.

"I have no idea. You would have to ask the Architect." The Shrike gave a smile that made it clear that he did not think she would do anything of the sort.

"Which of Sebastian's belongings did the Architect want?" asked Not-Triss.

"Something tied to his death, I believe." The Shrike shrugged. "The Architect never told me much more than that, but I would guess that it was something he needed to fulfill his half of the deal."

"That's . . ." Not-Triss thought of the tormented tone of the letters. "That was a cruel, horrible trick! He must have known they thought Sebastian would come home! And now he's trapped somewhere . . ." She thought of the way the Crescent family had ruptured and folded in on itself, like a paper hat in the rain. "Wasn't that enough? Why did the Architect kidnap Triss as well? Hadn't he done enough harm?"

The Shrike looked genuinely surprised by her outburst.

"The bargain you make is the bargain you make," he said with a shrug. "If Crescent didn't heed the wording, more fool him. He wanted to believe a lie, so he did. And maybe there were arguments when he didn't get what he expected, but he had enough sense to keep his side of the bargain and build the Architect's designs. Until a few months ago, that is."

A few more pieces slotted into place. The article in the newspaper. The mysterious conversations Not-Triss had overheard between Piers and Celeste.

"He stopped building what the Architect wanted, didn't he?" she said slowly. "He started working on that Meadowsweet suburb instead . . ."

"He *broke the bargain*." The Shrike's voice was suddenly pure venom, as if he was naming a sin far beyond the pale. Not-Triss remembered the Architect's reaction when Pen suggesting "telling" and going against the terms of her deal with him. She shuddered as she recalled his wild, childlike loss of control.

That would be breaking our bargain!

"There's nothing in this world more likely to drive the Architect insane than *that*," commented the Shrike. "And that's what he is now, where it comes to the Crescent family. Vengeance is on his mind, pure and simple. He has some plan for young Theresa—something that will see its end in a few days, if you ask me.

"Because that's where *you* come in. He needed *you* to stand in for little Theresa, just long enough for him to do whatever he plans to do. Now, usually when there's a switch of this sort, it's enough to leave an ordinary doll cloaked with a simple glamour . . . that is to say, a touch of something to fool the eye. The doll doesn't need to think. If it's a baby doll, it just squalls and asks for food, then withers over the course of a week. If it's older, it lies there as if it's in an impenetrable sleep and wastes away until it dies. But Crescent knows about the Besiders, you see, so the Architect wanted you to be more convincing. Much more convincing.

"*That* one"—he nodded toward Pen—"brought us everything we needed. Diaries to supply memories. Things dear to her sweet sister, all with a power to them. I wove them all into my masterwork. And then I pushed my craft to its limit . . . and I gave you the power to think. To remember. To believe you were Theresa. To act. To feel. And I cloaked your body of thorns, straw, and borrowings with the most powerful spell I had, to make you move and look human. That's why my dolls here started to move when you drew close. They came within range of the spell. They don't have a mind the way you do, but they can mimic having one, just while the spell touches them."

"So all my memories come from Triss's diary entries?" Not-Triss tried not to wonder what would happen if those pages fell out through her sides. "But . . . then I would just remember what was written down, wouldn't I? I remember more than that—what things looked like and how it felt to be there. I remember . . . Sebastian."

"The diaries were invested with Triss's memories," answered the Shrike. "They're a link, if you like. You only remember events written down in her diaries, but you remember them as *she* remembers them.

"There." He broke the thread and examined his handiwork. "Those seams should hold." He gave Not-Triss another shrewd glance. "And . . . I cannot help noticing that there's matter in those innards that *I* never put there. Other things belonging to dear Theresa, are they?"

Not-Triss flushed. It had not occurred to her that the objects she had swallowed might be visible to the Shrike through the holes in her side.

"So that's how you did it! That's why you're still so spry. By now, I thought you'd be flat on your sickbed, barely able to raise your head or talk. Clever girl. Won't make a difference in the end, of course, but good for you."

His manner was bright and approving, and an unacknowledged little flame went out in Not-Triss's heart. He was her maker, but he was not her father. He had the pride of a chef who revels in seeing his masterpiece but does not care what happens to the remains after the banquet. He would not help her.

"Triss?" Pen stared at her. "What does he mean, 'It won't make a difference in the end'?"

"Oh." The Shrike looked from one face to the other. "How sweet. You haven't told her, have you?"

Chapter 26

A SURPLUS GIRL

"WHAT DOES HE *MEAN*?" PEN SAID, GLARING AT Not-Triss.

"I'm afraid she's not designed to endure," the Shrike explained, with a tiny shadow of regret in his voice.

"I'm falling apart, Pen," Not-Triss said quietly. "I'm made of pieces, and I'm losing them, little by little. That's why I'm hungry all the time and keep losing weight."

"What?" For a moment Pen looked totally lost, then she turned on the Shrike. "Then . . . put more stuffing in her! Take bits from them!" She pointed around at the other dolls.

"It wouldn't work," the Shrike responded promptly. "Sticks and stones may strengthen her bones, but all that is keeping her on her feet is objects closely tied to your *real* sister. And even that will not help her in two days' time, when the enchantments all run out."

The rooster squirmed in Not-Triss's grip and gave a muffled abortive squawk. The Shrike visibly flinched and cast a glance toward one of the narrow windows.

"Dawn is coming," he muttered urgently. "The two of you must go—quickly! If you are here when the sun rises, that bird will give a full-hearted crow and . . . well . . . that will be the worst for all of us."

Remembering the way gravity had started to reassert itself during the cockerel's crowing spree, Not-Triss had some idea what he meant.

"Come on, Pen!" She managed to take the younger girl's hand again. "We've got to go."

"But . . . you don't mean you'll *die* in two days, do you?"

"Pen, please! If we don't go, we'll die *now*!"

As Not-Triss left by the door, Pen in tow, she saw the Shrike lift one hand to his brow. Perhaps it was a lazy sort of salute. Or perhaps he was adjusting his hat.

Outside on the street, some of the restlessness had returned. There was a nervous crackle and rustle, as if everything was made of brown paper and had sensed the fizzle of sparks.

The rooster made another attempt at crowing, and in a reflex of panic Not-Triss squeezed the bundle under her arm like an accordion, cutting the call short and occasioning some very annoyed clucking. Faint rays of light could be seen creeping out of the folds of the cloth, as if Not-Triss was grappling a little swaddled sun.

There was a voiceless whisper from every corner, every cobble. It rose in pitch, in volume, in ferocity and urgency.

Get out! Get out! Get out! GET OUT!

"Run!" shouted Not-Triss. She set off at a sprint with Pen beside her. The buildings parted before them, unseen hands pushed at their backs and then snatched them up and bore them on, so that their feet hardly touched the cobbles. The streets were a blur, a distorted mosaic of fleeting faces and clutching fingers . . . and then the world fell backward off its chair, there was a sickening second of weightlessness, and they were crashing into a heap onto cold paving stones in a darkened alley.

The voices were gone. The clutching hands had gone. Not-Triss was lying in Meddlar's Lane, and beside her lay Pen, who was struggling to sit up. The cockerel had taken advantage of Not-Triss's flailing fall to recover his liberty and was strutting in ruffled confusion a few yards away, head twitching. Its flopping comb and tiny perplexed eye made her want to laugh and laugh when she remembered how it had terrified everybody in the Underbelly.

Looking up, she could see only the dark, graceful arc of the bridge's underside. When she tried to move her eye along its length toward the secret upside-down village, however, something in the lines of the architecture twisted, straining and tiring her eyes so that she could not help closing them. She had heard of tricks of the light. Here the light seemed to have been thoroughly hoodwinked.

The girls tried to capture the cockerel again, but it slipped between a pair of iron railings into a trim garden a little farther down the road. Not-Triss was wary of following it, now that the sun was easing into the sky.

Looking at Pen, Not-Triss could see that the younger girl's collar was torn, and her clothing covered in dusty handprints. Not-Triss drew Pen into a park where she knew there was a fountain, to repair the worst of the damage. She expected resistance, but to her surprise Pen submitted, closing her eyes tight and turning her face upward so that Not-Triss could wipe at it with a drenched handkerchief. She ran her fingers through Pen's hair, to loosen the worst of the tangles, and the smaller girl winced but did not complain. It occurred to Not-Triss that they were playing the parts of little and big sister, and she felt a crushing sense of loss, as if somebody had shown her something immensely precious and then taken it away forever.

She's eleven years old. And what happened to Triss wasn't because of her. She was just a pawn. It was all about Sebastian.

Sebastian, trapped in an eternal winter. "Stopped" between life and death. As Not-Triss thought of this, she again remembered the single snowflake floating down to land between Violet's feet, and the ice on the inside of the windows. Snow and ice. Did Violet fit into this strange picture somehow, and if so, where?

"That's good enough." Not-Triss finished wiping Pen's face. "We should go back and talk to Violet."

As they were leaving the park, Not-Triss looked back to find that Pen was stooped, scrabbling at the grass.

"Pen, what is it? What have you got there?"

Pen ran to catch up, face set with concentration. She held up her hands toward Not-Triss and opened them. They were full of dead leaves, twigs, bits of string, a damp and trodden trading card, and a ragged piece of a paper bag.

"They were on the ground," declared Pen earnestly. "On the road behind you, when we were walking—and on the grass in the park. I think . . . I think they're probably bits of you, so I picked them up. So that we can put them back."

Not-Triss looked at the litter in Pen's small, grubby hands and felt cobweb sting at her eyes.

"Yes," she said gently. "I think you're right. I'll . . . I'll take them and put them back in later. Thank you, Pen."

Just as the two girls reached Violet's street, Not-Triss found that Pen had fallen back once more. When the younger girl caught up again, she was carrying two pairs of shoes, one in each hand.

"Pen! Where did you get those?"

"It's just borrowing!" protested Pen. "Like the cockerel!"

Not-Triss sighed, feeling that she was perhaps not setting the best example as fake big sister.

"Besides," Pen went on, "you *need* shoes. And I brought an extra pair so that you can eat them if you're hungry."

Nothing would persuade Pen to return them, or even discuss where she had found them. As Not-Triss put on a pair of the stolen shoes, she tried to console herself with the thought that Pen was probably right. In order to avoid looking like a half-wild thing, she *did* need shoes.

As they approached the door of Violet's boardinghouse, Not-Triss became aware that they were too late to sneak back in. The brass knobs of the front door were being polished by a middle-aged woman in a floral-print dress and long strings of beads. Her body was pear-shaped, and looked as if she was made of wax and had melted a little in the sun. There was nothing soft or warm about her expression of concentration or brisk gestures, though.

Not-Triss and Pen came to a halt on the street and stared, uncertain what to do next.

The woman gave them a brief, hard glance.

"We don't have trouble with flies, thank you," she declared curtly.

When the girls showed no sign of leaving and every sign of confusion, she gave them another pointed look. "Well, I assume you're here to catch flies, standing there with your mouths open. Now close them up and take yourselves off. I don't run a peep show."

"We're here to see Violet Parish," said Not-Triss, hoping that the name might gain them entrance. Presumably this was

Violet's landlady, the one she had described as "an old crab."

"We're her cousins," Pen added promptly.

The landlady narrowed her eyes and looked down her slab-like cheeks at Pen.

"I thought her family . . ."

"Yes, they threw her out!" Pen resumed enthusiastically. "But . . . our father sent us because he wants to bury the hatchet."

The landlady examined them both, and Not-Triss saw suspicion replaced by a beaky look of curiosity.

"Well, if I know Miss Parish, she won't be out of bed yet . . . but why don't you come in and wait for her? My ladies are just having their breakfast at the moment. How about a little bread and butter?"

What can we do? We can't stay out on the streets.

"That would be very kind," Not-Triss answered meekly, and they were shown into the boardinghouse again, but this time not as intruders.

Walking into the parlor was a bit like entering a large plum-colored, cloth-lined trifle. There was an elderly upright piano, perfectly polished but with no stool. Along the top of it clustered photographs of royalty in tortoiseshell frames.

The "ladies" turned out to be Mrs. Waites, who had lost her husband in the war, and Mrs. Perth, who had lost her husband "in Africa." Mrs. Waites's forward-sticking teeth made her tea slurp and her smile look hungry. Mrs. Perth was a watery-eyed old woman who sat up perfectly straight, ate her breakfast with care and dignity, and said almost nothing.

The two girls were given stools so low that the table edge came almost up to their shoulders.

As the landlady placed a plate of bread and butter in front of her, Not-Triss felt an all-too-familiar surge of ravenousness. Her right hand started to lunge for the bread of its own free will, but Pen pounced, seizing her wrist with both hands and holding it fast.

"Triss!" Pen hissed urgently. "Don't!"

"Are you called Triss, dear?" asked Mrs. Waites. "What a curious name!"

These words shocked Not-Triss out of her haze of hunger with a snap. They had only been in the house a minute and already they had dropped one of their real names.

"I didn't say 'Triss.'" Once again Pen was riding to the rescue, like a mounted knight through a minefield. "I . . . said . . . Tris . . . ta. She's called Trista."

"How beautiful!" Mrs. Waites beamed toothily. "Is that from the French?"

"Yes!" Pen declared impulsively, then paused, eyes burning with curiosity. "What does it mean in French?"

Not-Triss winced slightly, but Mrs. Waites was eager to show off her knowledge and did not seem to notice the oddness of Pen's question.

"'Triste' is French for 'sad.' Sorrowful."

"My name is Ruby," Pen announced, through a mouthful of bread. "Ruby Victoria—like the old queen."

"They're cousins of Miss Parish," the landlady explained, quietly but with emphasis, "come to try and smooth over *family differences*."

"You dear lambs!" Mrs. Waites responded promptly, and proceeded to pour tea for both "Trista" and "Ruby."

"Well, I do feel sorry for poor Miss Parish. Her fiancé was lost in the war, is that right?" There was a gleam of sympathy tinged with satisfaction as the girls nodded. "One of our surplus girls."

"What's 'surplus'?" asked Pen.

"It means 'left over,' dear. On the shelf." The landlady spoke confidingly, as if discussing a medical complaint. "So many young men died during the war, you see, that now there are a million young women who cannot find a husband."

"They should all go to the colonies," declared Mrs. Perth in a high, husky, genteel voice. "There are plenty of eligible young men out there in need of healthy wives."

"I do not think Miss Parish has *quite* the standing or means," demurred Mrs. Waites. "No, she should eat humble pie and go back to her family. It hardly seems right for a girl from a respectable home to be *working* the way she does—"

"—so many men out of work right now—" contributed the landlady.

"—breadwinners and heads of families, some of them ex-soldiers," continued Mrs. Waites smoothly. "It was all very well women pitching in during the war, keeping the country running . . . but sad to say, some of them got a taste for it."

"A taste for the money is more like it!" exclaimed the landlady. "Vaunting around in their sealskin coats!"

"Where *does* Violet work?" Not-Triss cut in.

"Where has she *not* worked!" The landlady raised her hands and gave heaven a quick and knowing glance. "She has been a waitress at Lyons café, a shopgirl at half a dozen places, a personal assistant . . . but it is always the same. She turns up late, leaves early, and is never there when they need her. She cannot keep a place for more than a month."

"And *now*"—Mrs. Waites looked the two girls over, apparently judging whether they were equal to her next revelation—"now . . . she calls herself a courier. Skimming around on that motorcycle of hers, working for any Tom, Dick, or Harry who offers her a job. And she is *extremely mysterious* about her deliveries."

"Rude, in fact," sniffed the landlady.

"Tell me, in past years, did Miss Parish ever show any signs that she might turn out a bit . . . wild?"

Before the girls could answer, however, a sleep-fuddled figure appeared at the parlor door. Violet's hair was tousled, her makeup hastily applied, and her frown deep enough to suggest that she had overheard the last few words.

"Yes," she declared, in answer to the hanging question. "I spent my entire childhood completely naked." As she glanced around the room, the sight of the two girls seated at the table seemed to jar her into alertness. She gave them an interrogative glare.

"Cousin Violet!" called out Pen with slightly manic enthusiasm. "Father sent us to talk to you, so you can eat humble pie and come back to the family!"

Violet gave a faint groan and pinched the bridge of her nose.

"Oh, he did, did he?" she muttered. "How tip-top of him. Why don't I take the pair of you out to buy an ice cream so that we can talk about it?"

The three women at the breakfast table looked disappointed as their morning's entertainment disappeared stage left to play the next act in the wings.

Violet said nothing to the two girls as they left the boardinghouse but looked tight-jawed and angry. She led them across the road into a dull, dust-windowed tea shop. It was almost empty, so it was easy to find a solitary table. When the elderly proprietor had brought them some weak tea and sad-looking biscuits, then shuffled back into the kitchen, Violet finally let out a long breath of exasperation.

"Of all the silly pranks!" She pushed back her hair in frustration. "Pen, I told you that I was taking a risk letting you stay with me without telling your parents. I could get into a lot of trouble. A *lot* of trouble, do you understand? And I told you that I expected to hear an explanation of all of *this*"—her eye fled to Not-Triss—"when I woke up. Instead, both of you disappear from my room. And then I come down and find you eating breakfast with my landlady!"

"But we didn't tell her that we were in your room last night!" protested Pen.

"We were already outside when she saw us," added Not-Triss. "She invited us in."

"So you told her that you were my cousins?" demanded Violet.

"But it doesn't matter!" Pen protested. "They believed us!"

"Of course it matters!" Violet shook her head. The bell of the tea-shop door jingled, and she flinched, glanced toward it, then continued in a lower tone. "If those nosy old crows ask questions, they'll find out I only have male cousins. And now you've been seen here, visiting me. Do you understand? If your parents think to come to my lodgings asking questions, somebody will tell them that you were here. I could get into trouble with the *police*, Pen. Now, tell me what the . . . the deuce is going on, and give me one good reason why I should not take you back to your parents *right now*."

"Actually," said a soft and earnest voice behind the two girls, "that would be the best thing you could possibly do."

Not-Triss spun around in her seat but already knew what she would see. There, not two paces away, was Mr. Grace the tailor.

Chapter 27

THE TRUE COLORS OF VIOLET

MR. GRACE WAS RIGHT THERE IN FRONT OF HER, with his gentle smile and kind, earnest eyes.

At the sight of him, Not-Triss's world turned white and terrible. Her body seemed to act of its own accord, and she watched as it leaped from the chair, scrambled around the table to be away from Mr. Grace, and dived into the corner behind Violet. Not-Triss's skin was tingling with the heat from remembered flames. She could barely recall how to breathe.

"It's him! It's him!" Pen was screaming. "He's the one! He tried to burn Triss! He told Father to throw her in the fire!" She too scampered to Violet's side, so that now all three of them were facing Mr. Grace over the table, with the wall at their backs.

"Miss Parish!" The tailor was trying to talk over Pen, in his calm and carrying tones. "Miss Parish, please listen—"

"Will everybody *shut up* for a moment!" Violet bellowed, jumping to her feet, and was rewarded by an unwilling hush.

During the pause the old woman who ran the tea shop opened the door from the kitchen and glanced around quizzically, apparently to investigate the source of the sound, then raised her eyebrows and withdrew.

"That's better," declared Violet, her voice somewhat uncertain, as if she had not quite expected to be obeyed. "Now—you seem to know my name, sir. And I am absolutely bloody sure that *I* do not know *you* from Adam. So who *are* you, and what the *hell* is going on?"

"Perhaps you should read this." Mr. Grace did not advance, remaining a pace away from the table, but pulled out a letter and carefully held it out toward Violet. With an air of reluctance and suspicion, she took it, unfolded it, and began to read.

Standing behind Violet, Not-Triss could see very little of her face, but just enough to observe that her frown was deepening. Parts of the letter were visible, however, and Not-Triss recognized the handwriting of Piers Crescent.

. . . are asked to assist the carrier of this letter, Mr. Joseph Grace, in recovering my daughters, Theresa and Penelope . . .

It was all happening again. Violet would listen to Mr. Grace now. Everybody always listened to Mr. Grace. All the adults did. Violet was louder than he was, but he was calmer, and his calmness would win out over her loudness in the end. It was all happening again.

Not-Triss had to run. Everything was an enemy. For the moment she pushed herself back into the corner, hard enough that the walls bruised her shoulders.

"Miss Parish, you have done nothing wrong." The tailor continued to talk in a steady, measured voice, maintaining eye contact with Violet. He kept his hands slightly raised and spread, as if Violet's temper was a gun. "I am sure the girls turned up on your doorstep in a state of distress. You have been looking after them and trying to calm them down so you can decide what to do next. Any reasonable and humane person would have done the same.

"You have kept them both safe, and I am sure their parents will be very grateful. But as you can see from that letter, I have been sent as a representative of Mr. and Mrs. Crescent, who are desperate to recover their daughters. Miss, I am sorry to trouble you further, but I must ask for your help—we need to take Penny and Theresa home."

"Don't listen to him, Violet!" shouted Pen.

"Pen, will you *be quiet*!" snapped Violet, then turned her attention back to the tailor. "Mr. . . . Grace, is it? This letter"—she flicked at it with a forefinger—"says that you've been sent by Pen and Triss's parents, right enough. But there are a lot of things it doesn't tell me. I still don't know who you are, or what happened to make *both* these girls run away."

Mr. Grace hesitated, pressing his lips together.

"There are certain delicate family matters that I would be uncomfortable discussing without the permission of Mr. and Mrs. Crescent," he answered carefully.

"Well, you'll damn well have to if you want to get past me!" Violet's temper seemed to be slipping its reins, all attempts to moderate her language in front of the girls forgotten. "Triss is terrified by the mere *sight* of you, and I want to know why!"

Through the numbness of her terror, Not-Triss felt the wheels of disaster catch on an unexpected stone. Mr. Grace had played a trump card, and his victory was inevitable. However, somehow the inevitable did not seem to have happened quite yet.

"Very well." Mr. Grace sighed. "So be it. The family does not want this widely known, but . . . there is a problem with young Theresa. You know she has been ill for some time?"

Violet nodded.

"Perhaps," continued the tailor, "you are also aware that sometimes a severe brain fever has . . . lasting effects. Theresa was very ill recently, and since then she has been, well, unpredictable. *Extremely* unpredictable." His tone was delicate but meaningful. "She urgently needs the proper treatment—for her own sake, and the sake of everybody around her. Unfortunately it looks as if the first course of the treatment scared and confused her, so she ran away—"

"VioletVioletViolet!" Pen was dragging at Violet's sleeve, almost on the verge of tears. "Don't believe him, Violet! You *can't* believe him! You *can't*!"

But Not-Triss knew that Violet could believe him and would. On the one side there was Mr. Grace, a respectable adult carrying the authority of the great Piers Crescent, and on the other a mad girl, whose words could no longer be trusted. There was still Pen, of course, but nobody would ever, ever listen to Pen.

With the odd lucidity of panic, Not-Triss's gaze flitted round the room. *Hot tea in the pot. I can throw that at somebody if I have to. Door to the kitchens. But there might not be a back way out. Front door . . .*

There was something hanging from the OPEN/CLOSED sign that had not been there when she entered. A small set of scissors. The tailor had blocked her retreat.

"I need you to take Penny home," the tailor was continuing. "I will look after Theresa. I know I am a stranger to you, but you *must* trust me."

"This treatment," Violet said slowly, "did it involve . . . fire?"

Mr. Grace hesitated a moment too long. "Fire?"

"Yes, fire." Violet's voice had an edge of steel. "Triss is terrified of it. I noticed that last night. And she's scared witless of *you*. Why would that be?"

Mr. Grace nodded slowly, as if surveying a chessboard and

realizing the inevitability of checkmate. His look of sadness deepened.

"Because of these," he answered, before pulling handfuls of small metal objects out of his pockets and casting them onto the table.

Some of the pairs of scissors fell open as they landed. Many were old and blackened, a few looking as if they had been hammered into shape by hand. All sent something singeing in Not-Triss's veins. They hated her. Their blades could sense her skin.

The wail that had been trapped inside her since the appearance of Mr. Grace finally escaped. Wallpaper bulged, burst, then peeled away. In a dresser by the door, crockery exploded like plates at a fairground rifle range.

Violet swore violently and spun to look at Not-Triss. The color drained from her long face.

"Look at her!" called out Mr. Grace. "Miss Parish—take a good look at her! I am sorry to have misled you before . . . but I wanted to avoid this scene, for your sake. Now, *please*, take Penny's hand and lead her away from the creature in the corner. It is *not* Theresa. I think you can see that now. Quickly! You are both in danger!"

"Triss!" hissed Pen, urgently and vainly. "Don't! Don't! You need to stop it!" The younger girl's face was a picture of dread, but Not-Triss only made sense of her words when she looked down at her own hands and saw the long thorn-claws extending from her fingertips and the fine, deep grooves they had already etched in the wall. She knew that her mouth must be a horror of thorns, her countenance wild and unchildlike.

Violet's eyes were fixed on Not-Triss's face. They were a dark, wet-weather gray, and they had a question in them.

Not-Triss managed to find her own tongue again.

"I'm sorry." Her voice was still hoarse from the scream, and fluted strangely, like a breeze in a chimney flue. "I'm not Triss. I can't *be* her. I'm something else, and I can't help it. And when they found out I wasn't their little girl, they tried to burn me. They thought it would bring their daughter back, but it won't. It will only kill me."

"It *is* pitiable," murmured Mr. Grace sadly, as if answering an unspoken thought. "Its instinct is to tug at the heart, even after the mask has slipped. Like a cuckoo trying to sing."

Violet stared at Not-Triss, apparently hypnotized. The wet weather behind her eyes was on the move, clouds shifting formation. Then her scowl deepened again, and she turned back to Mr. Grace.

"All right," she growled. "I'm convinced. She's not Theresa."

Mr. Grace's tension seemed to subside slightly into relief. "Thank you, Miss Parish—"

"Which means," continued Violet with the steely relentlessness of a torpedo, "that she isn't Mr. Crescent's daughter, and he has no rights over her. Which means you don't either. So she'll be coming with me."

Suddenly Not-Triss's lungs were full of too much air, and she did not know what to do with it all.

"Please do not do this!" exclaimed Mr. Grace. "Think of Penny! At least let me take Penny back to her parents! Remember, that letter gives me authority—"

"No, it doesn't." Violet crumpled the letter and thrust it into her pocket. "Not anymore." She leaned forward and jutted her long jaw. "So I don't think you'll be taking Pen either. Now get out of our way, or I will start screaming the place down. They know me in this tea shop . . . and they won't know you from Jack Frost. Who do you think they'll believe?"

Watching Violet and Mr. Grace stare at each other across the table, Not-Triss realized that they were about the same height. It baffled her, for Mr. Grace had quietly become a towering figure of fire in her imagination. Only now, when he no longer seemed unstoppable, could she see that he was not that tall for a man. Violet *was* tall for a woman, stubbornly lanky like a thistle.

"Violet," piped up Pen, "he keeps looking at the *clock*."

Belatedly, Not-Triss realized that Pen was right. Mr. Grace had been glancing repeatedly at something on the wall behind them.

He was clock-watching. He was waiting for something to happen. Perhaps when he had seen the three of them walk into the tea shop, he had not followed them in immediately. Perhaps he had sent off a hansom cab or message to somebody . . . maybe even Piers Crescent.

There was a frozen moment during which the truth sank in, and everyone realized that everyone else was about to do *something*. The next moment, of course, everything happened at once.

Mr. Grace leaped sideways, arm outstretched to block any attempt at escape, just as Pen threw her cup of cold tea into his face. Violet brought her knee up hard against the underside of the tabletop, tipping it onto its side and sending crockery, scissors, and everything else tumbling to the floor. The tailor leaped backward reflexively, and Violet gave the table another kick, knocking it onto its back like a turtle.

"Run!" she shouted.

There was now a path across the overturned table. Pen and Not-Triss leaped for it without more prompting. Out of the corner of her eye Not-Triss thought she saw Mr. Grace make a lunge for her, but suddenly Violet was there as well and crockery was breaking and his fingers did not reach her after all.

At the front door, fear jerked her to a halt, and she stared paralyzed at the hanging scissors. The next moment, however, Pen had flung open the door, and the scissors could only clatter at Not-Triss harmlessly from behind the glass. Both girls hurled themselves out onto the pavement and ran for Violet's motorcycle.

"Get into the sidecar!" Violet burst from the tea shop and pelted after them, her face red and her hair awry. The girls obeyed, Pen scrambling in after Not-Triss with painful haste. Violet did not bother with her goggles or hat but straddled the bike.

She brought down her heel on the kick-starter, and the world filled with the triumphant roar of the motorcycle engine. The forward surge was so sudden it yanked back Not-Triss's head, jarring her neck.

The roads were full of traffic, and Violet did not seem to care about any of it. They weaved between two carts, dared a car head-on, clipped over some tramlines, and came perilously close to the broad, downy feet of a shire horse. At the end of the road Violet ignored the furious waves of a policeman and cut across the path of a large mint-green Sunbeam that Not-Triss recognized all too well. For a fleeting second Not-Triss thought she saw Piers Crescent in the driver's seat, frozen behind glass like a photograph.

Then they were past and through the next gap, and nothing that ought to stop them did. The traffic just seemed to part for them again and again, like cows for a terrier. There was dust in Not-Triss's mouth, and her mind was spinning and singing like a gramophone record. The wheels of disaster had fallen foul of a rut. The unavoidable had been avoided.

At last Violet stopped the bike on a quiet dockland street. After the engine had faded away she did not dismount but sat for a few minutes with her face in her hands, almost as if she was praying. If it was a prayer she was muttering, however, it was one full of all the swearwords that Not-Triss had ever heard, and quite a few she had not.

"What happened to Mr. Grace?" demanded Pen, breaking the silence.

"He'll be fine," muttered Violet, without looking up.

"What did you do to him?" asked Pen in hushed tones.

"You'll work it out someday," Violet growled. "But *I'm* not going to be the one to tell you." She glanced across at the two girls, her face grimy with dust, and gave a small grimace. "Hop out, then."

They "hopped out," and Not-Triss's legs promptly gave way. Her mind was still spinning and singing, not helped by the engine fumes, and her limbs were shaking uncontrollably. When she tried to speak, she found her mouth was still full of thorn-teeth. Without meaning to, she started to sob, her eyes filling with cobweb. The world misted from view.

Suddenly there were two strong arms around her, holding her tightly, more tightly than Triss's parents had ever dared to hug Triss. Violet smelled of oil, cigarettes, and some kind of perfume. Her coat was rough against Not-Triss's face. Not-Triss could feel Pen there too, scrambling to be part of it, resting her head against Not-Triss's back.

"You're all *thorny*," whispered Pen, shifting position.

"I'll hurt you both," whispered Not-Triss. "My thorns—they'll hurt you."

"What, me?" answered Violet. "Don't be silly. I'm tough as nails. I've got a hide like a dreadnought."

Violet did not feel cold or metallic like nails or a battleship. She felt warm. Her voice was a bit shaky, but her hug was as firm as the hills on the horizon.

Chapter 28

A WINTER'S TALE

THERE WAS A DESERTED BOATHOUSE ON THE water's edge, so Violet pushed the bike inside, the girls doing their best to help by putting their shoulders to the sidecar. The roof had not been mended for a long time and was full of bright squints where the sky crept through. The concrete floor was slick with old puddles.

Against one wall were stacked some crates that were almost dry, and serviceable enough as seats. Violet dropped herself down on one, wiping at her grimy face with her handkerchief and leaving red, rubbed swipes across her cheeks.

"Don't worry, nobody comes here," she said, evidently noting Not-Triss's quivering tension. "Not during daylight, anyway. It's too damp to store anything, and no one will be coming back for these." She patted the crates with the flat of her hand. "It's just a bundle of toys sent over from Germany a few years ago, handmade, part of their reparations for causing the war. The water got into the crates, so—oh, *Pen*! *Stop* that!"

Not-Triss settled herself on a crate-seat next to Violet. Her pulse was slowing to a normal rate now, and her teeth felt like teeth when she ran her tongue across them.

Violet put an arm around the shoulders of each girl.

"Now, then," she said quietly, and waited.

Pen and Not-Triss exchanged a glance, and in fits and starts began to explain.

It was only when Not-Triss described the encounter with the bird-thing, and the contents of the mysterious letter she seized from it, that Violet looked sharply across at her.

"The letter was from *Sebastian*?" Her tone was harsh.

Not-Triss trailed off, afraid that her new ally did not believe her.

After a couple of seconds, Violet seemed to realize that she was glaring and dropped her gaze. "Are you sure?" she asked more quietly.

"Yes," answered Not-Triss timidly. "It was his handwriting. And . . . it had that day's date."

Violet stared out toward the doorway and the crooked square of bright water beyond. She spent a few seconds sucking in her cheeks, as if around a gobstopper.

"Tell me," she said. "What did it say?"

Not-Triss recounted the words as accurately as she could.

"In the snow," Violet said at last, almost inaudibly. "He's in the snow." She hesitated and then very slightly shook her head. "But he can't be," she added, with soft finality. "He's gone. There was a letter. He died."

"But we found out about that!" exploded Pen. "He's—" She stopped abruptly, and gasped in a deep lungful of air. She stared at Not-Triss, all the color draining from her face.

"Pen!" called out Not-Triss. "Remember, we're not supposed to talk about what we were told at the—"

A moment later Not-Triss knew precisely what Pen had just experienced. Just as she was about to pronounce the word

"Underbelly," she felt a sickening sense of vertigo and imminent peril. It was as if she had one foot on the very edge of a precipice, and the other stepping out over empty and lethal space. Like Pen, she broke off with a flinch and a deep gasp of shock.

They had both promised not to reveal the existence of the Underbelly, or anything they had discovered while they were there. Now, for the first time, she understood the power of that promise.

"What is it?" Violet stared at the two girls in bewilderment.

"There are things we can't tell you," Not-Triss explained. "Just now we tried . . . and we found we couldn't."

"We made a magic promise, and now it's stopping us from talking!" Pen joined in, red-faced with frustration.

"Magic promises," muttered Violet. "Doppelgängers made of leaves. And letters from . . . people who couldn't possibly have written them. If I ever have to explain all this to the police . . ." She coughed up a small, dry husk of a laugh. But she was not laughing at them.

"Violet," Not-Triss blurted out impulsively, "are you . . . magical at all?"

"No." Violet gave a short snort and rubbed at her grit-reddened eyes. "A spiritualist once told me I had a 'soul like clay' because I made fun of her. No, I'm not magical."

"Then . . . why do you make places cold if you stay in them too long?" asked Not-Triss.

For a long moment Violet looked startled and alarmed. Then she dropped her face into her hands and shook her head.

"Oh, sweet Peter," she said through gritted teeth, "I only wish I *knew*." She looked up, and in her dark gray eyes Not-Triss saw anguish, incomprehension, and a sort of relief. When Violet started talking again, her words came out in a painful rush, almost stumbling past one another, like people escaping a burning building.

"It never used to happen! Once, I could stay in a place as long as I liked without the barometer tumbling. Then, one day, the news came—the news that Sebastian . . . was gone. There was a letter from his commanding officer, and another from one of the men in his regiment. They didn't say much. All they told me . . . all they said about what happened to him was that . . . he died in the snow.

"That's when it started, I think. It was winter then, so I didn't notice at first. I stayed in my house, and the snow came down a yard deep as if it wanted to bury everything, and I didn't care. I barely noticed—my head was full of the snow, and when I opened my eyes and looked out through the window there was more snow . . . It seemed to make sense. It was the bitterest winter in Ellchester anybody could remember.

"But then the spring came, and the winter didn't leave. Or at least it didn't leave *me*. I stayed in my parents' house, but after a while I started noticing the way that there was always fresh snowfall outside our home but little or no snow on the rest of the street. Guests shivered when they came in, and put their coats back on. There was always ice on the inside of the windows. I thought there was something wrong with the house at first. But then I started visiting more, getting out . . . and I realized it was *me*. Winter was following me.

"If I stay in one place too long, it starts to get cold. And if I still don't move on, it starts to snow. Just a few flakes at first, then more, then a blizzard . . . I always give up and run for it by that point. I just . . . keep running and running. I don't want people to notice what's happening and realize I'm a freak, but that's only the half of it. I'm afraid that it's *Sebastian's* winter chasing me. I'm afraid that if I let it catch up with me, and I get lost in that blizzard, then I'll find myself *there*. In *that* place, with the wire and the booming of the guns and blood on the snow, with no way of ever getting back."

She took in a little gasp of air, and Not-Triss might have mistaken it for a sob if Violet was the sort who cried.

"What are you doing, Pen?" Violet asked, in a much more normal tone of voice. Pen had her arms as far round Violet's middle as she could manage.

"Making you warm," answered Pen, her voice muffled by coat.

"Oh, good," murmured Violet wearily. "Problem solved." She gave Pen's tangled hair a brusque but affectionate ruffle.

"Is Sebastian *haunting* you, then?" Pen looked up at Violet. "Is that why you sold all the things he left you? Was it to make his ghost go away?"

Not-Triss winced. She briefly wished that there was some way of shutting Pen up *after* she had said something and sweeping away her words before anybody could hear them.

For a moment it seemed that Violet might become angry. Then she let out a long breath and looked tired instead. She gave Pen a little squeeze.

"No," she said. "I sold them because I needed the money. They were just *things*, Pen. They weren't him. And do you know something? He wouldn't have minded. Not one little bit."

Chapter 29

TRISTA

AFTER A LONG PERIOD OF SILENCE, THERE CAME a sense that hugging had solved all it could.

"We need a plan," said Violet. She let out a long breath and stared at the floor between her feet. For a moment she looked somewhat at a loss, then she sniffed hard and straightened.

"First of all . . . we need to decide whether we stay in Ellchester or leave right now and head to London. It's a bigger city. People hunting us might not be able to find us there."

"London?" Pen's jaw dropped. "Do you mean . . . we're *really* running away?" Her face was aghast, and Not-Triss was not sure whether to laugh or cry. Clearly, "running away" in Pen's mind had never previously involved not coming back.

"I can't leave." Not-Triss bit her lip hard. "I *need* to stay. I don't know if there is any way to stop me from falling apart, but I can only find that out here. All the secrets are in Ellchester. If I leave, then I *know* I'll die. And . . . and either way, I want to do anything I can to help *other* me. And . . . Sebastian."

Violet sighed again and rubbed at her temples.

"Yes," she muttered, "I was thinking much the same. We stay, then. It won't be easy—we'll have your parents, Mr. Grace, and maybe the police looking for us. And time is against us." She gave Not-Triss a brief, cloudy frown of concern. "Whatever we do, we have to act *fast*.

"This mysterious Architect—he seems to be the key to everything. The other Triss's kidnap, Sebastian's letters, and whatever is happening to *you*, Triss. We need to discover as much as we can about him—who he knows, where he's based. Perhaps we can even get some advantage over him."

Not-Triss glanced at Pen, whose mouth had drooped into a little pout of fear. When she thought of hunting down the Architect, Not-Triss remembered the towering blurry silhouette that had loomed over her strange birth, and her insides felt watery with unease. But what other choice was there?

"Triss—you said you talked to that bird who brought that letter, didn't you?" exclaimed Pen. "If you understand birds, you should ask them where the Architect is. They fly everywhere."

"I don't think I understand *real* birds," admitted Not-Triss. "Just the scary ones with people-faces . . . and they're working for the Architect."

"Let's try another approach, then," suggested Violet. "What do we know about him?"

"He's *evil*," Pen declared helpfully. "He tricks and lies and—"

"He has a black Daimler," Not-Triss cut in.

"Distinctive." Violet nodded slowly. "I can ask around after that. Anything else? Pen, you're our best bet."

Pen did have the good grace to look uncomfortable at the circumstances that had made her their best bet.

"I always met him at the park or the cinema," she mumbled, "and I talked to him on the telephone."

"But it's not through the ordinary operator, is that right?" Violet grimaced. "A pity, or we could ask them to track the call. I can look into that cinema, though. Did he ever mention having another base? He must have somewhere. A car means a garage means a house."

"No! You don't understand! He can—" Pen was brought up short and sat gasping, pink-faced. She met Not-Triss's eye, and they exchanged a look of helpless frustration.

The Architect was a bricks-and-mortar magician. He could build palaces in broom cupboards and had already hidden a small town on the underside of a bridge. He could have dozens of bases that were marked on no map and known by no postman. Violet knew none of this, and they could not tell her.

Worse still, they could not tell her about the Underbelly, the pact between Piers Crescent and the Architect, anything the Shrike had said about Sebastian . . .

"I hate magic promises!" exploded Pen.

"There are things we know about the Architect that we can't explain to you," Not-Triss said miserably. "We *want* to, but we can't."

Violet closed her eyes and muttered something under her breath.

"Never mind," she said at last. "Just tell me what you can. I know some people in . . . interesting places. If the Architect has crooked connections, some of my friends might have heard of him. Any detail might help. Tell me what he looks like—anything that might make him stand out."

"I'm not sure he really looks the way he looks." Not-Triss remembered the ominous glints of hidden features through the Architect's glossily handsome facade. "But we can try."

Piecemeal, Pen and Not-Triss described the Architect's treacherous appearance. Pen had seen him in other fashionable outfits, but always with the same strange gray ruffled coat over the top.

"Oh! I remember something else!" Pen bounced. "He wore a watch on his wrist—I saw it peeking out from under his sleeve. I noticed it because it didn't look right with his clothes. It was a funny-looking thing. Old and scratched, with a bulging face."

Not-Triss remembered that she too had noticed a gleam beneath the Architect's sleeve. She had entirely forgotten about that brief hint of metal.

"A wristwatch," echoed Violet flatly. "Old and scratched. With a bulging face." The color had drained from her face, and an angry tension was returning to her jaw. "Are you sure about that, Pen?"

"Yes!" Pen stared at Violet. "Why? What does it mean?"

"Perhaps nothing," Violet said grimly, "but I have a hunch about that watch, and more questions I need to ask somebody." She cast an eye over both girls, then stooped to scoop up her driving goggles. "You both look half dead," she said curtly. "Get some sleep."

Not-Triss realized that she was indeed exhausted. Two nights of broken sleep and a day of running on nervous energy had left her shaky and drained.

"Are your friends racketeers?" demanded Pen. "I'm coming to meet them!"

"No, you're not!" retorted Violet. "I don't like leaving you two alone here, but if there's a hue and cry out for you, then you're better off hidden. I'll be back before dark."

When Violet had driven away, Not-Triss and Pen gathered moldy patchwork blankets from the crates and made a nest in which they snuggled down as best they could. In spite of the daylight spilling into the boathouse and wooden doors banging in the wind, Not-Triss soon slipped into sleep.

When she woke, the light seeping in through the door had honeyed into a deeper gold, and she knew that it must be late afternoon, just ebbing into evening. Not-Triss was alone in the nest. She could see Pen sitting cross-legged over by the doorway, with her back to her.

As Not-Triss sat up, her hunger woke and roared, like a dragon in her belly.

She doubled over, wrapping her arms tight around her stomach. Inside her was a hole that felt big enough to swallow the whole warehouse.

She needed to eat. She *needed* it. Nothing else mattered.

Her desperate fingers clawed her hair and found no ribbons, then raked her pockets and found them empty. With claw-tipped hands she tore off her dress buttons and crammed them into her mouth, but that only sharpened her need. She scrabbled and yanked at the dress, hearing seams pop and threads rip, but haste made her too clumsy to pull it up over her head.

Socks. She pulled them off, repelled only briefly by the mud spatters and the foot smell. The first sock went down so easily it barely touched her tongue. It tasted like the smell of wet earth and wild strawberries with the rain on them. The second followed the first.

For a little while afterward, she hugged herself and shuddered. Her claws had left hasty red scratches on her shins.

As Not-Triss tottered over, Pen looked up and peered at the blanket Not-Triss had draped around herself. "Why are you shivering?"

"I'm cold," said Not-Triss, sitting down. She *was* cold, inside and out. "Is Violet back yet?"

Pen shook her head and carried on scribbling in the exercise book in her lap. It had blots of yellow on its pages, and a green cover curling with the damp. Not-Triss assumed that it must have come from inside one of the crates.

"Maybe she's found the Architect already," Pen suggested with grim relish. "Maybe her racketeer friends are shooting him with their guns."

"She never said her friends were racketeers, Pen."

"She never said they weren't," Pen pronounced with complete confidence, "so that must mean they are."

Not-Triss wished she could share in Pen's optimism. Her own head was full of fearful images of Violet being apprehended by the police. Now, with the clarity born of a few hours' sleep, she started to understand how completely Violet had made herself a fugitive. For the first time, she wondered what would happen to Violet if Not-Triss fell into a heap of leaves and sticks and the real Triss was *not* rescued. "Triss" would last have been seen leaving with Violet—seen by Mr. Grace and Violet's landlady and her "ladies." What if the authorities decided she had done something terrible to Triss and sent Violet to prison?

"Violet . . . doesn't know what we know." Not-Triss felt guilty uttering the words, but they needed to be said. "She thinks she has to have a plan because she's the adult, and she wants to look after us. But we know more than she does, so we have to have our own plans too."

"What sort of plan?" asked Pen suspiciously.

"You still remember how to call the Architect on the telephone, don't you?"

Pen's face became stony. She scowled at the book in her lap.

"Listen," said Not-Triss. "The Architect wants to help his people by finding them secret havens. All your father wants is to get Triss back safely. Maybe . . . maybe if we can talk to the Architect, we can set up another bargain. He hands back Triss, and your father carries on building places for the Besiders to live."

"But that won't stop *you* from dying!" exclaimed Pen. "Anyway, we can't trust the Architect! He's tricky, and sly, and . . ." She trailed off, looking very young.

"Maybe we won't need to," Not-Triss said quickly. "It's just something to try if we run out of other plans. And . . . I could always call him instead of you."

"Don't be silly!" Pen rounded on her. "I'm not a baby, Trista!"

A few seconds passed before Not-Triss realized what Pen had called her.

"What?"

Pen scowled at her, clearly readying herself for an argument.

"You're Trista now," she declared. "I decided while you were asleep. I saved your life, so I decide who you are, and you're Trista."

It hardly seemed worth retorting that the life Pen had saved was unlikely to last the week. Instead Not-Triss sat in silence, hugging her knees.

Trista.

She was not sure what she thought about a name that meant "sad" in French, but it was a name, a name of her own. It did not give her a little sting of guilt and pain, the way it did each time Pen called her "Triss." And it was a good deal better than "Fake Triss."

"All right," she said quietly. "I like Trista. I can be Trista."

"Well . . . good." Pen looked grudgingly satisfied. "If . . . if you behave, maybe I'll let you keep that name."

"What are you doing?" asked the newly named Trista, trying to peer at the exercise book.

"I'm making us disguises." Pen showed her the front cover. Across it was written "Ruby Wiles" and below that "St. Rainbow

School for Girls." "That man who wants to burn you will try to catch us again. But he's not Father, so he has to *prove* we're us, so we need to prove we're not. We need things marked with our names, to show we're somebody else.

"I'm Ruby now. And look at this!" Proudly she opened the book to show scrawled squiggles and additions. "I even put some sums in this one, with red-pen crosses for the teacher. Now if I say I'm Ruby and show people this, they'll believe me. We need to get something for you too, though."

She hesitated, then from her lap she pulled a fragile-looking necklace of little wooden beads strung on a length of cotton. She spent a few minutes scribbling on the beads with her pen.

"There! Put this on." The necklace was placed in Trista's hand. In careful, clumsy letters the name T-R-I-S-T-A was spelled out across the middle six beads, one letter per bead.

"Thank you," said Trista, and felt herself warm very slightly to her sad, awkward, made-up name.

To Trista's great relief, Violet returned just as the sun was descending toward the foothills on the other side of the Ell. She took Trista's renaming in stride and launched into her own report.

"The bad news is that nobody I've spoken to seems to know of the Architect or anybody matching his description. The cinema that nearly ate Pen is closed and boarded up now, so that looks like a cold trail. Some friends of mine are looking out for his Daimler, but that's a long shot.

"There's good news as well, though. I had a look at all the evening newspapers—the *Crier*, the *Ellchester Watchman*, the *Custodian*, even the *Wetherbill Herald*—and there's nothing in them about the two of you. I dropped into the library to check the morning papers too. Nothing. I don't know whether your father's gone to the police, but he hasn't gone to the press. At least we won't have half the city looking for you. I can probably risk driving you through town, if we're careful.

"The even better news is that I've tracked down a friend who owes me a favor. We should be able to hide out at his place tonight. And . . . there's more that I want to talk to him about. Get ready—we're going out."

Violet glanced at Trista, then performed a double take. "Trista, what happened to your socks—and your legs?"

Trista was searingly aware of her dress's ravaged seams and missing buttons, and the fresh scratches on her bare shins. She dropped her gaze and hugged herself in haunted, guilty silence.

"Oh." For all the softness of that syllable, there was a world of realization in it.

"I'm sorry," whispered Trista.

"No," said Violet quietly. "It's . . . it's not your fault. I should have . . . Never mind." Trista dared to look up and found Violet regarding her with a small, grim, weary smile. "I suppose this is likely to keep happening?"

Trista shook her head miserably. "I don't have anything else that belongs to the real Triss, except my dress. The underwear's too new—"

"You can't eat underwear!" exclaimed Pen in horror.

"After the dress is gone," Trista finished quietly, "I don't know what I'm going to do."

Violet chewed her lip and frowned, as if thinking hard.

"We'll come up with something," she said at last. "But next time you start to feel hungry, let me know."

They found Violet's friend on a corner in Dressmaker's Lane, a dingy thoroughfare not far from the river. There was something middle-aged about his stoop and the aimlessness of his stride. When they drew nearer, however, Trista realized that he was not much older than Violet. He wore a dark brown flat cap and a dun-colored jacket over his shirt and gray wool waistcoat. His hair had been cut recently and badly.

Looking at him, Trista knew that something had gone wrong with him, though she could not tell what it was. He had a good sort of a face, broad-jawed with wide-spaced eyes, but something had been knocked out of kilter. His gaze went everywhere. His mouth was tense and very slightly open, as if he was waiting for the right moment to say something important.

He gave Violet a nice smile. It came and went like a flash of winter sunshine. A moment later it was quite gone, and his face looked lost without it.

"The Belle of the Ell," he said. His tone was odd. He didn't sound as if he was flirting or being gallant. It was almost as if he was introducing her to somebody else.

"Jack," she said. "It took me a while to find where they'd put you. New corner?"

"Yes." Smile. Gone. "It's the usual game. Everybody tells the police to cut down on gambling, so they *had* to 'find' the old corner. Now they'll pretend they don't know about this one for a few weeks. You're not looking for a flutter, though, are you?"

"Not my sort of gamble." Violet didn't smile at Jack; Trista noticed that. She talked more quietly than usual, however. Listening to them, Trista had a peculiar feeling. It was like watching two people walking around a room full of fragile things, avoiding them without even looking at them. "Listen, Jack. Your corner can spare you for half an hour. Come and walk by the river with us."

Jack looked toward Trista and Pen, then back at Violet.

"Sebastian's sisters," she said, in answer to the silent question.

He dropped his gaze, then he nodded slowly.

The foursome strolled by the river along a short concrete promenade, watching the sunset turn the Ell to copper. Other families were abroad in the late light, mothers pushing perambulators, and the occasional governess leading a bored string of children.

Jack said nothing. He waited. Trista started to get the feeling that he was always waiting, like a pebble beach braced for the next wave, and resigned to it.

When Violet finally spoke, her voice was unusually hesitant.

"There are letters, Jack. Letters in his handwriting. They've been arriving for a while, and they always have that day's date."

"Letters to you?" Jack gave her a glance.

"No," answered Violet. "His family."

"Tell them to call the police," Jack answered promptly. "It's a hoax. I'll wager the letters are asking for money?"

Violet sucked in her cheeks, then took the sentence at a run. "I suppose there's no chance—"

"No." Jack cut her short, with sad, quiet finality, like a coffin lid settling on its velvet rest. "No, Violet. I'm sorry. I was there." He glanced across at Trista and Pen. "Do you really want to talk about this . . . now?"

It was only at this point that Trista realized what Violet and Jack were talking about, and what his last comment had meant.

"You knew Sebastian in the war!" exclaimed Pen. "Were you his friend?"

Jack looked as though he would have done anything to escape this conversation, even if it meant jumping out of an airplane hatch without a parachute.

"Yes, Pen." Violet answered for him. "Jack was a good friend to Sebastian when they were serving as soldiers together."

"He was brave, wasn't he?" Pen demanded, trying to catch Jack's eye.

Jack did not seem able to look directly at either Trista or Pen.

"Yes," he told their shoes, and tried to smile. "Like in the stories."

"Jack was the one who wrote to me," Violet added, cutting off Pen before she could ask more questions. "With the news about Sebastian. He wrote to your father too, and sent home some of Sebastian's things—his cigarette case and service watch."

There it was again, the old bone of contention. Sebastian's possessions, the ones that he had left to Violet, and which the Crescents had refused to hand over.

"Jack." Violet's voice hardened slightly. "What did his service watch look like? Could you describe it to the girls?"

"It was a wristlet," answered Jack, and actually managed to look Pen and Trista in the face now that the conversation was on safer ground. "Worn on the wrist. You might be too young to remember, but before the war, wearing watches on your wrist was . . . well . . . only women did it. Men had pocket watches—wearing a wristlet would be like . . . wearing earrings or a bracelet.

"But during the war, the services started giving some of the officers and men wristwatches. It kept your hands free, you see. You didn't have to fumble in your pocket. The air force started using them first, then the army. But the ones we had still looked like pocket watches, only with a strap. Big, bulging things, about so wide and this thick, not like the sort you see now."

"Does that sound like the watch you saw the Architect wearing?" asked Violet.

Pen nodded, and Violet's face darkened into a scowl.

"I knew it!" she said through her teeth. "I *knew* your father was stringing me along! That high-and-mighty talk about keeping Sebastian's possessions . . . and all the time he'd given that man Sebastian's watch!"

Trista felt a building excitement. The Shrike had told them that Piers had given the Architect one of Sebastian's possessions. If Violet was right, they now knew what it was.

"Hold on!" Jack advised gently. "Maybe this Architect of yours served in Europe himself and came by the watch honestly."

"Do you want to give me odds on that, Jack?" snapped Violet. "No, this all smells to high heaven. Jack—was there anything special about Sebastian's watch, to tell it apart from others?"

"He replaced the strap," came the answer. "It wasn't black—it was blue."

"Yes, that's right!" exclaimed Pen. "Oh, and the time on it was wrong! It must have stopped, and he hadn't wound it up again."

A strange, dark flower of an idea tried to bloom in Trista's mind.

"What time did it say?" she asked.

Pen crinkled her brow as she thought.

"Teatime," she said, after a moment. "It was just after lunch, but the watch said it was half past four."

"Half past four." Jack repeated Pen's words in little more than a whisper. Then he dropped his gaze and cleared his throat. "Violet," he said quietly, "half past four . . . That was the time when . . ."

The sentence slipped into silence, like a hearse turning a corner on the street. Everybody knew where it was heading, however.

That was the time when Sebastian died.

"Was it . . . ?" Violet stopped, wet her lips and continued. "Was the watch broken then, when . . . it happened?"

The question made Trista feel sick. It changed Sebastian's death into something real and physical. It wasn't slipping away beyond a gray curtain; it was a bullet or an explosion or collapsing tunnels, something that could twist metal or shatter a clock's innards.

But Jack was shaking his head.

"No. When I sent it back, it was still working."

Trista remembered the way that the Shrike had spoken of Sebastian.

He is not gone, *but he is not alive either.*

He is just . . . stopped.

At half past four, somewhere in the bleak and distant neverland of war, Sebastian had "stopped." On the Architect's wrist, Pen had seen a watch that had also stopped, at exactly the hour of Sebastian's death. Trista did not believe this was a coincidence. She did not know how these two facts were connected, but she could sense the link between them swaying in the darkness, like a submerged mooring chain.

Chapter 30

WASTE, WITHER, WANT

AS HOPED, JACK AGREED TO LET THE THREE fugitives stay at his place, a dark-bricked terrace building in a set of "back-to-backs" within reach of the river's reek. As it turned out, "his" house also contained his mother, his three sisters, his brother-in-law, his aunt, and his older sister's flock of children. His father was absent, and this had apparently been the case for years. His sisters, aged about fourteen, sixteen, and twenty-six, were dark-eyed and angular, with broad grins and voices that bounced around the faded walls, bruising some life into them.

His mother did not seem particularly surprised to see him bringing home unannounced visitors.

"I suppose they have something in their pockets?" she asked. "Your sisters pay for their board—I told you, I won't put up strangers for free." Violet placed money into her hand, and she counted it carefully, then nodded. "The attic room. No noise after ten o'clock." She looked Violet up and down, her expression carefully veiled. "I hear you were betrothed to one of Jack's comrades?"

"Yes." Violet's expression was similarly masklike. "He didn't come home."

"He's not the only one," said Jack's mother flatly. Her gaze passed over her son smoothly and coolly, like fingers stroking the marble of a sepulchre.

The house was in the throes of washday, steam and the smell of suds emanating from the kitchen. The yard and stairs were a maze of washing lines.

The attic was reached by a ladder. It was musty and cool, its sloping walls slathered in whitewash. There were three mattresses covered in blankets and old coats.

"We can't stay too long," Violet said, once she was alone with Pen and Trista in the attic, "but we should be safe here for a day or two." She tossed Trista a much-patched dress in faded blue cotton. "I borrowed this from one of Jack's nieces—it's a family hand-me-down. If you wear it, you can keep Triss's dress in a bundle, just in case you need to eat something. But . . . try to ration it, if you can."

She sat down on one of the mattresses and let out a long breath. "I don't understand," she said, as though thinking aloud. "Why would your father give Sebastian's watch to the Architect? Where does that leave us? What do we do now?"

Trista and Pen exchanged glances.

"We have a plan," said Trista. "And . . . I'm sorry, but we can't tell you about it. We need to use a telephone."

"There's one in the Eyelash Club," replied Violet doubtfully, "and the staff there know me well enough to let me use it. Who do you want to call?"

"The Architect," answered Pen, with undue belligerence.

"What?"

Violet's brow wrinkled as she looked from one face to the other. "Is that safe? Can he . . . *do* anything to you through the telephone? Could he get his magic operator to trace where you are?"

"I don't know," Trista confessed. "It might be dangerous. But if we can talk to him, we might persuade him to give back Triss—maybe the service watch as well. And even if he won't agree to that, we might find out *something*." As she spoke, Trista could not help wondering whether the Architect might also know some way to keep her alive. She felt a little thrill of hope at the idea.

"Is there any way I can make the call, instead of either of you?" Violet was clearly still wrestling with the idea.

"No," Trista told her, with a pang of sad gratitude. "You can't even be there, or the magic promise will stop us from talking. I'm sorry, but you don't know the same secrets. It has to be us."

A little before ten o'clock at night, three fugitives drew up in front of the Eyelash Club.

The club sounded and smelled as if it might be rather grand. Soft blue-tinted light seeped through its Venetian blinds into the darkness. The music from within was the polite, tamed jazz they had heard before, or "supper jazz," as Violet contemptuously termed it. There was a handsome young doorman with gold buttons who winked at Violet when she asked to use the phone and ushered them in conspiratorially.

The telephone had its own little room, with a heavy wooden door to allow its users privacy. The walls were covered in red baize, and the little table on which the phone stood was chrome and glass.

"Don't take too long," Violet said. "I'll be outside. As soon as you've finished, run out and jump into the sidecar. If we drive away fast, then even if the Architect can trace the call, he'll only know where you've been, not where you are."

The door closed behind Violet with a firm but polite *whump*, crushing the sound from outside to a thin ribbon. Pen and Trista were alone with the telephone.

"Are you ready?" asked Trista. She could not help whispering, as if there was already a danger that the Architect might overhear.

Pen nodded.

". . . not afraid of anything . . ." she muttered under her breath, and reached for the phone. It looked so large in her hands, the fingers of her left scarcely big enough to curl around its black stem. As Pen held the conical earpiece to her ear, Trista realized that she was trembling.

"Waste, wither, want." As Pen said the words, it seemed to Trista that the black phone in her small hands bristled briefly. Trista could just make out a faint whispery sound seeping from the earpiece like smoke.

"Penelope Crescent to talk to the Architect, please!" Pen's tone was too loud, too determined, and came out sounding shrill. Only then did Trista realize quite how terrified the smaller girl was.

Pause. Pause. A faint buzz of a voice, too indistinct to make out.

"That's not fair!" exploded Pen without warning. "*You* betrayed *me*! You *tricked* me into going near the cinema screen! You wanted to trap me, just the way you trapped S—"

Trista gave Pen a nudge in the ribs, not a moment too soon.

". . . the way you trapped Triss," continued Pen without even a hiccup's worth of a pause. "But . . . I . . . wanted to talk to you. I'm sorry I said I was going to tell everybody about our bargain. I . . . didn't mean it. I want to make a new bargain now." Her eyes slid toward Trista.

"Pen!" hissed Trista in alarm. There was an all-too-familiar combination of defiance and slyness in Pen's eyes. She was sliding off script again, and Trista had no idea in which direction.

"I want you to make the *new* Triss stay alive," Pen declared, ignoring the nudges in her ribs. "And then I won't chase you with cockerels, or tell the police."

Pause. A thin trickle of distilled voice.

"What do you mean, I'm not trustworthy?" exclaimed Pen. Pause. "No, you won't, because you don't know where I am!" Pause. "Well, if you find me, you'll be sorry! I'm not afraid—I don't care what you 'do to traitors,' I . . ."

Pen trailed off. The tiny voice creeping from the earpiece went on and on. The color drained from Pen's face, taking her bravado with it. Her lower lip trembled, but she seemed to be transfixed, still gripping the telephone even as her hands shook. Her eyes became shiny, and she flinched inward, suddenly seeming even smaller.

Trista could not bear it. She pulled the phone from Pen's hands and put one arm around her, pulling the littler girl into a hug. Pen buried her face in Trista's dress, breathing in quick, frightened little huffs.

Trista was flooded with a feeling of pure, incandescent rage. And thus her mind was quite calm and unafraid when she lifted the telephone stand before her face and the earpiece to her ear.

There was quiet at the other end. A couple of clicks. A few sounds of movement, translated into an electronic rasp by the intervening machine.

"Hello?" came a response at last. "Are you still there, Miss Crescent?" The voice was unmistakable.

"No," Trista answered, "she's gone now. It's just me here."

"Ah." A soft exclamation with a hint of warmth. "My little Cuckoo."

Chapter 31

ECHOES

SOMETHING STRANGE HAD HAPPENED TO THE anger in Trista's chest. It was still there, roiling away, but now it was mixed with an odd warmth. It was the way that the Architect had called her "*my* little Cuckoo." It was the unexpectedness of being told that she belonged to somebody.

"And that backstabbing little human brat, she's gone now?" asked the voice at the other end. His tone was bright, light, and unpredictable, like the leaping of windswept washing on a sunlit line.

Trista stroked Pen's head. When the younger girl looked up, cheeks damp and face still crumpled with distress, Trista gave her a small smile.

You can go if you want, she mouthed.

Trista had wondered whether Pen's usual stubbornness would prevail. However, this time Pen, still biting both her lips in an effort not to cry, gave a little nod. She slipped out through the door, leaving Trista alone with the telephone.

"I've sent her away," Trista answered. As she did so, it occurred to her to wonder *why* she had sent Pen from the room. Had it really been to protect the younger girl? Yes, but only in part. The Architect had sounded pleased when he recognized her voice, and almost conspiratorial as he spoke of Pen. Something in her had responded to that. It was the part of her that was not, and never could have been, Theresa Crescent, the part of her that was the thorns and leaves, and that remembered the merciless laughter of ancient trees. She had felt a tingle of kinship, a sense that she could talk to this man, but in ways that Pen would not understand.

"Good!" the Architect declared briskly. "What a strident little bell she is! Someday I shall have to hunt her down and cut out her clapper. I'm surprised you haven't already."

"She doesn't trouble me anymore," Trista said carefully.

"Oh, you have her trained, then, do you?" The Architect sounded pleasantly surprised, and Trista was in no hurry to correct his misinterpretation. "I hear she has some fine new stripes on those annoyingly cherubic cheeks of hers. I thought that must be your handiwork. Yes, fear works pretty well for a while with her sort, but she'll find a way to betray you sooner or later. That one couldn't steer a straight course if you tied her behind a locomotive—and believe me, I have considered it."

There was a pause, during which Trista thought fast. Should she go ahead with the original plan to try to broker a deal between the Architect and Piers Crescent? If the Architect had just refused to make a second bargain with Pen because she had broken the first, why would he have any more faith in Piers? If Trista tried the wrong gambit, she would waste this strange, uneasy moment of rapport.

A faint, dull clicking sound came from the other end, and Trista had a mental picture of the Architect idly tapping at his teeth. She wondered if they were human-looking teeth at the moment, or whether he was wearing another visage altogether.

"So . . . you ran away," he said at last. "That wasn't part of the plan." There was an unexpectedly hard edge to his voice.

"Nobody explained the plan to *me*," Trista answered sharply. The army of grievances in her mind roared and clashed their spears. This was the man who had thrown her into existence as casually as he might have tossed an apple core into a ditch, fully expecting her to wither away. This was the man responsible for all her trials, her confusion, her dangers . . .

. . . and her life.

But I hate him, she reminded herself. *I'm just playing along.*

"No," said the Architect, sounding interested and surprised by the thought, "I suppose we didn't. Still, it seems a little ungrateful, after we'd planted you in such a well-heeled family."

"They tried," Trista said through her sharpening teeth, "to throw me in the fire."

"Oh, *did* they?" Now the Architect's interest was clearly piqued. "Well, well. *That* old remedy. Why, I do believe the Crescents must have been talking to somebody. They would never have come up with that by themselves." There was now a hint of grim concern in his voice. "Think, my dear. Do you know who it might have been? I really cannot have people running around with that sort of knowledge."

Without warning, Trista found herself trembling on the edge of a terrible temptation. Could she give the Architect the name of Mr. Grace? Could she set her enemies against each other? Remembering the fate she had nearly suffered at the tailor's hands, Trista felt her face grow hot again, but this time not from the blaze of a hearth. Setting the Architect on Mr. Grace would be no worse than anything the tailor had tried to do to her. After all, Mr. Grace knew about the Besiders, so he would be better forewarned than an innocent party. Surely it would be nothing but self-defense.

"There *was* a man with them—and he *did* tell them to throw me on the fire," Trista conceded, then bit her lip. Much as she feared Mr. Grace, she knew that he believed he was doing the right thing. Could she justify throwing him to the Architect? "If you found him . . . what would you do to him?"

"Oh, terrible things, of course!" the Architect hastened to reassure her. "Don't worry, no swift or easy death. Perhaps I shall turn him into a string for a fiddle that will be grated by a bow for a hundred years until it breaks. Perhaps I shall keep him in a cage made of his family's bones until he is so old and stooped you could use him as a croquet hoop. Or perhaps I shall have him slowly strangled by ivy. Maybe you have some better ideas."

Trista's heart was beating fast. When she remembered her own terror as the hearth was stoked to consume her, all these forms of revenge had a certain ghastly appeal.

"Could you turn him into a loaf of bread and leave him in the park for the pigeons?" she suggested, and was rewarded by a gust of laughter from the Architect. The wild leaves that made up her flesh and marrow were laughing too.

"Of course!"

"Then . . ." Trista closed her eyes and resisted the temptation. "Then . . . I'll try to remember whether anyone ever said his name. If I do, I will tell you."

"Good." The Architect did not sound completely satisfied but did not push the matter. "Well, if you were in danger of being cooked, I suppose I cannot blame you for leaving. After all, you have done your job of distracting them far better on the run than you could have in the cinder pan. But I do hope that you had the chance to cause them some heartache before you left!"

"I nearly ate them out of house and home." Trista found herself matching the Architect's tone. "My food, their food, even things that weren't food at all." Remembering the Crescents' aghast faces when they first saw her thorn-toothed aspect, she even felt a small, wicked cat's tail of satisfaction curl in her belly. "I upset everything in Sebastian's room, where nothing can ever be touched. I *frightened* them."

"Well, you will be glad to hear that their pain is only beginning," the Architect told her soothingly. "Fancy the cruelty of it, trying to cut short your seven little days of life! Well, keep ahead of them, my pet, and you may yet outlive your namesake. Will that not be a fine revenge?"

His words yanked at the fibers of Trista's heart, and she realized that her feelings toward the real Triss were a strange and twisted tangle. Contempt. Resentment. Jealousy. Pity. Empathy. Kinship.

"A *very* fine revenge!" She tried to make her voice as gay and spirited as his. "Tell me, what will you do to her? Let me know the fun you are planning! Will you turn her into an apple and put her in a pie?"

"Oh no, a better joke by far!" The Architect was almost crowing now, and again Trista was jarred by the unpredictable childishness of his character. "There are certain things that I can do better than Mr. Crescent, and he seems to have forgotten that. He always did lack imagination and the ability to think around corners. For him, up is never down, and back is never forth, and in is always smaller than out." He laughed.

"But how—" Trista tried again.

"You ask a lot of questions." The Architect's voice was suddenly viper-intense and vibrant with suspicion. Before Trista could come up with an answer, there was an explosion of laughter from the other end of the line. "Ah, if you could see Theresa's face right now! What a miserable, puling little miss she is. How she whimpers when we go on our midnight rides! And yet her parents set such stock by her—I can *see* their love, tangling all around her like a cat's cradle."

"Is she there with you?" Trista asked quickly. "Is the other me there?"

"Oh yes, listening to every word I say."

"Can I speak to her?" Again Trista channeled her resentment of the Crescent family and made her voice hard and gleeful. "I want to tell her everything I've done. I want to tell her I've been sleeping in her bed, and eating her dolls, and making her friends and family hate her. Can I? Please?"

For a long moment, there was nothing from the earpiece but a distant, papery crackle.

"Why not?" replied the Architect.

There were a few scuffling clicks, and then Trista could hear shallow sobbing breaths on the other end of the line. She felt pins and needles tingle over her skin.

"Hello?" Trista could barely give the word breath.

There was a ragged gasp.

"It's *you*, isn't it?" And Trista could hear her own voice speaking to her, just a little higher in pitch, more wobbly and more miserable. "You're . . . the thing they talk about, aren't you? The thing pretending to be me! What have you done to my parents? *What have you done to Pen?*"

For a tiny moment Trista felt a burst of panic. They were too alike. There was only room for one of them. She felt an impulse to fight back and claim the one Triss-shaped space in the world. Then, with difficulty, she swallowed down the feeling.

"Listen!" hissed Trista urgently, before her other self could say anything more. "Can the Architect hear what I'm saying?"

"I . . ." The other girl's voice was tear-drenched, uncertain. "No, I don't think so."

"Good! Now listen—please! I've tricked the Architect into letting me speak to you—he thinks I just want to torment you. You must pretend that's what I'm doing. Please, while I'm talking, you have to cry as if I'm scaring you!"

"You *are* scaring me!" wailed the girl on the other end, so loudly that static crackled in Trista's ear.

"I know—I know I'm frightening—but I didn't ask to be made. I haven't hurt Pen or your parents. The Architect doesn't know this, *but I'm not on his side.* I want to rescue you! Is he still there with you, listening to what you say? Shout 'I hate you!' for yes, and 'stop it!' for no."

"I hate you!" It was screamed with enough tearful force that Trista was not quite sure if it was the signal or just a sincere declaration.

"So he's still there." Trista racked her brains. "Do you know where you are?"

"Stop it!" was faintly sobbed. The signal for *no.*

"Do you know anything that might help us find you?"

But how could Triss answer without the Architect hearing? And how could they come up with a message system in no time flat? Desperately Trista scanned Triss's memories, trying to see whether she and Pen had ever shared a secret language or code. No, they had not. Perhaps if the sisters had ever been closer, shared more memories . . .

Memories.

"Triss, listen! We share memories. If there's something you want to tell me, then give me a clue that's linked to it in your memory—*our* memory."

For a few seconds she could hear only sobbing, and then just very faint two words.

"The frog."

The frog? Trista floundered, wondering if she had misheard.

Click, click, rattle.

"Did you have fun?" The Architect sounded as if he was trying with difficulty not to laugh. "The poor creature looks more terrified than a mouse in a trap. Good work! The sight of that silly, trembling little face has put me in *much* better humor. In fact . . . little Cuckoo, I think I might do you a favor. Do you want to live longer than seven days?"

"Yes." *Yes yes yes yes.* But it was impossible. He was teasing her. He had to be.

"I'm surprised it hasn't occurred to you already, to be honest. If you are eating Theresa's dolls, then you must have realized the key to keeping yourself intact is to eat things that are important to *her*. And you will need more and more of them, as time goes by.

"If you are to survive longer than seven days, you will have to devour something very important to her indeed, something rooted into the very core of her heart and being. But you actually have something of that description. You *know* what I mean, don't you?"

Trista gripped the earpiece and tried not to know, even as the Architect spoke again.

"Theresa's little sister. Penelope. Eat her, and the future is yours."

There was a final click, and the earpiece went dead in Trista's shaking hand.

Chapter 32

SPITTING IT OUT

TRISTA COULD NOT MEET PEN'S EYE AS SHE LEFT the telephone booth. Her insides felt like gravel, and for once she was glad that there was no time for conversation.

He told me to eat you, Pen. As they hurried out to the motorcycle, the unspoken sentence lay like a penny on Trista's tongue, cold and metallic-tasting.

When they scrambled into the sidecar together, Pen all elbows and scraping feet, Trista could not help flinching away from the other girl. It had never occurred to her to think of Pen as something she could eat. Now she realized that Pen did have the same tingling, tempting quality as Triss's possessions, but a hundred times magnified. The gaping, ragged hole at her core told her that, yes, the younger girl would fit inside it, like a ring in the velvet niche of a jewelry box.

After they got back to the attic room, Trista tried to tell Violet and Pen all she could about the conversation with the Architect. Her words sounded flat and dead to her, however. They were cold after-dinner scraps, handed to people who could never have appreciated the meal.

All the while, she was trying to decide whether to tell them what the Architect had told her to do with Pen. The trust of each had been hard-won. What would they do if she transformed herself before her eyes into a child-eating monster, a creature of the darkest fairy tale? How could they bear to be near her if they knew her life might depend on gobbling up Pen?

She was going to tell them. She was not going to tell them. She had to. Yes, but later. No, now or never . . .

And then she reached the end of her story, and the coin still lay there on her tongue, numbing it. The silence stretched, and both Violet and Pen looked up, realizing that she had finished talking. Trista's heart sank into a morass of misery and self-loathing.

"Good," said Violet. "We've learned much more than I expected. Well done, Trista." Her smile was kind, but Trista felt a sting of self-reproach at its very warmth.

"You say Triss mentioned something about a frog—do you have *any* idea what she meant by that?"

"No," answered Trista. "It must be something she remembers, something that should be part of *my* memories too. But it doesn't mean anything to me."

"It looks like it means something to Pen, though," Violet remarked.

Sure enough, Pen had withdrawn into herself once more, like a belligerent little hedgehog, and was staring down at her own knees while kicking her heels against the bedpost.

"It was just a *frog*," she said defiantly. "And it wasn't my fault! I thought it was dead! I was trying to . . ." She let her face droop into a pout again.

"Oh." A memory seeped belatedly into Trista's mind. "Oh, *that* frog." She met Violet's questioning gaze. "It . . . it really wasn't Pen's fault. It was about two years ago. The cat caught a frog and left it on our doorstep. So Pen gave it a funeral, with rose petals, and a barley-sugar tin as a coffin, and buried it in the garden. Then, um, much later she dug it up again—"

"I just wanted to see if it was a skeleton!" protested Pen. "But it wasn't. It was just really . . . dead and dry and flat. And . . . and it wasn't in the same place in the box—it must have moved—it must have still been alive when I buried it . . ."

It was all flooding back to Trista now, the memory of the frog drama. She felt a wave of horrified fascination and sympathy for the poor frog that had suffocated alone in darkness, but just as strong was the tide of exasperation and pity for guilty, miserable Pen. The feelings were not new, nor were they entirely her own.

Then this surge of emotion changed course as she understood what Triss had meant.

"He's going to bury her alive," she said. "The Architect's going to bury Triss alive."

A few seconds passed before Violet broke the stunned silence. "That's . . . *medieval.* We have to stop him."

"We probably don't have long." Trista tried to remember the Architect's exact words. "He said that I might 'outlive my namesake'—and I only have a day or so left."

"But if they bury her in the churchyard, won't everybody hear her banging to be let out of the coffin?" asked Pen.

But Trista did not think that the Architect would be burying Triss in a coffin or in the churchyard. On the telephone, he had hinted that he would arrange Triss's fate through things that he could do better than Piers Crescent. She knew where his talents lay, had seen his space-twisting masterpieces of bricks-and-mortar magic. He was quite capable of building a fatal prison for Triss that Piers would never find in a million years, let alone in one day. With the Architect's strange gifts, he could hide a dozen such prisons within a space no thicker than a coin. If he *was* building such a prison for her, it could be anywhere in Ellchester.

Trista opened her mouth to say so, and once again choked on the "magic promise."

"Once he buries her, we'll never find her," she said instead. "But . . . he said something about taking Triss for 'midnight rides.' Maybe if we see them on the move, we can follow them—even rescue her."

There was a doubtful pause. It sounded like a forlorn hope even to Trista. However, they were short on more robust hopes, so after a moment Violet nodded slowly.

"There won't be many cars on the roads at midnight. If we can get to high enough ground, we might be able to spot the Daimler's headlights or hear its engine. It's a long shot, but it's worth a try. And thanks to your father, there's some *very* high ground. Come midnight we'll be on the Victory Bridge."

Needless to say, Pen was sullenly insistent that she was coming on the midnight mission. Pen was *not* tired. Pen was *not* going to bed. Pen was . . . asleep. So impenetrably asleep, in fact, that she was tucked into one of the attic beds without waking, to the relief of Trista and Violet.

Even when she was back in the sidecar again, Trista kept seeing in her mind's eye Pen's small, curled form under the thin blanket. There was a tempest in her stomach made up of guilt, anguish, conflict, shame, and dread. She hoped that there was no hunger in the mix as well.

The night streets were still warm, and Trista could not stop herself from twisting her head to peer at the lit windows of public houses, from which poured piano music and occasional gaggles of figures. Other worlds that she had never seen, by virtue of her age and the "niceness" of her family.

When the motorcycle rose up above the city on the vast, curved back of the Victory Bridge, the winds grew fiercer and more irregular. Remembering the Underbelly beneath them made Trista feel giddy, and she wondered whether this was really a wise vantage point.

At the crest, Violet let the engine idle, then stop. There was nobody else on the bridge, nobody to observe as Trista and Violet dismounted, walked to the barrier, and peered down at the nocturnal city.

It was not like looking at a map. The hills made Ellchester appear crumpled, lights nestling in dark folds like glowworms in the crags of a tree stump. The river was ink, jeweled by the tiny hurricane lamps of occasional boats. A few squares and streets flared with electric light, the whiteness like an ache. The dark outline of the new rail station cut a triangle out of the sky.

The wind blew Trista's hair around her face, and she caught at it to push it back. The stray tress turned to dry leaves in her hand. So little time left . . .

. . . so was that why she had not told anybody about the Architect's last words to her? Was she keeping her options open after all? Had she always been keeping Pen around for that reason, like a packed lunch?

What was she?

"Violet." It came out as a husky whimper.

"We've got a minute or two, I think." Violet had her goggles raised to her forehead and was scanning the scene. "Drat! I thought we'd be able to see more."

"Violet!" Trista's exclamation was a muffled yelp, and when

Violet turned to look at her in surprise, the rest came out in a tearful, choked gabble. "TheArchitecttoldmetoeatPen!"

"Do you want to try that again, but with words?" Violet suggested.

"The Architect—he said I could live longer than seven days. But . . . he told me I had to eat Pen."

Violet stared at her for a second, then gave a hearty snort of mirth.

"He really doesn't know you very well, does he?"

"But . . . b-but I *could* eat Pen," stammered Trista. "I know that now. I can feel it."

"You're not going to, though, are you?" answered Violet without hesitation.

"How do you know?" demanded Trista. In spite of herself, she found her horror receding a little in the face of Violet's tone of calm certainty. "*I* don't know. How can *you* know? I . . . I'm a monster. When I'm hungry, I might do *anything*."

"Oh no, of course I couldn't *possibly* understand you." Violet's shadowed face seemed to be wearing a grim and serious smile. "I know, you woke up one day and found out that you couldn't be the person you remembered being, the little girl everybody expected you to be. You just weren't her anymore, and there was nothing you could do about it. So your family decided you were a monster and turned on you." Violet sighed, staring out into the darkness. "Believe me, I *do* understand that. And let me tell you—from one monster to another—that just because somebody tells you you're a monster, it doesn't mean you are.

"Just now you told me what you did because you want me to stop you from eating Pen. If you were a real monster, you wouldn't have done that, would you?"

Trista's eyes stung, and she wiped strands of cobweb away with her sleeve.

"Idiot," added Violet, for good measure.

"Violet," Trista began again when she thought she could keep her voice steady, "can I ask you something?"

"Ye-e-es," came the answer, "but not right now. There's something strange happening down there—a sort of flickering. There! Can you see it?"

From the city below her, Trista could make out the sounds of church clocks chiming midnight, each voice lonely and cold.

She hurriedly cleared the remaining gossamer from her eyes and stared down into the city, following Violet's pointing finger. Down in the poorly lit docklands by the riverside, she thought she made out a moving glint, or perhaps a host of tiny glints, fizzing and zigzagging across a square like champagne bubbles.

Both Violet and Trista jumped when a wild surge of winged shapes burst from beneath the bridge on which they stood and flocked out toward the city, wheeling downward with cries like steel shavings.

"Gulls," gasped Violet in a half laugh. Trista said nothing, her tongue held by the magic promise. She saw white wings as Violet did, but she also saw wings of pale leather, glassy insect wings, wings made of paper and matted hair. Some of the things had riders. Some had two heads. None of them looked up or saw her. She was able to watch as the strange flock sped down to join the strange flicker on the streets.

The flicker itself was moving over a distant hill now, threatening to disappear behind the crest.

"We're going to lose sight of them!" exclaimed Trista.

"No, we're not," said Violet. "Get back in the sidecar. They're not the only ones who can move fast."

Chapter 33

THE TRAM

TRISTA GRITTED HER TEETH AS THE MOTORCYCLE weaved sharply through the streets, bracing her limbs inside the sidecar. Violet was leaning forward over her machine like a cat preparing to pounce. Trista could feel in her joints every bounce of the tires, each road crack.

Gas lamps whooshed past on either side like will-o'-the-wisps on a mission. Bridges swooped overhead, shadowing the sky for a second, then were gone. The motorcycle's headlights flashed in the sullen windows of closed shops. Buildings scrolled past at speed, like the visions of a zoetrope.

Trista tipped her head back as far as she dared and watched the sky, looking for a flicker of movement or a darker patch against the void of the heavens. The air caught in her throat. There was a smell that made her hungry again and filled her with an odd, shadowy elation. It was a crisp, treacherous twilight scent that reminded her of the Underbelly, the Architect, and the fight with the bird-thing. The Besiders were close by, and it set her blood alight.

The alleys twisting up the hill were cluttered with rubbish pails, zigzags of washing, and bicycles against the walls. The motorcycle swerved between them all, triumphantly erupted with a roar into a square at the top of the hill, and descended into the winding lanes beyond.

As they roared over a narrow bridge, Trista glanced down at the street below it, which was bathed in dull yellow gaslight. Cruising past beneath her was a large black Daimler. The light seemed to slide uneasily over it like water over wax. Its engine made no sound. As she watched, it turned a corner and vanished from sight.

"There!" Trista's desperate squawk was inaudible, but also unnecessary. Violet had seen the car. At the far end of the bridge, Violet took a right to follow.

There was a rustling sound at the back of Trista's mind, and for a little while she thought it might be coming from her own head. But this time it was not the laughter of her inner leaves. There were wings beating overhead and whispers on the breeze. Looking upward, she saw rapid shapes skim past at eaves' height. Some spread dark wings. Some had insectile legs akimbo, like water boatmen. Some clawed their way through the air, as if it was solid as earth.

Some skimmed away on spread wings and were lost from sight almost immediately. Others alighted briefly on this roof or that, then sprang away with the lightness and power of a flea.

Violet took a left, a right, a left through the shadowed streets. Scattered pubs cast halos of light from their bright windows.

Just as they were nearing a crossroads, there came the sudden *ting-ting-ting* of a bell. The sound was familiar but so spectral in the circumstances that Trista could not place it. Violet braked sharply.

The road ahead was briefly illuminated by headlights, and then a bulky oblong burst into view from left to right across their path. It was a familiar double-decker outline, its inner recesses brilliant with electric light. Only then did Trista recognize the noise as that of a tram bell.

The tram flashed past, followed by two large trailer cars, both double-decker like the tram but with their upper seating open to the sky. Instead of the usual red, the tram and trailer cars were jet black.

As each passed, Trista caught a glimpse into its brightly lit lower saloon, a gleaming yellow tableau that passed in an instant.

In the tram itself, a collection of long-nosed men in gray coats and dark glasses stared out through the windows with binoculars.

In the saloon of the first trailer car stood a coterie of women with red, red mouths and fox furs round their necks that might almost have been alive and sleeping.

In the saloon of the second trailer car sat the Architect in his smart sportswear with a green cravat, and beside him the hunched, miserable shape of Triss, in a white hat and coat.

There was no way to shout over the sound of the motorcycle engine. Instead Trista pointed madly after the disappearing tram. Violet forced the engine into a roar once more, surged forward, and then swung right to follow. Trista felt the tires bounce over the tram rails.

At the far end of the road Violet once again had to screech to a halt, this time bringing the motorcycle around into a sideways skid. The gleaming tracks had come to an abrupt end, as had the road. Beyond a wooden barrier lay a dark pit, piles of sand, spades, and the gaping mouth of a concrete mixer.

Violet stared all around, her expression hidden by her goggles, then cut the engine. Her breath was ragged and unguarded.

"It's the tram route they are still building." Her voice had a hard force to it, and Trista knew that she was battling with bewilderment and frustration.

The tram had simply run off the end of the unfinished rails and vanished.

"No!" Trista heard her own voice sounding raspy and hollow. They had been so close. She had *seen* the Architect and Triss. They had been within fifteen yards of one another, divided only by metal, glass, and momentum.

Trista scrambled out of the sidecar, legs shaking. She ran down the darkened road, ducked past the barrier, and scrambled over a sand heap, which gave softly under her tread. Then she was sprinting down the dark road beyond.

"Trista!" called Violet, then swore. Now two sets of footsteps were echoing down the road, but Trista did not stop until she was brought up short by a row of houses with innocently dark alleys to left and right. From straight ahead, the wind again carried to her the whisper of wings and a faint echoing noise like the sound of hoofs.

She stared up at the house before her. The roof looked low—she could catch at it, she was sure she could. She kicked off her shoes, bent her knees, and sprang. The motion felt as easy and natural as breath, or batting away a fly. As she rose, she instinctively raised her hands and caught at the edge of the guttering. Then she kicked out against the wall, yanked herself upward using her arms . . . and landed silently on the very edge of the roof.

Her bare feet made no sound. Her long toes somehow found a grip on the cold sloping slates. A few springing steps took her to the roof's raised spine, where she crouched so that nothing would see her outline against the sky. Trista could still hear Violet somewhere below calling out her name, but the voice seemed small and inconsequential now.

This was yet another Ellchester, a town of silvery-gray inclines, sudden precipices, and a chimney forest spewing scented plumes of smoke. She had no time to boggle at its beauty, however.

A hundred yards away, she could make out a convoy of shapes surging over the roofs. Three black carriages, each drawn by two night-black horses, were riding up and down the slopes of roofs as easily as if they were on the ground. The wheels did not disturb the tiles, nor did the horses' hoofs slither. Above and around them surged and flew and leaped a host of smaller forms that seemed to change shape as they passed in and out of the stray shafts of light.

In that moment, Trista's fear of losing her quarry pushed out all others. She scrambled down the roof, and at the edge felt her knees tingle with the sense of the hungry drop before her. Thankfully it was only a small jump to the next house, and she leaped it with only a slight spasm of vertigo. Over the ridge of the roof, down the other side . . .

. . . just in time to see the three black carriages drop off the lip of a roof and vanish into the maze of streets, like frogs disappearing off the edge of a lily pad. The swarm swooped down with them and was lost to view.

With new urgency, Trista sprinted and leaped, sprinted and leaped, zigzagging her way through the roof maze. She reached the place where she had last seen the carriages and stared around her, shivering.

Somewhere she thought she heard the *ting-ting-ting* of a tram and the beating of wings, but the breezes were fighting and she could not tell where the sound came from. The ride was continuing—but where?

Trista stared around her for a little while, her eye baffled by chimney-smoke mirages and the rapid passing of bats, before the unbearable truth sank in. She had lost track of the riders.

She hobbled to the edge of the roof, peered over, and felt her stomach flinch inward like a sea anemone. Caught up in the frenzy of the chase, she had not felt that she was so very high, nor had the distances between the roofs seemed so very great. Now, as she returned to her usual perspective, she almost seemed to see the street dropping away to a perilous depth below her, and the gaps she had so confidently leaped widening like opening mouths.

She was a good two stories above the ground, and her leaps from one roof to another had carried her the breadth of streets.

There was something flapping against her side. Staring down, she saw a loose ribbon trailing out of a tear in her flank. As she watched, the wind whipped it free and carried it away. Instinctively turning to follow it with her eye, Trista realized that she could see other oddments scattered over the roofs she had crossed. Wind-chased scraps of paper, twigs tumbling over the tiles, hazy tangles of pale hair.

No.

Filled with a new desperation, Trista scrambled after the fleeing fragments. The ribbon had wrapped itself around a chimney pot, where it trembled temptingly but flung itself free just as Trista's reaching hand was within inches of it. The other pale pieces bounded away with the jollity of the wind and were swallowed by the night.

Shaking, Trista sank into a crouch on the roof's edge, hugging her knees. It was a few minutes before she became aware of Violet's voice still calling and calling her name.

Chapter 34

A GAPING HOLE

TRISTA'S JAW SEEMED TO HAVE LOCKED SOLID, and minutes passed before she was able to call back. There was a pattering of steps down on the street, and then the tiny figure of Violet emerged in the road below her.

"Trista?"

Trista managed only a faint squeak in response. The street now looked terrifyingly far down, and the drop dragged at her stomach. She closed her eyes, hugged her knees, and couldn't move. The air was cold.

She was dimly aware of noises below, a rapping on wood, voices, creaks and bangs. Then something clacked loudly against the guttering near her feet. She opened her eyes, and her gaze settled upon the top prongs of a wooden ladder, shifting uneasily against the roof's edge. After a sequence of creaks, Violet's head and shoulders rose into view.

"Come on" was all she said, very quietly. Trista edged over and shakily followed Violet down the ladder. At the bottom, a stout man in a dressing gown viewed Trista with outrage.

"You said it was your *cat* that was stuck on my roof!" he exclaimed, glaring at Violet.

"Thanks for the use of the ladder," Violet answered him blandly.

"Here, wait! What was she doing—"

Violet turned on him.

"My daughter sleepwalks," she declared icily, "and I didn't want to spend an hour explaining that to you. What do you want me to do—put her back on the roof?" Before the enraged man could reply, Violet took Trista by the hand and led her back to the alley where the motorcycle was waiting.

Thank you. Trista mouthed the words but could not give them voice. *Thank you for coming to rescue me.* More than anything else, it was the way Violet had called Trista her daughter that set Trista's eyes prickling. It made her feel that she had something small, fragile, and warm to hold on to, something to put in the hole left by the fragments that the wind had chased across the roofs.

They rode back in silence. When they had slipped into the attic of Jack's house, they sat down on one of the mattresses and Trista told of the chase, in whispers to avoid waking Pen. Violet hugged her all the while.

"It's not over," Violet murmured at last. "We'll find them tomorrow. But now you need to sleep. You're pale as paper."

"But I'm afraid to sleep!" whispered Trista. "What if I fall to pieces before I wake up? What if tomorrow morning I'm just a pile of leaves and sticks tucked under a blanket? What if this is the last time I've got left, and I waste it all being asleep, then wake up dead?"

For a moment, Violet looked conflicted. Then her jaw set, and she took Trista by the shoulders.

"You won't," she said gently but firmly. "I'll make sure you don't. I'll be watching you sleep. And if your hair starts to turn into leaves, or anything like that, I'll wake you up."

"You promise?" Trista felt the icy, titanic force of her terror recede a step or two. "You . . . you won't leave me when I'm asleep and go out?"

"I promise," said Violet, with a firmness in her tone that allowed no doubt. Her dark gray eyes were resolute as flint.

The long path down to the Grimmer had changed. Now it was knobbly with the roots of twisted trees. Rotting apples puckered on the grass like ancient, wizened faces. There were words to the birdsong, and the leaves were softly laughing. Under Trista's bare feet she could feel a flutter in the turf like a pulse. Ahead through the trees she could make out the sleek, obsidian surface of the water. An inky threat, a coal-black promise.

You have nothing of your own, *said the Grimmer.* Everything you have is borrowed, and when it is paid back there will be nothing left. Even your time is borrowed, and it is running out. One day. One left . . .

The wind rose and became bitingly chill. Trista could feel it starting to tear her apart like a dandelion clock . . .

. . . and then she woke, shivering with the cold.

She was in one of the attic beds, tucked under a blanket. Nearby, Violet reclined in a chair, her face set in a frown, her head moving in the discontented manner of one who is nodding in and out of slumber. Beyond her, in another bed, Pen was still fast asleep. White morning light was creeping in through the skylight.

Morning. My last morning. Only one more day . . .

The thought stared back at her, bald, cold, and inescapable as the sky.

Trista's breath was steam. She sat up, chafing feeling back into her hands.

Violet started fully awake, glaring around her for a baffled instant with glass-eyed antagonism.

"Oh." She recovered herself and let out her breath. "Still with us, then?" She came over and studied Trista with a speculative scowl, then drew her fingers through Trista's hair, causing a faint, crackling rustle.

Violet stared down at the dead leaves in her hand, biting her lower lip hard.

"It could be worse," she muttered under her breath.

"It *is* worse," Trista said softly. She did not need to say anything more.

"We still have a day," Violet answered doggedly.

"What time is it?" asked Trista.

Violet strode to the skylight, peered out, and gave vent to a not-in-front-of-children word. Tiptoeing to her side over the chilly floor, Trista could see at a glance why Violet had sworn.

The window was covered in a delicate lacework of frost, and through it Trista could just make out a faint sugaring on the nearby roofs and some gleaming thread-like icicles drooping from the guttering opposite. The sky was an uneasy gray, tinged with sepia. Storm yellow. The heavy yellow of a sky full of snow.

Violet's face was masklike, but in her clenched jaw and the movement of her eyes Trista detected panic and a deep-seated dread. With a shock she realized how much she had asked of Violet the night before. For Trista's sake, she had stayed in one place for hours. Now winter, which had been stalking Violet in vain all these years, was settling upon Ellchester with unseasonable speed.

"You *cursed*!" A sleepy, querulous-looking Pen was sitting up in her bed.

"Right after breakfast, I need to go out," declared Violet. "I'll head to Plotmore Hill—that was where you lost track of the midnight ride, wasn't it, Trista? You two will have to stay here."

Both girls started to protest.

"No arguments," Violet told them flatly, with a concerned glance at Trista.

Breakfast was chaotic and sparse. Jack was apparently still asleep. His aunt and brother-in-law had already left for work, and his two teenage sisters were just hurrying out to their jobs at the laundry. His mother and eldest sister were getting ready to go to the market, so making breakfast was left to Jack's eight-year-old niece, who took care of it with the briskness of practice, pausing to wipe the faces of the younger children like a miniature mother.

Everybody's fingers were numb with cold, but the cover remained in place over the hearth. The tea tasted like puddle water. Breakfast was a slice of bread with margarine. Violet devoured hers in seconds and then fidgeted, waiting for everyone else.

"But I'm still hungry!" protested Pen. "Why are *they* getting more?" The younger children in Jack's family were being handed a second slice of bread and margarine, wrapped in paper.

"That's their lunch, Pen," muttered Violet with a wince. "They're taking it to school."

Whenever she got the chance, Trista tried to make eye contact with Violet, willing her to hear her mute appeal. *Please don't leave me behind with Pen! I don't know if she's safe with me!* But Violet seemed stubbornly determined to avoid her eye, and kept following Jack's mother and sister with her gaze.

Trista barely noticed the front door slam but was slightly

surprised when Jack's oldest sister came back into the kitchen, removing the hat and coat she had just donned.

"Mom's just gone to buy some bread and eggs," she said brightly, "so you can have a breakfast that's closer to what you're used to. I'm to stay and make you more tea. Wait there and make yourselves comfortable." She ran up the stairs, presumably to put away her hat and coat.

Instantly Violet rose from her chair, taking care not to let the feet scrape.

"We're leaving," she said softly. "Quickly and quietly. Now."

When the trio were back on the street, Pen stared back incredulously at the house. "Why did we leave? They were going to make us more breakfast!"

"We're in the newspapers," Violet said in a low tone. "I'll bet my hide on it. The paper arrived while we were eating. Jack's mother and sister read it, then went to whisper in the hall. Then Jack's sister came back to keep us here. Jack's mother must have gone to the police. There's probably a reward."

"She betrayed us for *money*?" Pen exclaimed in disbelief. "I'm going back to break her windows!"

"Don't you dare!" snapped Violet, then sighed and gave Pen a gentle exasperated look. "Pen . . . money only seems like a mean reason if you've never had to think about it. Most people have to think about it all the time. Money doesn't mean cake and diamonds; it means finally paying off what you owe to the landlord, the baker, and the tallyman. It means having coins for the gas meter, so you don't have to chop up your shelves for firewood. It means keeping the wolf from the door for a while.

"She didn't owe us a thing, Pen, and if she doesn't fight for her family, no one else will."

The wolf from the door. Hunger *was* like a wolf, Trista

reflected. She had felt its teeth savaging her innards many times now. She had been caught up in her own self-absorbed, frantic battle with it, and had never considered that many people might go through their whole lives with the wolf trotting a pace behind them. Perhaps she had still been trapped in Triss's conviction that the world revolved around her own needs and suffering. Her own story now seemed very small.

Then her personal terror consumed her again, and she snatched at Violet's sleeve.

"Violet! I left Triss's dress behind in the attic room!"

"Oh, *hell*!" Violet looked back the way they had come, clearly conflicted. "Trista . . . I'm sorry. We can't go back. It's just too dangerous. Let me know if you start to get hungry and . . . I'll think of something."

"So . . . are we going to meet racketeers?" asked Pen when they had parked the motorbike on Plotmore Hill. "Will they have guns? Are you their *gun moll*?"

"No, Pen!" Violet rolled her eyes. "Guns only happen in movies and America. And I'm not a moll, for crying out loud! Most of the time I just deliver things. That's why I have the sidecar, so I can load it up with anything or anyone that needs to get somewhere fast. And I'm a good mechanic who doesn't ask questions—even if the car I'm fixing is full of black-market tinned cheese."

"A mechanic?" Pen seemed uncertain whether to be scandalized or disappointed.

"Yes." Violet grimaced. "One of the things I learned during the war. Strange—the war was probably the best schooling I ever had. I signed up to help with the war effort, and first they sent me to work in one of those munitions factories. I made a lot of friends there—mostly other munitionettes—and it certainly knocked the corners off me. Many of the male workers didn't really want us there, you see, and there was a lot of bullying and name-calling. One girl even had her tool drawer nailed shut when she was out of the room.

"Then I was reassigned and found myself driving this clapped-out ambulance. I *had* to learn my way around an engine, just to keep the darn thing on the move. I didn't expect I would need the knowledge again after the war ended, but"—she shrugged—"what else can I do? Even if I could find a job where I didn't need to stay in one place more than three hours at a time, why would anyone give it to me when they can pay half as much to some fourteen-year-old fresh out of school?"

"Violet." Pen's brow was creased. "If lots of people don't have any money or work, why don't any of them want to be our kitchen maid? Mother says it's impossible to find *anyone*."

Violet walked on for a little while before answering.

"I'm sorry, Pen," she said at last, "but your mother has a reputation. She fires her servants at the drop of a hat and doesn't give references, which means they can't get another job. Clara Bassett says that most servants in Ellchester have been warned about your family."

"Clara Bassett?" Pen looked incredulous. "Do you mean *Cook*?"

Violet nodded. "I still talk to her now and then. Every time your mother hires a new maid or governess, Mrs. Bassett tries to take them under her wing. Apparently she always warns them to avoid you and Triss as much as possible—particularly Triss."

"Why?" asked Pen. Violet did not respond, but Trista thought she knew the answer.

Trista thought of Celeste jealously patrolling her children, unable to bear Triss showing fondness for anybody else. Cook had survived by remaining stubbornly and stoicially invisible in her basement. Discovering that Cook had opinions about the Crescents was rather like finding that a familiar wardrobe opened onto an entirely new house. Violet halted outside a shop, which the striped pole proclaimed to be a barber's. The bell tinkled as she entered, Trista and Pen a step behind.

Two young men with hair oiled to blackbird sleekness were attending to customers, one shaving a mustache and another brushing hair cuttings from a portly neck. Neither exactly smiled to see Violet, but neither looked unfriendly. One gave a small nod in the direction of a door farther in the shop. Violet returned the nod and strode through the second door. The girls followed, Trista giving the scissors on the table as wide a berth as she could.

The room at the back was scruffy but practical. A broad-set man with coppery hair was seated at a desk, scanning sports pages and marking results in pen.

"Frosty!" he said as Violet entered the room. "Always a pleasure to see you."

"Bill," Violet said without preamble, "I need to ask you something downright peculiar. I know you had some boys . . . working late here last night. Did any of them happen to hear anything odd go by at about midnight?"

"Midnight?" Bill narrowed his eyes. "Do you mean the geese?"

"Geese?" asked Violet.

"Great big flock of geese," replied Bill. "We heard 'em go over just after midnight. That's the fourth night in a row that it's happened too."

"Did you see where they went?" Violet asked promptly.

"They swooped over, then curved about and headed back

toward the center of the city." Bill looked at Violet narrowly. "Why are you interested?"

Trista felt a sting of relief. The overheard "geese" could only be the Architect's midnight riders, and if he had headed back to the center, then at least he had probably not taken Triss out of Ellchester.

"You wouldn't believe me." Violet grimaced.

"I ask because I'm rather interested myself," continued Bill. "Geese don't just circle like that for no reason. I think something's been frightening them into the sky each night. As you know, I got some runners placed down in the Old Docks—they tell me that about four days ago strange boats started turning up. Small, old-fashioned craft. They draw up at the quays in the afternoon and evening and let off passengers. By dawn they're gone again. Something's happening down there. I'd like to know what it is."

"What did the passengers look like?" Pen asked impulsively.

"That's the rum part." Bill scratched his head. "Nobody could describe them, not even how many there were or whether they were dressed shabby or ritzy. But they agreed on one thing: none of the passengers had any luggage."

Things half seen and half heard. People hard to describe. In between and misty, dancing fleet-footed across the numb places in people's minds. And these strange boats had started turning up at about the same time the Architect had begun riding over the city.

Trista made eye contact with Violet. *Besiders*, she mouthed.

At this point, one of the barbers from the shop slipped into the back room and cleared his throat.

"Mr. Siskin," he said to Bill, "there's a hare coursing that I thought might interest you, sir." He took up the paper on the desk, turned back some pages, then handed it to Bill with a meaningful look.

After the barber had left, Bill stared at the paper in his hands for a long moment. Then he sniffed and spread it out on the desk, beckoning Violet over.

"I've seen better likenesses," he said.

The photograph of Violet showed her as a sweet-faced girl in her late teens, with a lustrous flood of ringlets. Nobody glancing at that picture would have guessed how a few years could have pulled that face taut, giving it anger and angles.

The other picture was a photograph that had been taken of the Crescent family less than a year before. It was the standard family pose that photographers loved, mother seated, children arranged ornamentally on either side, and father resting a proprietorial hand on the back of her chair. Through Triss's memories, Trista could even remember posing for the photograph, having to hold still for what seemed an age while the image seared its way slowly into the film.

Pen had not held perfectly still, of course, so there was a slight ghostly smudge of movement to one side of her face, but she was still recognizable. Triss's purse-mouthed countenance, on the other hand, had a frozen clarity beneath its floppy white ribbon.

CRESCENT DAUGHTERS KIDNAPPED, thundered the headline. Trista's eye tumbled helplessly down the columns of inky lettering. Violet Parish sought in connection with the disappearance . . . no ransom demand as yet received . . . rumored to be retaliation after a financial dispute . . .

"We're not kidnapped!" protested Trista.

"It's all full of made-up stories!" stormed Pen.

"I'm good at softening the police," Bill murmured, "but I'm not *that* good. What is all this about, Violet?"

“Sorry, Bill,” she said quietly. “It’s a mess. But it’s not a kidnapping.”

“Well . . . that’s a shame.” Bill sighed and tutted under his breath. “It’s a crying shame I didn’t read this until an hour after you’d left. I could have used that reward.” He gave Violet a small twinkle, then frowned slightly. “You know where all my out-of-town friends are if you need a place to hide?”

“I know—thanks, Bill.” Violet gave him a small but genuine smile. She stood to leave, then hesitated. “Bill . . . do you mind if I take that paper?”

As they took to the street again, Violet handed Trista the paper.

“It’s a picture of Triss,” she whispered. “Could you eat that if you start feeling hungry again?”

At the very thought, Trista’s appetite rose like a shark to a smell of blood. *It’s all right,* she told herself. *I know what this is. I can handle it.* She braced herself for the wave of hunger and felt it sweep over her, but this time it continued to increase, consuming her. She was shaking uncontrollably. This was new. This was worse. She snatched the paper from Violet, her hands crushing it into a ball, and began to cram it into her mouth.

“Holy Moses! Not on the street!” hissed Violet. She grabbed Trista by the arm and quickly drew her into an alley. “I’ll stand out here and keep watch until you’ve finished.”

As Trista staggered toward the back of the alley her vision darkened and speckled. Something inside her was gaping wider and ever wider. As it did so, everything distorted, as if through a fish-eye lens. Everything became smaller, small enough to push into her mouth without trying. In fact, she would have to try hard not to.

She gobbled the paper, and for a second could taste the

photograph, but its Trissness was thin as gruel. For a moment her hunger dipped and waned, like a flame in a draft, but the next instant it surged to life once more. It was not enough. She needed more.

She had to eat. She *had* to eat. There had to be something she could eat.

Like a stray cat, she scrabbled through the rubbish in the alley, looking for more copies of the *Chronicle* with their pictures of Triss. There were none, so in the frenzy of hunger she scooped up half-rotted scraps and swallowed them.

"What are you *doing*?" Pen's voice was right behind her.

Trista did not turn round but remained crouched, only raising one stealthy hand to wipe a speck of grime off her lower lip. She did not want Pen to see her face, just in case it was a monstrous, thorn-mandibled mask of hunger. If Pen kept talking to her normally, then perhaps everything *could* be normal.

"I was . . . I was hungry, Pen." How inadequate those words sounded. "I'm . . . hungry."

"I'm still hungry too," replied Pen mournfully. Trista could hear the smaller girl dropping to a crouch next to her.

"I'm . . . I'm *really* hungry, Pen." Trista swallowed drily. "I think . . . I think it's because I lost bits of myself on the roofs last night when I was chasing the Architect. Those pieces left a hole, Pen. And I think that's why I'm so very, very . . ." She trailed off, clenching her hands into fists.

"Then eat more things!" Pen sounded dismayed. "I can get you leaves!"

"It's no good," Trista said through gritted teeth. "They have to be *Triss* things."

"You *can't* fall apart!" shouted Pen, as if it was something she could insist upon. "I . . . I won't let you!" Before Trista could react she felt Pen's arms thrown around her, with the desperate energy of a rugby tackle. "You *can't*!"

Pen.

Trista closed her eyes and held Pen tightly. She clung to the one thing that felt warm and solid in her strange, unforgiving world.

Suddenly Pen gave a squeak and wince.

"Ow! Triss . . . why are you *spiking* me?"

Trista's gaze dropped to her hands. The thorns were out, curling from her fingertips like bramble briars, digging in through the shoulders of Pen's light dress. Her tongue could feel the fine points of tapering teeth. And her arms were curled around something that was banquets, and lemonade on a summer day, and hot soup in winter . . . and there was a hole inside her like a bottomless shaft that a person might just tumble into . . .

She pushed Pen away as hard as she could. The smaller girl fell backward, hitting the cobbles with a yelp. Winded, she stared up at Trista, and her expression of outrage and shock slowly ebbed into horror and fear.

Trista dared not stay another moment. She backed away, then turned and sprang onto the top of the nearest wall. From there she dropped down on the other side into a neighboring alley, landing at a crouch with her heart hammering. Then she was away and running, head ducked down to hide her monstrous face.

Chapter 35

CRUEL MIRROR

OUTSIDE, THE AIR TASTED OF SNOW. THERE WAS something brittle in the jolting of the breeze, and the sky was so low Trista felt she could leap and draw her claws across it. Instead she continued to sprint down lane after lane, her shoes quickly picking up grime and leaf litter from the pavement.

Where was she? She did not even know. These were not the streets that made sense to the Triss part of her mind, with prim, trim rows of houses where everything was held modestly back behind painted front doors and venetian blinds. Here, in the roads between the back-to-backs, all the front doors were open and bold life poured out onto the street. It was like watching somebody eating with their mouth open. Children sped hither and thither in intense, smileless gaggles like starlings. Mothers in hairnets chatted and peeled potatoes on doorsteps, fathers sat and smoked.

She ran on, ignoring the front-yard cycle-repair shops, the children huddling outside the tobacconist to beg cigarette cards off strangers, and the salty reek of stalls selling oyster pie.

At last Trista glimpsed the outline of the Victory Bridge, a concrete rainbow bowing to the earth under its own weight. The sight of it set her internal compass straight. She was no longer running through a twisted labyrinth of her own mind. She was still in Ellchester, with the river somewhere to the right, and the town's slate-scaled hills to her left.

At last she stopped for breath in an enclosed alley full of the cold echoes of falling drips. She gasped, and sobbed, and ground her narrow teeth.

I hurt Pen. And what if I'd eaten her?

I'm a monster. A monster. Mr. Grace was right the whole time. And Violet was wrong.

But Trista couldn't think about Violet without feeling a warm, stubborn hope. She remembered the way that Violet had stared straight into her eyes with complete faith.

Maybe I nearly ate Pen. But I didn't. *And I won't. I won't hurt Pen, whatever happens. I won't make Violet wrong, not after everything she's done.*

Trista swallowed, and in her mind's eye she could see the smile of the Architect. How charming he had been on the telephone! And how slyly he had slipped in that suggestion that devouring Pen might save Trista's life. Perhaps he really had felt a shred of fondness for Trista at the time, but his real motive had been his desire to strike at Piers Crescent's heart as cruelly as possible.

"But you couldn't make me do it, Mr. Architect," Trista whispered aloud. "You lost that game. I'm not your tool, and I never will be. I'm free and I'm myself, until my pieces fall into the gutter. And I'm not ready for *that* to happen just yet either." She wrapped her arms around her makeshift body, with its ravening hungry hole at the center, and hugged her small, dark victory as tightly as possible.

I'll find something to eat. Something that isn't Pen. Something to stop me from falling apart before evening.

Her thoughts scampered, cunning and ravenous as mice. Where could she find something dear to Triss? Was there anywhere else outside Triss's own home that had been important to her? Unlikely. Triss's life had been lovingly enclosed by the walls of her house, like a pearl imprisoned in an oyster shell. Trista could have wept with frustration.

An idea struck her and took hold. It was Tuesday—and Celeste had told Cook that she could take the whole of Tuesday off. Piers would be at work, and Tuesday was the day Celeste usually played tennis and had tea with other members of the Luther Square Mothers' Association. Margaret would soon have finished her work at the house.

The disappearance of the Crescent daughters might have thrown the schedule into disarray. However, it was just possible that even now the house was empty.

When she thought of venturing near the Crescent home again, Trista's insides twisted into a black scribble of indescribable feelings. Her hunger won out, however. With new purpose Trista broke into a sprint once more. Her feet barely grazed the surface of the puddles, and her steps stirred no echoes.

The wind was Trista's friend, so chilly that it cleared all but the most dogged from the streets. It dragged up protective coat collars, and everybody hurried by, paying one another no heed. Shop owners were too busy battening down their displays to notice Trista. Nonetheless she kept to the alleys and side roads.

She began to recognize landmarks, street names, achingly familiar to the Triss part of her head. But now she saw everything through a filter of her own strangeness and wildness. The familiar did not welcome her. It stared at her aghast. She was not coming home. She was an insidious shadow falling upon the neighborhood, like influenza or bad news.

And then, at last, there it was. The little square with its tiny park in the middle. The glossy cars, now crystal-freckled with the first spotting of rain. The tall, pompous houses shoulder to shoulder behind their wrought-iron railings. Trista slunk along walls between hiding places, then skulked behind an unattended car.

There was a postman at the door. He knocked and waited, knocked again, then leaned back to peer up at the house.

Trista wet her lips as she watched him straddle his bicycle and depart. Nobody had answered the door. The house was empty.

She scurried from her hiding place, swift as a wind-chased leaf, weaving through the side streets until she was in the alley behind the houses. Pushing open the gate to the yard, she crept in, a pepper-tingle of fear sweeping across her skin. Triss's memories were everywhere she looked, and they chafed Trista like stolen shoes. They did not fit her. She could not understand how she had ever thought they fit.

The back door was locked.

Above her, the bedroom windows beckoned. Trista felt the leap as an electricity in her legs, even before she sprang. Her fingers closed on one of the sills, and she tugged herself up with ease.

She scrabbled at the window, her thorn-claws leaving scratches on pane and frame alike. Then she managed to heave up the sash and pushed her way in past the soft lavender-colored curtains. The room beyond smelled of powder, potpourri, and the slightly acrid scent of wine tonic. It was Celeste's room.

Trista ventured out onto the landing, then opened the door into Triss's room. Her heart ached as she saw how carefully the room had been tidied and aired, the bed meticulously made, with Triss's nightdress folded on the pillow. It was like the scene from *Peter Pan* where the Darlings discover that their rooms are poignantly waiting for them to come back.

But I'm not the one it's waiting for.

And as her hunger enveloped her, Trista tore the room apart.

She tipped the chest of drawers, so that all the drawers spilled out onto the floor, then scrabbled through the fallen clothes, rending them in her haste. Triss's false pearls crunched like sugar. Books were clawed from the shelves, torn, and swallowed, their leathery bindings dropped to the floor like discarded fruit husks. The straw boater and St. Bridget's blazer were bittersweet and heady and nearly choked her. The bedside table tumbled, and the medicine bottles smashed. Now the carpet beneath Trista's feet was covered in broken glass, colored pills, and sticky puddles of cordial and cod-liver oil.

All the while the dolls shrieked and clattered in outrage and fear, beating their fists of china and wood against their shelves. She grabbed a rag doll, feeling it twist and struggle in her hands, and heard it wail as her mouth engulfed it. Two clothes-peg dolls followed, then a porcelain Pierrot. The screams filled Trista's ears as she fed in a frenzy, hardly knowing if one of the voices was hers. She was barely aware of the cobweb tickle of her tears rolling down her cheeks. Her mind was filled with a white madness, and all sounds were meaningless.

She barely noticed when there was another noise beneath the hubbub, the sharp distant slam of a front door. Only the thunder of steps on the stairs roused her from her frenzy.

Fear sobered her in one drenching instant. Trista sprang for the bedroom door, leaping out onto the landing just as Piers Crescent came into view around the corner.

He stopped, stared. His color and strength seemed to leak out of him. Trista had never seen him look so hollow-eyed, so desperate.

"Triss . . ." It was a barely audible whisper. A tiny, miserable flame of hope ignited in his eyes, and he took an eager step forward.

Terrified, Trista recoiled, baring her thorn-teeth in a hiss. Her mind was a furnace. All thought singed and sizzled into nothingness.

It brought Piers to a dead halt. Trista took advantage of that moment to flee into Celeste's room. She had just leaped onto the sill of the open window when Piers's voice reached her.

"Wait! Please! *Please!*"

Trista cast a glance over her shoulder into the room behind. Piers had stopped in the doorway, holding out one hand as if he could detain her from a distance. Her knees were still bent, poised for the drop to the yard. Something in his face, however, made her hesitate for an instant.

"I won't hurt you," he said, with a steadiness that evidently took some effort. "Please—I want to talk. I want to make terms."

"Terms?" The word exploded from Trista, and the voice that spoke it was not that of a little girl. *"You tried to throw me in the fire!"*

If I drop now, I can outpace him, I know I can . . .

"Then your argument is with me, not with my daughters." Piers let out a long breath. "Your master's quarrel is also with me. Tell your master—or your father, or whatever he is—that I want to make a bargain. I will hand myself over to him and suffer whatever revenge he sees fit. All I ask is that my girls be brought home safely."

Master? Father?

Trista did not know what to feel. Triss-feelings of love, loyalty, hurt. Trista-feelings of anger, outrage, fear.

"You don't understand," she said, her bitterness softened by sadness. Her voice sounded more human this time but older than the hills. "You don't understand the Architect, or me, or your own daughters. You don't understand anything. You're a loving father, but you're blind. Blind enough to be cruel."

Piers was in the dimness of the unlit room, but Trista thought she saw a pucker of tension and outrage in his cheek. It must have been years since anybody dared defy him, let alone speak to him in such terms. He took a hasty half step into the room but halted when Trista tensed on the sill.

"Then tell me—what *can* I do to get my girls back?" His tone of desperation tore at her heart, in spite of everything. "What does the Architect want from me?"

"He wants you to suffer," hissed Trista. Even now, she feared that the bird-things might be nearby and overhear her talking about the Architect. "Once upon a time you were useful to him. But then you *broke the bargain*. Now all he cares about is making you wish you were dead, and he knows the worst way he can hurt you is through your family. If you try to make a deal with him, he'll pretend to listen, and tie you up in clever words, but he won't give up his revenge."

Piers stared at her for a few moments.

"Why are you telling me this?" he asked at last.

"I tried to explain before," Trista answered with feeling, "but you wouldn't listen. *I don't work for the Architect.* I'm not his child or his servant. He had me made to look like your daughter, so you wouldn't notice she was missing, and he gave me Triss's memories. But *I didn't know what I was.*" Trista could not keep the rage and pain out of her voice. "I thought I was Triss. When

I looked at you, I saw the father I *loved*. Then everything started going wrong with me, and I was terrified. I thought I was going mad. And I tried so hard to be well, so *you* wouldn't have to worry about your little girl.

"And then you tried to throw me on the fire. Do you know what would have happened if you had? I would have burned to death, screaming. That's all. It wouldn't have brought Triss back. Because the Architect doesn't care what happens to me."

Piers stood staring at her, lips pressed together as if the truth was a pill he was trying to avoid swallowing. He wanted to dismiss her words as changeling lies, she could see that, but even now she knew a hundred small details were falling into place in his mind with painful clarity.

For years the whole of Ellchester had held a flattering mirror in which Piers could see himself reflected. A man of vision and community spirit, a leading figure of the city, an ideal father and husband. Now Trista was holding up a very different mirror, with a twisted image he had never seen before. To his credit, however, he did not look away.

He made two abortive attempts to speak before managing to frame words.

"I was told that you—"

"And Mr. Grace believed what he said," Trista interrupted. "But he was wrong."

"I did not know." Piers dragged his fingers back through his hair. "I . . . All I thought of was my daughter. It . . . it seemed the only way to save her. That is all I care about—protecting my little girl."

It was not quite an apology, for what apology could Piers give to the feral thing on his windowsill? It was close, though. Perhaps this should have made Trista feel a little better, stirred her sympathies. Instead his words stung her to the quick.

This time it was not just rage on her own account but a turbulence of feelings—anger, pity, frustration, and pain. Her mind was full of her other self, whom Trista had envied and despised. Triss the cherished. Triss and her nervous ailments, swaddled to suffocation . . .

"I know." The bitter words were out before Trista could stop them. "She's your precious treasure. That's why you like to bury her."

"What?" Piers reddened around the neck. "What do you mean?"

"You and your wife," Trista answered starkly, "have been burying Triss alive for years. She's miserable. She has no friends. She hardly ever goes out and never gets to try anything new or difficult. She's twisted up inside with boredom, and it's poisoning her."

"How dare you!" Despite Piers's state of shock, this was evidently a blow too keen. "My daughter needs special care! If you had any idea of the pains my wife and I have taken . . . Theresa is *ill*!"

"Triss is ill because you and your wife *need* her to be ill!" snapped Trista. "Apart from Pen, your *whole family* is ill! None of you have been well since Sebastian died!"

She had broken the taboo and spoken the sacred name. A shocked silence followed. Piers seemed to be having trouble breathing. Trista knew her words were harsh, but they had the bitter taste of truth. They needed to be spoken, and there was no gentle way to do that.

"Sebastian died," Trista went on. It was too late to stop. "You were supposed to be in charge of the family, and in control. But he died, and you couldn't stop it from happening. You tried. You made your bargain with the Architect, and it made everything worse."

Piers had no answer. The tormented letters from Sebastian were in the very next room.

"I think you tried to make up for it." Trista was probing deep in the family's wound now, and she knew it. "Maybe you promised yourself that you would protect your other children from all danger. But you couldn't do that unless they were *in* danger. That's why Triss had to be ill—badly ill—so that you could save her, over and over again, the way you couldn't save Sebastian.

"I know you didn't plan it like that—you thought you were just protecting her. But really all this time you've been teaching her to be ill. I know—I remember it all. I remember being told, over and over again, *you can't, don't even try, you're ill, you'll make yourself unwell.* And I remember being scared of the way my parents turned cold and angry if I ever liked somebody who wasn't them, or wanted something that wasn't home." Trista had to pause for an instant. The memories were not hers, but they bruised as if they were. "If Triss wants love, presents, kindness, or her own way, she can get them by being ill. She can have anything she wants . . . as long as she doesn't want to make friends, go to school, leave the house, or get better. Of course she can't get well—deep down she's scared that if she does, her mommy and daddy will stop loving her."

"Triss could never believe that!" exclaimed Piers aghast. "She knows we love her!"

"Do you?" Trista felt a pang as she saw her not-father blanch. "Or do you love the eight-year-old Triss in your head, the one who never grows up, never looks at you differently, and always needs you forever? *She isn't real.* Your real daughter spends her life pretending to be her—it's like a horrible game she has to play or she loses your love. *Nobody* is 'your Triss' anymore. There's just a girl who playacts all the time, and makes herself believe her own lies, and torments Pen out of misery and envy. She's spoiled and spiteful and deceitful, and you have to *promise* that if I rescue her and bring her back, you will love her anyway, for the Triss she really is."

A few moments passed before Piers seemed to take in the full import of her speech. Then he mouthed the word "rescue" voicelessly to himself.

"You . . . intend to rescue her." His tone was flat, as if he did not dare imbue it with any hope or energy.

"If I can," Trista answered.

Piers looked utterly flabbergasted. "Then . . . you know where she is?" He took on a look of pained hope. "Where? Tell me! Is she hurt?"

"I don't know where she is, not yet. She's alive, or she was last night."

Piers let out a breath, and then another thought seemed to occur to him.

"And Pen? Little Pen?"

"I thought you would never ask," Trista muttered nastily.

"Where is she? Tell me you have not hurt her!"

"Hurt Pen? After she saved my life?" Trista could not keep the outrage out of her voice. "No. Never. But right now I think she's safer with me. I don't trust your Mr. Grace not to decide that she's a changeling too and throw *her* in the fire."

Piers looked anguished, perhaps at the idea that he could not be trusted with his own children. The thorny part of Trista's heart gave a skip of malicious satisfaction. She could not help it. But there was another part of her that watched him with sadness and pity. She could not help that either.

"If I find out where Triss is," Trista said quietly, "and if there is time, I will tell you, so that you can come to help rescue her. But now you must tell me everything that might be important—everything about your deals with the Architect."

Seconds passed, then Piers winced before the cruel mirror he had been shown, and dropped his gaze. He swallowed down his protests and his pride and began to speak.

Trista listened, and all the while the part of her that was Triss sobbed to hear her mighty father sounding so humble, abject, and destroyed.

Chapter 36

HUE AND CRY

"I FIRST MET THE ARCHITECT NEAR THE OLD cemetery district," Piers began. "The letter about my son's . . . passing . . . had arrived that morning. My wife . . . It took some time to calm her. When she was asleep at last, I went out, and walked through the streets without seeing them. I do not expect you to understand, but sometimes grief has a terrible energy . . ." He trailed off.

Trista understood, and said nothing.

"I was halfway down a dark, narrow alley when I realized that I could hear a second set of footsteps echoing against the walls. There was a man walking in step with me. He greeted me familiarly, and by name, so I answered automatically. I meet so many people, you see, and I cannot always recognize them afterward.

"He knew all about my work for the war effort—the harbor defenses I helped to design in Kent—and talked of them so knowledgeably that I knew he must be someone of my own profession, or something similar. Then he offered his condolences for my loss. I was too miserable to care how he had learned of it. I told him that my son's death was not certain, that mistakes were sometimes made, that perhaps another boy with the same name had died. Or perhaps his injuries were not as bad as had been thought, and that he might have recovered after the letter was sent. I must have sounded like a madman.

"He called me his 'poor fellow,' said that his house was nearby, and insisted that I step in for a brandy to steady myself. There was a beautiful polished front door at the end of the alley—I thought that was strange, even then. Inside was a great studio, with light falling in through high windows. There were architectural drawings everywhere, on walls and easels. All my training told me that there was something wrong with the angles of that room, like badly drawn perspective in an old painting.

"But I just stood there like a fool, drinking his accursed brandy and telling this complete stranger everything I felt. I told him that I would give *anything* to hear from my son again.

"For a while he just stood there watching me. Then he told me that he 'might be able to do something about that.' At first I thought he was going to recommend some spiritualist, one of those phony parasites who bleed the grief-stricken for money. But he laughed and said it was nothing like that. He told me that he could promise a nice, solid letter from my son within a week, if I did something for him in return. Then he led me over to look at his designs.

"They made my skin crawl. They were plans for impossible buildings made possible. When I stared at each individual part of the design I could see that everything fit, supported one another, and made sense. I knew that it would work. But as a whole, each design was madness, illogical. Trying to comprehend each as a building made my head hurt as if my brain was being twisted."

"But you agreed to build them anyway?" prompted Trista.

"Not at first," Piers answered. "It hurt my pride to consider passing another man's work off as my own. If he had tried to bully me into it I would have resisted. But he shrugged, told me that I should not leave my decision for too long, and then suggested we talk about something else. How could I banish his words from my mind?

"In the end I agreed. The Architect asked for a list of Sebastian's possessions and was immediately interested when I mentioned the service watch."

"Did he say why?" asked Trista quickly. Her spirits had leaped at the mention of the watch.

"He said that clocks were servants of time but could be taught to be *masters* of it." Piers frowned, as if focusing his memory on the precise words. "He asked when Sebastian had died and whether the watch had been on his wrist at the time. He was glad to hear that it had. When he examined it, though, he seemed dissatisfied and said that it was not as strongly tethered to Sebastian as he had hoped—he suspected that somebody else had owned or used it. He could still enchant it to control the flow of time, but he would need something else powerfully linked to Sebastian to bind it to my son in particular.

"I came back to his studio the next day and brought a lock of Sebastian's baby hair, from my wife's keepsake box. He opened the works of the watch and dropped in the twist of hair. The cogs jammed on it, and the watch stopped dead . . . at exactly half past four."

Trista wondered if the hair was the only thing caught in the delicate grip of those cogs. Perhaps in that second Sebastian's departing ghost had also been trapped, suspended in an eternal moment between life and death.

"Where's the Architect's studio?" she asked.

"Gone." Piers shook his head miserably. "I went back but found only a faded boarded door, and behind that a tiny cramped room covered in grime and cobwebs. I have been trying to find the Architect for days, with no success. Plainly he has no interest in talking to me.

"When I spoke to Mr. Grace this morning, he seemed to think he had a line of investigation, but . . ." Piers trailed off, his expression conflicted and uncertain. Perhaps he felt uncomfortable about revealing Mr. Grace's activities to Trista, even now. "But . . . he has chiefly been on *your* trail, so he has been tracing Miss Parish through her friends. We thought that would lead us to the Architect and my daughters."

"Can't you make Mr. Grace stop?" she demanded. "If you tell him everything I just told you—"

"He would not believe it." Piers shook his head with an air of finality. "Even if I added my voice to yours. He has a terrible history with the Besiders."

Trista remembered the black band around the tailor's arm.

"What happened to him?" she asked.

"It was before the war. His wife was a woman from a small village, brought up with all the old folklore. When she was very ill during childbirth, she told him that she believed she had accidentally angered the Besiders. She begged her husband to make sure that a pair of scissors was left in the cradle with the child to protect it. It seemed foolish and dangerous, so of course he did not.

"As a result, she became convinced that their baby had been replaced by a changeling. One day he came home and found her preparing to beat the little baby with a broom, so he called in a doctor who sedated her. She pleaded with him to at least keep the child away from her, but the doctor said that it was important for the body of the child and the mind of the mother that the suckling continued.

"He came home one evening to find his wife dead, her body looking, in his words, 'drained.' The cradle was empty, and rocking vigorously as though it had just been kicked. He heard the back door bang, and when he ran to look out, he could see a white shape fleeing through the darkness. It was the size and shape of a tiny baby, but it leaped with unnatural agility. It turned for a second to look back at him, then vanished into the night. He says it was smiling."

Trista was lost between despair and pity. Her hopes of convincing Mr. Grace softly shattered.

"What about the police?" she asked.

"I never wanted them involved in the first place," answered Piers, "but last night I argued with Mr. Grace. I wanted to find the Architect and make terms; he said it was hopeless. He told me he was taking matters out of my hands for my own good. He went to the police and now the investigation is beyond my control."

"Do what you can to stop them, Mr. Crescent," Trista said bluntly. "Triss's life probably depends upon it." She turned away from Piers and dropped swiftly from the sill. Her feet struck the ground as lightly as pine needles.

"Wait!" shouted Piers as she sprinted for the back gate. "There are so many things I need to ask you!"

Trista did not linger for his questions but plunged into the network of alleyways, racing through turn after turn. She had to find her way back to Violet and Pen.

The birds in every tree she passed were as restless as the breeze. Her distracted brain made out the words in their rasps and chirrups, and she realized that they were not true birds at all. Glancing at a tree gray with beating wings, she thought she saw wizened, featherless faces leer back.

Traitor! Traitor! We heard *you. Crescent's little helper. Plotting against the Architect.*

Wait till the Architect hears! Wait till we tell him what the thorn-doll said!

Traitor! Traitor!

There was a jubilant viciousness in the tone, as the last word was tossed to and fro between them like a child's ball. Perhaps throughout her conversation with Piers, the bird-things had been lurking in the eaves, their wicked, tiny ears sucking up every word.

With a needle-thin shriek of derision, the winged shapes erupted from the trees, flung themselves upward into the sky, and were gone.

Trista felt chill. The bird-things would report back, and the Architect would know that she was not, after all, to be counted among his friends. The Architect, with his wild, tenacious rages and his vindictiveness toward any who betrayed him.

But she had no time to think about that now—she had to find the others . . .

"Trista!"

At the sound of her own peculiar name, Trista turned and was astonished to see Violet straddling her motorcycle parked at the edge of the main thoroughfare. Pen was standing up in the sidecar waving both arms. Trista's heart swelled with relief and love, and she ran over.

"Are you all right?" was Violet's first question, her gray eyes earnest and concerned. Trista had been braced for an angry tirade and could do little more than nod.

"Trista ran away!" pointed out Pen. "Why isn't *she* in trouble?"

"Because it was my fault, not hers," Violet answered levelly.

"How did you find me?" asked Trista in a small voice.

"Pen told me what happened," Violet explained, "so I guessed you would head back to the Crescent house to find something to eat. It's what I would have done in your shoes. Though that doesn't mean it was a good idea. Quick—get in. We don't want to be hanging around this close to Pen's home."

When Trista was back in the sidecar, Violet kicked down on the starter viciously, as if it had caused all their troubles.

Chapter 37

STORMS AND TEACUPS

THE OLD DOCKS HAD NOT FADED GENTLY. THEY did not look sad, like the primly peeling paint of the Victorian bathing huts you sometimes saw in coastal towns where the tide of luck had gone out. Neglect had given the Old Docks a dangerous air, like that of a half-starved dog.

Violet drew up on a riverside street where a drab chorus line of three-story houses stared out across the water. For the last five minutes, the motorcycle's roar had been punctuated by occasional stutters, and this time as she killed the engine it died fretfully.

"Fuel's low," she muttered with a frown. "And the police may be watching out for me if I try to buy more petroleum."

"Why doesn't Father stop them?" demanded Pen. "Triss—you said he was on *our* side now! He *can't* let them arrest Violet!"

"He's not in control anymore." Trista could not bring herself to explain further. Piers's harrowed face was still clear in her memory. "But perhaps he will try to help."

"And he wasn't angry with me?" Pen asked.

"No, Pen," Trista answered gently. "He wasn't."

"Then I expect it's a trick," Pen declared in a matter-of-fact tone. "He's *always* angry with me."

"You've been missing for two days," Violet reminded her. "Perhaps he's starting to forget how annoying you are."

Even now that her hunger had been sated, Trista still shivered at the memory of her last conversation with Pen. The smaller girl, however, seemed to have shrugged off the whole episode.

Trista was aware of a growing sense of unease as she looked around her. It was not just the down-at-the-heels area that was gnawing at her instincts, she realized. To her ears the breeze had a faint dry buzz to it. The sky looked like china.

"Is something wrong?" Violet asked her quietly, with a frown.

Trista swallowed.

"There are Besiders here somewhere," she whispered back.

"Are those the boats?" asked Pen in carrying tones, as she scrambled out of the sidecar and headed toward the water.

Some of the wooden jetties had not yielded to time and the waters, and still jutted out onto the river. Sure enough, moored to them and around them were a number of vessels. By far the largest was a shabby-looking barge, the glass of its portholes fogged with grime. There were some open fishing boats, each with a solitary slender mast, and a number of small rowing boats.

Trista climbed out of the sidecar and hurried to keep pace with Pen, who was running for the nearest jetty.

"Careful, Pen!" she called. "The boards might be rotten!"

To Trista's surprise, Pen gave her a shy glance and slowed, waiting to take Trista's hand. Pen ignoring her, Pen shouting at her—these were easier to deal with than Pen's matter-of-fact trust.

Somehow the safety of another person, a smaller person, had been thrust into Trista's hands. It frightened her. She wondered if mothers felt scared at having so much power over their children.

Perhaps they did. Perhaps they wished there was somebody to tell them if they were doing things wrong. She felt a sudden, unexpected sting of sympathy for the Crescent parents.

While Violet hid the motorcycle down an alley, Trista and Pen walked stiffly down the jetty, glancing at the boats. Trista tried to read the names painted on the sides, but the peeling paint had obliterated each and every one. One boat appeared to be called the *Si--er Wy-m*. Next to it nestled the *Ch----r* and the *Wail--g Gh---*.

"Where are all the people?" hissed Pen.

"I don't know," Trista whispered back. The boats all had an abandoned look, like empty peapods. And then, all of a sudden, one of them was not so empty after all.

There was an imperceptible moment of shift. It was like that instant where a patch of earth flutters and shows itself to be a brown bird, or a leaf twitches and becomes a lacewing. Somehow, in the jumble of sun-bleached deck chairs, rope coils, and old crates painted with curling slogans, there must always have been a man and woman sitting on the barge's deck in plain view. Now they stood up and became obvious.

Trista swallowed to smother her surprise. Pen gave a short, sharp squeak.

Neither of the strangers was young, but it was hard to be sure how old they were. Their skin was pale and grayish, with a tired, wet-weather look to it. Their hair was the color of damp sand, and something about their eyes made Trista think of oysters.

Both were wearing floor-length gray-brown coats that set bells ringing in Trista's memory. After a moment she remembered the coat the Architect had worn in the room behind the cinema, and realized that these coats were made of the same strange dull fabric. The other garments she glimpsed were *wrong*. The woman wore an old-fashioned plum-colored dress with a bustle, like the sort Trista had seen a grand lady wearing in a chocolate-box label. The man had seemingly normal trousers, but there were brown ribbons crisscrossing up them, binding them to his legs.

"Are we in Ellchester, pretty ladies?" asked the man. A flock of passing gulls made his voice hard to hear, and Trista had to shake her head to clear it. She felt as if somebody just behind her was whispering in her ear, telling her that the gentleman had actually said something perfectly normal, and that he did not have a smile like a sick wolf.

"Yes!" Pen declared with a boldness that told Trista she was frightened.

The woman's gaze trickled down Trista's face like cold oil.

"The little one," she breathed, "is she yours?"

Again the imaginary whisper was busy at Trista's ear, or rather inside her mind, telling her how charming and unthreatening the woman was.

"She's my sister," Trista answered as brightly as she could, while taking step after step backward. "It is so nice to meet you, but we . . . have to go back to our mother now."

The two girls turned about and returned to Violet, steps brisk. All the while, the back of Trista's neck tingled as she listened to sounds from the barge.

". . . such nice shinbones . . ." she heard the woman whisper.

Trista and Pen clung silently to Violet's sleeves as the couple approached them along the jetty and then walked past, proceeding up the road with a careful, stilted gait. Violet glanced down at the girls with a question in her eyes.

"They're Besiders," whispered Trista, once she was sure the pair were out of earshot.

Violet's expression barely changed, aside from a pucker of

tension at the corners of her mouth. She did not look over her shoulder at the strangers.

"How can you tell?" she murmured very quietly.

Trista stared at her. "Can't *you* tell?"

"They're like bonfire guys come to life!" hissed Pen. "Didn't you notice?"

Trista dared a glance at the couple, who had come to a halt outside a tearoom. The man seemed to be having some trouble working out how to use the door handle.

"I think they're doing what the Architect does to make people see him as handsome," she whispered. "It's probably the same thing the bird-things do, so everyone thinks they're just birds. Lying to people's minds without saying anything. But those two over there . . . I don't think they're very good at it."

"I had an odd feeling about them, but . . ." Violet trailed off, frowning.

"It's as if they're wearing a lie, but it doesn't *fit* them." Trista tried to straighten her thoughts. "They haven't buttoned it the right way, so it's baggy in some places and coming away in others."

And maybe Pen and I can see through it more easily because we've had more dealings with the Besiders, she added silently in her head. *I'm almost one of them, and we've both been to the Underbelly. It's as if we have a stamp on our passport.*

"Well, we can't stand here on the street," muttered Violet, looking warily about her. She gave the tearoom an appraising glance, then pulled off her gloves and strode resolutely toward it, Trista and Pen keeping pace.

The tearoom looked self-possessed but a little weatherworn. Celeste would probably have sniffed at it for being "plain" and "frequented by all sorts." Compared to the pretty Lyons tea shops with their fancy cakes in the window, it did look a bit drab.

Violet pushed the door open, and the girls filed in behind her. They traipsed through the ground-floor bakery, then up the stairs to the first floor.

The tea shop itself had walls the pale color of egg custard, interrupted by occasional paintings of nursery-book scenes where wispy fairies danced with mice. There were about twenty square tables, two-thirds of them occupied. Two women in aprons hurried to and fro bearing plates of cake and making ready the pots at the corner counter, with its row of great steel urns, spotted with age.

A smell of cooking sausages made Trista's stomach leapfrog. With a shock she realized that it was probably lunchtime. The day was seeping out of her fist like so much dry sand.

"I'm *really* hungry," declared Pen in a half growl, half whine.

Violet chose a table in the corner by the window so that they could keep a discreet eye on the street.

While Violet ordered crumpets and tea from the waitress at the counter, Trista cast a careful glance across the dining area. At a distant table she saw the mysterious couple from the boat, heads stooped together in earnest conference. Then her eye strayed to the next table, and the next, and the next . . .

A twitch of the head that was too rapid, too hawklike. A flash of silver in the eyes. A furtive licking of a jam knife with a long tongue. Boots that in shadow seemed to have toes . . .

"What is it?" murmured Violet, as she returned to the table.

"Other Besiders," breathed Trista.

Violet nodded very slowly, taking in the information. "How many?"

"Do you see the waitresses?" whispered Trista. "And the two ladies eating bacon over there? And the old man in the worn-out hat, and the young man with the newspaper?"

Violet nodded.

"Well . . ." Trista hesitated. "I think those are the only ones who *aren't* Besiders."

Violet grimaced and hissed her breath in through her teeth.

The tea shop was filled with a commonplace-sounding hum of conversation, but when Trista focused, she could hear what her fellow diners were really saying to the waitresses who came to take their order. It was like those moments when Triss's father tuned the family wireless and brought voices magically into clarity.

"Bring us butter! Butter! Never mind the bread."

"Good afternoon. I am not here to devour you. Now bring me sweetmeats so that I may pass as one of your kind."

"A glass of your tears, my honey. What? Oh. Tea, then."

The two waitresses were young, tired-looking women, and Trista noticed that both of them seemed tense and strained. They made mistakes, miscounted money, occasionally knocked over a milk pot or rattled their trays. The other non-Besider customers had the same air of confused unease.

"We should have brought a rooster!" hissed Pen.

Trista blinked hard and realized that the strange, seated figures had something else in common. All of them were wearing overcoats or long shawls in shades of gray or brown, made of the same dull, tufted fabric. As she watched, a woman at a far table yawned, and her coat seemed to ripple and flutter in a way that was familiar.

"Look at their coats!" Trista murmured. "I know it's difficult—your eye doesn't want to see them—but *look*. I think they're made of feathers. *Bird-thing* feathers."

All three of them jumped when a tea tray was set down with a slight clatter. Trista flinched, wondering how much the waitress had heard.

“I love children.” The waitress winked at Violet. “They always have a world of their own, don’t they?” She set out the crumpets, butter, and jam in front of the threesome and gave Trista and Pen a broad, indulgent smile. “You girls make the most of it while you can, that’s all I can say.”

Trista and Pen stared back at her with dark, round, exhausted eyes.

“I want a spoon, please,” said Pen dourly.

The waitress had barely turned her back when another figure drifted into the room. At first glance she looked like somebody’s smartly dressed aunt, in a tweed hat and coat. As Trista stared, however, the illusion split like the skin of a rotten fruit. She saw beneath it the red doll-cheek circles painted onto the drowned-looking face, the cat’s tails knotted into the floor-length black hair. The woman drifted like a mote on the breeze and came to a halt by their table.

Cowslip-yellow eyes passed over Violet and Pen, then fixed on Trista.

“These two—are they yours?” asked the woman. Her voice seemed to be made of the sobs of children in some distant cavern. Her gaze crept pointedly toward Violet and Pen.

That’s almost exactly the same question the couple from the boat asked. What does it mean? And why are they all asking me that?

Because they’ve seen something in me that is like them. They think I’m a Besider too. And they want to know if Violet and Pen are my . . . friends? My pets?

“Yes,” Trista said defensively, hoping she was giving the safer answer. “They’re mine.”

“I’m n—” began Pen, then gave a yelp as Trista kicked her. “Ow!”

"I'm still training the small one," Trista said quickly, recalling the Architect's words on the telephone. *Oh, you have her trained, then, do you?*

Violet put an arm around Pen, perhaps to comfort, perhaps to restrain. Her gaze flicked from Trista's face to that of the stranger, and her brow furrowed in frustrated concentration.

The woman appeared to accept Trista's answer, giving a slight nod, then put her head to one side.

"Where is your coat?" she asked, in her eerie, echoing voice. "I was told we were all to wear coats on arrival. So that we would not . . . cause remark." The last words were pronounced carefully, as if she was reciting them from memory.

"I don't need one." Trista watched the woman closely for any sign of reaction. "I didn't arrive today—I was already here."

The woman's yellow eyes became butter-bright with interest. "You have been living in this . . . *town*, then? And is it true about the bells?"

Trista nodded. "They cannot hurt us."

"I wanted to believe," breathed the woman. She shook her head. "I had no choice but to believe, to take a chance. Are you one of our guides, then, for the ride tonight?"

"No." Trista sipped slowly from her teacup to give herself time to think. "But I might join the ride . . . for fun. How much have you been told about it?"

"Only that we should disembark here and wait, and go no farther into this town, and draw no attention . . . and at midnight the Architect will arrive in his chariot and lead us to the haven."

"Is the haven the—" Pen began, then cut off with a little gasp of fear and frustration. Trista guessed what the smaller girl had wanted to ask, for the same question had flitted through her mind. *Is the haven the Underbelly?* Because of the magic promise, however, she could no more ask the question than Pen could.

"How much have you been told about the haven?" Trista asked instead, desperate to know if her guess was correct.

"Nothing—only that it is safe." The woman narrowed her eyes and gave Trista an inquisitive look, clearly inviting her to say more.

"It *is* safe," Trista whispered, hoping that she sounded confident. "I shouldn't say any more about it here, though. You will see it soon enough."

The woman inclined her head and drifted on through the tea shop. Trista was unnerved to notice the stranger talking to a number of the other seated Besiders, each of whom turned to gaze at Trista and give her a small, deferential nod.

"I . . ." Violet shook her head and rubbed at her eyes. "I . . . didn't catch all of that. It was like listening through fog."

"These Besiders are all newly arrived from outside Ellchester," Trista whispered. "I don't think they understand towns, and they can't blend in well, so they've been told to stay here and wait to be picked up. *That's* why the Architect is leading midnight rides—it's so he can lead them to a new home—a haven."

"By leading them over the roofs?" Violet raised an eyebrow.

"It's probably the only way to get them all there safely," Trista murmured back. "I certainly wouldn't trust them to follow a map. Look at them—some of them are having trouble with *spoons*.

"But the important part is, *the Architect is starting the midnight ride here tonight*. We already know that he takes Triss with him when he rides. It means that I might have a second chance—if I'm still alive at midnight, I can follow the ride across the roofs and try to save her!"

"Don't let her, Violet!" squealed Pen with deafening force. The waitresses glanced across at her with curiosity, and she dropped her voice again to match the whispers of the others. "She'll get hurt!"

"Pen's right—it's out of the question!" Violet's eyes were wide and serious. "Trista, last night the chase nearly tore you apart, and you *still* lost them! We . . . we'll have to find a way to follow them on the motorbike."

"But . . . the fuel tank's nearly empty . . ."

"It will *have* to last!" retorted Violet, and this time Trista caught the edge of panic intertwined with the determination.

Of course. Violet without her motorcycle was Violet with her wings clipped. She needed her wings, so as to be ever on the move. Her nightmares were always a step behind her. The unending, all-swallowing blizzard, the iron skies and forests of thorned wire, the hungry tempest of ice and darkness and loss . . .

. . . and snow. Soft, treacherous, all-covering, all-revealing snow.

"Violet," Trista said softly, "when you stay still, how long does it take before the snow starts to fall?"

"It varies." Violet tipped her head back and studied Trista interrogatively. "Sometimes as many as five hours, sometimes as little as two. Why?"

"I . . ." Trista bit her lip. "I've just had an idea. It's true, I *did* lose the riders last night. They dropped, and rose, and changed direction so quickly I couldn't keep track of them, not without moving fast enough to rip myself to pieces. But I *saw* them, Violet! Some of them were flying, but others were leaping from roof to roof, like me. And the Architect's car was driving—up walls, over roofs, along the roads. They touch down—and if there's *snow*, they'll leave tracks."

Violet stared at her. "Are you seriously suggesting that I . . . ?"

She broke off, and was uncharacteristically speechless for a moment. "But I can't!" she hissed at last. "I don't *control* this. I don't summon the snow, it *chases* me."

"I know." Trista glanced furtively around the room, then clasped Violet's hand in both of hers. "You're so brave, and fearless, and . . . and I know you're ready to drive into any kind of danger. I know you'd fight the Architect and Mr. Grace and the bird-things and the police and everybody until they were black and blue. And I know this is the one thing you *don't* want to face, and it's really scary and difficult, but—"

"But you want me to stop running." Violet finished Trista's sentence and cut it dead. "You want me to wait for the snow."

Trista hugged one of Violet's arms and buried her face in her jacket.

"I know you want to protect me," Trista said very quietly, "but you can't. Whatever you do, I only have this day. I want to make it matter. Please, please let me do some good with it. Let me *choose*."

Violet said nothing. Nothing was not a yes, but neither was it a no. Trista felt Violet's hand gently rest on the back of her head. Just for those few seconds their silence felt like a little fortress against the world.

"Pen," said Violet, in tones of affectionate irritation, "will you *please* stop doing that?"

Trista looked up in time to see Pen with her hands pressed against the window, sticking out her tongue at somebody down on the street.

"He started it!" Pen exclaimed defiantly. "It's rude to stare!"

"Pen, the Besiders are staring because they think I'm one of them!" Trista pointed out.

"But it wasn't one of the Besiders." Pen dropped back into

her chair and filled her mouth with crumpet. "It was the man who didn't eat his lunch."

"What?" A spider-tingle of alarm crept up Trista's spine.

"He was over there." Pen pointed to a nearby table. "And they brought him sausages, but he didn't eat them. He just went away."

"Violet," Trista whispered urgently, "that's where the young man was sitting—the one with the . . ."

The newspaper. Over on the abandoned table, draped over the neglected plate, was a copy of the *Ell Chronicle.* The trio exchanged glances.

"We need to get out of here *right now,*" hissed Violet. She rose from her chair and then froze, still half stooped. Looking down onto the street, Trista could see exactly what had caught her eye. Two policemen were hurrying across the road toward the entrance of the tearoom.

Violet pressed the heels of both hands against her temples and stared down onto the street. She was breathing quickly, in a way that made her nostrils flutter.

"Violet . . ." Pen's voice was a rising curl of panic.

"I'm thinking," Violet said through her teeth. Some resolution clicked into place behind her gaze, and she gave a short, sharp nod. "Follow me—quick!"

The three of them weaved hastily between the tables toward the back of the dining area, to the dark doors of the "conveniences."

"In here!" Violet shoved open the nearest door, and the girls bundled in after her.

Immediately Trista knew they were in the wrong place. The walls were a somber olive instead of powder-pink. It smelled strange, a little like cologne and men's hair cream . . .

"Violet, this is the wrong—"

"Shh!" Violet braced herself against the door. Her gaze fell on Trista and Pen, and she gave them a dark, wry smile. "Both of you—listen to me. When I say run, you *run*. You don't wait for me. You find somewhere to hide. Do you understand?"

"But—"

"Take care of each other." Violet turned to place her ear to the door, eyes closed as she listened. "And, Trista—good luck in the snow."

Outside came a soft tumult of steps, then a thunder of knocks at a door, but not the one to which Violet's ear was pressed. Trista guessed it must be the door to the ladies' convenience. *Of course it never occurred to them that we would come in* here.

"Miss Parish?" It was a male voice, polite, youthful, and slightly out of breath. "If you would be so kind as to come out, we can avoid a scene."

Violet's mouth twitched with the shadow of a grin, her hand curled around the door handle.

"Miss Parish?" A different male voice, deeper, gruffer, and a bit uncle-like. "At least send those children out. Then perhaps we can talk more calmly."

A long pause. A sigh. Then the sound of the ladies' convenience door being barged open and a clatter of boots on a tiled floor.

Violet's reaction was instant. She flung open the door and leaped through it, closely followed by Trista and Pen. The two policemen who had charged into the ladies' powder room turned in time to see Violet slamming the door behind them. She grabbed a chair from beside a neighboring table and wedged it under the door handle. The door jerked in its frame, and there was the sound of pounding fists and irate voices from the other side.

"Run!" she shouted.

Dozens of Besider eyes stared as Violet, Trista, and Pen sprinted back through the tearoom, knocking over chairs as they went. They all but tobogganed down the stairs, stumbling, slithering, and bruising knees. The bread girls gaped as they raced down the aisle to the front door.

The young man with the newspaper was loitering outside, but was apparently not expecting the three of them to barrel out onto the street. He tried to call out, and made a snatch for Pen, but Violet used her momentum to shoulder-charge him. Violet and the stranger hit the pavement in a sprawl.

"Keep running!" she shouted, elbowing her opponent in the head.

Trista grabbed Pen's hand and kept sprinting, taking turns at random. She did not know where she was or where she was going. All that mattered was that they kept moving. The riverside kept appearing solicitously on the right, like an overattentive nanny.

Her feet were silent, but Pen's steps echoed with painful clarity. How obvious they were! *Tell me, have you seen two girls running?* They needed to hide.

"There!" she hissed, and pulled Pen over to one of the jetties, beside which a rowboat bobbed. She clambered down into the boat and helped Pen in after her. Then, pulling at the underside of the jetty with all her might, she managed to drag the boat under it, so that they were hidden from casual view. There was a sodden blanket in the belly of the boat, which she pulled over them for good measure.

As they lay there gasping, trembling, listening, a familiar sound reached Trista's ears. It was a guttural, rebellious rumble, the sound of a not-too-distant motorcycle engine throbbing to life.

"It's Violet!" squeaked Pen in stifled excitement. "She got away! She got away!"

The motorcycle's tune rose into a crescendo, accompanied by the percussion of running steps and shouted demands. A roaring ribbon of sound . . . and then a long screech of distressed rubber, and a sustained, painful rattle of impacts. There was a *ting, tinkle, clatter* of settling fragments, followed by a gouging silence.

The hush held its own for seconds, then gave way to a growing murmur of voices, a bubbling swell of concern and curiosity, punctuated by urgent shouts.

Chapter 38

GREEN BOTTLES

TRISTA LAY IN THE BOTTOM OF THE BOAT WITH her arms tightly around Pen, feeling as if all her bones had been turned to jelly. She could hear Pen making little hiccupy noises that sounded like sobs.

"Violet . . ." whispered Pen. "She crashed—she *died*."

"No, she didn't," Trista said very quickly. She clenched her eyes tight, but that did nothing to shut out the deluge of imagined images. A body flopped over the bonnet of a car, or perhaps a broken windscreen with reddened shards . . . Just for an instant she hated Pen for saying aloud everything she was trying not to think.

But Pen was too little and miserable for her to hate. Instead Trista tried to take her few rags of hope and wrap them around the smaller girl.

"Violet isn't dead," she told Pen and herself. "She had a plan, and her plan wouldn't involve being dead."

Silence. Snuffle, snuffle.

"What was her plan?" asked Pen, her tone of misery tempered by a touch of reluctant hope.

Trista stared into the darkness of the blanket, desperately trying to make sense of Violet's last words.

Good luck with the snow.

"She *decided* to let them catch her." Trista blinked at the revelation, and clung to it. "She *let* it happen, so we could get away, and so they would put her in a police cell. That way she stays still . . . and the snow comes. Now hush, Pen, please hush! Or they'll find us!"

For what felt like an age, there were sounds of running steps on the street and conversations in urgent tones. Occasional words and phrases were audible.

". . . ambulance . . ."

". . . two girls come by this way?"

At one point she actually heard several sets of feet walk out onto the jetty directly above them. Trista tensed, and even Pen's snuffles became more muted.

"Please take a moment to think, madam." It was the voice of the younger policeman, the one who had asked Violet to surrender. "The two little girls—where did they go after that?"

He sounded harassed and concerned. In an odd, distant way Trista felt sorry for him. She wondered if he had a nice face, and a wife who would be sympathetic when he got home after a hard day. At the same time she wondered what would happen if he found her, and whether she would have to bite him in order to get away.

There was a pause, and then the response came in a voice that sounded like the combined sobs of children in a distant cavern.

"I remember quite clearly. They carried on running down the street—that way. Then they got into a car. A yellow car." It was unmistakably the drowned-looking Besider woman from the tearoom.

"I saw them too," insisted an unfamiliar voice, which rasped like crab shells chafing against each other. "Definitely a yellow car. It drove away."

"Yes," agreed a hiss like sand seeping through an hourglass. "A yellow car. The girls are gone. Take your snooping elsewhere."

Trista could hear the faint scratching of pencil on paper. She wondered how many of the Besiders' actual words the policeman could hear with his conscious mind, or whether he was jotting down ordinary-sounding statements.

The Besiders were lying, to send the police off on the wrong trail. Why? They believed Trista was one of them, so perhaps they were protecting their own. Or maybe they did not want police paying attention to the Old Docks while it was full of Besiders.

To Trista's enormous relief, the young policeman seemed to heed the statements given by the witnesses, and his footsteps creaked off the jetty again. For a while she made out his voice asking the same questions of passersby, then she heard him no more.

There were still many sounds of hubbub and inquisitive exchanges in the road above, however. Perhaps the Besiders would not turn them in, but there were plenty of ordinary people on the street, who would doubtless soon connect the policeman's questions about two young girls with the missing Crescent daughters in the newspapers.

"We have to stay here for now." Trista racked her brain, trying to form a plan. "We'll wait for the snow. It'll be easier to walk around without people spotting us when there's snow."

"What if it *doesn't* snow?" demanded Pen, sounding only slightly mollified.

"It will."

It has to snow. If it doesn't, then it means that Violet isn't sitting still in a cell, or even a hospital. It means that she's on the move still . . . or that she's dead.

The next few hours were the longest that Trista could remember. They were also painful in a very real sense, because Pen fidgeted hopelessly, sighing every minute or so and shifting position in ways that always involved elbowing Trista.

There were whispered complaints too. Pen was bored. She was hungry. It was damp, and the blanket smelled funny. Trista was taking up all the room.

Trista told Pen to sing "One Hundred Green Bottles" in her head. Pen settled for whispering it huskily to herself, and soon Trista regretted making the suggestion. There was something terrible about the countdown. The last hours of her life were falling away from her and smashing silently like so many imaginary bottles, and she was stuck in a musty boat watching it happen. She tried not to think about the fact that her not-sister was full of unspent years, like pips in a robust little apple.

After a long while, however, she noticed a change in the atmosphere. The bobbing of the boat altered its rhythm a little, betraying a shift in the direction of the wind. The blanket flipped and flapped. Pen was now complaining of being *cold*. At last Trista dared to tug aside the blanket and peer out.

The September sky had curdled and was now an intimidating yellow-gray, its tobacco-stain hues reflected in the shivering surface of the river. Stray gusts of wind tore in from the estuary with a shark-bite fierceness and a chill that made her eyes stream. The riverside road was now all but empty of pedestrians.

"Pen," she breathed, "it's cold. It's *cold*. Violet did it! She did it, Pen!"

Violet's alive! She could not voice the words, though, without admitting to Pen that she had been in doubt.

"Look!" Trista drew back the blanket a little, and Pen blinked mulishly in the meager daylight. "There's nobody on the street. We can probably sit up a bit now." She expected Pen to be as pleased as she was, and was a little surprised when she directed a surly glare at the lowering sky. "The snow's coming. It'll be here soon, Pen, I promise. We just need to wait."

Pen sniffed hard and half sat up, disarranging the blanket.

"No!" she hissed. "I don't want to! I don't like these docks! I don't want us to stay here anymore!"

"Pen, you're being . . ." Trista let out a breath and started again. "You know I *have* to be here at midnight, so I can follow the Architect."

"No, you don't!" Stars of reflected light gleamed in Pen's eyes, her shadowed face creased with earnestness. "We could sail away, in this boat! We could go to France!"

"What?" Trista could barely keep her voice to a whisper. "Pen, of *course* we can't. And what would happen to Triss?"

"I don't care!" And Pen, who had faced down moving cars and yelled at the Architect, was shaking, face crumpled, tears spilling out of her eyes. "I don't want you to go! And . . . and I don't want *her* to come back!"

"Pen!" Trista exclaimed, appalled. "You don't mean that!"

There was a growled, snuffled response that might have been "Yes, I do."

To be loved, to be *preferred* . . . The very thought gave Trista a painful little stab of joy. A moment later, however, she thought of the jagged rips that crisscrossed the Crescent family and felt only sadness.

“But she’s your sister, Pen! I’m not. I’m just a bundle of sticks that looks like her.”

Pen did not answer straightaway but wriggled herself closer, so that her damp face was buried in Trista’s shoulder.

“Do you remember what happened after . . . after I dug up the frog and found out it had moved?” Pen’s voice was hesitant and defiant, but with a touch of slyness.

It took a second or two for Trista to adjust to the change of subject and comb through Triss’s memories.

“Yes . . . yes, I do.” Trista stroked Pen’s head. “You were so upset you couldn’t cry, you just went around *staring* at everything. You couldn’t sleep, even. And so . . . one night I remember sitting on your bed and telling you that the frog was in frog heaven, where there were no cats, and where all the lily pads were lovely and soft. And I said that the frog wanted you to know that it was happy, and that it didn’t blame you for anything because you were only trying to help.”

“And you hugged me when I cried,” mumbled Pen. “And after that I went to sleep. Didn’t I?”

“Yes, Pen.” Trista sighed, and let go of the stolen moment. “But *that wasn’t me.* That was Triss.”

“But . . .” Pen pulled away and looked into Trista’s face, and her expression was a startling combination of determination, desperation, and pleading. “But what if it *was* you? Maybe that’s why you remember it so well? Because perhaps”—she gabbled on with increasing speed, as if afraid of interruption—“perhaps we were wrong all the time, and you weren’t just made out of sticks a week ago, perhaps there were *always* two Trisses, a good one and a bad one, and you’ve always been the good one, and I only sent away the bad one . . .”

Oh, Pen.

With a surge of pity and exasperation, Trista started to understand the fantasy Pen had cobbled together in her head. So this was why Pen had slipped into calling Trista "Triss" repeatedly. This was why Pen had scowled whenever anybody talked about rescuing her real sister, and why she had tried to bargain with the Architect for the life of Trista instead. All this while Pen had been building a make-believe version of reality where she hadn't *really* betrayed her sister to a terrible fate, just sent away a *bad* version of her . . .

"*Pen*," groaned Trista, tenderness battling against frustration, "that doesn't make *any sense*." She gave Pen another squeeze. "Life isn't that simple. *People* aren't that simple. You can't cut them into slices like a cake, then throw away the bits you don't like. The Triss who was kind about the frog and the Triss who spoiled your birthday—they're *the same person*."

"But she *hates* me!" roared Pen. "And if she comes back, she'll tell Mommy and Daddy what I did, and . . . they'll send me away to prison or an orphanage or school . . ."

And that was it, of course. If Triss returned, reality would come knocking. Pen would no longer be able to pretend to herself or to her parents that she had not been responsible for her sister's kidnapping. She would have to face up to what she had done.

"Triss doesn't hate you." Trista could almost feel the strands of Pen's affection, and knew that they had been flung out to her in desperation, like a swift grab made by a falling climber. Now, with a sense of sadness, she realized that she needed to detach them and reattach them to Pen's real sister, where they belonged. "When I talked to her on the telephone, she was shouting at me—asking what *I* had done to *you*. She wasn't angry with you. She was *worried* about you."

Pen had no answer. Instead she gave in to a torrent of ragged, tormented sobs.

"I don't want to go to prison!" she wailed at last. "I want my mommy!"

"I know," said Trista, who had no mommy. "I know."

She was still rocking Pen in her arms a few minutes later when the first tiny flakes of snow began to float down from the sky.

The boat-bound fugitives sneaked occasional peeks out from under their blanket as the sky grew dimmer. At first the snowflakes were tiny like ash flecks, dying as soon as they touched the ground and leaving freckles of damp. A few people opened their windows for a while to laugh and wonder at the unseasonal sprinkling. The temperature kept dropping, however, and soon the windows were closing again.

The wind stilled and the flakes fattened. Before long the air was a ballet of chill tufts, each the size of a farthing. The first settled on the earth and melted, falling in on themselves. Their successors left a skin of fine, gray slush. But there were more and more, falling faster than they could melt, and soon the whole scene had a downy pallor. Both girls in the boat were shivering now, and Trista was glad of the blanket.

"I haven't had my tea," Pen muttered mournfully as supper smells seeped from dozens of houses.

"We don't have any money," Trista reminded her.

"There's snow! We could go carol singing, and people might give us food if we look sad." Without further ado, Pen began pulling at the underside of the jetty, so that the boat began to swing out from beneath it.

"Wait!"

"You said we could get out of the boat when it snowed!" protested Pen.

"All right, but be careful getting out, and stay close to me!" Trista helped Pen climb up onto the jetty, the smaller girl tottering slightly with stiffness. Trista wrapped the blanket around the pair of them, so that it shrouded their heads and figures like a cloak. "Let's keep this over us, so people don't recognize us."

At the back of the tearoom, a kindly under-cook passed some leftover currant scones to the girls through the kitchen door, telling them that she shouldn't really, but it was a shame for them to go to waste. The girls stood in an alley and munched the scones, watching the whirl of white around them. The few scant gas lamps on the streets were now surging into solemn, flickering life, each illuminating a halo of flurrying flakes.

"I'm *cold.*" Pen hiccuped down the last mouthful of her scone, then peered into the darkness. "I bet *they* would let us sit by their fire."

Following the direction of Pen's pointing finger, Trista made out a reddish gleam in the shadow of an abandoned auction house. Against the wall she could just see a stumpy black crate that had been pressed into service as a brazier. Around it stood three figures, hunched against the cold.

"All right," she whispered back. "But let's creep over, in case they're Besiders."

"Besiders like you, don't they?" Pen frowned.

"They won't when they hear I'm against the Architect," Trista muttered. "And they'll find *that* out as soon as they talk to the Architect's people. They might know already."

Trista and Pen padded down the powdered road, keeping to the darkest parts of the street and avoiding the pools of gaslight.

Finally they found a shadowed doorway from which they could watch the firelit group with more ease.

The murmur of voices from beside the brazier was subdued but sounded human. There was no eerie overlay, no sinister under-voice. The figures seemed to be dressed in ordinary jackets and coats, furthermore, not the strange feather-garments the Besiders in the tearoom had worn.

"They seem—" Trista began.

"Shh!" hissed Pen furiously.

Trista shushed, and a voice from the group at the brazier floated over to her.

"They were definitely here. That much is certain."

The speaker had his collar turned up and a scarf wrapped protectively around his chin, hiding most of his face. Nonetheless, there was no mistaking the voice of Mr. Grace.

Chapter 39

A SHEEP IN WOLF'S CLOTHING

"THE GIRLS WERE IN THE TEAROOM WITH MISS Parish," Mr. Grace continued. "We are not likely to get a statement from *her* anytime soon, of course." He sighed. "I still think she might have been an innocent dupe in all of this. I did try to reason with her when we first met, but she wouldn't listen."

Trista's heart gave a flip-flop of anxiety. What did he mean, Violet would not be giving a statement anytime soon? *Please let him mean that she's being stubborn, or just unconscious! Don't let her be dead!* She had been so sure that the snow meant Violet was alive. Now she felt the chill of doubt.

"But everybody says the children left again," remarked a girl by the fire, rubbing her hands frenetically over the dull embers of the brazier. "In a yellow car." With a shock Trista realized that it was Dot from the cottage. Dot of the eggshells.

"Yes. Yes, they do." Mr. Grace pensively pushed more lengths of wood into the fire. "Over and over again. The exact same story. The firelight made his face look narrower and more haunted, a collage of sharp edges. "There is something odd about this place. Have you noticed that?"

"Yes. It's covered in snow. In September." The third figure at the brazier was a middle-aged man Trista had never seen before. He had shaky hands, thick eyebrows, and a mustache that made him look like a colonel. "Is that what you mean?"

"No," answered Mr. Grace, "though I dare say the snow is *their* doing as well. No, the snow seems to be falling all over Ellchester. But here, *right here*, there is a feeling . . ." He trailed off.

"People here make my thumbs prick," muttered Dot.

"Well put, Dot." The tailor gave her a smile softened by avuncular affection. "We are all feeling uneasy for a reason. There are Besiders in the Old Docks, I would lay money on it—and we have probably spoken to some in the last hour."

"Well, if you think the story of the yellow car is bunkum, then what—" The mustached man came to a halt abruptly, seeing Mr. Grace raise one hand in warning.

"Charles," the tailor said evenly, "it would seem we have guests."

Trista stiffened, ready to grab Pen's hand and run. However, she soon realized that Mr. Grace's gaze was not trained their way. Instead he was peering down the street toward two figures who were hobbling with a stilted but relentless gait toward the light of the fire.

Both individuals wore the strange gray-brown feather-coats, and peeping out beneath them Trista glimpsed a plum-colored hem and brown ribbon garters. It was the Besider couple they had met on the jetty.

"May we join you?" asked the woman, as she advanced into the halo of the brazier. "Your fire has such a *gentle* light." Her wet-looking gaze flickered disapprovingly toward the yellow aura of the gas lamps.

There was the briefest hesitation and exchange of glances among the huddled threesome before Mr. Grace hurried forward.

"Of course—let me find you something to sit on." He hastened around a corner and returned with a pair of crates, which he set down as seats for the newly arrived "guests." Trista was uncomfortably reminded of the way he had played gracious host to her during her visit to his shop.

There was a growing knot of tension in Trista's stomach. It was like watching a perilous scene in a play and desperately wanting to call out a warning. At this moment, though, she was not sure whom she wanted to warn.

Charles, the colonel-like man, passed a flask of brandy to everyone around the fire except Dot (who seemed a little disappointed). Everybody remarked on how peculiar the weather was.

"So what brings you out into the snow?" Mr. Grace asked the couple after a pause.

"We have just arrived in this town," answered the Besider man serenely. "We are waiting to be shown to our new home. The snow does not trouble us."

"Really?" Mr. Grace's smile was perfectly charming. "Then welcome to Ellchester! Are you and your wife traveling alone?"

"No," answered the woman in the plum dress. "We have . . . many . . ." She trailed off, and locked gaze with her companion for several seconds in silent communion. "Friends," she hazarded at last. "Many . . . friends."

At this revelation, Dot shot her human companions an alarmed glance. Charles paused in refastening the lid of his flask.

"Well, at least you are better dressed for the weather than we are, with those warm-looking coats," remarked Mr. Grace.

The Besiders' oyster-like eyes glistened uneasily in the firelight.

"You . . . noticed them?" inquired the Besider man, in a tone that suggested that this was surprising and unwelcome news. "Yes. They are useful to us." He leaned forward, and there was a new intensity and suspicion in his wet gaze. "And what brings the three of *you* out into this bitter night *without* such warm coats?"

Mr. Grace hesitated only briefly, as if choosing a card at whist.

"We are looking for a couple of children. Two little girls—"

"They got into a yellow car," declared the Besider woman promptly, without waiting for him to finish.

"And it drove away," finished her consort.

There was a long, uncomfortable pause.

"You cannot even see your city now, can you?" said the Besider man at last. It was true. The whirl of fat, feathery flakes hid anything more than twenty yards away. He pushed a stick into the fire, stirring the embers so that they cracked and sent sparks in a panicky dance. "The snow has a thousand, thousand fingers. Imagine them pulling apart your city, piece by tiny piece. Imagine that this little street is all that is left. Adrift. In darkness." He smiled, as though paying somebody a compliment.

"In the old days folk would have told stories," remarked his companion. "By the fire. To hold back the dark. But the dark always finds its way *into* the stories, does it not? The stories worth hearing, at least. The true lies."

"Everybody has dragged a tale to this fire," continued her male friend. "I can hear them whispering."

Charles cleared his throat, perhaps in an attempt to relieve the tension. "I've never been good at storytelling—not even when it comes to telling jokes at my club."

"Every person can recount their *own* story, even if they can tell no other," said the male Besider. His clammy gaze slithered to Dot's face. "What is *your* story, little fox cub?"

Dot swallowed nervously. Her laugh burst out forced and breathless.

"Me? Oh, you don't want to hear about me!"

"But I do," insisted the man in garters. "I want your story. *Give it to me.*"

With the last words, his expression changed to one of urgency and hunger. His eagerness tore through his false human facade like a fang through silk. In that instant, the tension of the scene snapped, like an overwrought violin string.

Eyes wide with panic, Dot recoiled a step from the gartered stranger, and Charles pushed forward, taking up a hostile stance in front of her. Both Besiders leaped uncannily to their feet, like two string puppets pulled up from a slump.

At the same time there was a faint silken *shunk*, like a sword being pulled from its sheath. It was not a sword that Mr. Grace had drawn from beneath his coat, however, but a long, wicked pair of blackened scissors. Trista's stomach tingled as she recognized them from the dressmakers'.

At the sight of the scissors, both Besiders sprang backward a step, making yowling noises like cats. The man flung out one hand as if sowing seeds, and the snowflakes around him started to fizz and frenzy with new purpose, diving for the faces of the humans. His female companion gave a soundless wail that made Trista's eardrums tingle and throb. Charles clutched at his ears and fell to his knees.

One arm shielding his eyes, Mr. Grace lunged forward, aiming the iron points at the face of the Besider man. The latter ducked and retreated, only to find the wall against his back. The tailor lunged forward once again, this time halting so that the points of the scissors were just resting on the man's chest. His captive gave a shriek like tortured chalk and froze against the wall, quivering.

"Tell that she-creature to stop singing!" demanded Mr. Grace. "Now!"

There was a short pause, and then the Besider woman closed her mouth and the terrible silent noise ended. She stood trembling like a flag in a breeze, her eyes fixed on the black metal of the scissors. Snow settled on her cheeks without melting.

Charles remained on his knees, dabbing at his ear with a handkerchief.

"It's your turn to tell tales, I think," continued Mr. Grace, regarding his prisoner without sympathy. "To begin with, how many of your friends are in the docks area tonight?"

The man opened his mouth, but only terrified gargling noises emerged.

"Twoscore," answered his female companion.

"And what purpose do these coats serve?" asked the tailor.

"We were all ordered to wear them." The female Besider seemed to be hypnotized by the scissors. "They baffle the eye and mind. They let the wearer pass without remark."

"And this home to which you are to be taken? Where is it?"

"We do not know."

A small, swift jab of the scissors poked two holes in her consort's coat as easily as needles through cobweb. The man gave a howl of pain and terror.

"We do not know!" protested the Besider woman again, twisting her fingers so fiercely it seemed they might snap. "They told us we had to wait until now because . . . because the haven was not ready. But that is all we know! That is all!"

Mr. Grace considered for a moment, then gave a small sigh.

"I believe you," he said simply. Then, with all his strength, he drove the scissors into the Besider man's chest.

Concealed in her doorway, Trista gasped, feeling as if all the air had been sucked out of her. Next to her, Pen gave a muffled yelp, then stood with both hands over her own mouth as if she could still hold the sound in.

There was no blood. The Besider man split like a cloud before the moon, and light spilled out, wet light that screamed as it came. His mouth opened wide, and ghostly ribbons spiraled out into the air, chittering forgotten tales. As they pulled away from him and vanished, he seemed to unravel, twitching. Soon there was nothing left but a gray-brown coat slumping to the cobbles.

The female Besider gave another of her soundless shrieks and flung herself wildly upon Charles. Her momentum bowled him over onto the brazier, where his coat caught fire and he flailed helplessly under her weight. Then Mr. Grace thrust the scissors into her back. There was a leaping of silver flame, one last inaudible cry that seemed to shake the frame of the world, and she too was gone. Charles tumbled off the brazier, and Dot helped bat out the flames in his clothes.

Trista squeezed Pen's shoulder. The smaller girl still had her mouth covered and was panting with shock.

Mr. Grace paused and looked up, staring out in the direction of the hidden girls. Perhaps he had heard Pen's yelp.

We could run. But then he would definitely *hear us. And he could follow our tracks.*

I don't want to fight you, Mr. Grace, but if I have to, I will. I will. I won't let you hurt Pen.

The tailor frowned a little, then turned his back on the shadows and hurried to Charles's side. He winced as he examined the older man's injuries.

"Charles, old chap, you're going to need a doctor," he said gently. "Dot—will you go with him? I don't think the poor fellow can stand by himself."

“What about you?” asked Dot, her face alight with concern.

Mr. Grace stooped and picked up one of the Besiders’ coats. It trembled and fluttered in his hand like a captive bird.

“Forty Besiders have just arrived in Ellchester,” he said grimly, “and it’s clear that they are setting up a stronghold in this city. I have to find out where it is, Dot. If we don’t locate it and destroy it, who knows how many more of the creatures will turn up here next week, or the week after?”

“What are you planning to do?” Dot helped Charles to his feet. Her face was a picture of anxiety, admiration, and trust. Just for a fleeting moment, Trista’s mind seesawed, and she could almost see Mr. Grace and the world as Dot saw them. The next instant Trista was back to her own perspective with a thud.

Mr. Grace slowly slipped on the coat. It brindled a couple of times, then settled. Occasionally it spasmed a little, its color turning patchy like scuffed velvet.

“You heard the creature, Dot. Some guides will be here soon, to lead forty newcomers to the Besider stronghold. Let’s hope they do not know the new arrivals by sight . . . and will simply be looking out for strangers in eye-baffling magical coats.”

Chapter 40

MIDNIGHT RIDE

FROM THE SHADOWED DOORWAY, TRISTA AND Pen watched as Dot helped Charles limp away. Mr. Grace carefully smothered the brazier and then stalked away into the night in his twilight-colored coat, his footprints neat and straight like a dotted line on a dress pattern.

"I feel sick," said Pen in a tiny voice. "I think I might *be* sick."

Trista found her hands were pressed to her own chest, perhaps in search of scissor holes.

"He just killed them." Her own voice sounded breathy and lost. "He didn't have to kill them."

"I didn't *like* them." Pen's face made crumple-shapes and her eyes were shiny. "But . . . they were scared . . ."

". . . and they didn't hurt anyone," finished Trista. "Not until everybody attacked them." Her mind was still playing the scene over and over. "Perhaps that old man *did* want to hurt Dot—Mr. Grace seemed to think so. But sometimes Mr. Grace is wrong. He was wrong about me."

"What do we *do*?" whimpered Pen.

Trista drew in a breath, then found she had no words to fill with it. What *could* they do?

If she did nothing to stop Mr. Grace, what would happen? If he succeeded in infiltrating the Besiders and found his way to their haven, he would stop at nothing to destroy the stronghold and everyone in it. If she warned the Besiders about him, though, she would almost certainly be signing his death warrant. And how could she contact the Besiders without giving herself away to the Architect?

"I don't know, Pen," she answered faintly. "I don't know."

Trista looked at her not-sister, at her small, round, crumpled face, the dusting of snow in her hair, her stocky legs trembling with the cold. Everything became a lot simpler.

Maybe later I'll end up choosing sides in the big fight, but saving people comes first. I have to free Sebastian's soul and let it escape from the snows. And I have to save my other self.

I have to save Triss.

For Triss's own sake, and for Piers's and Celeste's sake. For Violet's sake, so she doesn't get sent to prison for murder. For Pen's sake too, or she'll grow up knowing she caused her own sister's death. And for my sake, so that—whatever happens—my life will have mattered.

She closed her eyes and focused on the thought of Triss's fragile voice on the telephone. Triss, with her hints about the frog, her terror of being buried alive.

Buried alive . . .

Trista opened her eyes and was dazzled by the excited whirling of the snow.

"Pen—I know where the ride is heading! I know where the haven is, where the Architect is taking Triss!"

"What?" Pen's curiosity burned through her misery. "Where?"

"It's not the Underbelly. You heard the Besider lady—it's somewhere new, people have only just started moving in. It's the *new railway station*. Of course it is—we've been so *stupid*! And that's where the Architect is planning to bury Triss alive too.

"It's shaped like a pyramid, Pen. Pyramids are *tombs*. And tomorrow morning, your father will be in charge of the Capping Ceremony, lowering the point onto the pyramid *and sealing Triss in*." Trista's blood throbbed with certainty. The Architect would not have been able to resist the twisted elegance and irony of that solution.

In Pen's dark, horrified eyes, Trista finally saw realization dawn. At long last, Triss was no longer the threat, the twist of conflict in Pen's gut. Triss was the frog, hearing the deluge of earth on the lid of her box-coffin.

"Pen," Trista said quickly, "I need you to do something for me. It's difficult but really important. You have to go home. You have to find your father and tell him that the Architect is taking Triss to the station. If he doesn't hear anything of her or me by tomorrow morning . . . then I've failed, and he needs to find a way to stop the ceremony. He could tell everyone . . . that the station caught fire, or there's a dog trapped inside—anything to stop them from lowering the cap."

"But he never listens to me!" protested Pen.

"He will this time!" insisted Trista. "Everybody else will try to calm you down, and take you to doctors, and give you Ovaltine and tell you to have a nice night's sleep. But you *must* talk to your father, whatever happens."

Pen cast an open-mouthed glance over her shoulder at the snow-draped streets. She looked painfully small, and Trista felt a pang at sending her away through the city by herself at night. But the Old Docks were becoming more dangerous by the moment.

"You could come with me!" Pen exclaimed. "If we know

where the Architect is taking Triss, you don't need to chase them after all—"

"Yes, I do," Trista interrupted gently. "You saw how hard it was to get into the Underbelly! Once the Architect hides Triss in a secret part of the station, how would anybody ever find her? I have to try to rescue her *before* he can do that."

Trista pulled off her blanket and wrapped it around Pen's head and shoulders, making her look like a small Nativity-play figure.

"If you get lost or scared, find a policeman, or tell somebody to hand you in for the reward," Trista advised. "I didn't want to send you home before, in case Mr. Grace hurt you—but right now he isn't at your house. He's *here*."

"I'm not scared," said Pen with shaky ferocity, under her blanket robe. "I'm *never* scared."

"I know," said Trista. Their hug was quick, cold, and damp. "Go on, then! Quickly!"

Off ran the short blanket shape, like a robust little ghost, feet slithering on the fresh snow.

Good-bye, Pen.

Trista was alone. She felt cold and strangely light, as if Pen's presence had been a warming but heavy overcoat. She stepped out of her borrowed shoes without even thinking about it, and left them lying pigeon-toed in the alley.

The snow burned her soles with its cold, and she was alive, alive, feeling every second. She opened her mouth and tasted the flakes, feeling her tongue tickle and her teeth ache.

Now there's nobody to judge me, to tell me about myself. Nobody to impress, nobody to disappoint. Now is the time I find out who I am.

She searched the brazier for the Besider lady's coat, just in case there was still enough of it for her to wear as a disguise. There was nothing left, however, except some charred shreds and a smell of burned feathers.

She scaled the front of a boardinghouse, leaping up from sill to sill, and found a skulking point between the chimney stacks. The chimneys were hot with smoke, taking the edge off the chill, and she could watch the street without being silhouetted against the sky. There she settled to wait, crouched like a slender-limbed gargoyle, her damp hair feathered with falling snow.

Now and then, Besiders would drift down this street or that in ones or twos. None of them seemed to notice her. Their prints in the snow were misshapen, some leaving double grooves like tracks left by deer, or score marks from tails dragged across the snow's crust.

The human inhabitants withdrew, as if they sensed the strangers. Sound gradually died in the riverside public houses. No clatter of hoofs or stutter of engines interrupted the settling silence. The snow accepted its dominion.

Every time Trista blinked, there seemed to be more Besiders clustered on the street, mutely waiting in the cloud-colored coats. Soon they were huddled along every jetty, the base of every wall, in every doorway. A few lighted easily on nearby rooftops, folding wings away like umbrellas or preening them with toothed beaks.

When midnight approached, Trista could *feel* it. The snow whirled with its breath. The chill intensified as its shadow stretched long over the city. All over the Old Docks the Besiders raised their heads to stare into the darkness and gave a long, drawn-out hiss of excitement.

Elsewhere in the city, church bells released a muted jumble

of chimes. Trista barely noticed them. Her gaze was upon the jet-black tram that had suddenly, impossibly, surged into view, gliding down the rail-less road.

As it drew level with the jetties, it halted in a heartbeat without needing to slow. The twin trailer cars behind it came to the same unnatural stop without shunting each other.

When they were not moving, they looked eerily ordinary. Both tram car and trailer cars had corkscrew steps at front and back. Through the windows of the trailer cars, Trista could make out the usual wood trim and advertisements for hand soap. As with commonplace trams, they had open cabs at both front and back, so they could be driven from either end, and soulful, round headlights.

No oilskin-clad driver stood braving the bitter wind, however. There was nobody manning the tram's controls at all.

Half of the Besiders poured onto the trailer cars, finding seats inside the lower saloons or scaling the spiral steps to the open-air "balcony" seating on the upper level. Others gathered around the doors, twitching with eagerness.

The doors of the tram car itself did not open, nor did anyone make a bid to board it. Just for the fleetest moment, Trista saw the Architect at one of the lower windows, waving a gloved hand with gracious regality. Beside him was a shorter figure, face pale under her hat . . .

Ting, ting. The tram sounded its bell, a crystal note eerie in its mundanity.

Without warning, the tram was in motion once more, snaking away through the docklands with dizzying speed. The Besiders who had not boarded the trailer cars surged after it, like a tide of gray-brown floodwater, bobbing and leaping. From all the surrounding rooftops figures took to the air, some spreading wings like ribbon-cloaks or skeleton leaves, others springing light as fleas from roof to roof.

Taking a deep breath, Trista sprang from her hiding place and joined them.

The first leap was nearly her last. She had not appreciated how treacherous the snow would make the roof slopes. The white layer slithered away under her weight, so that she lost her footing and nearly plunged to the cobbles below. A timely snatch at a chimney steadied her, though, and she continued, landing on all fours each time so that her thorn claws could sink into thatch or the gaps between tiles.

Ahead, the tram took a sharp right away from the river and directly toward a row of houses. Without effort, it ran up the front of the nearest house, drawing the trailer cars after it, then up onto the roof, leaving two frayed grooves in the snow. There the tram and cars changed course again, speeding away along the row of roofs, tilted sideways by the tiled slope. A gray, half-seen mass of figures followed them, like a fog of giant gnats.

Trista gave chase, trusting to instinct, toe, and claw. She felt her hair stream with each leap, the wind chilling her clenched teeth. Her heart beat hard but did not seem to matter, like a loose oddment rattling in a forgotten drawer.

She barely saw the other members of the ride, but they were all around her. Their wings beat in her ears. Her feet scuffed their forked and twisted tracks across the rooftops. Occasionally she caught a flash of lichen-colored eyes, or teeth bared in a grin of fellowship. She tasted snowflakes and realized that her mouth was open, that she was laughing.

All at once it felt like a game. The tram weaved this way, that way, and she matched it, increasing her speed. She was a kitten chasing a twisting piece of string. She focused all her energy and strength, and pounced.

Trista leaped for the stepped boarding platform at the back of the rear trailer car. She judged the leap well and knew that she would land safely. Her knees reflexively bent, ready to soften the impact, and her arm stretched out to grab the pole. Before her feet could touch down, however, the whole trailer car changed before her eyes.

The engine thrum melted into a clatter of hoofs and the rattle of carriage wheels. Instead of landing feet first on a metal platform, Trista struck what felt like a slick wooden wall, jolting her jaw and knocking the breath out of her. She scrabbled for purchase, her claws leaving lean gouges in the black-painted wood, then lost her grip and fell.

She hit the sloping house roof and rolled down it in a froth of snow, before tumbling off the edge.

Only a last-minute snatch at the guttering with one hand stopped her from plummeting to the street below.

She hung there winded for a few seconds, her mouth dry. Below her she could see a few fragments of herself falling away, shocked loose by the impact and her exertion. Dead leaves, crumpled book pages, strands of hair . . . she did not have time to collect them.

With her long toes she scrabbled at the brickwork and with difficulty hauled herself up onto the roof once more.

Where was the trailer car turned black carriage? Where was its hissing, soaring entourage? Gone, swallowed by the blizzard. But on the roofs around her were tracks that even now the snow was trying to blot out. Fox paws, childlike bare feet, long loping prints . . . and among them the grooves from wheels and the crescent scoops of horses' hoofs.

Trista brushed the snow from her eyelashes and set off in pursuit once more.

She followed the tracks across the roofs of slum houses, then through the petite, well-groomed streets of the daintier shopping districts.

Now and then a tug in her flank that told her she had lost a twig, a trinket, a twist of paper.

There, ahead! Three black carriages raced over the roofs, amid a wider haze of flitting, leaping shapes.

Her legs shaking, Trista risked wider, wilder jumps as she fought to catch up. She sprang to the town-council roof, then to the tip of the war monument, and finally leaped for the back of the rearmost carriage once more.

This time her toes sought out the rear footboard, and she sank her claws into the woodwork of the carriage. She hung on even as the "carriage" changed shape again and again. One moment she was clinging to the spare tire on the back of a great black Daimler. The next she was hugging the tail of a huge black snake. At last her strange transport swelled back to trailer-car dimensions once more. She landed with a clang on its rear platform, grabbing the pole to steady herself.

Gasping for breath, Trista risked a glance through the glass of the nearby door, into the lower saloon of the trailer car.

She was confronted with a suspiciously innocent scene. Electric light poured from small round lamps in the ceiling. Above them, pink and green posters advertised SHRIKE'S REMOVAL SERVICES and ELLCHESTER, YOUR HOME AWAY FROM HOME! Every seat was full, the passengers well-dressed and silent, most staring down into their laps or across at each other with mute serenity. All wore gray-brown coats, gray-brown shawls, gray-brown hats. Some were reading, but the lettering on their books and newspapers swarmed and seethed. Trista could make out the drowned-looking Besider woman from the tearoom discreetly powdering her nose with the aid of a compact.

At the far end of the carriage sat the Shrike, licking butter from his silver box.

She could not risk walking through the compartment. Perhaps the newly arrived refugees did not know who she was, but the Shrike would. The only way to get past without him seeing her was to climb to the upper level.

Just as Trista ducked back out of sight, she had an impression that one of the other figures had moved, that a head had raised, that a pale face had turned to look at her.

Legs shaking, she scaled the spiral steps while snow blew into her eyes and her clothes whipped in the wind. At the top, the racing air grew fiercer still. The roofless "balcony" was covered in rows of hard wooden benches, slick with meltwater. Clinging to these were a handful of smokily indistinct figures, who were thrown to and fro as the car veered and bucked. Sometimes they lost their grip and were flung clear, beating desperate wings in their attempts to catch up and recover their seat. None paid any attention to Trista.

Dropping to all fours to escape the worst of the snow-filled wind, Trista crawled forward past the benches, snow thickening in her hair and burning her ears. When she reached the front, she quickly clambered onto the safety rail, gripping it tightly with her fingers and toes, and prepared to leap to the next trailer car.

The gap was not large, but it opened and closed unpredictably as the cars tilted and swerved, and she hesitated, trying to judge the jump. At that moment, the trailer cars sheared through a thick column of chimney smoke, blinding her and making her splutter. For a short while she could only cling to the rail, eyes clenched, trying to stifle her coughs.

As she blinked the cobweb tears from her eyes, she heard a faint clatter of footfalls from the spiral steps behind her. She turned in panic, fearing that she might see the Shrike coming after her.

Somebody was indeed edging toward her along the roof, one arm shielding his face, his stolen coat flapping, his hair ruffled by the unforgiving wind.

It was Mr. Grace.

Chapter 41

FIND THE LADY

NO! THERE MUST BE FIFTY *BESIDERS HERE—WHY is he still chasing* me?

With the energy of desperation Trista leaped, and landed safely on the balcony of the next trailer car. She crawled to the front, not daring to look around, then darted for the spiral stairway back down to the lower level. She half slid, half jumped down, then leaped across the shifting gap to the rear platform of the leading tram itself.

She heard a rattle of steps, and then Mr. Grace came into view, slithering down the stairs she had just descended, blinking as snow buffeted his face, his teeth bared in a wince.

"Stop it!" she entreated him, under her breath, as he clattered his way down the steps. "Stop it, Mr. Grace! You'll spoil everything!"

There was a small grim pucker of humor at the corner of the tailor's mouth.

"That is rather the plan," he said, and launched himself toward the platform where Trista was standing.

An idea streaked through Trista's mind, even as he jumped. One well-timed kick or swipe with her claws, and he would be knocked back and fall. He would drop to the street, and lie there broken like Angelina. And nobody would know she had done it, just as they had never found out about the doll.

But she did not let the thought lead her limbs. Instead she froze, and the next moment Mr. Grace was landing with a clang on the metal platform beside her. All too fast, and everything changed. He was huge now, and she was the small, frail doll.

"Don't!" she squeaked and ducked his attempt to grapple her.

Shunk. The long black scissors were out and in his hands. He was the nightmare again now, the red-legged tailor from the nursery-book of horrors.

He lunged, and she dodged but too slowly. One point of his scissors pierced the cloth of her collar, pinning it to the wooden frame of the tram door. The other blade the tailor held poised, ready to cut horizontally toward her neck.

"Listen, please!" Once again she was the miserable child-monster begging, cobweb tears clouding her eyes. "I'm on your side! I'm trying to save Triss too! If you only listen, we can defeat the Architect together!"

Mr. Grace looked at her carefully for a second, his eyebrows rising slightly. He was out of breath from the chase, his fingers blue with cold. His hair was thick with snow, and trickles of meltwater ran down his face like tears.

"You creatures really will say anything to save your own twisted lives, won't you?" he murmured softly. His eyes were as dark as a thousand years of rain.

The death of his wife and the loss of his child. That was the crevasse of bottomless grief that stretched between them. With despair Trista realized that, for all her changeling agility, this was one abyss that she could not jump.

“Architect!” shouted the tailor at the top of his lungs. “I have your—”

Your daughter? Your servant?

Trista did not wait to discover the end of the sentence. With a strength born of panic she yanked herself to one side, rending her collar and leaving only a rag of dress fabric pinned by the scissors. Before the tailor could react, she leaped upward onto the smooth, closed roof of the tram car and scrabbled away on all fours, out of sight and reach.

Behind her, she heard the tram door thrown open, perhaps by the tailor, perhaps by somebody inside. She had no idea what was happening below her. All she knew was that, for the moment, it was no longer happening to her.

The air smelled damp. Looking over the side, Trista realized with a shock that the tram was skimming over the river, above its own blotchy and surprised-looking reflection. A flock of gulls split giddily before the tram and veered away in panic, the wings of one grazing Trista’s cheek.

Buffeted by the rush of air, Trista slithered forward along the roof, then clambered down the front of the tram, using the destination panel and trimmings for footholds. She landed softly next to the empty driver’s cab, then peered in through the window of the door, into the tram car’s lower saloon.

The tram car was more lavish than the trailer cars, the seats covered in what looked like green velvet, the windows set in frames of golden-brown wood, the lights hooded with little green shades. It was empty but for three figures.

At the far end of the carriage was Mr. Grace the tailor, with the open door behind him. He still wore his dripping feather-coat, though it was fluttering madly as if trying to tear itself away from him. His hair was plastered to his face, which bore a look of ice-cold determination. In his hands he held the great black pair of iron scissors.

Mere yards from the dripping tailor, standing as if to confront him, was a taller figure. Even from behind, Trista recognized the smooth, honey-blond hair, the debonairly cut coat, the Oxford bags, and the blinding, sunbeam aura of nonchalant panache. It was the Architect.

Far closer, seated with her back to the window, was a small girl of about thirteen with light brown hair. She wore a white hat and coat and sat with her shoulders nervously hunched, hands twisted in her lap.

With an effort of will, Trista retracted her thorn-claws and reached down her free hand to tap at the glass of the door. The girl started, turned to look around the compartment, then glanced across at the door and saw Trista's visage.

Trista stared in at her own face, pale and miserable amid its glossy, careful curls. As she watched, the small pink mouth drooped and wavered in shock and fear, with an expression that Trista had felt on her own lips so many times.

Triss. Triss, quailing at her own face staring in from the night.

Trista beckoned, and mouthed a desperate instruction.

Come closer!

Triss hesitated, casting a fearful glance toward the Architect.

Please! mouthed Trista. *Quickly!*

Triss began furtively sliding along the seat in Trista's direction, watching the Architect all the while. Meanwhile, Trista gently eased her door open. As she did so, the conversation inside the tram became audible to her.

"Do you know, sir," said the Architect, in his smooth, musical, slightly excited voice, "I have the funniest feeling that you do *not* have a ticket for this ride."

"I hoped *these* would satisfy any inspectors." The tailor raised the scissors, his tone steely rather than playful. "Do you wish to raise the matter with the Ministry of Transport?"

The Architect's laugh was like a saw blade drenched in honey, and halted just a little too suddenly.

"Oh, hardly. Well, I suppose I should be flattered that you are so determined to take your place in my carriage." His voice was dangerously pleasant. "Perhaps you would like to join us and relax—take a little refreshment?"

"I think it only polite to tell you," the tailor said through his teeth, "that your arts are wasted on me. I see you as you are, Architect."

"*Do* you?" Again there was an uncomfortable sense of something only just under control, a teacup cracking as it tried to contain a storm. "Do you, scissor-man?"

Both Mr. Grace and the Architect seemed too engrossed in their confrontation to glance down the carriage. Trista decided to risk a whisper.

"Triss—I've come to rescue you! Take off your hat, shoes, and coat! Quick! While they're distracted!"

Triss looked perplexed but hastened to obey, fingers fumbling with her buttons.

"So," continued the Architect, "you think you see the world clearly?"

"Compared to most of my fellows," the tailor answered drily, "I see it clear as crystal." He had moved his feet into something like a fencer's stance, but Trista could not tell if he was planning a sudden lunge or a hasty retreat.

"And that, I fear, is your problem," sighed the Architect. "For the world, my friend, is *not* clear. It is cloudy as a blood pudding. So if you see it crystal clear, there is something wrong with your eyes. Or perhaps you do not *use* your eyes. Perhaps you see with your scissors instead.

"Vile things, scissors. They are only made for one purpose. To divide, cleanly and falsely. Snip, snip. Everything on one side or the other. Nothing in the middle."

When the Architect said the word "scissors," the melodiousness of his voice broke, like a needle skipping over a scratch on a record.

"Better than hiding in a gray fog of lies," declared Mr. Grace sharply.

"But you are *wearing* our gray!" laughed the Architect. "You have made yourself a bird of *our* feather! And"—his voice took on a discordant edge, like a shift to a minor key—"*I think it suits you.*"

The Architect's gesture toward Mr. Grace was so casual, he might have been tossing away an invisible cigarette butt.

As he did so, however, the tailor gave a gasp as if he had been punched, and doubled over. The scissors fell from his fingers and clattered to the floor. The feathers of his coat fluttered madly, spirals ruffling and rippling through it like patterns in wind-flattened corn. He coughed, and each gasped breath filled the air with tiny dust-colored feathers.

His dark hair was receding, receding, until it left only a grayish scalp. The panicky motions of his head became convulsive, rapid, birdlike twitches. From his collar, sleeves, and the bottoms of his trousers poured ash and fine gray feathers. Then even his head was dwindling in size, shriveling to the size of a coconut, an apple, an egg . . .

"Triss!" hissed Trista, seeing her double gaping at the transformation. "Come out here! Quickly!" She held open the door, and Triss made a dart for it.

Triss gasped as she emerged into the mouth of the wind and took in the vista of the rushing river. Trista snatched the coat, shoes, and hat from her hand and quickly put them on.

"What do we do now?" asked Triss. "Where do we go?"

Trista's heart stuck in her throat as she stared around her for inspiration. Any moment now, the Architect would notice Triss was missing.

"I'll show you," she said abruptly. "Come—stand here with me." She pulled Triss away from the saloon door, toward the edge of the boarding platform.

"What is it?" Triss asked, eyes watering. "What am I looking for?" The tram was starting to veer toward the bank, the black edge of the New Docks closing in on their right.

"Sorry," murmured Trista, and as the tram skimmed over the shallows, she pushed her other self in the back with all her might. Unprepared, Triss pitched forward into space. The roar of the air swallowed her startled yelp and the soft splash that followed.

She can swim, Trista told herself as she leaned out, frantically scanning the dark water for signs of life. *I know she can. I remember learning to swim. And I dropped her in the shallows . . .*

Yes, there was a splash of foam, a small head, and a flailing of white limbs not far from the nearest jetty. Trista closed her eyes, as her mind flooded with relief.

A large hand was laid on Trista's shoulder and firmly pulled her back from the edge.

"Now what in the world were *you* planning?" asked the Architect, his voice sleek with playful malice. "Were you thinking of jumping in the river? In *your* state of health? Or were you perhaps hoping to call out to someone?"

Trista said nothing but kept her face lowered as he led her back into the saloon and guided her to sit down on the green velvet seat. She twisted her hands in her lap, the way Triss had done.

Something was flitting around the room, bumping against the lamps like a moth. It was a bird-thing, a large one, but getting smaller by the moment as it molted feathers and ash.

"Sciss-sciss-sciss-sciss!" it hissed and buzzed, as it battered itself against walls and glass. Its tiny pale face was mad with hate. On the far side of the tram carriage lay a heap of Mr. Grace's clothes. There was no other sign of the tailor.

"Look at you now, with your wet hair," the Architect commented, as he sat down beside Trista. "You could catch your death, Miss Crescent."

Trista's heart beat wildly inside her chest, like the Mr.-Grace-bird-thing battering the walls.

I couldn't jump out with Triss. I couldn't. He would have noticed she was missing and gone back to find her.

Besides, I have to get that watch.

Chapter 42

TIME RUNS OUT

THOUGH TRISTA TOOK PAINS TO KEEP HER HEAD bowed, now and then she darted a look through the window. Ellchester tore past below, ghostly in its white garb. Lit windows flew by, frail and tiny as fireflies.

Then the tram was dipping, descending. It touched down with a shudder, and Trista became aware of a new set of sounds. A steady, metallic scraping that rose in pitch each time they cornered, and a *ker-thud ker-thud* like a heartbeat. It was the sort of noise heard on a train, the muffled jumping of the railroad ties.

Seeing a level-crossing sign pass on one side, Trista realized that the tram must be running along the unfinished railway track that led to the new station. The view outside was replaced by scaffolding, raised boards, rickety fences. Trista felt the tram slow and stop.

"You really do not enjoy travel, do you, Miss Crescent?" The Architect reached over and patted the back of her hand. "Do not worry—that was your last journey." He took hold of her wrist so tightly that Trista could see her fingers turning pink. She did not resist as he pulled her to her feet and led her to the saloon door. As they stepped off the tram, she kept her gaze on the

Architect's wrist through the curtain of her hair. Under his crisp shirt cuff was a bulge of the right size to be a service watch.

The station loomed before her, its snow-covered slopes dimly luminous in the darkness. Its shape was blunted, the point missing from the top. It looked too mighty for its surrounding scaffolding. Staring up at it, Trista could not imagine why nobody had realized that a vast spectral tomb was being built in the middle of Ellchester.

The other Besiders were pouring out of the trailer cars, and dropping from the sky, striking powder clouds of snow from the ground. They wasted no time but seethed toward the station. Ignoring all the obvious arches and entrances, they scrabbled, leaped, and soared their way up the sloping sides of the pyramid.

The Architect led Trista to the base of the pyramid at a stately stride, and as they reached it, a swarm of gray bird-things frothed in ahead of them and clustered to form a few rough, flickering steps made of shifting, living forms. With utter unconcern the Architect began to climb these, forcing Trista to do the same. She could feel the bird-steps squirming and squealing under her weight. As each step was left behind it dissolved with a flutter, the bird-things flitting up to provide the next step for the ready foot of the Architect.

And so they climbed the pyramid on bird-back steps, right up to the square, gaping hole at the top. There was a pause, and then the Architect toppled forward into the darkness, pulling Trista with him. There was a plummeting sensation, and a moment where the world pulled itself inside out. When Trista's head cleared, the two of them were still standing, but they were inside an enclosed room where the angles seemed to be glaring at each other like affronted cats.

The torrent of other Besiders surged past them, disappearing through a torchlit archway into what looked like a cross between a banquet hall and a jazz club. Candles glinted in chrome; wild whinnies tangled with saxophone trills.

"Oh, that place is not for *you*, my dear," murmured the Architect with quiet savagery. "All that light, all that sound! Think of your headaches. No, you need quiet and dark."

He reached out and opened another door she had not noticed, then dragged Trista into a narrow stone-walled corridor. Brackets in the walls oozed silver flame that moved sluggishly and barely revealed the room, like a sad memory of fire rather than fire itself.

The corridor forked again and again. The Architect chose this turn, that turn with dizzying speed as he weaved through the labyrinth.

"Faster! Exercise is good for young limbs." The Architect's stride accelerated to a long-legged lope, then a run. He almost dragged Trista off her feet as he pulled her through antechambers, past walls carved with a hundred eyes, up and down twisting steps.

At last he burst into a large, domed room, whose floor sloped down to a round shaft in the center. With a forward sweep of his arm, he flung his prisoner to the ground so hard that the breath was knocked out of her and her hat fell from her head.

"Welcome to your new home." There was nothing smooth or debonair about the Architect now. He was seven foot of trembling malice, silver eyes brighter than the false torches. "*Your father* made it for you, and come the dawn he will seal you into it. By all means try to find your way out—you will fail. If you wish, you may sob here until you starve or stifle. If you wish for a quicker death, throw yourself in that pit. The fall never ends, but you will. It will pull the screams out of you until you unravel, leaving nothing but the screams."

"No!" His captive flung herself at his feet, desperately clutching at his hand and arm. "Don't leave me here! Please!"

For a few moments the Architect was content to let the girl sob and cling, but then he gave a noise of distaste and pushed her roughly away.

"What a pitiable object you are," he muttered. Then his eyes fell to his hand, sticky with gray strands instead of tears, and his wrist, which was now bare of all but shirt cuff.

With astonishment and rage, his silver gaze flicked to his captive and the scratched service watch gripped fiercely in her small, slim hands. The girl raised her head, and the Architect looked into a smile full of thorns.

"Hello, Daddy," said the Cuckoo.

The Architect's shriek of rage was the fluting at the heart of a hurricane. The domed room shivered, cracks running across its paint-spiraled ceiling. He lunged at her, but she leaped out of the way, landing on all fours with her thorn claws extended.

"Where is she?" he demanded.

"Long gone," hissed the changeling. "Can you even guess how long? Can you guess how long I have been by your side, laughing at you?"

The Architect threw back his head and gave another terrible, infantile shriek, and the whole room tipped and swung like a bell, trying to hurl Trista toward the dark and gaping hole at its heart. He came after her as she fought to keep her balance, as the slabs shifted and bucked under her bare hands and feet. He seemed larger than the room, darker than the twisted stem of a tornado. And yet he was still man-shaped, with pale eyes that scorched and hands that snatched for her.

The room flung her this way and that, and she was battered painfully against wall and floor. She felt her sides rip like cloth seams. She tumbled and sprawled, coughing up brooches and thimbles. But always she found her feet again, just in time to dodge the Architect's next grab. The watch never slipped from her grip.

This was one of the Architect's places, where he had more control than in the wider world. And yet again and again his fingers raked empty air, for in this moment of rage the Architect was not in control of himself.

But I'm weakening. Every leap was taking more effort. *I'm getting slower. I'm running out of time . . .*

One painful sprawl too many. She was too slow to rise. She felt strong fingers grasp a handful of her hair. She clawed at the Architect's hand in vain as he dragged her relentlessly along the ground toward the shaft . . .

. . . and then his grip loosened as the fistful of hair became a fistful of leaves. Trista sprang to her feet, unexpectedly finding herself directly behind her towering attacker. She hurled herself against his back with all her might, and as the room lurched, the pair of them pitched forward. Trista landed on her belly, digging the claws of her fingers and toes into the floor cracks to stop her from sliding.

The Architect, however, tumbled onto his side and rolled, vanishing over the edge into the dark, abysmal shaft. His scream made her curl up and clutch her ears. It went on and on, thinning and fading until there was nothing left but a tingle in the ear.

Trista lay sobbing for breath on the stone flags, looking at the watch she was still clutching in her shaking hand. She sat up slowly and painfully, hearing the rustle as straw seeped out of her seams.

With her claws, she prized open the back of the watch. There, amid the works, was a small strand of faded brown hair. Carefully she teased it out, and as it finally pulled free, the tiny mechanism began to move.

She closed her eyes and imagined a spirit slipping free of the imprisoning cogs, escaping the terrible weight of winter. She thought she heard the wind surge softly, as if in a sigh, and then fall silent.

"Good-bye, Sebastian," she whispered.

The Architect had enchanted the watch to be a master of time, instead of just a servant. Sebastian's hair in the device had bound him to it, and when the watch was stopped, he had been trapped between life and death. But the watch was not linked to Sebastian alone. Sebastian had left it to Violet, the woman he cared about more than any possession. So it had trapped her too, binding her to an undying dead man and his unending winter.

The ticking of the watch was freedom for Sebastian, freedom for Violet. But now it was biting away the last seconds of Trista's life.

I'm out of time, she thought, as leaves fell past her face like confetti. *I'm out of time.*

And then the Architect's words forced their way into her mind once more. *Clocks are servants of time but can be taught to be* masters *of it.*

She stared at the watch, barely daring to understand her newest thought. She was running out of time, but in her hand lay something that perhaps could *stop* the inevitable. If she could bind the watch to her . . . put something in the works that belonged to her . . .

But what did she have that was hers? Her hair was leaves, her body fragments of another's life. Everything she had was borrowed, just as the Grimmer had said in her dream. She was litter and leavings, not a person in her own right.

"But I *am* a person!" she wailed, the room throwing back derisive echoes. "I'm real! I am! I've got a name!"

A name. Inspiration struck at last. With fingers that felt increasingly like twigs, she pulled off the bead necklace on which Pen had scrawled her new name. That at least had been given to her, and her alone. As her eyes started to blur, Trista pushed a loop of the cotton into the works. The cogs bit the cotton, gently jammed, and . . . stopped.

The sounds woke her. A roar of engines, juddering and thundering. The hiss of sand. Shouts and orders. Gear clashes, the grinding and shrieks of metal defying its limits.

Trista opened her eyes, and found still she had eyes to open. There was a watch in her hand, and there was still a hand to hold it. She sat up with difficulty, clutching at a rent in her flank. She was weak and in pain, but there was still a Trista to *be* weak and in pain. There was a strange numb lightness in her head that wanted to become joy but was not yet sure how to go about it.

It took her a moment to realize what the noises must mean. Those were not Besider noises. Those were the sounds of a construction site. Somewhere out there, ordinary hardworking people were preparing to place the cap on the pyramid of the station. She was still running out of time.

She clambered unsteadily to her feet, tucking the precious

watch into a pocket, and staggered to the doorway, stooping now and then to scoop up fragments from her innards. Beyond it lay the Architect's stone-walled labyrinth.

By all means try to find your way out, the Architect had told her. *You will fail.*

But the Architect had not reckoned on the trail that Trista had left, all too unwillingly, as he dragged her down corridor after corridor. Her wake had been scattered with scraps and stray leaves. Now, leaning against the walls for support, Trista followed them back.

She would not be fast enough. Outside she could hear megaphone speeches and applause from a crowd. Then a deep, juddering thrum that had to be the engine of the great crane . . .

. . . which cut out again. There was silence, and then a discontented, puzzled hum of voices that went on and on. New speeches followed, apologetic in tone.

They've stopped. They've stopped!

Pen, wonderful Pen! You did it! You made them stop.

At long last, she found the little door through which the Architect had dragged her. With a painful, incredulous surge of hope she pushed it open, and then stopped dead.

The room beyond was filled with figures. A montage of Besider faces glared at her, stripped of all disguise, their features twisted by anger and grief. At their head stood the Shrike, his eyes burning under his bowler hat.

"The Architect!" was the whisper that ran through the crowd. "The Architect! The Architect!"

Trista remembered the long, resonating scream, and her heart plummeted. They had all heard it. They knew what had happened. No tears or pleas would placate them for the loss of their hero, their savior. And so she did not weep, and did not plead.

Instead, she looked straight into the eyes of the Shrike.

"They've stopped work out there—have you noticed that, Shrike? Piers Crescent won't let them put the cap on the pyramid until he knows I'm safe. And if he doesn't, this building will be unfinished. Unsafe for all the people who want to live here."

A tremor of uncertainty passed through the crowd, and all faces turned to look at the Shrike. As Trista had guessed, in the absence of the Architect, the Shrike was the obvious leader.

His bulldog features twitched with suppressed feeling. Again she thought she sensed behind them a curved beak, this time itching to snap her in two, or crack her like a nut. All that he needed to do was give the word, and his fellows would rip her to shreds. But, she realized, that was the last thing he could do. He was bound by a magic promise not to harm her, either directly or indirectly.

"If you don't make peace with Piers Crescent," Trista went on, as calmly as she could, given that she was using one hand to stop her insides from falling out, "it will mean disaster for everybody sooner or later. For him, and for you and your people. Will you let me talk to him for you? Or will you make the same mistake as the Architect, and tear apart everything for revenge?"

The Shrike bristled for a few more seconds, then made a curt, angry gesture to the others, who reluctantly fell back toward the banquet hall. It was not simply wrath that was brightening the Shrike's button eyes, however, as he scrutinized Trista's living, breathing form like someone analyzing a conjuror's trick.

"*How* did you . . . ?" His gray gaze flickered with something that might have been respect.

"Maybe you made me better than you thought," answered Trista.

He glared at her, then shook his head.

"Somebody get the lady a ladder," he barked, his tone heavy with reluctance. His gaze passed over her rents and tears, and he winced fastidiously, conflict visible in his face. In the end, impulse triumphed over restraint. "And . . . and while we're waiting, my needle and thread!" He gave Trista the angriest smile in the world.

"We are not friends, Cuckoo, but if I *am* letting you out, you will not emerge looking like some seamstress-in-training patched you together with her eyes closed. I am a craftsman, and I have my pride."

Chapter 43

LETTING GO

FOR THE NEXT FEW DAYS, THE CRESCENT FAMILY was front-page news, but the stories about them were very confusing. It was public knowledge that both the kidnapped Crescent girls were safe and well, but there were wild and varied reports of their rescue.

Most agreed that the youngest girl had been discovered wandering in the snow by a policeman on the beat. She had subjected him to a dazzling deluge of tall tales, the tallest being that she was the missing Penelope Crescent. Fortunately the constable had been patient enough to check this story, which had turned out to be true.

The rescue of the older girl was a far more sensational matter. Those who gathered to witness the Capping Ceremony to mark the completion of the new railway station were forced to wait as the proceedings stalled for inadequately explained reasons. It was later revealed that Piers Crescent, the civil engineer who had designed it, had suddenly demanded that everything halt, since the snow would make the placing of the apex too dangerous.

While the crowd became restless, and the organizers tried to convince the increasingly irate civil engineer that his fears were groundless, a solitary figure had been noticed at the very top of the pyramid, weakly waving its hand. Hundreds watched as several men, including Piers Crescent, clambered up the scaffolding and came down again carrying a frail-looking young girl. Those who saw her recognized her from her photograph as the missing Theresa.

In spite of all this evidence, however, there were still some newspapers that insisted that Theresa had actually been rescued the night before, when she was discovered dripping and disheveled on a dockland jetty.

There was just as much confusion about the identity of the girls' kidnappers. All the papers that evening had carried stories on the arrest of Violet Parish, with lurid details of her rumored criminal contacts. Having painted her scarlet as blood, the same paper' accounts of her the next day were short and rather furtive. The Crescent girls and their family were apparently adamant that Violet was blameless and that she had in fact been injured in her attempts to protect the children.

Indeed, it seemed the one person who had pointed the finger at Violet Parish was a tailor named Grace, and he was no longer to be found. As the days stretched with no further word, the papers alternated between describing the kidnappers as "mysterious" and hinting heavily that the missing tailor might have been one of them.

It was a week of wild stories, however. Everything, including the seasons, seemed to have gone mad for a time. Crazy reports of children seen on roofs, mysterious wild-fowl behavior, ghost barges, and missing dressmakers seemed not out of keeping with the freak miniature winter that had descended on Ellchester within hours, and which yielded to an Indian summer within days. After a while, "Wild White Week," as it became locally known, was dismissed as a time that didn't count, a period when the usual rules had temporarily stopped working.

The Crescents certainly had nothing to tell the newspapers. The reporters tried for a while to trace Violet Parish, but Piers had paid for her to be moved from the city hospital to a private clinic outside town, and no details of her location were forthcoming. The Crescents, after all, could afford a high quality of discretion.

The clinic nestled in the lap of three hills and had a peaceful, coddled feel. Its lawns were neat but not severely so, and there were crazy-paving paths through its little orchard. The apple trees had suffered during the freak blizzard, however, the weight of the snow ripping away many boughs. The grass was lush and green but still had a saturated, sodden look. Like the patients within, the gray-stone clinic was suffering its own share of recovery pangs as workmen struggled to mend a damaged roof and pipes that had burst during the freeze.

To anybody who knew her, it was clear that Violet was suffering from impatience and boredom more than from the splint on her leg. The orderlies had quickly learned that her repeated demands for news on "when it would be fixed" were questions about her motorcycle, not her leg. Violet had been lucky, suffering only sprains and bruises rather than any fractures.

"I bounce," she explained to anybody who asked, with a savage grin.

She refused to believe there was any good reason for the splint ("They're just afraid I'll chase the male orderlies") or for her to be denied cigarettes ("I'm choking without them"). The staff tolerated her jibes but refused to yield to any of them. Violet was at least allowed visitors. She seemed happiest in the company of another patient, a young girl who had been admitted at the same time with the conveniently vague complaint of "nerves."

On the first morning in September, that same young girl could be found in Violet's private room, leaning out of the window to hear the church bells chime.

Trista never tired of hearing them. Clocks fascinated her now, the way they ticked and told the hours without her dying. Suns that set and rose again, without a countdown. Mornings without the whispers and snickers of mortality.

The last soft chime throbbed into silence, and Trista stepped back into the room with a slightly rueful smile.

"Are you going to do that every hour for the rest of your life?" asked Violet. She was disheveled and shiny-faced without her makeup. The books and magazines that people had given her to relieve the tedium had avalanched onto the floor and been left to sprawl there.

"It still isn't boring," Trista answered, slightly embarrassed. "I'm enjoying meals as well, now that I can just eat a normal amount." Then, a little more boldly: "Are you going to keep moving around, now that it's not chasing you?"

Violet puffed her cheeks thoughtfully and wiggled the toes of her imprisoned leg.

"Probably," she said at last. "Habits die hard. I *love* the fact that I *can* stay still if I want, and sleep a full eight hours in the same bed without causing Ragnarök. But . . . it turns out I love speed, motion, and change too, and without them I go stir-crazy. At some point, that became part of me. However, now I'm the one who chooses. I can move toward something, instead of just running from a past I can never escape."

Violet peered at Trista through narrowed eyes.

“I . . . saw him that night,” she said carefully. “The night of the snows.”

Trista did not ask who “he” was, nor did she exclaim or prompt. She came over and sat by Violet’s bed, giving her friend a silence to fill.

“It was bitterly cold in the hospital, and the sisters had run out of blankets to pile on us. And then the windows all burst open, and the rooms filled with the blizzard. Not just gusts of flakes, but a real snowstorm so thick it was as if we were all outside. I felt as if the world had melted away, and all that was left was winter, with me and my bed in the middle of it.

“Then I saw a figure walking toward me, through the snow. And it was . . .” Violet trailed off, and laughed under her breath.

There was a long pause, and Trista realized that no more tale would be told. There was only a snow-blank page for her to fill in herself.

“And . . . he seemed . . . happy?” was all she could think of to ask.

Violet gave the slightest nod and a very small smile that made her look younger and slightly shy.

“He says he likes my hair short,” she said, under her breath.

“I’ve been thinking about the watch.” Trista bit her lip, then made herself unbite it. The mannerism gave her a funny feeling now that she had seen Triss do the same thing. “It was mainly linked to . . . to him through his hair. But it was linked to you because it was *yours*, and because he wanted you to have it. That means it still *is* linked. I’ve stopped time running out for me, but it’s possible I did the same for you. I . . . don’t know what that means.”

Violet pondered this, brow creased, hands behind her head, then finally gave a shrug.

"Well, it isn't stopping me from healing. It sounds as if we'll have time to think about that, anyway." She grinned. "And potential immortality isn't the worst problem we've had to face recently, is it?"

There was a knock at the door.

"Miss Parish?" A nurse put her head around the door. "Those visitors you're expecting—they're here."

Despite herself, Trista found herself straightening and readying her mental armor as the Crescent family entered the room. The armor was almost immediately dented as Pen pelted across the room and flung her arms around her.

"Trista!"

Trista picked her up and swung her to and fro so that her legs waggled in the air, then remembered that she was displaying strength unusual for a slight thirteen-year-old girl. The other three members of the Crescent family waited by the door, looking pale-faced and uncertain, as if they thought there might be lava under the floor.

It was Piers, of course, who braved the lava first, finding a chair for his wife to sit down, then walking over to shake Violet's hand and ask if she was being well looked after.

It was Piers also who went on to talk and talk, filling the gaping silence that was waiting to happen. His voice sounded confident, but Trista knew him too well to believe that. He was treading carefully, knowing he was walking along a riverbank full of sleeping crocodiles. All the while, Violet listened with a crocodile smile and helped him with a wry remark now and then.

Trista was not really listening. She was looking at the Crescents, watching for hints and signs. Their little family jigsaw had been torn apart, and the pieces had suffered strange adventures, growing into new and unexpected shapes. Yet there they were, sitting in the same pose as the newspaper photo, the classic family. Mother demurely seated, children on either side, father standing behind with one confident hand placed on the mother's chair. Had the pieces been slammed back into place, forced to take up the same shapes as before and form the old picture? Would they pretend that nothing had happened?

No. She did not think so. A few tiny changes caught her eye.

Pen was as bold and impulsive as ever, of course, but she was not silenced at every step. Her parents occasionally muttered a restraining or reproving word, but it no longer had the same reflexive force, the same weary exasperation. The reins seemed to have slackened, and Pen's boisterousness was enthusiastic instead of angry.

Celeste looked older. There was something slightly off-kilter about her, as if she had lost her balance and was not sure how to regain it. She tried to give Trista a smile, but it fractured and went wrong, and Celeste dropped her eyes. Looking at her face, Trista could only think of Celeste walking out of the farmhouse kitchen and shutting the door behind her so that horrors could happen.

I don't know why I find her harder to forgive than Piers, who was ready to throw me in the fire. Well, at least he was willing to face up to what he was doing. But I do feel sorry for her. She will always be the person who walked out of that door . . . and she knows she can never come back through it.

There was a hollowness in Piers's confidence now. He halted himself now and then, glancing at others to gauge their feelings, their approval or disapproval.

And then there was the fourth member of the family, in her powder-blue dress and hat, sidled up against her mother's arm, the tip of her nose red and a thick scarf wound under her chin.

How did anybody ever mistake us for each other? I'm taller than her! No, perhaps I just stand up straighter than she does.

It was still eerie, looking into a face that was so like her own and yet animated by another mind. Triss clearly found the experience unnerving too. Her eyes glassed over as she looked at Trista, then she dropped her gaze and gave a little involuntary shudder.

Trista felt a pang of hurt, but rallied. *She saw me walk out of the Grimmer*, she reminded herself. *I frightened her family, and tore apart her room, and ate her dolls, and made her sister like me, and pushed her into a river. No wonder she's scared of me.*

Then Triss lifted her eyes again, met Trista's gaze, and hesitantly managed a small smile. It was a bit nervous and tight-lipped but still a real smile, not a parentally enforced smile-to-show-you're-friends-now.

Trista smiled back, guessing that her own smile looked much the same.

"Obviously, there are problems," Piers was saying. "If you and young . . . Trista stay in Ellchester, both of you are likely to be hounded by the papers. Idle people, foolish questions—you know how unpleasant such things can be."

"I can see it might be embarrassing to have to explain how you grew a spare daughter overnight," remarked Violet, with a paper-thin air of sympathy. "Perhaps you could claim that one was a draft version?"

"Miss Parish, you understand the way people's minds work, the sort of scandal—"

"Oh, I think I understand what you're worried about, Mr. Crescent," said Violet with a slightly unpleasant smile.

"Our family owes you both a great deal," Piers went on. "And we want to make sure young Trista has the best possible prospects. There are excellent schools—"

"Boarding schools?" asked Trista. Her reward sounded a lot like being locked away and tucked out of sight.

Without even thinking about it, she reached out for Violet's hand, knowing it would be there. It was, and curled warmly around hers.

"No boarding schools," said Violet. "She needs a home—people who understand who and what she is."

The Crescent parents exchanged appalled glances. They began the terrible, apologetic disclaimers, trying to explain without explaining. *Of course we would love to have Trista, but . . . but . . . but . . .*

"Why?" demanded Pen. "Why can't she come home with us?"

"Because she's coming with me," answered Violet.

There was more talk after that, of course. Piers would help. Lawyers, adoptions, a story—perhaps that Trista was an orphaned daughter of one of Sebastian's comrades? If Violet was looking for work in London, Piers could provide references, contacts, possibly even a place somewhere. Trista could only think about the strong, long, nicotine-stained hand holding hers.

"And . . . if we can help with money . . ." Piers suggested.

Trista's "no" coincided with Violet's "yes." Trista glanced at Violet and changed her own "no" to a "yes."

"Well, we should let you both get some more rest." Celeste rose from her chair. Her ever-busy fingers made their usual adjustments to Triss's clothes, pulling her scarf warmly around her, drawing her protectively close . . .

. . . and without unkindness, Triss pulled away from her mother slightly. She did not even appear to notice she was doing so.

"Mother," she said shyly. "Can I . . . talk to Trista alone? In the garden?"

They walked side by side, darting only occasional glances at each other. On an unvoiced impulse they had linked hands as they left the building and were now uncomfortably connected. Sometimes Trista felt Triss try to pull away, and reflexively tightened her hold. At other times the strangeness of it made Trista want to let go, only to find Triss hanging on stubbornly.

"Thank you for rescuing me," said Triss at last.

"That's all right." Trista gave her a sideways glance. "Sorry about pushing you in the river."

"You could have asked me to jump," Triss replied in a small voice. "I would have."

"Would you?"

The Triss that Trista could remember being would not have jumped. She would have wailed, clung to somebody, and demanded to be taken home. But that was Triss before she was kidnapped by the Architect, not the girl who stood before her now.

I only remember the Triss she was, not the Triss she is now. And people can change a lot—sometimes in as little as a week.

"It doesn't matter," Triss said quickly. "I really wanted to ask you something. When you're in London, can we write to each other?"

Trista was taken aback.

"Yes," she said, as soon as she had recovered her wits. "I . . . can't promise I won't eat some of your letters. I lost a lot of my stuffing, and I don't know what will happen if more falls out. I *would* like to write to you, though." She paused before continuing. "I already promised Pen I would send her letters."

“Pen misses you.” Triss looked down. “Every time she looks at me, I know who she would like me to be.” Her expression was one of thinly veiled hurt.

“Pen just needs an older sister,” Trista said quietly.

“But . . . but *I’m* her older sister!” exclaimed Triss, her eyes shiny with tears of frustration and sadness.

“Then steal her back from me.” Trista smiled her thorny smile. “*Be* her big sister.” They walked on, and Trista gave Triss another curious glance. “Do you think your parents will mind the two of you writing to me?”

“I don’t know.” Triss shook her head. “They won’t *say* they mind, but . . . I think they want to forget everything that happened and go back to the way things were.” She gnawed her lip. “We can’t, can we? Everything’s different . . . not the way I thought . . . broken.”

In her heart of hearts, Trista knew that it would have been far easier for Piers and Celeste if Trista herself had died. It would have made things simpler and neater. They did not wish that on her, of course, but hers would have been a poignant tale with an ending. They could have closed the book, detached her in their minds from their beloved Triss, and tried to return to the comfort of their rut.

But she had *not* died, and nothing was simple. She was still drawing in breath after troublesome breath, and nobody would have the luxury of forgetting about her. There was a strange new piece in the jigsaw of the Crescent family, pulling it into a different shape, and they would have to deal with that now and always.

It might have been easier for the Crescents if Trista had died. But easier, she reminded herself, was not the same as better.

“I don’t think they know what to do,” Triss went on. “*I* don’t know what to do.”

"You should ask your parents to send you back to school," Trista answered impulsively. "Ask them now, while they can't say no to you."

"What?" Triss paled. "But I haven't been to school for years! I don't know how . . . I mean . . . I can't!"

"Listen to me," said Trista, turning to face her other self. "Triss—I'm asking you to jump."

Violet's bruises healed, and she stalked about angrily with a walking stick until her doctors relented and released her. Piers paid for the repair of her motorcycle, and when she left the clinic with Trista at her side, there it was waiting for her, gleaming, ugly, and glorious.

Trista climbed into the sidecar. It felt strangely cavernous without Pen sitting painfully in her lap. *But I'll grow to fill it*, she told herself. *Or will I? Perhaps I'll just stay this age forever, like Peter Pan but with sharper teeth.*

"Typical," Violet snarled, then glanced at Trista and laughed. "Tucked away in a hospital for a month. We're the awkward ones—the ones who spoil things and don't fit. So they hide us away and call us ill."

Trista's mind drifted to other misfits. The displaced Besiders, under the grinning, pragmatic leadership of the Shrike, who now had an uneasy truce with Piers. And Jack, who had taken the news of Violet's imminent departure from Ellchester with solemn calm, telling her it was "about time she let go."

What happens to the outsiders? Are we like windfalls, rotting when we fall off the main tree?

"We're like ghosts," Trista said aloud, feeling sad. "The real world goes on—jobs and families and newspaper stories—and we're outside it."

"No, we're not," said Violet, with surly defiance. "*They're* the ghosts. Piers and Celeste and the others like them. Trying to cling to the past, to the way things were, pretending nothing has changed. *Everything* changes and breaks and stops fitting—and *we* know that, even with our stopped clock. The world is breaking, and changing, and dancing. Always on the move. That's how it is. That's how it has to be."

And Violet kicked down on her motorcycle's starter, like a bull stamping a challenge. She crouched forward as the engine gave its ugly, cackling roar, and then the pair of them were on the move and speeding, hedges fleeing past them as if outraged.

The sky was a tearless blue, stung with the white motes of birds. The sun blazed pitilessly on the smashed golden fields, where workers tried to make the best of the snow-crushed harvest. Cars swung around the corners without warning, their horns lowing, their windscreens dust-spattered. Signposts gleamed white, and promised London.

Trista's eyes stung with dust, and joy, and the cobweb tears that she was beginning to accept. Her lungs and mind were full of life—life as it was, not as anyone said it should be.

This second is mine, and this, and this, and this . . .

There was an invisible necklace of nows, stretching out in front of her along the crazy, twisting road, each bead a golden second. She had no idea how many there were. Perhaps a hundred million of them, perhaps fewer than ten.

And she laughed, knowing that with every risk, every corner they took at speed, the necklace could be broken, its beads spilled and lost in the gutter. All was *perhaps*. Nothing was certain.

And that, that was wonderful.